GUARDIAN ANGELS

JOSEPH A. CITRO

Contents

Part Four: The Pinnacle

From the *Tri-Town Tribune*, a weekly newspaper, published in Antrim, Vermont, Special Evening Supplement, Wednesday, December 28, 1983:

WHITCOMBE CHILD UNHARMED IN TRIPLE SLAYING

ANTRIM—The bodies of Clint Whitcome, 41, his wife Pamela, 37, of Antrim, and Elizabeth McKensie, 75, of Chester, were discovered at seven o'clock this morning at the Whitcome residence by Antrim Police Chief Richard G. Bates.

Eric Nolan, 36, of Long Island, New York, a cousin of Mrs. Whitcome's, was taken into custody. Although no one has been charged with a crime, Chief Bates stated, "Looks like we've got a few murders on our hands."

Antrim's triple slaying is the latest in a series of mysterious deaths and disappearances that have plagued area residents since late November, beginning with the vanishing of Antrim Police Officer Justin Hurd. Other apparent victims include Perly Greer and William Newton of Antrim, and Dr. Carl Sayer of Duxbury.

When asked if he believes the cases are related, Chief Bates stated, "They all happened in my jurisdiction, that makes them related."

State police were summoned to the Whitcome house on Tenny's Hill. Media and curiosity seekers were banned from the area, where new-fallen snow might reveal footprints or other evidence.

Clint and Pamela Whitcome were lifelong Antrim residents. Whitcome headed the Antrim Highway Department for fourteen years. The couple's four-year-old son, Luke, was found unharmed at the crime scene.

He was sedated and released in the custody of his uncle, Peter Whitcome of Antrim.

Elizabeth McKensie, Chester historian and occasional contributor to this newspaper, was well known for her Vermont essays and poetry. She had served for nine years as president of the Chester Historical Society. Mrs. McKensie had been confined to a wheelchair for many years.

State's Attorney Geoff Mellors, Sergeants Bill Schubart and Carl Yalicki of the state police, and Chief Bates worked on the case throughout the day. Their most important clues included discharged firearms and a flattened penny found in the possession of the boy.

Bates said that they had uncovered additional evidence as well, but declined to be more specific.

If the authorities knew of any motive for the triple killings, they did not make it public.

Nolan, who had been visiting the couple since November 21 of this year, is unemployed and is known to have recently suffered psychological problems. According to New York state police, Nolan has never been charged with a crime. His wife was recently killed in a car and train collision.

Chief Bates stated that any remarks made by Nolan at the crime scene are confidential.

When asked about the condition of the bodies, Chief Medical Examiner J. Howard Kunstler said that they had suffered extensive damage, but declined to be specific about the nature of the wounds.

PROLOGUE

Joe Grant felt a satisfying crackle as the squirrel's skeleton flattened under the heavy wheels of his pickup.

He smiled, his approaching eruption of laughter cut short by a beer-fragrant belch. It bubbled from his stomach, rumbled up his gullet, and dribbled onto the barrel-round front of his sweatshirt. Joe made a face, spat mightily out the window, and wiped his mouth with the coarse side of his hand. Then he dried the hand on his shirtfront.

To sweeten his mouth, Joe swigged from a sixteen-ounce Black Label—he called it his "pounder"—and squinted into the night.

For a moment, his eyes rested comfortably at half-mast until the pickup started to wander lazily toward the shoulder of the road.

Joe snapped awake, slapping the wheel, directing the truck back to the right-hand lane. At the same time, he stomped the headlights from low to high. The white tunnel of light bore deeper into the black trees that lined the mountain road. Crazy shadows danced along the roadside as the pickup bounded over ruts and potholes.

Joe took another pull from his pounder and whooped out the window—"Whooooo-weeee!"—his cry of delight lost below the roar of his perforated muffler.

1

He felt good.

Everybody'd been feeling good tonight. The boys at the bar had bought lots of rounds. Joe was good and drunk, yet he felt thrifty. He was returning home with change from the ten-dollar bill he'd started with some five or six hours earlier.

Joe smiled again, his mind wandering. The pickup meandered from side to side, missing as many bumps as it took. The tail pipe banged loudly against the underside of the vehicle.

"Devil's knockin' to get in," Joe chuckled, as he bounced up and down on the seat.

Goddamn dark tonight, he thought. No more'n a dribble of a moon. Looks like a little cum stain on the sky. He hoped Mona would be awake when he got back to the trailer. If not, he'd wake her up; why not? She didn't have school tomorrow, did she?

What day of the week was this, anyhow? Friday? Saturday? "Can't be Sunday," Joe said. "Bar ain't open on a Sunday."

It didn't matter. Joe didn't have any job to worry about; he hadn't worked in nearly six years.

"You on one a them welfare grants from the gum'ment?" One of the guys at the bar had asked him.

"Way I figure it," Joe had replied, "they pay me *not* to work. Same way they been payin' them farmers not to grow wheat. I figure I'm doin' my patriotic duty; I'm sacrificin' my job for them that needs one more."

There were a couple of chuckles.

"Mebbe so, mebbe not," the guy had said, looking doubtful. "Least ways, somebody give you the right name—"

"Yeah, *Grant!*" Somebody else exploded with laughter, as if he just got the joke. Then the whole room was laughing.

Joe smiled as he remembered.

Yes sir, he'd had a great time tonight. He didn't care if people made fun of his name. Fact was, the joke was on them; they were the ones out scratching for a living, complaining about prices, kissing ass, and bitching about their bosses.

Not Joe; he was his own boss. All he had to do was meet with that lady from the welfare office a couple times a year, assure her that Mona was still in school and promise that he still hadn't been able to find a job. "I'm out there lookin', though," he'd tell her.

Yes sir, he did all right. He made a little under the table trapping beaver every fall, and in the wintertime he'd plow a little snow. Unlike most of his working buddies, Joe always had meat on the table. Ever since he'd replaced the pickup's front bumper with a railroad tie, he got two, maybe three deer a year without any damage to his vehicle. Maybe he'd get one tonight ...

Joe slowed down a little, watching for movement in the passing shadows.

There! In the road ahead—something moved! A rabbit?

Deer, rabbit, what the hell ...

Joe yanked the wheel to the left in time to see the fat body of a woodchuck disappear safely into the bushes, beyond the range of his high beams.

When he had straightened the wheel, he saw something else. This time the eyes were higher off the road. It was a bigger animal this time.

Joe blinked his own eyes to make sure they were working okay; he didn't want to be seeing things. He was liquored up, sure, but not enough for hallucinations.

Yup, they were still out there, all right.

This time, by Jesus, it must *be a deer.*

Joe gunned the accelerator, barreling toward the eyes at the roadside. They were just beyond the reach of his headlights. He was traveling sixty, maybe sixty-five, when the bright white beams washed over the figure.

It isn't an animal. Oh God! It's a human!

It's a kid!

3

Joe jammed his foot against the brake pedal. *Christ, what's a kid doin' out at this hour of the night?* The truck fishtailed on the road's gravel surface, grinding stones and dirt beneath its balding tires.

The kid's face showed a rictus of pain before the impact came. Little hands thrust forward, as if expecting to push the racing vehicle away.

"Shit ... Christ!"

Joe heard the collision more than he felt it. Almost instantly, the child was airborne.

The pickup ground to a stop, and Joe was out the door. "Hey ... hey kid, you okay?"

Joe explored the island of light in front of his rig. Nothing. Maybe he *had* been seeing things.

But maybe not; the blackberry bushes at the roadside were broken, flattened. Something had done that. Something bigger than a woodchuck.

"Hey, kid ... !"

Part of his mind told him nobody, especially a little kid, could survive an impact like that. But there was no arguing, the kid was nowhere around.

Joe peered into the black forest, searching the pits of shadow at the perimeter of the pool of light. Maybe it had been a hallucination after all.

Whatever it was, the kid was gone now.

Perhaps if he'd had a flashlight, he might have explored a bit farther. But what was the point? A direct hit like that couldn't have sent the kid more than twenty feet through the air.

Joe paced off about six yards and walked in an arc around the front of the pickup. He felt the irritating prick of the thorny bushes against his arms and hands, and heard the tiny tearing sounds as the prickers pulled at his trousers. But he saw nothing.

There was no kid.

4

Joe's shadow was long and massive, projected harshly against the trees by the twin bolts of light.

"Hey ... hey, kid?"

The only sound was his own uncertain voice in the tense darkness.

"Fuck it," Joe murmured. His beer-sodden brain made some hasty calculations: "Kid musta run off. An' if he run off, means he's okay. Besides, it's too dark for him to have seen who hit him. An' if he's dead, they ain't a Christly thing I can do for him now ..."

He reached a conclusion: "Probably the best thing to do is get the hell out of here before somebody spots me."

Joe Grant got back into his pickup and headed for home.

PART ONE
ANTRIM, VERMONT

But look at these lonely houses, each in its own fields, filled for the most part with poor ignorant folk who know little of the law. Think of the deeds of hellish cruelty, the hidden wickedness which may go on, year in, year out, in such places, and none the wiser.

—Sherlock Holmes, *The Adventure of the Copper Beeches*

CHAPTER 1
GOD'S COUNTRY

The only thing William Crockett liked about the possibility of moving to Vermont was that it might get him out of school a little early.

Lately, school was becoming a major bore. With two long months to go, Will wasn't sure if he could stand cramming for another test or researching another paper. It was the same every year; when the end of the school year was in sight, time started to crawl.

This year one thing was different, though: Will's friends were starting to bore him, too. It was as if they were changing; all they wanted to do was hang out at the mall, eat ice cream and flirt, or maybe link up with somebody old enough to drive and cruise around every evening, looking for girls.

Not that there was anything wrong with girls; they certainly weren't boring. The ritual of connecting with them, however, could be tiresome as hell. Sometimes Will thought boredom might be the natural state of things. Perhaps everything in the world was boring, it was just a matter of degree: some things were simply more boring than others.

Surely nothing in all of creation could be more boring than being forced to leave home and move to some beat-up old farmhouse in Antrim, Vermont.

Well, maybe it wouldn't happen. There was always a chance. At least he could hope.

Will looked out the window from the back seat of Dan's Renault. They were on Interstate 91, somewhere north of Greenfield, Massachusetts. Last time Will had looked out the window a sign said:

Brattleboro, VT 25 mi.

Maybe they were in Vermont by now. Will didn't much care.

Vermont. The thought conjured images of little white towns, black-and-white cows, and rosy-cheeked kids in blue denim overalls fishing off covered bridges.

No way, Will thought, shuddering. *I can't let them do this.* He looked down at the copy of *Heavy Metal* on his lap. Even the big-breasted alien in the skin-squeezing jumpsuit couldn't hold his attention.

Back to the window again—nothing to look at but trees. Trees, and a big flat ribbon of water off to the right: the Connecticut River. Although it was mid-April, patches of snow still littered the ground. Clumps of it clung, dirty and solid-looking, to black tree trunks, or spread like columns of spilled plaster along the roadside.

Will could tell already, Vermont was nothing to get excited about. First, it was so *rural*; probably there were no video stores, no libraries, not even a goddamn shopping mall to go to, even if he went in for that kind of thing. And second, what did people actually *do* in Vermont besides fish off bridges? Just milk cows, eat cheddar cheese, and slurp maple syrup. And for fun, what? Go skiing, maybe? When Will tried to imagine what Vermont girls were like, the thought grossed him out.

No question about it, the whole thing really sounded like the pits. Somehow, he was going to have to talk them out of this.

"You're awfully quiet, Will." Dan glanced back over his right shoulder, careful not to take his eyes too long from the road.

"Got nothin' to say."

"Still don't like the idea of country living, huh?"

"The idea's okay. I just don't wanna do it."

Sheila entered the conversation, her voice hopeful. "Maybe, once you see the place, you'll change your mind."

He was going to argue—after all, she hadn't seen the place either—but when she smiled at him, Will couldn't help smiling back. He liked the way his mother looked when she smiled. Her nose sort of crinkled at the bridge, and a series of little wrinkles— they looked like a stack of smiling mouths—appeared at the center of her forehead.

"Yeah, maybe."

Will remembered a time when he'd thought he'd never see his mom's smile again. Three years ago, well before Dan had entered the picture, Will's real father had died of a heart attack. Alan Crockett had been a young man, only forty-two. Understandably, Sheila had taken it badly. She'd become very upset, chronically tearful, entering a cycle of depression that threatened to last a long time. Her downward spiral was interrupted when she visited a therapist, Dr. Gudhausen, on State Street. He recommended she process her feelings at the keyboard. After that, Sheila spent long, solitary hours at her writing; she seemed to vanish into it, and when she came back, she'd be tired and cranky.

For a long while Will had feared he'd lost not only his father, but his mother, too.

Still smiling at her, Will hit his mother with their private joke. "I think you just want to buy this place so you'll have something new to clean."

Sheila's eyes widened in mock outrage. Dan gave a halfhearted chuckle.

11

Will realized they were just humoring him, trying to get him out of his funk.

The funk only got worse when, at last, they arrived in the town of Antrim. They were all pretty beat after the three-and-a-half-hour drive from Boston. In spite of himself, Will experienced some relief when Dan pulled the Renault into a yellow-lined parking place in front of a shiny little white building with a picket fence around it. Although this one-story structure was obviously quite new, it was fashioned to look old, a prefab replica of its colonial neighbors. In the front yard, an inverted L-shaped post was driven into the ground. To Will it looked like a gallows for midgets. A little swinging sign hanging from the horizontal post said:

Gordon F. Carey
Land Sales

Dan got out of the car. After fumbling to open the gate, he trotted up the walk to the door. Looking back, he waved and vanished inside. Will and Sheila, road-weary and silent, waited in the car.

Pretty soon a green Scout nosed its way out from behind the little white building. Will thought of an alligator crawling out from behind a rock. Momentarily, Dan jumped back into the Renault. "The place is about five miles out of town," he announced happily.

Sheila nodded, smiling.

Dan followed Mr. Carey's Scout through the tiny town of Antrim. Will took everything in as they passed the drugstore, the inn, a squat brick post office, and a grocery store. He bit his lip.

It's a death sentence, Will thought. *I'm going to die of boredom.*

12

The two-vehicle caravan held to a modest thirty-five miles an hour as they wound along four miles of pitted blacktop. Slate-roofed, two-story houses in contrasting degrees of repair appeared now and then; most had a barn for companionship. Wide-eyed cows stared vapidly from behind single-strand electric fences, their heavy heads turning slowly to track the progress of the passing traffic.

Finally they arrived at the place where Tenny's Hill Road branched off and up.

They drove along another mile of steep, twisty dirt road, flanked by thick greenery, until the house came into view. It stood all by itself at the top of the hill, separated from a barn-board garage by a sloping, gravel-covered yard.

Will's heart sank. Sheila was silent.

Dan parked beside the Scout, and everybody got out.

Will felt cramped from the long drive. He stood up straight, stretched, and yawned. He saw his mother do the same thing. When she leaned backward, her round stomach strained against her loose-fitting top.

"Good to meet you, Missus," said the realtor, without being introduced. "You too, sonny."

Mr. Carey seemed a little too eager to shake everybody's hand. He kept flashing one of those tooth-heavy smiles; it felt as if he were hitting Will in the face with it. The realtor's spiky-looking teeth were stained brown from tobacco. *He isn't smoking now*, Will thought. *Probably abstaining for our benefit.*

Almost immediately Mr. Carey started waving his arms around, pointing things out. He referred to the gravel parking area as a "dooryard." He called the garage a barn, and the porch a piazza. This was Will's first exposure to any kind of Vermont dialect. He had the feeling Mr. Carey was laying it on a little heavy, maybe for the same reason he wasn't smoking.

From the moment he set eyes on the place, all Will could think about was escape. If they actually moved here, he'd want to get away as often as possible. He wouldn't be able to drive a car until he was sixteen, almost a year from now. Till then, he'd need a bike to get back and forth to town. Too bad his Schwinn ten-speed had been stolen last summer. Too bad he hadn't gotten another one.

Trapped.

Will looked at the house with a feeling of horror. It wasn't scary-looking, that wasn't the problem. It was just a dump. The windows were bashed in, the front door was boarded up and the whole place needed a paint job.

He didn't even want to look inside. He was sure his mom and stepfather wouldn't, either. With any luck, now that they'd seen the place, seen it for the wreck that it was, they'd decide to turn around and go home. Maybe they'd even give up this crazy idea of moving to the country. He cringed at the thought of another three-and-a-half-hour drive back. It'd be worth it, though.

"Let's have a look," said Dan. Was the enthusiasm in his voice real or forced? Will searched his stepfather's face for a clue. Dan's eyes were sparkling below his rimless glasses—a bad sign.

Mr. Carey led the way, walking with a slight limp. It suggested there might be at least one interesting story connected with this overeager little man. Maybe a war wound? Maybe a hunting accident, or a fight? Dan and Sheila kept pace with him across the gravel yard and up the rickety steps to the porch.

Will tagged along, reluctantly.

"It ain't been lived in for about four, maybe five years." Mr. Carey told them.

"I can see why," Will muttered, but a stern look from his mother discouraged further comment.

The realtor opened the door, which was cracked down the middle and nailed back together with planks and bent spikes.

What could do such a thing to a door? Will wondered—*frost maybe?*—but he didn't really care enough to ask.

"Looks like the vandals have done a little bitta damage," said Mr. Carey, as if tuning in to Will's thoughts. "Sorta thing can't be helped these days, not even way up here in God's country."

God's country, yeah right.

Inside, the house was dark and damp and smelled like the dirt basement of their brownstone duplex in Boston. ("I shoulda come up here earlier, aired the place out," Mr. Carey chattered.) Faded blue linoleum peeled in tar-rimmed triangles from the floor. ("Nice wood floors under there. Pegged pine. Oak in the other room.") Paint scrolled from the doorframes and wainscoting. ("Dunno why they'd wanna cover up the woodwork like that.") Here and there, fist-sized holes in the walls exposed a skeleton of lath below plaster muscle and wallpaper skin. ("Little paneling'll fix that right up in pretty good shape.")

It's a goddamn slum, Will thought.

Upstairs was no better than the downstairs, and the cellar was the worst yet. It was like a cave designed to store witless children.

The whole place gave Will the creeps. He was profoundly surprised when Dan made an offer on it.

———

"Twenty-five thousand dollars, for a house and fifty acres, it's a steal!" Dan told his wife and stepson on the ride home.

Gotta do something, Will thought. "But Dan, the place is a disaster area …"

"We can put twenty grand into fixing it up and still come out ahead of the game."

"But there's no TV …"

"There is too, didn't you see that old antenna on top of that broken-down windmill in the back?"

15

"Jeez ..."

"Mr. Carey said it'll pull in Channel 3 out of Burlington when the wind's blowing just right." Dan winked at Sheila.

"Sure, one channel, big deal."

"So we'll get a satellite dish; how does that suit you?"

"But what about my karate lessons?" Will persisted. "I bet there's no place around here to practice."

"That's because people around here don't fight," Sheila said.

Goes to show how much you know about karate, Will thought, staring out the window again. He didn't say anything more. He had argued the best he could, but he'd lost.

They bought it anyway.

CHAPTER 2
SCHOOL'S OUT

Not counting the driver, Mona Grant was the only person on the school bus as it puffed and chugged its way toward the intersection of Tenny's Hill Road.

Hers was the last stop on the route.

She looked out the window, watching for small animals at the roadside, birds in the trees, anything to break the green monotony of the fifty-minute ride home. She knew she should be feeling happier—this was, after all, the last day of school—but mostly she felt lonely.

As always, she was making the trip alone. Just once it would be great if a friend came home with her. Some of the other kids brought their friends home on the bus, but not Mona. Never Mona. And, because this was the last day of school, all she had to look forward to was a long and friendless summer. She lived too far out of town for anyone to visit, and besides—she had to admit it—there was no one who liked her well enough to come to her house.

Maybe next year things would be different. She knew for sure that things were starting to change.

It wasn't her imagination; the changes were real, visible, she could see them in her mirror. Her tall, gangly body was beginning to fill out; her hips were rounding, softening, her breasts—finally—were beginning to grow.

This morning, while she had studied herself in her bedroom mirror, she had smiled at her changing image, and—at least to her—the smile had been more like a woman's than a little girl's.

Now she had the whole summer to let the changes run their course. She'd let her hair grow all the way down to her ass, by God, and she'd save every bit of her bottle money to buy makeup and pretty earrings. Next fall, on the first day of her freshman year, she'd be a different person. Maybe the other girls would like her then. She was sure the boys would; they were already starting to notice.

The bus driver, "Rapid" Rollins, cleared his throat as he downshifted. The bus lurched a little, and Mona crossed her legs, her denim skirt riding up to expose the sleek early tan of her thighs.

She smiled to herself when she caught Mr. Rollins looking at her in his wide rearview mirror. With a new optimism she realized that not only boys, but grown men, were starting to take notice. And this wasn't the first time she'd seen Mr. Rollins looking at her.

He cleared his throat again. Coughed loudly. His cough sounded wet, just like Pa's, probably the result of too many cigarettes. At least Mr. Rollins didn't smoke on the bus; that would be awful. Mona wished she could get Pa to quit it, or at least to stop smoking in the trailer. It made the whole place stink!

Mr. Rollins's voice cracked when he finally spoke. "Almost home, Mona."

"Yup."

"Bet you're pretty excited 'bout school bein' over."

"I s'pose."

"What ya gonna be doin' with yourself all summer long?"

Mona saw his hopeful eyes in the mirror and smiled quickly at him. Then she snapped her head forward so her hair closed around her face like a curtain. Looking down at her lap, she

18

muttered, "Dunno. Guess I'll do some readin' an' take care of Pa's garden."

"Ain't you got no boyfriends to help you pass the time?"

Mona shook her head, smiling secretly behind the barrier of her hair.

Mr. Rollins passed the turn-off, stopped, backed the bus onto Tenny's Hill Road, and stopped again. Mona stood up, gathered her notebook and used lunch bag, and walked between the rows of empty seats toward the front of the bus.

Rapid Rollins still hadn't pulled the handle to open the folding door beside the driver's seat. Instead, he turned his body to look at her.

Mona kept her face down, clutching the book and bag against her body. She pushed it tightly against her stomach, knowing it made her breasts stand out.

Mr. Rollins cleared his throat again. "Now suppose," he stammered, "… suppose I was to take a little drive up here in my car someday this summer. How'd you like it if you an' me went out for a little ride sometime? Think you might like that?"

Mona stopped and stared at the door, waiting for it to open. "Where to?"

"Why, anywheres you like, that's where to. Do you good to get out once in a while. Go for a little spin, maybe over to Springfield for an ice cream?"

"I dunno. Maybe …"

Glancing back she saw him smile. His black and white whiskers looked like tiny arrows stuck in his face. Mona saw that most of his teeth were missing. His wet tongue probed at a gap between two yellow teeth.

"I gotta go now," she said.

Mr. Rollins grabbed the door lever. "Okee-doke, but don't you go forgettin' now. I owe you one ice cream cone, an' I always pays my debts." He winked at her and pulled the handle. The

19

door folded open. Mona slipped past him, but not quickly enough to escape a pat on the butt.

When she was on the ground, she didn't turn around to look at him. She was smiling, though, and the painless tingle on her bottom felt good—promising.

She had started walking up the hill when she heard the bus door close and the engine rev. She glanced back to see the clumsy old bus rolling down the hill toward town.

From here it was a fifteen-minute walk to her trailer. Tenny's Hill Road wound around like a big "S," so it was faster to cut through the woods than to follow the road.

Mona took off her loafers and stepped onto the warm dirt path that veered off into the forest. In a moment she was beneath the green tent. Sunlight dappled the trail and the surrounding ferns, giving them almost a surreal florescence. A tiny lizard crossed her path; she lost sight of it as it scampered behind a boulder.

A stand of evergreens was ahead. She had often thought about how old they must be; they towered, it seemed, nearly to the clouds. Sometimes she imagined they were ancient pillars, holding up the sky. High above her, their branches, long, thick, and intertwined, wove a living fabric that the sun could barely penetrate. She stepped into the evergreen forest, and it was like stepping into evening. The light seemed to vanish, and she was in a strange twilight world with balsam-scented air.

Mona filled her lungs with the comfortable fragrance, and suddenly she was in no real hurry to get home. Pa would probably be there, stinking of beer and sweat and cigarettes, and wanting to get friendly.

"Come on, Babydoll," he'd say. "Come give ole Pa a smoother."

Sometimes she'd give him a quick peck on the cheek, sometimes she'd go directly to her room and lie on the bed with the headphones on. If she kissed him, he'd grab her; if she went to her room, he might come in and … Well, she hoped he wasn't drunk, at least.

No, she wasn't in a hurry to get home …

Mona sat down on the brown pine needles. She could feel their prickle against the backs of her legs. Leaning against the trunk of a tree, she closed her eyes, breathing in the relaxing odors of the forest.

She could almost fall asleep. Here, in this wonderful place, her loneliness didn't matter. She felt fine now. The solitary months ahead didn't bother her, either. *Maybe it's better I'm alone,* she thought. If a friend were with her, she couldn't enjoy the forest as much; they'd be talking, or laughing, not feeling the crispness of the breeze or inhaling the pleasant-smelling air. They'd be mindless of the erratic song of the birds, or the scratching of tiny chipmunk claws in the branches overhead.

Relaxed now, eyes closed, she might have dozed off, but she felt her nipples beginning to harden against the fabric of her cotton blouse. She ran her palms along her naked arms—goose bumps!

Had it suddenly become cold in the forest?

Mona looked around, expecting to see branches waving in the wind. But everything was still, motionless. She listened; all the woodland noises had stopped. Her eyes explored the tree limbs overhead, looking for birds or squirrels or chipmunks.

Nothing moved.

Then she heard a twig snap.

She looked in the direction of the sound and saw a shadow disappear behind a tree trunk.

Mona stood up, facing the direction of the movement. She squinted into the half-light of the pine forest, trying to see what had moved.

Pine needles crunched. She jerked around, trying to pick out the source of the sound. Again the crunching noise, like footsteps moving closer.

Cold tension seized her. Muscles taut, she held her breath, listening, watching.

Another crunch.

Oh God, she thought. *Rapid Rollins is coming back. He's parked the bus, and he's coming back!*

She turned in the direction of her trailer and took a tentative step. Pine needles crunched under her own bare foot. The noise seemed strangely loud.

Another shadow jumped, to her right this time. It was a quick, dark movement in her peripheral vision, hardly visible, then gone.

Her legs started moving on their own. A few cautious steps at first, then her stride lengthened, and she was running.

Wind seemed to build around her. She heard it overhead. Long pine boughs moved as if tugged by puppet strings. It wasn't the slow, graceful swaying of a spring breeze; it was abrupt, jumpy, as if small animals were scampering in the branches above.

Thump! Something dropped out of a tree fifty yards to her left, then darted behind the trunk. Another thud, as something behind her hit the ground.

She couldn't look everywhere at once!

Mona ran, mouth open, arms stretched out in front of her. Something was after her, something that made the air cold and made trees move in the windless air.

She caught occasional glimpses of stunted forms darting from tree to trunk—like apes, almost—never remaining in sight long enough to identify.

Maybe they're kids, she thought, *maybe they're playing some kind of trick on me.* In a more rational part of her mind she knew this could not be so; there were no kids around, no houses even, except for that creepy old place at the top of Tenny's Hill.

Mona was maybe half a mile from the safety of her trailer. If she called out, could Pa hear her at such a distance?

"Paaaa!"

There was movement all around her now, in the trees, on the ground. Noise and motion inspired confusion, then panic.

Pine needles bit into her feet, as if the earth had teeth. An exposed root caught her foot; Mona pitched forward and felt her wrist snap as she caught herself, trying to prevent her face from colliding with a boulder.

"Paaaa! Hellllp meeee!"

She tried to get up, but something grabbed her hair from behind. It hurt like crazy. She jerked her head to the side, trying to see what was holding her. A wave of pine needles sprayed across her eyes as if tossed by a wind. As she tried to shake the gritty twigs from her face, something dropped over her head. A bag? A blanket?

God! She couldn't see! Everything was black!

"Paaa!" The muffled sound was useless within the smelly fabric. Mona whimpered and struggled. Her body thrashed like a landed trout. She felt hands, lots of hands, all over her …

PART TWO
THE HOUSE

ECHOES

"You believe in God? I thought not. An' if you don't believe in God, you don't believe in the devil, neither. An' you don't believe in his kin. There's so damn much evil in the world nowadays, you start to see it as normal. You figger, hell, if it's normal, it *can't* be the work of Satan …"

—Perly Greer, 1983

CHAPTER 3
POPBEADS

Sheila Crockett stood at the bottom of the stairs, hands on hips, looking around and smiling. Sunlight blasted through spotless windowpanes, and the bright air was rich with the fragrance of Pledge. *The place looks great*, she thought. *Even Will has to admit it looks a whole lot better.*

By the second week in July, when the family had actually moved in, the contractors had completely transformed Will's "dirty old farm," into something of a showpiece. Will had said, a bit reluctantly, that it was like moving into a brand-new house.

Now, almost three weeks later, Sheila felt that everything was finally in place. She walked across the glowing wood floor of their carefully furnished colonial living room. She slid her fingers across the smooth, almost flesh-soft surface of Dan's rolltop desk, then paused, captured by the panorama to the west. The view was beautiful, breathtaking—rolling green countryside, distant mountains—framed like an oversized landscape painting by sliding glass patio doors.

She opened one of the doors just enough to slip out onto the newly constructed deck. Inhaling deeply, she enjoyed the cedar-fragrant odor of sawdust from the freshly cut lumber below her feet.

Sheila felt good. Wholesome. The therapeutic effects of the country air made her tingle with confidence. Things would be fine now. At last the family was in exactly the right place. There could be no better spot in all the world for their baby to be born.

She took a few steps to the far side of the deck, leaned against the railing for a moment, then turned around and looked up at their house. The colonial red siding was so bright it almost hurt her eyes. A flicker of pride exploded into a tremendous feeling of success. After all, it was her money that had made it all possible.

But it wasn't right to feel possessive, she knew. It was selfish and boastful. It was Dan's house, too. And Will's. Still, none of it could have happened so quickly if it weren't for Sheila's books.

In all fairness, it was nothing she could take credit for, not really. It was luck, pure and simple. Oh, maybe there was a modicum of talent thrown in, but mostly it was luck—and a gifted editor.

In the last seven years, Sheila had published three novels.

From the time she was a little girl, Sheila's one enduring ambition was to be a writer. Eight or nine years ago she'd worked up the courage to take the first hesitant step toward fulfilling her dream; after much talk and more procrastination, she finally put pen to paper. Her intent was modest, she would write a book for teenaged girls. An adventurous editor at Allen House Publishers took a chance on her novel, *Popbeads*. It was released in paperback, targeted for young adult readers.

Excellent reviews followed. Film producers chomped at it like hungry piranha.

Feeling more adventurous now, the editor had it reissued, this time completely repackaged for a general audience. Adults started reading *Popbeads*. It caught on; it took off.

Sheila sold the film option on her second novel, *Charm Bracelet*, for what she had once thought of as a year's pay. Her third novel, *Toymaker*, earned such a big advance they were able to buy this house outright.

It was something to be proud of, all right. But Sheila felt a little ashamed, almost guilty, about any kind of pride.

Whenever she experienced this, or any other ignoble emotion, Sheila always did the same thing for release: housework.

It was a problem, she knew, yet she had come to tolerate, if not accept, her near obsession with cleanliness. It was the last carryover from that terrible time when her first husband had died. It remained the one thing about Alan's death she still hadn't been able to put into some kind of manageable perspective.

At least hers was a harmless preoccupation. Dan even teased her about it sometimes. Once at dinner he said to Will, "Your mother depends on that vacuum cleaner the way a kidney patient depends on a dialysis machine."

Will had smiled wanly, probably not getting the joke. Sheila saw the humor—thank God she could laugh at herself—but it hurt a little just the same. Cleaning was, after all, compulsive behavior; she couldn't help it.

She'd beat it though; she was determined to get it under control. With the baby coming, it was essential she learn to relax. The housekeeper Dan would find through the want ads would be a big help.

A housekeeper! Sheila thought, *what yuppies we're turning into.* Yet she was eager for the help, and for the company.

———

Will let the kitchen door slam, announcing his arrival. He found his mother in the living room, trying to hang some variety of long-leafed plant from a little bronze-colored hook in the ceiling.

Her long, blonde hair was a tightly braided golden rope; it dangled parallel with her spine as she stood on a ladder-back chair. Arching slightly backward, she stretched toward the ceiling. Her stomach was so round it looked as if she were smuggling a basketball beneath her blouse.

Will felt a little ashamed every time he looked at Sheila and saw her, not as his mother, but as a woman. Still, he couldn't help noticing how her breasts seemed to be growing larger every day. Probably it was a little warped to be checking out your mother's breasts, but he had to admit it, she was a good-looking woman. Lately, she appeared so much calmer, too. Her face was relaxed, peaceful. Somehow, she looked younger and very pretty.

Will remembered how Dan was always telling her to rest more. The move itself had been hard work for a pregnant woman. That was behind them now, of course, but Mom still couldn't slow down. Will knew she wouldn't be able to rest until everything in the house was just so.

"Why don't you let me help you hang those plants?" he asked.

She looked down from the chair and smiled. She acted a little surprised by the offer. "You must be awfully bored if you've stooped to helping with the housework."

"Naw," said Will. "I'm just a great guy."

Sheila handed him the red clay flowerpot and climbed down off the chair with one long, painful-looking step. Will took her place, picking up the plant by the attached cords. He had to reach way up, stretching on his tiptoes, to loop the string over the ceiling hook.

Will wasn't especially tall for a fifteen-year-old—only about five six. Although Dan and Sheila assured him he'd grow some more, Will wasn't too sure. As it was, he wasn't even as tall as his mother; she was five nine. To Will, it was important to be at least as tall as his mother.

"What else you want me to do?" he asked.

"You want to ride into town with me? I'm going to do a little grocery shopping. I want to have something special for dinner tonight. Kind of a celebration."

30

"Celebration? How come?"

"'Cause all the papers are signed. Today is Dan's first day as the official new owner of the *Tri-Town Tribune!*"

"Oh yeah, right." Will knew it was all part of the master plan. The whole rationale for their being here wasn't simply a whimsical relocation from Boston to Antrim, Vermont. It wasn't just a poetic quest for solitude so Mom could continue her writing career.

More than anything else, the move was for Dan's benefit.

In Boston, Dan had worked as a reporter for a daily newspaper, *The Olympian.* Since he and Sheila had gotten together, Dan had been talking, more and more enthusiastically, about how great it would be to move to the country and run his own newspaper. Sheila liked the idea and became almost as excited about it as Dan. Pretty soon the discussion became a plan.

Then they actually did it! Sheila got her solitude; Dan got his paper. But what did Will get? Nothing.

Well, that wasn't exactly true. Dan had offered to let Will do a column for the *Tribune* once school got started. He could be the reporter assigned to high school news. Might be a good way to meet some people and to make a little money at the same time. Besides, Will had always like to write. Maybe it ran in the family.

Sheila made sandwiches while Will mixed iced tea from an envelope, the kind with the sugar already in it. Then they sat down on the deck to have lunch.

"So, are you going to ride into town with me after lunch?"

"Yeah sure, why not." Will heard himself answering, all the while knowing he didn't want to go into town; there wasn't much of anything to do there. He didn't know why he was agreeing. Maybe he was just trying to please his mother.

They sat quietly for a few minutes, looking out at the swaying green grasses in the nearby meadow, watching the shadows shifting slowly on the mountain.

Finally Sheila said, "Will"—she always began a sentence with his name whenever she had something really serious to say—"we've been here almost a month now, and I'm wondering, are you honestly as bored as you're trying to act?"

Although it took him by surprise, it was a fair question. Will reflected for a moment. After all, being bored was something you didn't normally think about, you just did it. "It's just that there's nothing to do. I don't know anybody."

"You'll meet people fast enough when school starts."

"Yeah, I know. But I just don't see what anybody's supposed to *do* around here."

"What do you suppose country kids do?"

"Who knows? Go walking in the woods, maybe?"

"Or hunting, or fishing ..."

Will had the feeling his mother didn't know what country kids did, either. She seemed to ponder the question a long time. Sipping her iced tea, she never took the glass from her lips, just tipped it back a little every now and then as she looked out over the mountains.

Finally she said, "I guess it's pretty much a matter of what we can and can't do. To tell you the truth, Will, I'm not sure I can enjoy all these simple country pleasures any better than you can. I mean, I *can't* enjoy them right now, but I want to *learn* to enjoy them. Do you know what I mean?"

Will felt confused. "Guess so," he told her.

"I mean, it's a big change of life for all of us, you know?"

Will nodded, polished off his tea and wiped his mouth on the back of his wrist.

"So, you coming into town with me or not?"

Will's gaze wandered out across the pasture, over the stone wall, and into the forest. "Maybe not," he said. "Maybe I'll try going for one of those hikes in the woods."

His mother seemed surprised that he hadn't accepted her invitation. She stared at him as if she were trying to determine how serious he was. When she had decided, she said, "Do you think you really should be going off into the woods by yourself? You're really not used to—" Then she started laughing. Her face turned red and tears dripped from her lower eyelids.

Will had no idea what she was laughing at.

When she caught her breath, she said, "What a pain in the rear we mothers must be, huh, kiddo? First, I tell you to start getting into country life, then when you do, I tell you not to. No wonder adolescence is such a mixed-up time."

She gave Will a pretend stern look. "But I've got to say it, Will. I can't help myself. You be careful if you go hiking. And I mean it. You're not used to the woods—"

"Yeah, yeah," he said, and they both started laughing. Sheila reached over and mussed his brown hair. Her belly pressed firmly against the patio table, as if it were taking a big bite of the tabletop.

The camera Will took with him was a little 35mm made by Canon. Dan and Sheila had given it to him soon after their marriage. They said it was a wedding present. Dan explained that Will had gotten married, too, so why should they get all the gifts?

Gestures like that were what had eventually solidified an uneasy friendship between the boy and his stepfather.

At first Dan tried a little too hard to get Will to like him. He always wanted to play catch, or take Will to Red Sox games.

But Will had never liked baseball.

Finally, Dan and Will discovered they both enjoyed Sherlock Holmes stories, science fiction movies, and all sorts of lore and legend of the arcane variety.

Will figured not too many people knew who H. P. Lovecraft was, but Dan knew. One of the happiest days of his life was when Dan presented him with an Arkham House edition of one of Lovecraft's books. It was from Dan's own collection! Suddenly they really had something to talk about.

It was then that Dan finally admitted he didn't like baseball that much either. They started going to scary movies instead of Red Sox games, and by the time Sheila and Dan got married, Dan and Will were pretty good friends.

Living with Sheila was a little like getting a massage from someone wearing a barbed ring. Most of the time it felt great, but every now and then—when the barb caught—it hurt like a son of a bitch.

Dan Wilder smiled, satisfied with the analogy. It seemed to describe their marriage very well. Right now they were going through one of the best periods ever; it seemed as if everything was falling perfectly into place.

So why didn't she answer the phone?

Holding the receiver away from his ear, Dan could still hear the far-off purr at the other end of the line. It repeatedly told him Sheila and Will were not at home. *Odd,* he thought, *where could they be?*

Dan wanted to talk to his wife, tell her that the meeting and the signing had gone smoothly. He wanted to share his good mood and hoped to invite his wife and stepson for a celebration dinner.

Still the phone rang. With each trill his joy inched slowly toward minor irritation. Looking up from his desk, Dan gazed at downtown Antrim through the dusty storefront window.

He felt his face split into a smile.

Must be ESP, he joked to himself. *Isn't that Sheila's station wagon coming up Main Street?*

———————

The woods began about a hundred yards in any direction from the house. It was as if the house, the garage, and the mowed lawn comprised a little island of civilization in the middle of a vast, unchartable sea of wilderness.

Will walked out behind the garage where a disused trail led across a flat, rocky plane and up to a stone wall. Dan had once explained that the stone walls had been built for sheep. In the early eighteen hundreds, this whole area had been heavily involved with sheep farming. Of course, that was before Vermont had become a dairy state.

He hopped easily over the stone wall and started walking among the trees. He noticed how much darker it was in the forest. It smelled good, though, kind of like Christmas.

Which way to go? Without a specific destination, it was difficult to make choices. If he walked to the right, the land got steeper and led up to Pinnacle Mountain. They owned a lot of that mountain—just how much he wasn't certain—but not the whole thing.

To his left there was a brook. He could hear it rushing and splashing, but couldn't quite see it yet. *The brook might be interesting*, he thought, and decided to take a look.

After walking two hundred feet or so into the forest, he could see the brook winding through the trees. The water splashed over brown, slippery-looking rocks, spraying tiny halos of mist into the air.

Stray beams of sunlight spilled through an opening in the branches far above the water. The beams fell and struck the halos, turning them into little rainbows.

It was pretty. He wondered if he could get a picture of it. Stretching out on the riverbank, he got his head, and the camera, really close to the water, trying to fix the miniature rainbow just right in the viewfinder.

Snapping a couple of pictures, his mind switched to fish.

He didn't know much about fish. There was cod, of course, and mackerel, and all the other kinds you eat. But those were ocean fish.

What kind of fish might live in this water? Dan had sometimes talked about taking up trout fishing. Quite possibly, Will concluded, this was a trout stream.

He jumped to his feet, bounded out to a large flat rock in the middle of the stream, and sat down. A pool of water collected around the downstream side of the rock. It looked fairly deep, maybe twelve or fifteen inches, easily big enough for a fish to live in. But too much sun on the stream's sparkling surface made it almost impossible to see what was happening underwater.

When his shadow fell across the pool it killed some of the reflections. Now he could make out rocks and leaves and small stiff branches twitching in the current below.

If a fish came by, he hoped to get a picture of it.

After waiting patiently as long as he could—maybe five minutes or so—nothing had swum by.

Discouraged, he decided to follow the brook down to see where it went.

In some places it had cut so deeply through the earth that trees and bushes grew right up to the water's edge. When that happened, Will jumped off the bank and hopped from stone to stone, making his way right down the middle of the brook. Once he slipped and got a sneaker full of icy water. He gasped and swore and after a while decided it hadn't felt all that bad.

In a little while, he started to get thirsty. The day was hot, and he was sweating. He wasn't sure if this brook water was safe to drink, so he just rubbed some on his face and neck.

After making his way farther downstream, the running water started to sound strangely loud. About fifty feet in front of him the stream narrowed, funneling between two huge ledges, where it disappeared.

As Will got closer, he saw he was standing above a waterfall. Climbing carefully across one of the funneling ledges, he peered over the side.

The thick column of water shot downward for about twelve feet, crashing and bubbling where it collected at the bottom in a big churning pool.

That's when he saw the girl.

She was stretched out languidly on a flat rock at the side of the pool. The sunlight was bright on her. It looked as if she had just been swimming; the rock she was lying on was dark with dampness, her T-shirt was wet, clinging tightly to her body.

Lying on her stomach, she was posed like some girl in a magazine. Will could tell from the way the shirt stuck to her that she wasn't wearing anything underneath.

Interest piqued, he crouched down a little. He felt self-conscious and hoped she couldn't see him. Probably his brown hair would blend in pretty well with the colors of the forest; he didn't need to be worried.

But might she hear him? No, not a chance; it would be impossible above the roar of the waterfall.

Confident he was adequately camouflaged, Will lay down on the rock and made himself comfortable. Unabashedly, he watched her for a while, even considered taking her picture, but somehow that just didn't feel right.

Who was she? What was she doing out here all alone?

Squinting to get a good look at her, he hoped to determine how pretty she was. It was impossible to see her face because it was buried in her folded arms. Her back looked nice, though, and her legs were long and very tan. In addition to the T-shirt, she was wearing microscopic denim shorts. Nothing else.

Nothing!

When she rolled over he got a better look at her. He watched, fascinated by the way her breasts moved under the wet, white fabric. Even at that distance, Will could see her nipples, hard and brown, below the cloth. The T-shirt had some faded writing on it, but he couldn't see what it said.

All of a sudden she stood up and pulled off the T-shirt. Will fought the urge to take a picture then.

He marveled at her breasts; they were large and bouncy. Part of him wished he'd brought his binoculars instead of the camera. The fact was, this was the first time—outside of magazines, of course—he'd ever seen a girl's breasts.

He began to feel himself becoming aroused.

He remembered some of the guys back home, scummy guys like Phil Lubio, who said they'd actually done it with some girl. Will didn't believe it. He didn't even believe the guys who claimed they'd seen a girl's tits, unless it was their sister's or something. Will knew most of them were just bragging.

But was bragging any worse than spying?

He'd almost resolved to tear himself away when the girl started to take off her shorts. He got a quick glimpse of the dark patch of hair between her legs before she jumped into the water. Then he could hardly see her at all because she was churning up the pool.

Watching her for a minute longer, he suddenly started to feel funny. Could he be some kind of pervert? The words "peeping tom" came to mind.

Will turned away, sweating, resisting a final urge to take a picture.

Then he went home.

CHAPTER 4
UNDER OBSERVATION

"God damn it all to Christ!" Police Chief Richard G. Bates stripped yard after yard of tangled monofilament from his open-faced reel. It was bunged up worse than he'd thought; he was going to have to cut it. Calculating quickly, he figured he was about to lose at least twenty yards of line, not to mention the brand-new Mepp's spinner that had come off when the line snapped.

Sliding a moist palm across his forehead, Bates discovered he was sweating. He was breathing hard, too. And his heart was thumping.

Hell, he wasn't simply annoyed, he was out and out angry.

"What the hell's eatin' me, anyway?"

Less than a half hour ago, he'd parked the cruiser up by the road and had walked down to the bank of the Connecticut River to try a couple of casts. Why not? People took smoke breaks and coffee breaks while they were on duty. Why not a fishing break? Maybe it would calm him down.

It hadn't worked. He was still edgy as hell. Christ, lately everything he'd tried to help him relax had backfired. He wasn't supposed to smoke; drinking—coffee or alcohol—was prohibited; eating, especially when he did it to calm his nerves, was against the rules; and now even fishing got him all riled up. What was left?

40

Bates shook his head from side to side, violently, like a dog trying to throw off the weight of a rainstorm. That didn't work, either. No matter what Bates did, he just couldn't shake his uneasy feeling.

It had been with him for days now, floating just below the surface of his thoughts. It tainted everything he did, colored everything he said. The awareness of the feeling was everywhere, making it impossible to concentrate.

Uneasy? Listless? Bates couldn't find the word to describe the sensation. All he knew for sure was that he couldn't get rid of it. It was like one of those irritating little tickles in the back of the throat. But this tickle wasn't in his throat; it was in his mind.

And it was building, getting stronger.

He took a deep breath, turned from the river, and wandered up the pebbled path to the police car. He should probably head back to the office; he'd been avoiding it long enough. The way his luck was running, Bates was positive the new town manager would be there waiting for him, acting real buddy-buddy and confidential, encouraging him to lose more weight. "I'm not thinking about the job, Dick, I'm thinking about your health." Goddamn little pisshand.

But the town manager wasn't the problem. Why couldn't Bates figure out what it was?

No matter. It was probably the beginning of some kind of powerful hunch. Bates had always been a firm believer in instinct. When he often said—"a policeman's job is more gut work than head work"—he was serious. Maybe he was even right. In his twenty-five years of police work he'd come to rely on his ample gut every bit as much as he did his cruiser, his radio, or the .357 he had strapped to his belt.

Bates eased his bulk into the driver's seat and wrapped the tight-fitting seat belt around his waist. The steering wheel burrowed into his fleshy abdomen, reminding him of his most

41

recent, and typically unsuccessful, attempt at dieting. When he'd weighed himself this morning the scale had said 345 pounds. That was 7 pounds more than when he had started the diet. *Christ*, he thought, *if I keep this up I'll have to weigh myself on the grain scale down to Agway.*

Ah, what the hell. What's another bad habit.

With fingers big as bananas, he probed the pocket of his sweat-damp shirt. Nothing. Then he reached under the seat and pulled out a pack of Camels. Isolating a single cigarette, Bates removed it from the wrinkled pack and tapped it against the dashboard.

He lighted it and exhaled against the dirty windshield glass.

Driving slowly along Antrim's quiet Main Street, Bates put out the cigarette before he came within sight of the town offices.

Somethin's gonna happen, he thought.

As he scanned the silent buildings, the slow-moving traffic, the kids on bikes, his attention was arrested by the newspaper office.

Maybe it's got something to do with those new people, thought Bates. *Maybe it's got something to do with them and that old house they moved into.*

Bates's mind flicked back to that horrible December morning in 1983. Snow-covered bodies littered the dooryard making it look like a battlefield.

The unnamed instinct throbbed painfully, like a wounded finger.

———

When Will Crockett returned from the waterfall, he saw cars in the yard: Dan's Renault and the big Chevy station wagon his mother had bought for their move to the country.

He stood beside the garage and watched. What the hell was going on? Mom and Dan were standing on the porch, surrounded with brown grocery bags. They were doing something strange with the front door. First they opened it, then closed it, then opened it again.

He saw his mother shake her head, shrug and follow Dan inside. Almost immediately they turned around and came back out.

Then they looked at the door again.

Will couldn't imagine what they were up to. When his curiosity wouldn't allow him to observe any longer, he walked across the yard and toward the porch.

"What're ya doin'?"

Dan jumped at the sound of Will's voice. When he looked down, the boy was smiling that goofy, disarming smile. How could Dan be angry with him?

Luckily, Sheila spoke up before Dan was forced to. "Will, didn't Dan and I both ask you to lock the door when you go out? Don't we always keep the house locked?"

The boy's expression immediately became blank.

Dan hated any sort of confrontation with his stepson; he was uncomfortable with discipline. Nonetheless, it was his husbandly duty to provide backup for Sheila. Parental agreement and consistency were highly important. "Your mother and I have mentioned this time and again, Will. Don't you understand, it's simply *because* no one's around that our house makes such a perfect target for thieves—"

Will shook his head. "But I did lock it," he insisted, holding up his house key as if that would somehow convince them. "I *always* do."

43

Dan looked at Sheila, then back at Will. He peered over the top of his glasses like a stern schoolmaster, but couldn't think of anything to say.

"Are you sure, William?" Sheila asked.

Will nodded. "Absolutely."

Dan believed him. The boy was imaginative, but he wasn't a liar. He wasn't even particularly forgetful.

"Come here and look at this," Dan said. He wasn't content with Will's looking so much like an outsider, standing alone in the yard under two sets of accusing eyes. He felt some kind of relief when the boy ran up the steps to join them on the porch.

"What do you think, Sherlock?"

At Dan's encouragement, Will examined the front door. "I guess somehow it came unlocked. Maybe because it's an old lock, or something … ?"

"Maybe," Sheila said, skepticism heavy in her voice.

"Not one of your more brilliant deductions," Dan chuckled, "but you demonstrate a firm grasp of the obvious." He looked at his wife. "We'll have to get a new lock, Sheila."

She nodded, raising frightened eyes toward the open door.

Dan cleared his throat, choking back his nervousness. "Guess we'd better go inside and have a look around."

Everyone was graveyard quiet as, single file, they followed Dan into the house. Separating—but not too much—each looked in a different direction. Dan watched his wife moving cautiously, as if she expected something to jump out from behind the furniture.

He was surprised at how uneasy he felt. It was no big deal; the door was unlocked, so what? Probably Sheila just forgot, or maybe Will was the culprit after all.

Sheila tapped Dan's shoulder and pointed to the cellar door—it was slightly ajar. Inching over to it, swallowing nervously, he grabbed the brass knob firmly. *Strangely cold*, he thought. Another deep breath, and he yanked the door open.

He'd expected the door's sudden motion to surprise whoever might be lurking behind it. Instead, it was Dan who jumped. Tripod, their three-legged cat, snarled savagely and bolted from the dark cellarway.

Sheila gasped; Will leaped backward, his hand jumping to his throat.

Heart pounding fiercely, Dan forced a nervous laugh and flicked on the basement light. As he peered down the shadowy stairs, the musty odor from below filled his nostrils.

Could he force himself to go down there?

With Will and Sheila watching, could he refuse?

"Be careful, Dan," Sheila whispered.

Taking each step carefully, as if it might break under his weight, Dan descended about halfway. Bending forward, he looked around.

He held his breath. Fear grew stronger in the back of his mind; *what if someone had come into the house? What if he's still here?*

Bracing himself, he continued his descent. But nobody was in the basement; a quick walk around proved it.

Dan returned to join his wife and stepson at the top of the stairs. When they all trooped into the living room, Will said, "Look at that! The sliding doors!"

Dan saw the glass doors to the deck were closed. "So what, Will?"

"Well, they're closed, just the way they're supposed to be. That's good, isn't it?"

Dan chuckled in spite of himself. "Okay, Sherlock—"

"Look Dan, the spider plant," Sheila voice was shrill. "We just put it up this morning!"

Plant, pot, and hanger had shattered on the floor. Black potting soil spread in a three-foot circle on the rug.

Sheila walked quickly to it and slowly lowered herself, moving awkwardly because of her big stomach. She began to pick up pieces of the red clay pot, placing them beside her in a neat pile.

"The hook must have pulled out of the ceiling," Will said.

Dan looked at the jagged hole in the spotless plaster above his head. "Looks like ..."

For a few moments they stood there, puzzled, watching Sheila as she picked up the red pieces of clay. "Look at this, Dan," she said.

She pointed at a scuff mark in the dirt. It looked like something had been dragged through it.

"A footprint!" Will said.

"Probably Tripod," Sheila said. "Do you think he could have done this, Dan?"

Sheila looked around. So did Will and Dan. They were trying to identify a spot from which Tripod might have jumped.

Although Tripod had only three legs, Dan knew he was a regular cat in every other way. If you dangled something in front of him, he'd swat at it. He'd climb on the furniture if he thought he could get away with it. It would have been completely in character for Tripod to jump onto the flowerpot. But there was a catch; the plant had hung too high off the floor. It would have been impossible for Tripod to reach it. As Dan looked, he realized there was nothing near enough for the cat to have jumped from.

No, they couldn't pin this on Tripod. The only other explanation was that the plant was simply too heavy; it had fallen under its own weight. Somehow, Dan wasn't satisfied with that explanation either.

"Do you think we should call the police, Dan?" Sheila asked.

While he thought about it, he paced around the room. Stopping by the patio door, he pushed his glasses higher onto his nose and peered out across the waving grass beyond the deck.

Then he made a little puffing noise, exploding air between his lips. "No, no I guess not. There really isn't any sign of a forced entry. I don't want to get off on the wrong foot with the police. I don't want them to think I'm one of those paranoid outsiders who'll call them every time he hears an owl hoot."

No one argued, but Sheila didn't look too pleased.

Further inspection convinced them nobody was hiding in the house.

In a way, Dan wished they'd found somebody. Not a thief, or anybody dangerous, maybe a kid, or a neighbor. Otherwise, there was no explanation for the open door and the fallen plant, just a lot of speculation.

Dan hated speculation.

———————

That night Will had a hard time falling asleep. He tossed and turned in his bed, his mind racing. It kept jumping around, from the sexy girl in the woods, to the unlocked door, to the broken flowerpot.

He *had* locked the door. He knew he had. It was a habit. One he'd acquired—and very thoroughly, too—back in Boston. Besides, he could clearly remember wrestling with the ancient lock.

Suddenly, Will was aware that his hand was on his throat. His spirits sank a little when he felt it there; he thought he'd broken that habit.

Like his mother's compulsive housecleaning, this was Will's carry-over from his father's fatal heart attack. Lately, Will hadn't been worried about his own heart too much, not the way he used to be right after Dad died. Back then he'd spent a lot of time with fingers on his neck, feeling his pulse, making sure his heart was pumping the way it was supposed to. He'd discovered that at night, if he lay on his pillow in just the right position, he could hear his heart beating in his ear. He used to listen to it before he could go to sleep. When it thumped away at a regular beat, and when he was sure it wasn't going to stop, he'd fall asleep.

He couldn't sleep now, he was too nervous.

Will knew Mom and Dan were worried, too. They were whispering in the next room. He couldn't tell what they were saying, but the sound continued for a long time.

He kept straining his ears, listening to every tiny noise.

Outside, he could hear a high-pitched cheeping. Dan had told him this was the sound of peepers, young frogs whose shrill chorus rose and fell long into the night. Dogs barked somewhere far away, their relentless yapping amplified and sharpened by the night. The night was full of noises, really, but Will remembered when he'd thought of it as quiet. He'd been accustomed to city noises; these were country sounds, something totally different.

In fact, the house itself played a whole symphony of sounds. Boards creaked, expanding or contracting with the changing temperature outside. When the wind was right, a branch from the nearby maple brushed his window, like bone-dry fingers scratching to get in. The big ventilator fan Dan had installed for cooling whirred like the engine of a spaceship.

And there was something else.

Had Will's imagination started to run away with him? He kept thinking he heard footsteps on the roof. If so, what could be up there? A squirrel? No—it sounded heavier than that.

Whatever it was, at least it was outside; it couldn't get in.

Will wondered who might have a key to their house. Supposedly, just the three of them. It worried him to think that some unknown person could come and go as he pleased.

Will would definitely remind Dan, first thing in the morning, about changing the locks on the doors. Maybe he'd even offer to do it himself. He could do a simple job like that.

Then, from nowhere, a frightening thought popped into his head: maybe it wasn't that someone had come *into* the house; maybe somebody had gone out.

Maybe someone was in here all along, and they had to wait until we all left before they could get out.

That would explain why the door was unlocked; somebody had done it from inside. Then left.

It could have happened that way.

Will got out of bed, went to his door and closed it. Now the cooling fan wouldn't do any good, but he didn't care. When the door was secure, he put a chair against it for good measure. Then he tried to go to sleep again, thinking about the girl by the waterfall, listening to his heart.

CHAPTER 5
THE PASSING OF TRIPOD

A lone with her new word processor.

Sheila sat staring at the blank screen, wondering where to begin. Should she catch up on her letter writing? Make some notes for her nonfiction book? Or should she plunge right into the new novel? She couldn't decide.

The cursor winked steadily, distracting her with meaningless flirtation.

She was all by herself in the house. The guys had gone into town. Will was going to clean the basement at the newspaper office while Dan supervised both operations, upstairs and down. It was a workday, and everybody was working. That is, everybody but Sheila.

The big green eye of the computer screen was like an all-seeing taskmaster, applying unstated pressure for her to produce. *How can I write under this kind of scrutiny?* she joked to herself. The easiest thing, of course, would be to escape into household chores; it had always been a successful dodge. Since they'd moved in, Sheila had devoted untold hours to organizing and cleaning. Painting. Pestering the contractors. It had been easy to pretend she had no time to write.

Now, eye to eye with the screen, there was no excuse at all.

What to write? Where to begin?

———————

"Dan, somebody to see you."

Dan looked up from his desk and nodded a distracted "thank you" to Alicia Faye. As she stepped back toward her own work area, Dan could see the little woman waiting for him at the front of the office. She was petite and wrinkled, with gray-brown hair bunned at the top of her head like the cap of a mushroom. Simply but neatly dressed, she wore light blue slacks and a cream-colored flowery top. As she waited, looking around the office, she clutched a rolled copy of yesterday's *Tribune*.

"Hi," Dan said cheerfully, walking over to her. "I'm Daniel Wilder."

She cleared her throat, her fingers tightening around the newspaper. Dan saw ink smudges on her fingertips. On some sympathetic level it bothered him that this frail-looking little woman should be nervous in his presence. For some reason she made him think of his mother, and he wanted to put her immediately at ease.

Her voice was high-pitched and musical. "You the gentleman's looking for a housekeeper?"

Dan smiled broadly. "Yes, ma'am, someone to help my wife—"

"Well, housekeepin's somethin' I'm good at. Done it all my life. First for my husban', 'fore he died. Now for myself an' anyone needs me. I can give you references, or you and your wife can jest come right on over and inspect my place, have a cup a coffee with me while you're at it."

He had pegged her wrong. This woman wasn't timid at all. She was confident, businesslike, and properly aggressive.

He cleared his throat. "Well, first I'd like you to meet my wife, Sheila. I mean, I put the ad in the paper, but she'll do the hiring."

"That's jest as it should be." The little lady nodded. "I've wrote down my name and phone number"—she handed him a sheet of yellow lined paper—"and this here's a list of people I've worked for. You can call 'em up, then you give me a call when you're ready to talk business."

She held out a moist, ink-stained hand and Dan shook it. "Nice talking with you Mr. Wilder."

"Umm, yes, nice talking to you, too, Mrs.—" he looked down at the paper—"Mrs. Menard ..."

The cursor winked at Sheila from the empty screen.

She imagined herself poring over a tight, terse, colorfully detailed account of the family's day-by-day adjustment to country living. "Back to the Earth," she'd call it, or "Back to the Land ..."

No, she smiled, each of them sounded too much like a euphemism for death. She wanted her journal to be something uplifting, something enduring, like *Walden*, or Marjorie Kinnan Rawlings's *Cross Creek*.

She tried on a new excuse: she hadn't learned to use her new word processor yet. The manual did no good. It was like trying to pilot a submarine using "Cliff's Notes."

The idea of "processing words" still struck Sheila as kind of funny. It seemed as if these days one "processed" just about everything: words, food, even emotions.

She tentatively placed her fingers on the keys, then typed:

After my husband died, I spent hours at the typewriter—the suggestion of my therapist. "Writing's the way you best express yourself, Sheila," he had said. "Why not write out everything you're thinking and feeling. You can show me what you want, we'll talk about it. You can show me nothing at all …"

It was a good suggestion. As Dr. Gudhausen told me, I "processed" my feelings; as Dan was quick to point out, the old fart "processed" himself right out of a job!

But there had been a good side to it: This "processing" had evolved into a bestseller. The only difference was that today she didn't have any "negative feelings" to process. Nothing like her husband's death.

She typed:

Listen to me! "My husband's death." I wonder how Dan would feel about that choice of words? He was touchy enough when Will and I decided to keep Alan's name. But the fact is, an awful lot of people will lay down their $14.95 for a book with *Sheila Crockett* on the cover. No one has ever heard of *Sheila Wilder*.

Okay, so maybe I'm superstitious about it, but why change when you're on a roll?

She stopped typing—another false start. A waste of time.

Writers, Sheila concluded, are great time wasters.

As much as she wanted to begin, she just couldn't find inspiration in stone walls, or front doors that unlocked themselves, or crashing spider plants.

Yet, she was convinced there was some vital aspect of country living to address. Where was all the adventure they'd anticipated? Where was the drama? What was the real conflict in their lives just now?

Sure, country living allowed her plenty of time to write, but that was all. It certainly offered nothing like a good death in the family!

A grisly thought, but it started the dominoes falling.

There *was* something after all! She should at least get it down on paper while it was still fresh in her mind. She was sure she'd be able to hammer it into shape and use it sometime. What she couldn't understand was how she'd overlooked it even for a minute—it had happened just this morning.

Sheila typed:

THE PASSING OF TRIPOD

Tripod didn't come home last night, so this morning the three of us organized into a search party and looked for him.

Dan didn't seem nearly as concerned as Will and I. Of course, he hasn't known Tripod as long. "He's probably taking to the back-to-nature stuff faster than we are," Dan said. "I bet he's off stalking some bird, or chewing the head off a field mouse."

I cringed, just the way Dan knew I would.

We dismissed the problem—perhaps too quickly—guessing that Tripod had acquired new, more exotic tastes, and that a rebirth of instinct had replaced his dependency on a daily ration of Cat Chow. From now on, we concluded regretfully, we could plan on seeing less and less of him.

I had no idea how prophetic that phrase would be.

For a moment I felt sad, anticipating how I'd miss his smug feline squint, but generally—at least right then—we were not uncomfortable with Tripod's absence ...

That is, until Dan started the car ...

Will and I could hear Tripod's screech from the kitchen. We thought Dan had backed over him

Instead, sometime during the night, Tripod had apparently crawled up through the wheel well and into the engine compartment of the Renault. There he'd found a cozy place to snooze somewhere near the fan belt. When Dan started the car, it was if he'd put Tripod in a food processor.

When Dan opened the hood, I cringed again at the mess he'd made.

I know Dan was upset. Will was shaken up a bit, too. None of us could figure out why or how it had happened. Tripod had always been afraid of the car; far as I know, he'd never gone near it before. At least, not of his own volition.

I think Dan came up with the best explanation. "I've heard about cats doing that in the wintertime," he offered. "I guess when it gets real cold out, they like to crawl up under the hood; they snuggle up against the heat retained in the engine after it's been running."

Dependable old Will, as always, immediately carved a hole in Dan's theory, "Jeez, Dan, it's August. It wasn't even cold out last night!"

Sheila felt an easy satisfaction as the narrative began picking up steam. There was a story in here someplace. Then—for no apparent reason—the screen went blank.

The power was off.

CHAPTER 6
DOING BUSINESS

Will Crockett couldn't put off the dirty deed any longer. He looked up and down the main street of Antrim, hoping a new form of diversion would present itself. Guilt was quickly overriding avoidance. No way did he want to clean the *Tribune*'s basement. No way. But he'd given his word; he'd promised. Reluctantly, Will braced himself for the inevitable, and, hands in pockets, he headed back through town.

Antrim, Vermont, was small by any standards. The inhabitants were scattered far and wide, among back roads, hillside farms, and hidden valleys.

The population was sparse enough to suggest far fewer than the U.S. census listing of 2106 official residents.

The center of town was nothing more than a cluster of buildings around a village green. The most imposing structure was the Medford Inn, a monstrous three-story affair built in the mid-nineteenth century. Dwarfed around it, like chicks around a wise old hen, stood a pharmacy, a general store, and a regiment of well-kept wooden houses, many of which had recently been broken up into apartments. Directly across from the inn was the newest building of all: the red brick post office.

This town's soooo boring, Will thought as he walked along. *But it's pretty, a kind of postcard pretty, if you don't have to look at it any longer than you would a postcard.*

The building housing the *Tri-Town Tribune* looked more like a hardware or grocery store than a newspaper office. It was an ancient, unpainted storefront that, Will figured, may never have been a store. Dan had told him the newspaper was 105 years old and had operated out of the same place all that time.

The entire operation was in one big room. A painted, note-covered, plywood divider separated the quieter activities "up front," from the heavy, noisy machinery—presses, mechanical folders, cutters and other big black mysterious looking monstrosities—"out back." One of the presses made a loud clicking sound as it turned.

In the middle of the big room was the lay-out area, with its back-lit glass tabletops and crusty-rimmed jars of rubber cement. Old oaken file cabinets formed a makeshift partition around the typesetter's work space. The office was full of strange mixes and matches; everything was either very old or very new. The dark walls and ancient printing machines contrasted with modern, high-tech equipment, like Dan's new computer, the Ricoh photocopier, and the typesetting machine.

There was a reception area at the very front near the street. People came in to place their advertisements, renew their subscriptions, or pick up copies of the paper for thirty-five cents. They also came in to chat. Dan didn't like that too much because it took work time away from the *Tribune*'s four staff members.

There was Marcie Twombly, the typesetter, Gary Provost, the reporter, and a business manager, Alicia Faye. Dan was the editor/publisher. Will always marveled that it took so few people to get out a weekly newspaper. He was used to visiting his stepfather at the three-story building in Boston, where crowds of people put together the *Olympian*.

When Will walked in, Dan was talking to a policeman. He was a tall, heavyset man—fat, actually—with a pleasant, youthful-looking face. There was something careless about the way he was dressed. It wasn't simply that his uniform looked like he'd been sleeping in it; it was that, in spite of his size, everything seemed too loose, too big for him. Maybe he'd recently lost some weight, or maybe he'd just bought new, larger clothes, expecting to expand some more. Dan introduced him as Chief Bates.

"I hear you're the fella's gonna be handlin' the back-to-school beat," the chief said to Will. He extended a big right hand to shake. His fingers felt like a handful of hotdogs.

"Yes sir," Will said, shaking the sweaty hand. "I guess that'll be a good way to get to know the teachers and kids and everything."

"Same way your pa here's gettin' to know the townspeople. I see he's breakin' you in right, already gettin' you to think like a reporter."

Will had to bite his lip not to explain that Dan wasn't really his pa.

"I hope you an' your ma are settlin' in comfortably," the chief went on. "Bet you find this a considerable change from city livin'. But I'll tell you somethin', you can feel real safe up here in Vermont—ain't that right, Daniel?—ya don't have to worry all the time about keepin' everything locked up tight."

That seemed like an odd thing to say, Will thought. He looked guiltily at Dan. Had he told the chief about their unlocked door? Dan smiled at him noncommittally.

Will liked Chief Bates immediately, but he wasn't sure why. Maybe it was because the guy didn't look like a cop. Will couldn't imagine him chasing anybody, for example, although around here he probably never had to.

It was a good thing he liked the chief, too, because, like him or not, Will knew he should show him a special deference. Dan had explained that the police were the first people a newspaperman had to get to know. The "blotter," or police report, was something everybody in town would want to read. It was a strong selling point for the paper. A reporter had to keep on the good side of the police, or risk losing a lot of news.

"So, what'cha think of Antrim, son?" the chief asked.

Dan winced a little, probably expecting Will to start railing about how bored he was. Instead, Will smiled. "I like it," he said, "but I think I've got a lot to learn about country living."

The chief chuckled through his nose and winked at him. "Now that you mention it, I suppose you do. Small town might take some gettin' used to at that." His face brightened, and his round cheeks lit up like red Christmas bulbs. "I got an idea might get you off on the right track," he said. "How'd you like to join me and my son Mark for a little fishin' someday before school starts? Fishin'll make a country boy of ya quick as anything. I got one of them little aluminum boats. By God we'll take it right out on the Connecticut River—"

"Sure, that sounds good," Will said.

The chief chuckled, looking pleased with himself, and slapped Will's shoulder. "Then we'll just do 'er, son, an' you can count on it."

Will hoped the chief meant it. A lot of people gave kids invitations they never planned to carry through on, but Will had a feeling the chief was on the level. He came off as a sincere kind of guy. Maybe fishing would be all right, too, but Will wasn't so sure. It sounded boring.

The chief looked at Dan. "Well Daniel, I'm off to continue my never-endin' war against crime. My best to the missus. Good meeting you, William."

He shook Will's hand again, this time in a very formal manner, then he left.

"Will," Dan said, "do me a favor before you get started on that basement … Run down to the store and pick up a pound of coffee, okay? We're all out, and I want to avoid a newspaper strike." He pointed to the empty Mr. Coffee machine on a table by the copier.

Delighted at the stay of execution, Will was out the door in a second. Not wanting to hurry the errand, he watched Chief Bates amble across the road and continue in the direction of the old railroad station where the town offices and police station were located.

Again, Will marveled at the chief's size. *He seems like an awfully nice guy*, Will thought, *but how much help can he be in an emergency?*

———————

Sheila blinked at the empty screen. This time the cursor didn't blink back. It was gone! Disappeared. No light at all.

Everything was dead. The page of text, just a second ago so clear and perfect on the screen, had instantly compressed into a point of light and vanished into oblivion.

"Shit!"

She listened for the whir of the computer's cooling fan. Silence.

"It's broken."

Then she had an idea; she tried the desk lamp. Nothing.

"Goddamn power's off, God *damn* it!" she said, slapping her fingers on the desktop. She realized she'd lost every single word she'd electronically composed.

Four, almost five pages, gone!

She tried to calm the rising fury and frustration. The real estate man had warned them the power would go off occasionally—"No storm or nothin'. No reason t'all. Power just goes off ..."—only she hadn't realized what an occupational hazard it would be.

The whole saga of the processed cat, just gone ...

Sheila stared immobile at the shiny black screen. An odd thought occurred to her; it was like staring into the eye of a dead man, unresponsive, distant, though strangely watchful and intrusive.

The deeper she looked into the unblinking eye, the more she was able to see as the reflected room began to open up behind her. Definite, recognizable shapes started to materialize. First, there was the familiar dark image of her own head, but much less distinct than in a mirror. Over her reflection's right shoulder she saw the bright rectangular outline of the window.

Something moved there.

Something was in the window … and then it wasn't.

A hot rush of alarm coursed through her lungs as Sheila turned in her seat, not quite believing her eyes. Now she was looking directly at the window. It was empty.

Strange.

She really had seen something. Hadn't she?

Yes, by God. There could be no doubt. Something round had been clearly reflected in the monitor. Something had been in that window, something that shouldn't have been there, something in the shape of a head.

"Impossible," Sheila said, getting up, walking over to the window for a better look.

"Impossible," she said again, looking down at the ground far below.

She was almost convinced she'd been hallucinating when she heard a noise.

———

A narrow driveway separated the pharmacy from the general store. As Will approached, he heard voices long before he could see who was talking. He resisted an urge to stare into the passage. Instead, he glanced casually over his shoulder as he walked past.

There, snugly tucked in the alley, was an old white convertible with two guys in the front seat. They were talking to a girl carrying two bags of groceries.

Will hadn't gotten a good look at the people, but something about them stuck in his mind. It was as if he'd recognized one: the girl. Something about her—her hair maybe—looked familiar. Could she be the one he'd seen by the waterfall?

He didn't want to stand and stare, but he was curious. He leaned against the wall of the general store, just outside the alley, and listened.

"So whyn't ya let us give ya a lift with them groceries? You ain't gonna *walk* all the way out there to your place, are ya?" It was a guy's voice.

"I'm waitin' for my pa. He'll be 'long soon enough."

"Not if he gets waylaid at the bar, he won't. You could be waitin' here all night. You gonna do that, you might's well wait with Spit an' me."

Will heard that ugly, mocking laughter he associated with bullies; it was a sound he'd always tried to avoid. When it stopped, the car door opened.

"Come on now, Mona, let me take them bags for ya."

Her voice rose, sounding urgent. "No. Stop it Reggie, you'll rip it."

Will heard paper tear. A crash. Glass shattered.

"You've ruined everything. Look! Two quarts of orange juice … lookit them eggs! That's fifteen dollars' worth of food. Pa's gonna kill me!"

"You got food stamps, don'cha. You can jest buy some more …"

The other guy snickered. It was a horrible, taunting sound.

The girl's voice was really shrill now. "Damn it Reggie, you let go of me … Git yer hands offa me!"

"Come on Mona, get in the car. We'll get you some more groceries."

She was fighting with them, Will could tell from the sound. He hated the confusion it inspired in him. Part of him wanted to ignore the situation, just go into the general store and buy the coffee. Another part wanted to help the girl.

But did he dare?

He looked around to see if Chief Bates was still in sight. He wasn't. Nobody was.

It was up to him.

He turned into the alley. The ugly scene registered all at once. Both guys were out of the car now. They were trying to drag the girl into the front seat.

What should he do? He knew what would happen in books and movies. When a girl gets in trouble the hero rushes in and rescues her just in the nick of time. But, even with a few karate classes under his belt, Will knew he was no hero.

"Hey, come on you guys, leave her alone." He blurted out the words. In his own ears they sounded louder than a P.A. system. Once they were out, there was no hauling them back.

The bigger of the two guys let go of her and turned to face Will. "What the fuck . . ?" he said.

This was Reggie—Will could tell by his voice. He was over six feet tall and quite a bit older than he sounded, maybe nineteen or twenty. Reggie had long, limp hair, slick with grease. Randomly placed blotches of pimples distorted his scowling face. The feature that made the biggest impression was his lips. They were bright red and weird-looking, as if there was a smear of lipstick where his mouth should be.

Reggie didn't say anything more, just stared at the intruder as if he couldn't believe his eyes, as if Will were some kind of ghost that had magically materialized.

Then the little guy, Spit, released Mona and stepped forward. He slipped aggressively around Reggie, who was filling up most of the space between the car and the wall of the drugstore, and took a couple of steps toward Will.

Will was cringing on the inside. He knew what was coming, and desperately wanted to avoid it. There was the issue of face — could he save his in the eyes of the girl?

Spit was a horrible little guy. He wore a dirty T-shirt with what first appeared to be a college logo printed on the front. Carefully designed calligraphy nearly disguised the shirt's message: FUCK U. Will guessed it was Spit's comment on higher education, his greeting to people in general.

At first Spit seemed to be wearing some kind of punk hairstyle. On closer examination it was more like some do-it-yourself home hack job. The tattoo on his right arm looked homemade, too.

"Well, whatta we got here, Rambo, or somethin'?" He glared at Will, sneering. The space between his front teeth was big enough for a rat to crawl into.

Will knew the trouble was getting closer, and he had asked for it. How easy it would be to duck out of the alley and disappear. Suddenly, cleaning the *Tribune*'s basement didn't sound so bad.

But he couldn't back down, and he wasn't sure if he could fight. Unconsciously, his hand moved to his throat; trembling fingers searched for a pulse beat.

He tried to think fast, but no action came to mind. The only thing left was to talk. "I'm not Rambo, and I don't want any trouble. I just got a message for Mona. From her father —"

"An' I got a message for you, Rambo. Butt the fuck out."

Spit took a step toward Will. He'd come completely around the car and stood next to the rear bumper. With luck he'd come no closer, but Will didn't feel lucky.

Little guys were likely to be troublemakers. He'd seen them before: belligerent and mouthy, backed up by a big guy like Reggie. A friend of Will's once pegged little guys pretty well: "Trouble with them is, their brains are too close to their assholes."

"Come on, Mona," Will said, "your dad's waiting out front in the car."

"In the car, huh?" Spit looked wide-eyed, his mouth forming a silent "O," as if he'd just received startling news. "What color car?"

Will just blinked, feeling confused.

Spit turned, looking cautiously at the girl as she hugged the remaining bag of groceries. With mock interest he asked, "When'd your pa get a car, Moaner?" Then, turning to Will, he shouted, "Her dad don't have a car, dip-shit, he's got a truck."

Will's bluff had been called. He felt his courage sinking like a stone in a pond. He took an involuntary step backward, pushed by a sense of the approaching altercation. Desperately, he tried to force his mind to speed up; he had to get the better of Spit who, just maybe, wasn't as dumb as he looked.

By now Reggie had moved up behind the little guy. They were both trying to stare Will down. His stomach knotted. He felt hot all over, as if the juices in his body were starting to boil. He was afraid he might throw up. Nausea weakened his legs and his sense of resolve.

"Whyn't ya step into the alley a little more," Spit said.

Mona suddenly spoke up. "Whyn't you jest back off, Spit. Your fight ain't with him. He ain't done nothin'." As she talked, she was inching her way around the other side of the car. "What difference it make what my pa drives? Huh?"

Will appreciated her attempted intervention, and he clearly saw what she was up to. If she could just keep them occupied a minute longer, she'd be able to inch her way to the opening of the alley and slip out. With any luck, Will could join her.

65

The prospect of running away sounded damn good.

Just as he began feeling hopeful, something plowed into his back. Wind blasted from his lungs as he lunged forward, off balance. Reggie grabbed him and spun him around. With a quick, pain-inspiring jerk, Reggie locked Will's arms behind his back.

Yanking him upright, Reggie forced him to face the guy who'd shoved him from behind.

"Wha'd'ya say, Norm," Spit said, grinning like a psycho in a horror movie.

Norm didn't say anything, he just loomed there, a tall, sinister shadow in the alley. He wore black denim jeans tucked into black cowboy boots, and a black western shirt. His cigarette looked as if it were glued to his lower lip. His jet-black hair was frozen motor oil.

"What the fuck's goin' on here?" Norm said to no one in particular.

"Come on, you guys, leave him alone," Mona pleaded, but nobody paid any attention to her. In the corner of his eye Will saw her pick up the remaining bag of groceries and hold it over her head.

Norm took a threatening step toward Will just as Mona slammed the groceries against the hood of the car. The crash immobilized everyone. They watched in frozen surprise as she dashed away.

Will felt some relief that she was safe; he wished he were.

Reggie tightened his hold on Will's arms. They felt as if they might tear from their sockets. "This guy was fuckin' with your car, Norm," he said.

"No, I—"

Norm's facial expression never changed. Very slowly his right hand came up, greased-stained fingers plucked the cigarette from his mouth. He flicked it at Will.

Arms locked in place, Will was unable to duck. The glowing butt shattered against his cheek, painlessly. Burning shards of tobacco fluttered downward and out of sight.

"This here's Rambo." Spit pointed with his thumb.

"Rambo's new in town," Reggie said.

"Looks like we got some gettin' acquainted to do," Norm drawled in his best Clint Eastwood. He stepped forward.

Spit got out of the way as Norm began to remove his wide leather belt. Precise and unhurried, he wrapped it around his hand, leaving the heavy silver buckle dangling on the outside.

Another menacing step.

Will took a couple of deep breaths through his mouth, trying to calm down. *If I fight these guys,* he thought, *they'll really cream me. At least Mona won't be around to see it.*

"Look, I don't want a fight," he said. He hated his voice, it sounded high-pitched and weak.

"You don't always get what you want," Spit giggled from somewhere behind him.

Norm didn't say anything; he just raised the belt.

Oh shit, Will thought. He might have cried out, he wasn't sure; everything seemed to happen automatically. Even though Reggie was holding his arms, Will was able to jump high enough to kick Norm in the face. Norm's cheek felt soft under Will's sneaker. Staggering backward, hand to mouth, Norm looked more surprised than hurt.

Will came down, landing squarely on both feet. Without pausing he thrust upward, using all the strength in both legs to force his weight backward. Reggie went off balance, slamming into the side of the store. He yelled "Ooof," and Will was free.

All three guys were in fighting positions. They crowded around him, closing in. Will looked from one to the other, wondering who would be the first to charge.

67

Norm had unwrapped the belt and was swinging it around his head like a lasso.

Turning to run, Will's escape was cut short when a noisy pickup truck screeched to a stop blocking the alleyway.

Mona got out of the passenger's seat. A huge man in a filthy ripped undershirt leaped from the driver's door. He didn't look around; he didn't stop to consider. He moved awfully fast for a big man.

"Fuck," Norm said as the man grabbed him. His belted hand rose defensively. The man snatched the buckle in his left, the arm itself in his right. He brought Norm's stiffened arm down across his knee. Will heard a loud crack. Norm wailed.

Spit ran toward the back of the alley. Reggie scrambled for the driver's seat of the convertible.

The man slammed Norm's arm a second time. Now it dangled the wrong way at the elbow. He pushed the hysterical cowboy away like a sack of garbage.

Vaulting over the back of the car, he seized Reggie around the neck.

"No!" Reggie whimpered.

The man pulled Reggie out of the car, dragging his back across the door. He kept on pulling until Reggie's head collided with the wall of the drugstore. Still controlling him with a kind of headlock, the man scraped Reggie's face up and down on the clapboarding. The dirty white wood got dirtier with blood.

Will stood beside Mona, watching helplessly, too nervous to feel sick or angry or afraid. He saw Reggie, limp as withered celery, drop out of sight behind the car.

The big man walked over to Will and Mona, his right hand, smeared with blood, extended.

His voice was a low rumble, like an engine. "For what you done for my daughter," he said, "I'm obliged."

That was all he said. He pushed Mona toward the pickup. They got in and drove away.

Alone now, his heart pounding like a snare drum, Will ran back to the newspaper. He shook as he considered the horrible things that might have happened; he thought more about the things that did. He'd never been in a fight before, not a real one anyway. He'd never even seen one. The violence of it shook him up pretty badly—that man, Mona's dad, had really destroyed those guys.

Will knew he had made some enemies in town; it was a scary feeling.

———————

As Will opened the door to the newspaper office, the telephone rang.

"For you, Dan," Alicia said. She was one of those heavily-rouged, serious-faced women who said everything with a sigh, as if speaking were a lot of work.

Will watched Dan walk over to the phone. This would give him a few minutes to decide if he should say anything about the fight. His hand was sticky with blood from the handshake. He wiped it on his pants.

"Hi, Sheila," Dan said. Then he was quiet for a long time. The smile faded from his face, and he seemed to be getting whiter. "Okay. Are you sure you're okay? We'll be right up. You sit tight."

He hung up.

"Come on, Will. We gotta get up to the house."

"What's the matter?"

"I'll tell you in the car. Let's go."

They drove the five miles to Tenny's Hill in what seemed like five minutes. The Renault sailed over the blacktop and bounced along the gravel without slowing for turns or stopping at stop signs.

CHAPTER 7
LOOKING BACKWARD

With tires grinding noisily on the gravel driveway, Dan's car jerked to a stop. He slammed the driver's door and rushed up the steps, Will right behind him. His shoes clattered loudly on the porch floor as they raced to the door.

"Hurry, Dan," Will said.

Dan turned the knob and pushed against the solid wooden door. It was locked. While fumbling in his pants pocket for his keys, he caught the worried look on his stepson's face. Just as Dan's fingers closed around the keychain, he heard Sheila calling from inside, "Dan, is that you?"

She pulled the door open before he got his key into the lock. Sheila looked scared. Her face was pale, almost colorless. Streaked mascara shadowed red-rimmed puffy eyes. He knew she'd been crying.

Something in him locked, left him stunned. A long-buried dread returned as he recognized something frightening in Sheila's hollow gaze.

His mind flashed to the many times he'd seen a nearly identical expression on his wife's face: still agitated, but flat, deflated, drained from crying. During the first tempestuous months of their marriage this replica of a face had shrieked groundless accusations at him.

He'd hoped never to see such a look again.

71

"What is it, Sheila? What's going on?"

Could she still be terrified that Dan, like Alan Crockett, might one day leave her? Was she again transforming her fears of death into suspicions of infidelity?

Putting his own fears aside, Dan took his wife into his arms. She held on tightly, whispering, "God, I'm glad you're home."

Good, no accusations—no questions even. But he was wary ... "What's happening, Sweetheart, tell me ..."

"Let's sit down," she said.

Sheila led them into the living room and sat beside Dan on the couch, close together. Will sat across from them in the canvas director's chair with his name on it.

Even though it was still quite sunny outside, Sheila had pulled the drapes across the glass doors and closed the shutters on all the windows. Dan looked around, feeling uncomfortable.

"There were people out there, Dan," she said.

"People! What people? Who?"

"I don't know. I don't know who they were." She pulled her legs up onto the couch and made a face, as if her stomach were hurting. Dan thought perhaps the baby was kicking inside her.

"You all right, Sheil?" He took her hand.

He was asking about the pain in her belly, but her answer included far more than that. "Yes. Sure, I'm okay. I'm shaken up, but I'm okay." She was referring to her hysteria; she was telling him it hadn't returned. He was grateful and relieved. But still cautious ...

Dan squeezed her hand. "Did they say something, Sheila? Did they ... do anything to you?"

"No they—"

"What's frightening you, can't you tell me?" He waited for her to answer, but she didn't. "Try to relax, Babe. Want a drink?"

"I shouldn't be drinking—" She gently placed a trembling palm on the mound of her stomach.

"You shouldn't be scared half out of your wits, either. Tell me about it, Sheila. It's better if you tell me."

Sheila sat up perfectly straight. Her long, golden hair fell behind her shoulders as she took a deep breath through her mouth. "Maybe it's nothing," she said. "Maybe it's my hormones or something. Maybe it's being all alone up here ..."

Sheila patted her eye with a Kleenex. When she spoke it was quietly, slowly, as if she were trying to remember something. She told about the electricity going off, then, each word uttered with a writer's precision, she told Dan about the strange movement she'd seen reflected in her computer screen.

"Something moved in the window?" Dan was uncomfortable with the notion. It sounded ... impossible ... irrational. "Could it have been a bird or something?"

"No, it wasn't a bird. It was round, like a head. I think somebody was watching me while I was writing."

Dan tried to keep himself from appearing incredulous. "But that window's upstairs, Sheila. There's no roof outside it. There's nothing out there but a fifteen-foot drop, straight down. If someone was watching you, he'd have to be standing on a ladder."

"There was no ladder, Dan. I went over to check; I wasn't so scared then. Whoever it was had gone, and there was no ladder."

"Maybe it was some kind of animal," Will suggested.

"I don't know what kind of an animal could climb up the side of a house," Dan said. "And even if they could, their claws wouldn't work on the vinyl siding."

Sheila exhaled loudly. "Maybe I will have a drink," she said. "Just a light one. White wine, maybe."

"I'll get it," Will said. He hurried to the kitchen, eager to help.

"Did anything else happen, Sheila?"

"Noises. I heard noises. First on the porch. I came downstairs to see if anybody was around—"

"And was there?"

"No. Nobody I could see. But then I couldn't tell where the noises were coming from. I heard something running across the porch roof."

"The porch roof! Could it—"

"I know what you're going to say, Dan—could it have been an animal? I don't know. I asked myself that, of course, and I don't know. It didn't sound like an animal, though. It sounded like it was moving on two feet."

"Then what … ?"

"Then nothing. Then I started getting scared. That's when I called you. It really bothers me to think I was sitting up there all alone, oblivious to everything, and all the time someone was watching me from the window. That's really creepy, Dan."

"That *is* creepy."

"And actually hearing things running. I mean, seeing the reflection, that might just have been a trick of the light. I could have talked myself into believing that, anyway. But hearing something, that means something was really out there …"

Dan had to stop himself from asking Sheila if it might have been her imagination. Although it would be the first thing to come to anyone's mind, Dan knew the question would have unpleasant connotations for both of them. Still, the whole thing sounded too strange, he didn't want to believe it. The only alternative was to pass it off as a new symptom of her old problem. But that was too convenient. Above all, it wasn't fair. This was different. This was new; it was real. Sheila had a writer's creativity, but Dan was convinced this wasn't a product of her imagination.

No, something had happened up here.

Sheila moved closer to him on the couch. She spoke softly, as if trying to keep Will from hearing. "Then, the more I thought about it, the more scared I got. I went around locking the doors and windows. I pulled down all the shades. When the power came back on it scared the shit out of me."

She embraced him, her moist lips touching his. "Thanks for coming home, Dan," she whispered. "I love you so much."

Before he could return the kiss, Will came back with a glass of wine for each of them. Sheila drank hers very quickly. Then she drank most of Dan's.

CHAPTER 8
INTIMATE CONVERSATION

J oe Grant enjoyed talking to himself, but only when completely alone.

These days, it seemed, he was too often alone — "God damn it all" — either in his trailer, or in his truck: the two places where he spent ninety percent of his time.

"Man shouldn't hafta be home alone alla time. Ain't right"

He walked from the night-dark, plastic-covered window — a winter heat-saving device he'd never bothered to dismantle — to the refrigerator (icebox, he called it) and helped himself to a beer.

"Cocky little bitch oughtta be fetchin' 'em for me."

Sitting heavily in the recliner he designated as *his*, Joe pulled greedily on his bottle, slurping, dribbling amber and foam onto his stained T-shirt. He jumped a bit when some of the liquid found a rip in the material, stinging his bare skin with coldness.

"Christ," he said. The crotch of his pants was worn smooth and stained dark from the near constant massaging of his rough, dirty right hand. Some of the beer landed there. Absently, Joe worked the droplets into the material.

Right now, with Mona nowhere to be found, he could allow himself the pleasure of his own company. He didn't even have to keep his voice down.

"Where the hell is that friggin' girl?"

To Joe's way of thinking, talking to himself was a secret thing. He tried never to do it around his daughter, and never—God forbid—in the presence of outsiders. In other people, Joe was convinced, talking to yourself was a symptom of mental illness. Not in him, though. But just to be safe, he kept his own habit well guarded and private.

"By the Jesus, no one's gonna mistake *me* for crazy."

Mental illness had always been a much-feared thing to all the Grants. To Joe, it was far more frightening than heart disease, or cancer, or even that ema-zeema his doctor kept warning him about every time he browbeat Joe to quit smoking.

With the thought of smoking, Joe lit one up and inhaled deeply. He tossed the match onto the floor.

"Christ, my own pa was crazier'n a shithouse rat," he blurted to the walls of the silent trailer. Joe was thinking about his father, Lawrence, who'd lived in an abandoned railroad caboose not far from Antrim center. Here the old man had stayed rent free for many years, totally alone, his only company, his senility.

Pa had died ten years ago, at least that's what everyone thought. Joe remembered the times he used to drive past the caboose and find his father charging down the road, sometimes dressed, sometimes not, but always with that same glazed look in his eyes, heading off toward Springfield.

"Where ya going, Pa?"

The old man would look up into the cab of the truck, his pale—they were almost white, washed-out looking—blue eyes squinting and confused. Obviously he didn't recognize Joe.

"Goin' into town, get me some pussy!"

"But Pa, town's back the other way ..."

One night, in the midst of a snowstorm, the old man had just wandered off into the woods. Or so Dick Bates theorized. In any event, Pa never turned up, and they never found him. Heavily falling snow erased his tracks and with them any accounting of how he had met his end.

But it wasn't the storm that killed him. And it wasn't cancer or a bad heart. It was the mental illness, the—what had they called it?—Ole Timer's Disease? It was an awful thing. Joe trembled at the memory.

Thoughts of Mona, back-to-back with thoughts of his father, made it difficult to get properly angry.

"Where the fuck is that girl?"

It bothered Joe that his daughter would leave the trailer without getting his permission, without even telling him face to face. She'd been doing that altogether too much lately, almost every night, sneaking out while he was taking a shit or napping in his chair.

"Gettin' too damn big for her britches, too Christly independent."

Especially tonight. After what happened this afternoon— three young pecker-heads crowding her like that, sniffing around her like horny mutts—you'd think she'd stay home where she belongs and not go out looking for more trouble.

For the twentieth time Joe got up, paced over to the door, and gently kicked it open (the latch hadn't worked right in months). He looked out at the dark wall of trees surrounding his property, the moon bright in their branches, and wondered if his daughter had lit out on foot, or in a car with some pimply-faced faggot or teenaged slut from town.

"Christ, s'almost ten o'clock!"

If Mona was with some little bitch from town, they were probably off squeaking and giggling, pointing their little tits around, trying to light a fire in the pants of some farm boy with a driver's license.

But if she was with a guy—and this thought really pissed Joe off—the little prick was probably pawing at her like a drowning man grabbing at a life raft. Well, by God, Joe could do the same thing for any snot-assed little prick that he'd done for those boys earlier today. And in no uncertain terms.

"God damn it all, she oughtta be right to home with her Pa."

He drained the last of his Black Label—on special, just $2.69 a six-pack at the P&C in Springfield—and staggered a bit.

"Stuff does a good job for the price," he said, momentarily distracted by the quality of the beer, holding up the empty bottle like a trophy.

A mighty belch almost rocked the trailer. Joe smiled, pleased with the sound.

Then the smile faded as he thought of Mona again. When she got home, by Jesus, he was going to tell her just where the bear shat in the buckwheat. He was going to pull down her tight little blue jeans and …

"Gonna paddle that little behind of hers till it shines like an apple."

He smiled again at the thought.

And then, just maybe if she was sorry enough, if she cried and asked real nice, he'd show her how he'd forgive her.

CHAPTER 9

GHOSTS

Will wasn't sure when he first suspected their house might he haunted, but Friday evening he started to believe it.

After dinner he'd been restless. He'd prowled around the house, pouting and feeling cheated; a guy his age should have something more interesting to do than stay at home with his parents.

Dan and Mom were outside, sitting on the deck. Dan had suggested a night out, and Will had brightened at the prospect of driving to Springfield for a movie. His hopes were dashed when Mom insisted she wasn't nervous anymore and was enjoying talking, watching the sunset, and sipping iced tea.

Yeah, right.

Bored with rambling from room to room, Will ended up on his bed, trying to read. He'd smuggled in the August issue of *Playboy*—there was an article on UFOs that he wanted to read—but he couldn't concentrate.

In part, he was worried about his mother. Who could she have seen at the window yesterday? At first, he'd figured it was that trio of geeks: Reggie, Spit, and Norm. They were definitely pissed at Will; maybe they'd come up to take things out on Mom.

No—the timing wasn't right. They couldn't have gotten here fast enough.

Most likely it was just Mom's nervousness. She wasn't used to the country; she'd said so herself. And Will believed pregnancy could do strange things to a woman's head.

He scanned another paragraph, but he couldn't seem to block out competing thoughts. After reading the same sentence three times, he gave up and flipped through the photo sections: taut, tan bodies, sparkling with ocean water, made him think about the girl, Mona. Will's mental picture of her sunbathing at the waterfall was as hot as anything on the glossy pages. How terrific she'd looked! How—

The image of the fight intruded: brutality, broken bones, big kids crying. Will rubbed his hand against his pant leg, as if the blood were still on it.

Sooner or later he'd have to tell Dan about the fight. It just hadn't seemed important after that panicky call from Mom.

Will tossed the magazine under his bed and sat up. *I've got to do something,* he thought. *I've got to move around.*

Then he remembered the attic.

Back in April, when they'd come up from Boston to look at the house, Will had briefly seen the attic. Since moving in, he hadn't bothered to spend any time up there.

He decided to go up and check it out, see if anything remained of the house's previous owners.

Stepping from his bedroom into the little upstairs hall, Will could hear the faint sounds of his parents talking and moving around downstairs. Across from him, the door to their bedroom was closed. Beside it, Mom's writing room was aglow with the fading western sun.

The door to the attic was like the door to a time machine. On the hall side, the door was freshly painted and looked brand new. When he opened it, however, the renovation work ended at the threshold.

Narrow, long-unpainted steps led up a dark passageway to the third floor.

Groping for a light switch, he discovered there was none.

Will peered upward, straining his ears against the whir of the cooling fan. The bone-dry wooden steps squeaked as he climbed.

At the top of the stairs he looked around. On either side of him, brown, unfinished boards formed the slanting roof. Dull tips of black nails protruded here and there. The dimly lit attic was like an ancient thing, a crude settler's cabin placed on top of their modern house. It was as if he had stepped back in time. If he looked out the window, perhaps he'd see Indians stalking game in the neighboring fields. Will's pre-colonial fantasy might have been complete were it not for the very modern stacks of cardboard boxes, junk they'd lugged from Boston and would probably never unpack.

There was a dirty window at the far end of the attic. In spite of the fan, mounted in its lower half, the upstairs was hot. Sun had beaten against the slate roof all day long, leaving little islands of warm, unmoving air amid rushing currents of ventilation.

Beyond the stacked boxes, the ancient wide-planked floor was covered with an accumulation of dust. *Guess Mom hasn't cleaned up here yet*, Will thought. He could see patterns traced in the dust by the moving air.

Stepping back to where the dust was thickest, he inspected the floor in the dim light. What he saw there had to be footprints. Three of them were scuffed and indistinct; the fourth was nearly perfect. It was no more than six inches long, clearly showing the imprint of a heel and five toes: a child's footprint in the undisturbed dust.

The kid who used to live here must have played in the attic, Will thought.

A melancholy feeling took hold of him as he thought of the ancient fossilized footprints of dinosaurs—beasts long gone, their footprints seemingly fresh and new.

Something skittered across the roof, rapid little claws that must belong to a squirrel.

Startled, Will stood up. He held his breath, eyes aimed at the ceiling. Straining his ears, he listened for every sound in the shadow-filled attic.

The fan whirred. A grating creak sounded from somewhere in the shadows, no doubt the house groaning under its own weight.

Tense now, the hairs on the back of his neck prickling, Will had the uncomfortable impression that someone was close by, hiding, watching.

He looked around, not daring to venture another step.

Old houses make noises, he reasoned. But an irrational echo came back: *old houses are haunted.*

Haunted?

Will's mind clung to that idea. Hundreds of ghost stories he'd read over the years returned like photographs to his memory: headless specters, evil ancestors, wandering spirits forever trying to atone for things they'd died and left undone.

What if we bought a haunted house?

Will took a step backward. Then he ran down the stairs.

———————

Back in his bed, the sheet pulled protectively around him, Will tried to clear his mind of frightening thoughts. He couldn't help wondering about the people who'd lived here before. Which of them used to sleep in Will's room, staring out at night through the same window?

He remembered Mr. Carey, the real estate man, saying something about a family. The man and the woman had died. The son went to live with relatives somewhere in the area. Will's family had bought the place from them, but it was all done through a lawyer. They'd never met the people.

He wished he had paid better attention. Had Mr. Carey said the parents died here—in this house? He couldn't remember. If they had, maybe someone had died right here in Will's room.

Will shivered, moving his eyes from side to side. Was it a change in the air or the thought of death that made him suddenly feel so cold?

He looked up. Were those footsteps or settling floorboards overhead?

Perhaps he could learn a little about the history of the house by checking the files at the *Tribune*. Or he could ask Chief Bates; he seemed like he'd been around for a while.

Will had often read about houses built on top of Indian burial grounds. Could Indians have lived on this land long before the earliest settlers arrived in Vermont? Could they still be here, in spirit form?

Realizing he was working up a good scare, Will tried hard to fix his mind on other things: what school would be like; how soon they could get their satellite dish; how he was going to get his driver's license the minute he turned sixteen.

When his mind flashed back to Mona, it stayed focused on her. She'd looked so pretty lying there in her clinging wet T-shirt, her sun-warmed legs tan and glistening.

Aroused, Will reached for his magazine. Mona's image was vivid in his imagination. It seemed to hover like a ghost between his eyes and the provocative photographs. He reached under the sheet and touched his erection, but he stopped, too inhibited to exorcise the sensual vision.

He felt like he was being watched.

The night passed slowly, almost sleeplessly.

Will watched the sun come up, a little at a time. The trees far outside his window turned from dark, motionless shadows to green moving forms, like giant shrouded figures lined up for some kind of ritual.

When his alarm clock said five-ten, Will decided to give up on sleep. He got out of bed, pulled on his jeans and sneakers, grabbed a clean T-shirt, and headed out. Before going downstairs, he paused in front of Mom and Dan's bedroom. Their door was open a crack, so air could circulate, and it was dark inside. He couldn't hear them at all, so he figured they were still asleep.

Maybe he should go out for a walk. He felt as if he had some thinking to do and figured he could do a better job of it in the fresh air.

He decided to head down the road and pick up the mail. Supposedly, it arrived by five o'clock every morning, but Will had never tested that claim. He'd find out today. With luck he'd get a letter from one of his friends in Boston.

Birds were singing happily, and the sun was bright enough to sting his eyes. Dew rose like conjured ghosts from the misty fields on either side of Tenny's Hill Road. Will wondered whose job it was to cut the brush back so grass and wildflowers could grow.

It was a surprisingly long walk—almost a mile—down to the "T" where their dirt road met the highway running between Antrim and Springfield. The junction was where their mailbox stood. If Will went all the way down, got the mail, and came back, it could take at least forty-five minutes, maybe more. Even on Saturdays, Dan was an early riser because of the newspaper. Will should have left a note. It would freak them out if they got up and he was gone.

Better hurry, Will thought.

The mail hadn't arrived yet; so much for the post office's claim about early delivery. As Will started back up the hill, he saw something in the woods, a building or something. It was set back far enough from the road so he'd never have noticed it when they went barreling by in the car.

He walked down the highway a little to check it out. Soon he discovered a nearly invisible road—more a driveway, really—that led through the trees and back to a trailer. It was an old trailer, green-colored and rust-spotted, with a small wooden porch built on to the side. The yard was extremely cluttered, but Will couldn't see with what.

He didn't dare go too close but got near enough to see a familiar pickup truck in the yard.

"Hi!" a voice said from behind him.

Will gasped, jumping involuntarily. He felt his heart whacking at the inside of his chest. Whirling around, he found himself in a fighting position.

"God, Mona, you scared me!"

"I know," she said, smiling. "Know your name, too: it's William, right?"

"Yeah, William …"

"William Crockett, right?"

"Yeah … how'd you know?"

"You're new in town. Everybody knows about new people." Will couldn't think of what to say. He felt surprised, yet bashful at the same time. He had often felt tongue-tied around pretty girls.

"I don't know your last name," he managed.

"Name's Grant. We live here." She pointed her thumb at the trailer.

"I thought so; I saw the truck."

She looked really good, better than he remembered. The skin of her face seemed to shine, as if a bright, clear light radiated from within; her blue eyes, too, shone like twin stars. They were the sharpest, most alert eyes Will had ever seen. She was tall, nearly as tall as he was. He couldn't guess her age, though. She seemed younger than he, yet strangely old. Whatever her age, her appearance made Will forget all his doubts about Vermont girls.

"What are you doing out so early?" he asked, and immediately thought it was a pretty dumb thing to say, too nosy, and definitely not cool.

"Don't sleep much anymore," she told him. "Guess I'm one of those folks don't need much sleep."

"I didn't sleep much myself last night …"

"You was upset, I bet. 'Cause of the fight."

Will blinked at her; she was right, but it embarrassed him a little. "Naw, it didn't bother me that much."

"It's okay to be upset about the fight. Upset me, too. You was brave, and I wanted to thank you. If you hadn't come along, them guys mightta … well I don't know …"

She was right about the fight's upsetting him, but only partly right. He wondered if he should tell her about the other half of the problem: Mom getting scared; the strange noises in the house. "Mona, did you know the people who lived in our house before we moved in?"

She looked around, pulling her lower lip between her rows of straight white teeth. "Kind of. That was a long time ago, though. I was just a little kid. I mean, I seen 'em once in a while, though I can't say I knew 'em."

"Do you remember what happened to them?"

"Wha'd'ya mean?"

"I heard they died, or something."

She glanced at the woods again, looking strangely uncomfortable, as if the question had somehow frightened her, as if …

Will's mind leaped to the time he'd been in the class play, the time he forgot his lines. He'd frozen up and gawked around, waiting for the prompter to bail him out. *That's it,* Will thought, *Mona looks like she forgot her lines.*

"I guess they died," she said slowly, not meeting his eyes. "Don't really know. Don't remember."

A loud voice, anger-filled and piercing, sliced the morning air. "Mona!" It cut off their conversation—"Monaaaa!"—ending their growing intimacy.

Mona's fingertips shot to her mouth. Eyes wide, she whispered, "Oh shit, that's my pa." There was a sharp undertone of fear in her voice. "Prob'ly wants his breakfast or somethin'. You'd better get on out of here, William."

Remembering what Mr. Grant had done to those three guys, Will decided not to argue. "Yeah, okay. See you later, maybe … ?"

He turned and started back up the hill; the bellowed name, "Mo-naaaa," ping-ponged around in the clear morning.

"Hey William," she called after him.

Will turned. "Yeah?"

"I seen you watching me the other day." She gave him a sexy smile, suggestive beyond her years, then she ran through the brush toward the trailer.

———

As early as that evening, Will began to think Mona had an uncanny knack for catching him alone.

Mom and Dan had gone to what Dan referred to as "Baby College," the childbirth classes at the hospital in Springfield.

Will had stayed—a bit nervously, he had to admit—alone at the house.

It was about seven o'clock, seven-thirty at most. Madonna wailed from the radio. Will was playing it really loud, louder than his folks would permit if they were at home. He stood in front of the refrigerator, drinking orange juice directly from the carton, another thing he wasn't supposed to do.

He wiped his lips on the back of his arm and put the carton back. Then he swung the door closed and turned around, all in a single dancelike motion.

Mona stood there, right in the middle of the kitchen.

Will jumped. His heart raced. He hadn't heard her come up to him because of the music.

"Jesus!" he blurted.

She smiled at him, looking clean and fresh and slightly mischievous. "I thought maybe you'd like to go swimmin' with me tomorrow."

Will couldn't answer right away; he was feeling too frazzled. Instead, he stared at her, thinking—*feeling*, actually—how really nice she looked. Evidently she'd washed her hair and put on some lipstick.

Not knowing what to say, he just kept looking at her, dumbly. She wore a sweatshirt with the arms and neck cut off. This modification allowed him to see the tops of her breasts. Her sweatshirt was cut off at the bottom, too, so he could see her tight, tanned stomach. The short denim skirt stopped halfway to her knees where lovely straight legs stretched all the way down to her bare feet.

"Tomorrow's Sunday," Will stammered.

"So?"

"So we go to church on Sunday."

"Water up there never gets too warm. Prob'ly warmest in the afternoon. Why'n't ya come by about two. That okay?"

"T-two?"

"You be back from church by then, won'cha?"

"I—I think so ..."

"Think ya can find the falls again?"

Will's face might have reddened a little. It embarrassed him to have her come right out and admit she'd seen him watching her. But it was enticing, too; she knew he'd seen her naked, and she was inviting him back to the falls. Will wished he could be more poised, or say something clever. He could think of nothing.

"Well, can ya find it? Or should I come by for ya?"

"No, that's okay. I can find it again."

She smiled, and took a step toward him. Then she reached out, grasped his shoulders in her hands and kissed him right on the mouth.

Even while it was happening, Will knew he was pretty limp-lipped about it. It had surprised him, that's all, and he wasn't ready.

He tried to do it again, to do it right, but she pulled away. "I gotta get back. Pa's in a temper tonight. He don't like me bein' out so much, an' he ain't a man to get riled."

And then she was gone.

CHAPTER 10
SHEILA'S CYBER NOTEBOOK

August 9

I want to get this down before we leave for church. It's so amusing I think there's the makings of a short story in here someplace, maybe an article for *Yankee* or *New England Monthly*.

Last evening, when Dan and I left for our Saturday birthing class in Springfield, we saw a man putting up a mailbox next to ours at the bottom of the hill.

"Stop a minute," I said to Dan.

"What's the matter?"

"Let's talk to this guy."

"Why, Sheila? We've got to get to Springfield—"

"He must be our neighbor, Dan. Don't you think we should meet our neighbors?"

"Well sure, but why now?"

I decided to come clean. "I want to see if he's been bothered by prowlers, too. Maybe he can tell us something about what's been going on lately."

Dan gave one of his tolerant sighs, making it very clear that he was humoring me, and pulled the car over to the side of the road. I got out and walked across the highway, approaching the man. Dan stayed put.

He was a rotund, poorly-dressed rustic, apparently unused to the minor physical exertion required to screw a mailbox to the top of a pole. The dome of his bald head was glistening with sweat in the soft golden rays of evening light.

The black-lettered name on his mailbox was "J. Grant."

I managed to walk all the way over to him and stand right beside him without attracting his attention. He was either ignoring me, or he was deaf. I waited patiently a moment. Still he fidgeted with the mailbox. Finally I spoke up.

"Mr. Grant?"

He didn't look at me, just kept working and grunted, "Umm-hmm?"

"I'm Sheila Crockett. My husband and I are your new neighbors from the top of the hill ..."

He straightened up and faced me at last, shoving the pliers and screwdriver into the back pocket of his dirty green work pants. He was well over six feet tall with a thatch of black hair wriggling out of the collar of his T-shirt like a herd of worms. His hammer was in his hairy left hand.

He didn't say anything; he simply stood there, apparently waiting for me to explain my intrusion. There was a sad, almost idiot vapidity in his lazy-browed eyes.

"I'd like to ask you something, if I may," I told him. Already I saw that my veneer of social grace was totally useless in this situation.

He blinked at me, spat toward the side of the road, and moved his lips a little before the words started to come. "You can go ahead and ask," he said.

The Yankee twang was heavy in his speech. I'd heard a lot about these taciturn Vermonters; perhaps this was the first genuine specimen I'd come across since moving up here.

Feeling, well ... a little foolishly feminine all of a sudden, but no less determined, I decided to press on with my questions. "Mr. Grant, you live around here, right?"

"No point puttin' up a mailbox if I don't."

In the interest of accurate reporting, I must admit I giggled nervously at that. A little wrinkle of a smile split his lips, and I could see the tips of an incomplete row of dark, irregularly spaced teeth.

He went on—"Used to have a post office box in town, but the welfare says I gotta have an address. That's my place over there." He jerked his head back to indicate a trailer, nearly invisible among the trees.

I took a breath and went on. "Mr. Grant, have you folks been bothered by prowlers or anything like that lately?"

He blinked at me again, not seeming to understand. It made me uneasy, so I may have babbled a little, something like, "The other day I was all alone up there, and I kept hearing things around the house. Noises. Footsteps. Has there been any trouble with break-ins, or vandals, or anything like that? I mean, I don't want to bother you, but you're our nearest neighbor, and I thought … well … I saw you here, and I thought I'd ask you …"

"Nobody'd want nothin' out of my trailer." He kept blinking at me as if I were crazy. I got a little more frightened when it occurred to me that if someone actually were poking around our house, it might have been Mr. Grant.

I wanted to get away then. I started to excuse myself and looked back at the car where Dan was waiting. "Well, thank you," I said. "I'm sorry to bother you—"

"Mighta been an animal," he said.

"An animal?"

"Coon, maybe. Maybe a pork-a-pine …"

"Will they come right up to a house?"

"Course it coulda been a bear." He pronounced it bay-ya. "Bear'll come around sometimes. You always gotta be careful a bears."

All of a sudden I realized what he was up to: he was playing with me, trying to scare me, having his little joke. A vague twinkle in his dark eyes alerted me that it was all in fun. "Okay, Mr. Grant." I smiled, I hoped knowingly. "We'll be careful of bears."

He smiled, too, and the whole character of his face changed. All of a sudden he looked like a good-natured giant. With slow deliberate motions, he wiped his right hand on his pant leg and held it out in front of him. "Nice to get to know you, Mrs. Crockett. Hope you'll be happy up here."

I shook his hand, thanked him and went back to the car. Mr. Grant went back to his project.

On the way to Springfield, Dan and I had a good laugh. Dan kept repeating Mr. Grant's lines in that stupid-sounding Vermont accent of his. I laughed terribly hard, not at what Dan said, but at his attempts to say it.

We almost made it to the early church service this morning. We would have, too, if we hadn't got to laughing after seeing the punch line of Mr. Grant's joke.

We found a piece of paper tucked under the windshield wiper of the car. I picked it up and read the large, blocky, childlike scrawl:

To Attract a Bear

1. build a fire
2. heat up a square of tin
3. in it dump a mix of bacon grease, honey and anise oil on the tin and on the bushes and ground around it
4. hide
5. when the bear comes all the way into the open, shoot the son-of-a-bitch in the neck.

Somehow, I have the feeling I should chalk this up as my first REAL introduction to Vermont culture. I must admit, I'm eager to see more of Mr. J. Grant.

I just hope he was joking about the bear.

CHAPTER 11
A PHANTOM INTRUDES

Chief Bates was the first person to leave the church. He rose from the back pew and charged through the double door, fumbling in his pocket for a cigarette.

Outside, Bates studied face after face. Two by two, a steady procession of people filed from the big white Congregational Church. He knew most of them, not all anymore, but most.

Leaning back, he rested on his car. He felt his buttocks flatten against the driver's door and remembered — too late — that he was sure to pick up a coating of road dust on the tails of his brown suit jacket.

Least I'll keep the car clean, he joked with himself, trying to relieve some of his tension.

This was the first time he'd been to church in weeks. He had anticipated guilt-producing stares and snide remarks. Additionally, being out of uniform and not driving the cruiser made him feel strangely out of place. His old brown suit just compounded the feeling. This morning, when he had tried to fasten the coat, the middle button had taken off like a champagne cork. Another thing: he didn't like the white collar of his scratchy shirt biting into his neck. It was like somebody trying to strangle him; he'd always hated the idea of strangulation.

Still, Bates guessed he looked no more ill at ease than many of the people around him. His eyes scanned all those sweaty, craggy-faced men in their once-a-week suits. They clustered together, smiling, their stocky red-faced wives, wearing print dresses and flowered sun bonnets, at their sides.

Finally, Bates located his cigarettes—*too many damn pockets to keep track of*—fished one out of his inside pocket, and started to light it. *Maybe not*, he thought, *don't look too good to be smoking on a Sunday morning right outside the church.*

Furtively, he dropped the unlit cigarette to the ground beside him. Then he thought better of it, picked it up and returned it to his pocket, hoping no one had seen.

He started looking around again, searching for the people he wanted to talk to. They'd been in the church. They should be out any minute.

On the left hand side of the stone walk some women had set up a table and were having a bake sale. Cakes, pies, brownies, and plates full of colorful cookies appeared from brown bags and square wicker baskets. Maybe he'd just mosey over in that direction.

A striking blonde-haired woman in a loose-fitting blue dress, a real traffic hazard of a woman, was in the process of buying a blackberry pie. "For our Sunday dinner." Bates heard her say to someone over her shoulder.

"Good thinking." Dan Wilder smiled, as he materialized out of the crowd.

God, thought Bates, *is that Wilder's wife?* He tugged at the tight shirt collar. As he pulled it away from his Adam's apple, the button launched into orbit.

Shit!

Lots of people said hello to Dan. Some came over to be introduced to the pretty woman and the boy, William. Bates waited impatiently, shifting his weight from foot to foot, listening to all the chit-chat about the new house and the baby. Most people said they hoped it would be a boy. The blonde woman seemed to bristle about that, but didn't say anything, just smiled prettily and nodded. *I'll have to be careful of that,* Bates thought, *she's probably one of them women's libbers, or whatever they're callin' themselves nowadays.*

After a few minutes of glad-handing and palaver, Dan's family separated from the crowd and began moving across the lawn toward their car.

That's when Chief Bates started to move in.

He felt a wave of nervousness waft over him like an unpleasant odor. Something in his gut kept telling him ... telling him what?

"How do, folks," he said, as Dan was unlocking the passenger's door of the Renault. Bates caught the boy's puzzled expression. Although they'd met only three days ago, he probably didn't recognize the chief out of uniform.

Recognition lit Dan's face. "Chief Bates!" he said with a smile and an extended right hand.

The boy was still frowning as he nodded uncomfortably.

Bates nodded to the woman. "This must be Sheila. The descriptions I've heard of you fit you to a tee; I could pick you out of a line-up." He found himself looking at the blackberry pie. *One of Mrs. Tessier's,* he thought, *wouldn't mind a piece of that, myself.* Embarrassed to be so distracted, his mind scrambled for something to say. He looked at Will. "Looks like you're gonna have a little brother pretty soon, son." It had just slipped out.

"You can never tell" — Sheila smiled — "it might just be a little sister."

"It might at that, ma'am." Bates cleared his throat, then wiped the back of his hand across his sweat-slick face. His town, and he'd never felt more out of place in it.

How was he going to get to the point?

"Ahhh, folks," he finally said, "I wonder if you'd mind hanging on a minute. I got something on my mind, and I'd like to talk to you about it. Was plannin' to drive up to your place after the service—"

"What is it, Chief?" asked Dan, interested. "Is something wrong?"

This was what had brought Bates to church on a day that wasn't Christmas, or Easter, or a wedding or funeral. Whenever one of his heavy-duty hunches proved true, it made him feel somewhat spiritual. It reminded him to say his prayers; it reminded him of church.

"Well ... not wrong, exactly ..." At least he hoped not.

"What is it then? Can we talk about it here?"

"Maybe here's not so good. Maybe we don't want nobody listenin' to us."

Dan eyes widened. "If it's business, how about your office? Or mine?"

Bates thought about it until Sheila spoke up. "Maybe you'd like to come up to the house, Mr. Bates?" Sheila smiled warmly. "You said you planned to anyway. I could offer you a cup of coffee and a piece of pie."

The chief eyed the blackberry pie and considered the lady's offer. He thought of the nagging sensation that had been prodding at him lately, the feeling that something was about to happen, about to go wrong. He recalled his screaming telephone, rousting him from sleep at the ungodly hour of two o'clock this morning. "Yup," he finally said with a single nod of his head. "That's a mighty temptin' offer, Dan, Sheila. And I'd jest soon take a drive up to your place. That's probly the best place to talk about what I got to say."

Dan and Sheila looked at each other. Dan said, "Of course, Chief, let's go."

———

During the drive back to Tenny's Hill, Will sat glumly in the back seat pouting out the window, his fingers on the throbbing artery in his neck. He was scared. Unconsciously, he tried to replace fear with anger. Anger directed at Dan.

Why had Dan made him go to church? Why?

It wasn't that Will didn't believe in God, it wasn't even that he hated church, or found it especially boring, it was just that Dan never forced him to go when they lived in Boston. Now, Dan insisted, church attendance was an important part of getting established in a small town. And Mom went along with it! She said Will should do it for Dan.

Will had agreed, had kept his mouth shut, too. But still it seemed a little two-faced.

And now it had gotten him into trouble. He was sure Chief Bates was after him.

"What do you think the chief wants, Dan?" Sheila asked.

"I really don't know, Sheil, but he sure is acting mysterious about it, isn't he?"

Will kept looking over his shoulder, watching the chief's car following theirs. He tried to imagine what it would be like if he were a big-time criminal with the cops on his tail.

All this had something to do with those guys who got beat up; Will was sure of it.

As the Renault got closer to home, Will became more and more frightened. Maybe the chief was going to blame him for the fight. Maybe he was in big trouble.

It wasn't his fault. He hadn't started it.

Falsely accused.

Life on the run.

Will took another look at the car behind them and swallowed loudly.

Will squirmed in his seat and asked for permission to leave the table. Dan said no, responding to an almost invisible shaking of the chief's head.

Sheila made coffee. Dan repeatedly caught the chief stealing glances at the pie on the counter. When would Sheila get around to offering him a piece? Dan hoped soon but said nothing.

As his wife set out the cups, Dan made small talk about the *Tribune*, and how he was going to launch a big advertising and subscription drive.

"Sounds good, Daniel." Bates conversed halfheartedly. He didn't seem as cheerful as usual. Often his smile looked more worried than mirthful.

When finally Sheila joined them at the table, the chief took over the conversation. He started by clearing his throat, just as if he were about to address an audience. "Now, first thing I wanna say is this: don't go takin' none of this to heart. It ain't gospel. Matter of fact, I ain't much worried about it, myself. But the right thing to do is to alert you folks to what's goin' on ..."

Sheila's smile flattened, the perky, red glow vanished from her cheeks. Dan witnessed the transformation but didn't know how to diffuse it. Almost instantly his wife's eyes began looking tense and hard, her fingers closed into fists which she let drop into her lap, out of sight.

Dan understood. The last time she'd been approached so earnestly by a policeman, it was with news of her husband's death. She was struggling to keep calm, and Dan admired her for it.

He sipped his coffee, trying to influence her by looking relaxed. He peered over the tops of his glasses as he often did at the newspaper office when he was talking to somebody on the phone or across his desk. *Don't worry Sheila, this is business as usual ...*

"It's like this," the chief continued, "a fella from the hospital up to Waterbury—fella name a Nolan—well, the way I hear it, he just walked right off the grounds—"

"The hospital at Waterbury?" Sheila's words were tiny and soft, like cat's feet before a predatory leap. "That's a mental hospital, isn't it, Mr. Bates?"

"Well, yes it is, Ma'am." The chief fidgeted in his seat like a truant schoolboy.

"Are you saying this Nolan was *locked up*, and he *broke out*?" The tension in Sheila's voice made her sound hostile, Dan thought.

"That's right, Ma'am." Bates cleared his throat and dabbed his mouth with a paper napkin. "Anyway, he'd been up there—locked up, as you say—for about four years now, and ... well ... he's out now, and some folks figure he might be pretty dangerous ..."

"So what's all this got to do with us?" Sheila shook her head, confused. "I mean—"

"Sounds like a good story, Chief." Dan cut in. "You could have told me about it at the office, though, don't you think?"

"Guess I coulda." The chief's eyes drifted to the blackberry pie again. "I don't know how much you folks know about what went on up here 'bout four, five years back."

"Here at the house?" Sheila asked, some of the edge gone from her voice.

The chief nodded.

"About the kid whose parents died?" asked Dan.

"That's right."

Dan was interested. The reporter in him wanted to take notes. Will was curious, too, by the look of him.

"I don't know a great deal about it—" Dan glanced at his wife—"I just know that's why the place was empty. The kid went to live with his uncle, or something ..."

Dan reached for the coffee pot and refilled his cup.

"Well, fact is, it was a pretty bad scene. The little fella's parents didn't just die, they was murdered. Same for an old woman, helpless old cripple in a wheelchair. She was in her seventies, for pity sake, couldn't a been more helpless. I seen it myself day after it happened—I discovered it, actually—a real bloodbath, real sick-o stuff ..."

Sheila's gaze fixed on Dan. An etching of worry around her eyes. Dan reached across the tabletop and took her hand.

"That happened *here*?" she asked, her voice was a quavery whisper.

"That's right, Ma'am."

"Why didn't anyone tell us? Why didn't Mr. Carey say something ... ?"

"Folks don't like to talk about it much, Ma'am. Some figure what's done is done."

"Just the same, he should have said something. A realtor has a responsibility. Don't you think he should have said something, Dan?"

Dan shook his head as if to say, I don't know. He squeezed Sheila's hand and looked at Chief Bates. "So this guy, Nolan, he's the one who did it?"

"That's what most folks think, yes."

"Oh, that's just great!" Sheila yanked her hand free of Dan's. She was on her feet, pacing in front of the stove, putting more water on to boil.

"He never come to trial, though. Judge sent him to the hospital for an evaluation, and that's where they kept him. Nobody had enough hard evidence to bring him to court, and he was too wacked-out to be released."

"But now he's out," said Dan, "and you think he might come back here; is that it?"

103

The chief was twirling his cup on his saucer. It made a clattering sound. "He might. I just can't say. I thought I'd better tell ya."

Sheila slammed the tea kettle down on the stove. Everyone jumped. "That's GREAT!" she said, her eyes filling with tears. "That's all we need is a goddamn psychopath hanging around up here."

"Now, Mrs. Crockett, logic says he won't come anywheres near here. Nolan's from down country, Long Island. If he goes anywhere, it'll prob'ly be back there. Either that, or he'll just try to lose himself and head off for parts unknown."

Sheila glared at the chief, as if the whole thing were his fault. "But just in case the murderer returns to the scene of the crime, you thought you'd drive up and warn us; is that it?"

The chief seemed ashamed. He looked down at his nearly empty coffee cup and stirred it with his spoon.

"The chief's just being cautious, Sheila—"

"That's right, Ma'am. It's only right I should warn ya ... I don't really 'spect nothin' to happen."

"Well, maybe something's already happening." Sheila sniffed, bracing her shoulders for control. "Maybe the other day I caught someone looking at me through the window ..."

The chief's guilty-little-boy look vanished. Suddenly he was intense, professional, an instant and total transformation. "When? What other day?"

"Three days ago ... Thursday."

Mr. Bates's features relaxed. "Couldn't a been Nolan. This just happened last night. I got the call 'bout two this mornin'. Woke me up. Maybe you shoulda called me about the prowler, though. I can't do nothin' for folks when I don't know what's goin' on."

For a second Dan thought Sheila and the chief were going to go at it. He spoke up. "So what about this Nolan, Chief? Did he do it? What do *you* think?"

The chief shook his head, sadly, slowly. "I don't know. No one knows. When I drove up here that morning, Nolan was sitting right out there on the front steps, just waitin'. He coulda run off, but he didn't. Clint Whitcome and the old lady, Mrs. McKensie, was dead at his feet. Pamela, that's Clint's wife, was out in the yard. She was pretty tore up. They all was. It was an awful thing, an awful ugly thing ..."

"But if Nolan didn't do it, he must have seen what happened," Dan pressed.

"I suppose he did."

"So what's his story?"

"He never give a statement. He never said nothin' for the record. Maybe he don't remember. Or maybe he remembers and just won't talk. That's parta the reason they kept him locked up: he never talks, never says nothin' ..."

"Didn't he say anything to you when you got here?"

"Nothin' that made no sense."

"What'd he say?"

"He said little people done it."

"What?" Dan and Will said it together.

"Nolan said little people come out of the woods and killed the family."

"Like elves, or something?" Will asked.

"That's what he said, son."

"That's crazy," said Sheila.

"That's right, Ma'am."

Sheila sat back down at the table. Everyone remained quiet for what seemed like a long time. Finally, she asked, "So, what do we do if this guy shows up?"

"You call me, that's what. Don't toss it off like you done the other time, with your prowler. If you see anybody strange—if you just *think* you see anybody strange—call. This Nolan ... the thing to remember about him is he's got bright red hair, red's a pumpkin. You see him, you see anybody, you call me at once. That's what I'm here for. That's the only way I can help you."

Sheila nodded, her gaze dropped to the floor. "We will, Mr. Bates, thanks."

The chief stood up, walked over to the counter and looked down at the blackberry pie. "I'm sorry I had to get you folks all upset like this. Helluva thing to hear about a place you jest move in to. Most likely it's a false alarm; most of 'em are. Nolan may or may not be crazy, but I'll tell you one thing: he ain't dumb. My guess is he'll high-tail it outta state and get as far away from Vermont as possible."

Dan got up and walked the chief to the door. "I'll stop by the station tomorrow, get a statement for the paper."

"That's fine, Daniel. But let's keep this little chat off the record, okay? No point in gettin' folks' heads all in a spin. That's why I didn't want to talk down there in front of the church."

"So, Chief Bates," Sheila said, "who do you think it was at my window the other day?"

"No way I can say, Ma'am. You shoulda called me."

He walked out without another word.

Will got up and stood beside Dan at the door. They watched Chief Bates through the screen. The backs of his coat and pants were covered with white dust. When he was halfway to his car, he stopped and turned around. "Place looks good, Daniel. You folks done a fine job on 'er."

"Thanks, Chief."

Bates pulled out a cigarette, lighted it, eased himself into the car, and drove off.

Suddenly, Sheila was at Dan's side. She slid her arm around him and pulled him toward her. He opened his arms for a powerful embrace.

Looking over his wife's shoulder, Dan gazed into the kitchen. Somehow, the whole house seemed different.

CHAPTER 12
DIRTY WORK

Will waited a long time at the waterfall, but Mona didn't show up.

He'd had to argue, nearly plead, to get permission to leave the house. Luckily, Dan had intervened, "There's no point in everyone getting paranoid, Sheil. The chief said Nolan's not likely to be around here. We can't live in the country and stay locked up all the time."

Sheila had begrudgingly relented.

"I'll be careful, Mom," Will promised her. He didn't like seeing his mother so upset, but he left anyway.

Will bounded down the porch steps, ecstatic with relief: Chief Bates's visit had nothing to do with him. There was no mention of the fight. Will was a free man! Totally in the clear!

Soon he was running through the woods. He glanced at his watch: plenty of time to make their two-o'clock rendezvous.

He almost burst with anticipation as he vaulted over a fallen log. He was aching to get to the falls, painfully eager to see Mona again. All morning her soft-contoured image had glowed vividly in his mind. Her sensual vision had taken on clarity during the church service, until—while Chief Bates talked—Will could almost smell the woodland fragrance of her hair.

He checked his watch again; it was one-forty-seven. Soon he fully expected to enjoy pleasures only hinted at last night during Mona's appearance in the kitchen.

Where is she? Will sat down on a rock to wait.

Far below the rock on which he sat, Will could see his reflection in the water. His image shimmered eerily, transparent and otherworldly. It was as if he were seeing his own ghost.

His preoccupation with Mona had forced the haunted house idea right out of his mind. Now, waiting alone by the falls, he considered it again.

"Our house is actually haunted," Will whispered to his watery twin. He was trying on the possibility, checking to see how it fit, as one might try on an unfamiliar article of clothing.

Until two nights ago, he hadn't given much thought to ghosts. He'd always been interested in the idea of them, but he'd never come to accept their existence as fact. From Will's point of view, it was all pretty simple: If he ever saw a ghost, then he'd believe. Until then, he'd continue to entertain himself with scary stories and an occasional helping of speculative "nonfiction" like *The Amityville Horror*.

From what Chief Bates had said about their house—the horrible murders committed there—it seemed as if conditions were perfect for a haunting. Suddenly, Will found himself struggling not to believe.

He dropped a pebble and watched it fall. Nearly out of sight, it splashed in the water below. The ghost-Will vanished, transformed into rippling circles.

So where's Mona?

Peering into the woods and listening to the water, Will began to feel nervous and uncomfortable. It wasn't the possibility of confronting an escaped psycho. It wasn't the idea of ghosts, either. It was just that all of a sudden he realized things weren't getting off to a very good start in Antrim, Vermont.

Was he being too impatient?

Maybe. He tossed another pebble. He'd known all along living in Vermont would take getting used to, but the fates had thrown him some horrible curves: his mother was miserable; he'd made three enemies who probably wanted to beat the living crap out of him; and his house was the scene of a mass murder, maybe haunted.

And now his only friend, Mona, had stood him up.

Fuck her, anyway … This time he hurled a stone into the pool below.

Splash!

He checked his watch; it was almost three o'clock.

Still, he hoped she'd show up. Any minute now she'd probably sneak up behind him—her footsteps lost in the sound of the crashing water—and tap him on the shoulder.

Will kept looking around, hoping to spot her, not wanting to let her get the drop on him a third time.

After a while, a nagging feeling of rejection warred with his faltering optimism. *Maybe she thinks I'm a nerd, or something.*

The best thing to do, he decided, was to walk down to Mona's trailer. Maybe she'd forgotten their date. Maybe her father wouldn't let her come out.

Maybe she was sick.

There were thousands of reasons why she might not have shown up, but Will was positive he knew the real reason: she'd decided she didn't like him.

Okay, if that's it, I'll just give her a chance to tell me to my face.

Full of resolution, he took off through the woods, heading downstream in the direction of Mona's trailer.

Dan understood how his wife felt; after Chief Bates's visit, the house had subtly changed for all of them.

It still looked the same, of course, but now there was an uneasiness about it, a heaviness in the air. Partly, it was attributable to Sheila's frame of mind; she was upset and who could blame her? Discovering a whole family had been butchered in your home can quickly take the hominess out of it.

"We should have stayed in Boston, Dan." Her back pressed solidly against the kitchen counter. She wasn't crying, but her face was tight and her eyes darted back and forth as if she were in a panic. "We didn't need to move all the way up here to get peeping toms, and psychos ... and ... and, as if that weren't enough, we pay twenty-five grand for a place that was the site of a massacre! Jesus Christ, Dan, you're a newspaperman, couldn't you have checked or something?"

He got up from the table and walked over to her, hands gesturing uselessly in front of him. "I had no reason to check, Sheila. And Mr. Carey *did* tell us about the deaths, don't you remember? He just didn't say where they died, or how."

"And you didn't ask him? I can't believe that, Dan. You always ask stuff like that."

"You didn't ask, either—" Dan felt like a kid for using such a sophomoric tactic. He was dodging because Sheila had him pegged; the fact was, he had asked, he had checked. He had known all about the killings. He'd just kept it to himself.

"Suppose we had known, Sheil, what difference would it have made?"

"We'd have known what we were getting into, that's what. We'd have known what everybody else in town already knows."

"But this is such a great place. Babe. It's everything we talked about, everything we wanted. And it was so *cheap*. If we had known, maybe we'd have passed up the best deal of our lives."

She looked at him. Her eyes were calmer now. Her fist unclenched, and she delicately combed her fingers through her silky hair. "It *is* a nice house," she said, looking around.

"It's a beautiful house, Sheil. And don't forget, lots of old places have a 'history,' that's what gives them their charm."

Sheila smiled weakly. "Some charm ..."

"I'll bet people have died in just about every house in town. I mean, we can't blame the house ..."

She placed her hand on Dan's chest and kissed him on the cheek. "You're right, Dan," she sniffed. "I'm overreacting."

Dan breathed a sigh of relief as Sheila walked over to the screen door.

He followed. Standing behind her, he put his arms around her waist. Together, they looked out across their yard and into the forest.

"I hope Will's okay," Sheila said.

Will followed the brook. Even when the water was beyond seeing distance, he still made certain he could hear it. He was pleased to find he was developing a pretty good sense of direction in the woods. Before he knew it, he was able to discern the outline of the Grants' trailer through the trees.

Moving toward it slowly and carefully, from tree to tree, Will briefly imagined he was an Indian stalking a settler's cabin. The pickup truck in the yard spoiled the fantasy; something about it made him nervous. Was it because he was scared of Mr. Grant?

For a while he went no farther, just studied the place from a safe distance. He thought, emphasizing the words in his mind, *This is where Mona lives*. It occurred to him then, he guessed for the first time, that Mona was a poor person. Their trailer wasn't even close to new; it was old, battered and rusty. Will knew it sounded stuck-up, but he couldn't help thinking that, all and all, the Grants' trailer was a pretty shitty-looking place to live.

The Grants didn't have any kind of lawn, just a stump-littered, semi-cleared area, wheel-rutted and cluttered with old tires, parts of engines, the skeleton of a ski-mobile, and various unidentifiable pieces of junk. The rusty top of their septic tank was exposed, with dirt piled in a half-circle around it. It looked like someone had dug it up—maybe to clean it—and hadn't bothered to fill it in again.

An ancient, weather-beaten shed stood in the back, its door swinging open. Will could see cut lengths of firewood piled haphazardly inside.

The unpainted porch on the side of the trailer leaned dangerously. It was partially closed in with fake wood paneling that had started to peel, forming wood-print scrolls where it was delaminating.

Will's gaze followed the rickety steps up to the porch and to the trailer's entrance. The door was open a little! Flies and small animals could have their run of the place, he guessed.

Moving up a little closer, he still couldn't see any movement. No one was out in the yard. There was no visible motion behind the windows, some of which were covered by sheets of cloudy plastic.

Maybe Mona and her father were inside. There was no way he could tell for sure without going right up to the door. He wasn't certain he wanted to do that though; his courage was slipping.

What would he say? How would he begin?

He decided the best thing was to be straightforward. After all, Mr. Grant had nothing against him. In fact, he had actually thanked Will for helping Mona. If Will knocked and Mr. Grant answered, he could just introduce himself, say that he'd stopped by to see how Mona was doing, to make sure she was okay.

It would be being friendly.

Yet, looking at the strange, still trailer, it was hard to work up his courage.

He moved cautiously into the yard and crossed it, stepping gingerly around a rusty amputated bumper and some cement blocks. The stairs up to the little porch were really creaky; the whole stairway swayed as he climbed it.

He peeked into the dark crack of the open door, knocking on the side of the trailer at the same time. "Hello, anybody here? Hello!"

No one answered. He listened but couldn't hear any movement inside. "Mona! Mr. Grant! Anybody home? It's Will Crockett!"

He pushed the door open a little more. The cool air rushing into his face smelled funny. It wasn't a clean smell; it was like old clothes and sealed rooms, and a hundred years of cigarette smoke ...

"Hello! Anyone here?"

... and it was dark in there. Some of the shades were drawn. What light there was lost its strength as it filtered through the plastic window coverings.

"Mona! Mr. Grant!"

Will didn't know why he did it. Maybe, simply because he'd started the thing, he wanted to see it through. Whatever the reason, he pushed the door open the rest of the way and stepped inside.

The place was extraordinarily messy; it would have been a nightmare for his mom: clothes all over the floor, dirty dishes here and there, on the stained carpeting, on the table, all over the kitchen. A big brown recliner, its arm split and threadbare, oozed discolored stuffing that tumbled to the floor. Overflowing ashtrays were everywhere.

"Mona! Mona, you here?"

An irritating dripping noise came from the kitchen faucet as it leaked into a frying pan full of brown, greasy water. A lava lamp, looking like a dead amoeba in a cylindrical aquarium, sat on top of an incongruously modern color TV set. A soiled cap had been thrown on top of the lamp. Several guns stood teepeed in the corner beside the slip-covered couch.

And it was chilly inside—real chilly. Will couldn't hear a fan or air conditioner running. Why should it be so cool?

He looked to his left where a dark and narrow hallway led to the bedrooms. That's where he saw Mr. Grant—although at first he didn't realize it was a person at all.

The man was lying among shadows on the floor, nearly invisible in the lightless hallway. He was on his back, head near the living room, right hand stretched out, as if reaching for something. If Will had taken one more step, he'd have stepped on twisted fingers.

When he realized the knot of shadows was a body, he jumped back, almost out the door.

"Mr. Grant ..." he said timidly, his voice shaking. He felt really weird just then, out of place and oddly conspicuous: he was in someone else's house; he wasn't sure he should be there; and all of a sudden somebody's on the floor, maybe sick, or drunk, or ...

It didn't take Will long to suspect that Mr. Grant was dead.

As Will's eyes got used to the darkness inside the trailer, he forced himself to take a closer look, just to be sure. He was caught up in a terrible blending of fascination and revulsion; he didn't want to look, but his eyes automatically pulled toward the death scene.

Fascination won out, and Will examined the body. Mr. Grant was dead all right, and Will began to get some vague idea of what had happened to him.

The first thing to arrest his attention was Mr. Grant's head. His eyes were two black and bloody pits. Dried blood masked most of the face, except the area between his mouth and the floor, which was crusted with vomit.

The front of his T-shirt had been ripped and peeled back, exactly like the ruined flesh beneath it. Mr. Grant looked as if somebody had taken a big knife to him, slicing him straight up the middle, like a steer in a slaughterhouse. Every surface of skin was covered with strange, crescent-shaped gouges.

Will started taking little stumbling steps backward. He felt sick. He wanted to scream, but something told him not to. It was the same prompting voice that was telling him to get out of the trailer, and fast.

But he couldn't. He was afraid Mona might be in there, too, maybe badly hurt. Maybe dead.

A picture of Norm and his two creepy pals flashed into Will's mind. Were they responsible for this?

Will stood helplessly for a few minutes, frozen, unable to move, unsure of what to do. He tried to keep his stomach under control, swallowing rapidly, tasting acrid liquid at the back of his tongue.

Looking around for the telephone—they must have had one hidden somewhere in all the junk—he wondered who to call. His mother? The rescue squad? Maybe he should call Chief Bates. Yes, that's what he should do. With that thought came another: *This must be the work of that maniac the chief warned us about ... Nolan.*

Maybe he's left here by now, maybe he's working his way up the hill, heading for ...

Mom! Dan!

The terrible possibility put a fire under him. First he'd call Mom and Dan, then he'd call the police. Will started tearing things apart, frantically looking for the damn telephone. He couldn't find it! It wasn't on the floor; it wasn't on the wall. Where the hell was it?

If it was anywhere at all it must be in one of those rooms on the other side of Mr. Grant's body.

Will pushed his back tightly against the wall of the little hallway. Fear pounded at his temples. His own breath seemed too loud, whistling through his nostrils. Carefully, he stepped over Mr. Grant's outstretched arm, then over his leg. There was a door on the right, just about even with Mr. Grant's foot. It was closed. Will opened it a crack. In spite of the deeper darkness beyond, he could tell it was the bathroom. No point looking for a phone there.

At the end of the hallway an open door led to a bedroom. A cigarette-scarred vanity attached to the wall supported a filthy mirror. It reflected an unmade bed, just a bare mattress and a tangle of dirty blankets. No pillowcase covered the blue-lined pillow.

And there was no telephone.

"Mona?" he said softly to the last unexplored door. It was directly in front of him.

Tension seemed suffocating as he reached out for the knob. He stopped when he heard a noise. He whirled and saw Mr. Grant's leg move!

Then he saw the foot that had kicked it. Mona's foot.

Will looked up. Mona was standing there. She had come out of the bathroom.

"Mona. God! Are you all right? What's happened here?"

She walked over to him, slowly, with shuffling steps. The brilliance was gone from her complexion; the radiance had vanished from her eyes. In the half-light of the bedroom, her face looked as flat and featureless as a doorknob.

As Will took a step to meet her, she flung her arms around him. "William, oh William, I'm so glad it's you."

"What's happened, Mona?" he pushed her away a little, but gently, leaving his hands for a moment on her biceps. "Where's your phone. We oughtta call the cops."

"No phone," she said.

He grabbed her hand, pulled. "Then we gotta get out of here. We gotta get up to my place."

She was resisting. She wouldn't come with him. "Come on!" he cried.

"No. Wait." She brought both her hands to her mouth, not looking at him, not looking at her father's body. Her eyes seemed as if they weren't seeing anything at all.

"Who did this Mona? Tell me—" Then a horrible thought slammed into Will's mind. "Not you ... Mona ... ? You didn't—"

"No, not me—"

"Who then?"

Her eyes flicked from side to side; she blinked rapidly. Will thought she was going to faint, so he stepped closer in case he had to catch her. "Who did it, Mona? Tell me? What if he's still around here someplace? Come on. We gotta get out of here."

She pulled back, not letting him lead her away.

"The boys. The boys did it. The boys came here, and they did it."

"What boys? Mona ..." Then he knew. "The guys your father beat up?"

She looked at him blankly. He held her by the arms, shaking her. "What boys, Mona?"

She nodded her head. "Yes ... yes. Those boys."

"Then we've got to call the police."

"No!" She said it loudly, great alarm in her voice.

Will thought maybe he should force her out of the trailer. They couldn't stay there. What if the guys came back? What if they were outside somewhere, waiting?

117

"Come on, Mona, please. Hold my hand, I'll take care of you. But we've got to get out of here. Now."

Mona thrust her weight against Will, backing him through the last door into the bedroom — her bedroom. Then she pushed the door closed, cutting off their view of the body and the dark, cool trailer.

She turned to face Will and threw herself into his arms. Tears finally came. "We can't go," she cried. "They'll come here, William. I know they'll come ..."

"Who, Mona? Who'll come?"

Her eyes darted around as if she were looking for the words she needed. She was obviously confused. Her mouth moved as if she were gasping for breath. "The ... the welfare people. They'll come here. They'll take me away, put me in an orphanage or something. I don't want to do that, William. Don't let them. You've got to help me."

He felt her trembling in his arms. Was she hysterical? Could he reason with her? "But Mona, we've got to get help. Those guys're crazy. Look what they've done. Suppose they come back to get you. Or me! We can't let them get away with this!"

"They *won't* get away with it. But if you call the police, I'm the one who'll get in trouble."

"What do you mean?"

"They'll take me away, put me in a home. My mother's gone, William. Pa says she's dead. I ain't got no relations. And I ain't old enough to live on my own."

Will knew he was doing it again; he was getting talked into something he knew he shouldn't do. But somehow, it all made a crazy kind of sense ...

No! He couldn't be thinking straight; maybe he was a little nutsy himself, because of everything that was happening. Crazy or sane, the fact was, he felt tremendously sorry for Mona; she was poor and didn't have much of anything. Now her father was dead.

Will was her only ally in the world.

Again he wrapped her in his arms. With a comforting hand he pressed her face into the pocket formed by his shoulder and neck. He held her for a while.

Will knew what it was like to have a father die. He'd been through it. But for Mona it would be different; the next day nobody'd be there to take care of her. When Will's dad died, his mom was always right there for him.

Suddenly, Will knew it was up to him to take care of her.

He hugged Mona tighter, not knowing what else to do. "It's okay," he said softly. "It's okay, Mona." Her body felt warm against his. He could feel her hot tears on his cheek. In spite of the situation, he noticed that her breasts felt soft and yielding against his chest. He just held her for a long time, trying to make her feel better, more comfortable. He felt the tenseness in her body ease until at last her crying stopped.

She pulled her head back and looked into his eyes. "I'm only thirteen, William. They ain't gonna let me stay here on my own."

"But we can't just let those guys get away with this." It was a weak argument, but it was the only one he had left.

"They won't. They'll get what's comin' to them. Maybe not for this, maybe not for what they done to Pa, but sometime, for somethin'. You wait'n see. They're no good, that ain't gonna change, but I'm the one's gonna pay if we let on what's happened here. I'm the one's gonna get locked up. I'll never see you again."

She buried her face in his neck, hugging him so tightly it almost hurt.

"What're we gonna do about your dad?" Will asked, looking at the closed bedroom door.

"I can take care of him. I'll bury him in the yard, just like in the old days."

"But won't people notice he's missing?"

"Pa ain't got no friends. Nobody ever comes around."

"But his job ... ?"

"Pa ain't worked in years."

Will was thinking about it. As crazy as it sounded, he was considering it. He knew how much he'd hate it if someone yanked him out of his home and put him someplace else. It was bad enough leaving Boston and moving to Vermont, but at least his parents came with him. Mona would have nothing, no one. If they called the police, she'd lose all say in what happened to her.

"Please, William, help me." Her eyes pleaded, her body felt warm and urgent. Right then Will would have done anything for her, gladly.

"I ... I don't know," he stammered.

"Please, William. You can at least give me until tomorrow. At least give me a little time to think about it. I gotta work something out ..." She looked into his eyes, deep into his eyes.

And he agreed.

CHAPTER 13
BURYING THE PAST

Over the next two weeks Mona spent a lot of time with the family on Tenny's Hill.

She never talked about what had occurred at the trailer. Several times Will tried, but couldn't force himself to bring it up. He didn't want to think about it, much less discuss it.

He even lacked the courage to ask Mona what she'd done about her father's body. The next time he visited the trailer, however, he noticed that the dirt had been filled in around the septic tank.

Yet, try as he might, Will couldn't avoid thinking about it. He realized he and Mona were breaking the law; they were covering up a serious crime. His sense of justice was assaulted every time he thought about those three punks getting off scot-free. They were *murderers*, for God's sake, actual murderers.

Will worried, too, that the murderers had left their work incomplete; what if they came back to get Mona? Or Will?

Strangely, the idea of another attack didn't upset Mona. She'd said the punks' argument had been with her father, and now it was settled. "You gotta understand how folks up here think," she'd explained. Still, Will wasn't so sure.

At the same time, the situation had at least one positive side: Mona was looking better every day. She seemed happy—if that could be the right word—and the sparkle had come back to her eyes. It was almost as if she was glad to be rid of her father. What could their relationship have been like? How could Mr. Grant's death cause such a change in Mona?

When Will visited her at the trailer, she had cleaned up the whole place, aired it out, and had mayonnaise jars and ketchup bottles full of wild flowers almost everywhere he looked.

Sometimes Mona would bring a big bouquet of brown-eyed Susans, daisies, and Queen Anne's Lace as a gift for Sheila. Sheila liked that, and Will was sure she liked Mona, too. She gave Mona an autographed copy of *Charm Bracelet*. The next day Mona came back and said it was the best book she'd ever read. Sheila wouldn't have been more pleased with a glowing review in the *New York Times*.

And Mona was full of questions about the baby. Will guessed it did his mother good to have somebody to talk to—somebody female.

Dan was the only one who hadn't seen too much of the girl. He was rarely around, the *Tribune* taking up most of his time. Almost every evening Dan worked at beefing up his advertising campaign. One night at dinner he announced that he'd made a big decision: he wasn't going to print the paper anymore, he was going to ship it over to Springfield to have it done photo-offset by Green Mountain Printers. This would be cheaper, he explained, and it would open up more space at the office because he wouldn't have to store those huge rolls of paper. He also planned to get rid of the gigantic web offset press that took up nearly the entire back room. The plan was for Dan and Will to tear it down, piece by piece, since it was too big to be moved out the door.

One Thursday night, after dinner, Dan and Will drove into town to begin disassembling the press. They had promised Sheila they'd be home before dark. She'd been brave about it, encouraging them to go, but at the same time she was still nervous about being alone in the house at night.

Will hoped Mona would arrive pretty soon to keep Mom company.

———————

"Where the guys off to?"

Sheila turned away from the dishwasher and looked at Mona. "Hi," she said smiling. "Come in. They're down at the paper." The screen door slammed behind her.

"Both your men desertin' you, huh?" Mona, dressed in cut-offs and a Pepsi T-shirt, walked barefooted across the kitchen and began helping Sheila collect the dinner dishes. "Let me load the dishwasher," she offered.

"You don't have to do that."

"I like to. It's fun. Y'know, the only dishwasher we got down the trailer is me."

Sheila chuckled as she sponged the counter. Mona stacked greasy plates and filmy glasses. "Easy to see which plate's Will's," Mona said. "See that, he don't eat his broc'li."

"But he packed away two hamburgers without much difficulty."

"So, what you plannin' to do tonight, Sheila? You gonna do some writin'?"

"I thought I would, but that was before I knew I was going to have company."

"Oh, I ain't gonna stay. I jes' come up to show you somethin'."

"Oh ... ?"

Mona forced her fingers into the tight front pocket of her shorts and pulled out a folded piece of paper. "I wrote somethin' for ya. It's a poem" — she pronounced it *poym* — "but I don't want you should read it till after I go ..."

"A poem? That's awfully nice of you, Mona." Sheila held out her hand for the paper. "But you don't have to leave now, do you? I thought maybe we could make some cookies for when the guys get back."

Mona's eyes lit up. "I guess there's always time for cookies."

Sheila put the folded paper in her own pocket and handed the detergent to Mona. Soon the dishwasher was humming in the background.

While Mona spooned cookie dough onto a sheet, Sheila sat at the table mixing a second batch of chocolate chips. She became suddenly aware that Mona was watching her. Turning, their eyes met.

"What are you thinking about, Honey?" Sheila asked.

"The baby, I guess. Won't be long 'fore you're gonna have that little one."

"Less than two months ..."

"You suppose you're gonna let me sit it sometimes? So's you and Dan can go out? I'd like to, you know. I'd be awful good to him. You wouldn't have to worry."

"That's a very kind offer, Sweetie—"

"You wouldn't have to pay me nothin', neither. I'd do it 'cause. Well, I'd do it 'cause you're a friend a mine. You an' Dan could go off two, three days at a time, even. I'd take good care of him ..."

Sheila experienced the pressure of unformed tears at the corners of her eyes. Her newfound friend seemed worried about being replaced when the infant came.

"Dan and I couldn't ask for a better babysitter, Mona. If you hadn't brought it up, I was going to ask you."

The two of them sat quietly for a long time, eye to eye. Sheila studied Mona's placid, almost frightened smile. It was as if the girl were working up the courage to say something more.

"Sheila ...?"

124

"What, Hon?"

"I can't never have no babies."

"Oh Mona, don't say that. You just have to wait till you're older, until the right man comes along."

"No. I used to be able to. But now I can't."

Sheila turned in her chair, her knees almost touching Mona's. She took the girl's hands in her own.

"What do you mean, Sweetie?"

"I mean … well … one time I got …" The corners of her eyes started to twitch. A glass film of water appeared along her lower eye lid. "I got … you know …"

"Pregnant?"

"Yup. I had to have a 'bortion."

"Oh, Mona …"

"They busted me up. Inside. And now … now I can't …"

Sheila leaned forward, taking Mona in her arms. "Oh, Sweetie," she whispered. She could feel the girl vibrating against her, crying silently. "Oh, Mona, it's all right …"

Mona's trembling subsided after a few moments. She sat up straight and wiped her eyes, smiling self-consciously.

Sheila wasn't sure if her next question was motivated by nosiness or true concern. It was an unnecessary question, but it just tumbled out, thoughtlessly. "And the father … ?"

Mona sniffed loudly and stood up. "I … I gotta go now, Sheila. I gotta go. I ain't supposed to talk about it."

The screen door banged again, before Sheila could get to her feet. By the time she reached the porch, Mona was gone.

———

They hadn't been at the office more than half an hour before Will's hands, arms, face, and clothes were covered with black ink.

Dan looked at him, laughing. "You look just like something out of a minstrel show." Then he got real serious. He pulled a coke out of the little refrigerator and poured it into two Styrofoam coffee cups. "Tell me something, Will," he said, passing a cup, "what's the story on that girl, Mona?"

"I dunno. Like, wha'd'ya mean?"

"You two are spending an awful lot of time together, aren't you?" He was trying to sound as if he were just shooting the breeze, but Will suspected he was leading up to something heavy.

"Well, it's not like I got a whole lot of friends to hang out with …"

"Have you ever been down to her trailer?"

"Yeah. Sure. Once or twice."

"What are her parents like?"

Will felt as if he were in some kind of vise, and it was squeezing shut. He knew the routine; any information he offered would just bring another question, if he didn't give enough information, that would look suspicious, too.

"Her mom's dead," Will said truthfully.

"What's her dad like?"

"I dunno. He's not around much." Will hadn't exactly lied to Dan yet, but he felt it coming.

"You mean he works?"

"He … ah … he drives a truck."

"So he's on the road a lot?"

"I guess so. I never really met him."

"So Mona is home all by herself?"

"Pretty much." Will thought fast, trying to find some way to reroute the conversation. "I guess that's why she comes up to the house so much."

"But you go down there, too. Is it all right with Mr. Grant that she's having you at the house when he's not there?"

"I dunno. I guess so." By this time Will was pretty sure he knew what was going on. Oh, he could go on playing dumb and telling his half-lies, but he didn't like doing it. Instead, he decided to jump right in, head first, "It's not like she's my girlfriend, or anything, Dan. I mean I like her, but she's not my girlfriend ..."

Maybe that was the worst lie of all. Will would love to have Mona for his girlfriend. It just hadn't happened yet, not exactly; the whole situation was too weird ...

Apparently his disclaimer had embarrassed Dan, though; he seemed to back off a little. "I know she's not your girlfriend, Will. But she is a girl, and not an unattractive one, I might add. I'm just saying that maybe it's not such a good idea for you to go down there when she's all alone. Mr. Grant might not like it, and frankly, I'm not sure I do either—"

"But Dan—"

"Before you start arguing with me, Will, just let me finish."

Will waited. He was sweating, more from nervousness than exertion. Drops of black were dripping from his forehead, splattering onto the floor.

"All I want to say is this: Mona's welcome at our house any time at all. You two kids seem to get along well, and your mother likes her. I'm just asking that you not spend time alone with her at the trailer, not unless her father is there, and he approves, okay?"

It really wasn't okay, but Will figured arguing would just prolong the discussion. He was eager to change the subject, so he agreed. Will understood that Dan was actually worried about two things: how it would look for them to be hanging out in the trailer; and sex.

Dan and Will had never talked about sex. Will wasn't even sure Dan knew how he felt about girls in general. Sex was one of those things that wasn't easy to talk about with a parent. *What am I supposed to do*, Will wondered, *just run into the house one day and announce, "Okay guys, it's finally happened—all of a sudden I'm attracted to girls?"*

Will had often laughed at the way his parents always wanted everything neatly laid out and carefully scheduled for them. Unless his puberty was penciled into an appointment book or written on the calendar, they'd never trust that it had happened. They'd think, "Oh, it's going to happen any day now," but they'd never come right out and ask. Instead, they'd just keep putting out these stupid little feelers and asking a bunch of dumb, indirect questions.

Will thought maybe some day he should have a real man-to-man with his stepfather. But not right now.

———————

It was totally dark when Dan called off work for the night. They'd pulled the big printing press completely apart and left it lying in giant puzzle pieces on the office floor.

Sweaty and tired, they drove home in the rain.

During the ride, Dan complained that he hadn't been able to sell the ancient press. He couldn't even give it away, not after dozens of phone calls to printers and even to museums. Instead, he'd ended up paying some guy $250 to truck it off to the dump.

Everything outside the Renault looked glassy and still. The wipers worked hypnotically, like twin metronomes.

Will felt relaxed until they drove past Grant's trailer. He saw that the lights were on. Apparently Mona was inside, rather than at the house with Mom. Considering his conversation with Dan, it was probably just as well.

Will was eager to see Mona, though. After being so evasive with his stepfather, he was more convinced than ever that what they were doing was wrong and had to stop. He and Mona were concealing too much. They shared too many ugly, potentially dangerous secrets.

Somehow, Will noticed, he always felt the most doubtful when Mona wasn't around. When she was with him, everything seemed okay.

The porch light was on when they pulled into the yard.

Sheila was waiting at the door. She'd made cookies, and the whole house smelled like a bakery. Will was relieved to see that his mother was full of smiles and looking really nice. She announced, with satisfaction, that she'd even spent about an hour at the word processor. Before that, she told them, Mona had dropped by and helped with the dishes. Then they'd made cookies. "She's an awfully nice girl," Sheila said. "But she's troubled, Dan, and I think we should talk about it."

"Okay, sure. Maybe we should start paying her for the work she does around here," Dan said.

Sheila smiled at the idea, then shook her head. "I want Mona to feel like our friend," she explained, "not like our employee. Besides, Mrs. Menard gives me all the help I need."

She kept giving Dan little hugs and kisses. Will got the strong feeling they'd like to be alone. At about ten-thirty he went upstairs, showered, and hung out in his room with the headphones on.

The loud rock music didn't drive Mona out of his mind.

Whenever he was alone, he got to thinking, and the cycle of concerns always followed the same course. Sure, he was worried about breaking the law, but it was more than that. Wasn't it strange no word about the fight had ever made it back to Dan? Must be no one had reported it, and that was further proof that Norm and his geeky friends had wanted to pay Mr. Grant back in their own way.

And that was even weirder, a real nightmare: the way they'd paid him back, the shape Mr. Grant's body had been in. It was the most sick and disgusting thing Will had ever seen. Even now—almost two weeks later—his stomach turned just thinking about it. Why hadn't they simply shot him, or stabbed him, or maybe just worked him over? Why did they punch out his eyes and slice him up the middle like that? And what were those other marks Will kept remembering? The ones that looked like bites? The whole thing was crazy—way out of proportion. Those kids were sick.

He understood Mona's not wanting to turn them in; she had too much to lose. Still, hadn't she seemed just a little too eager to let the whole thing go? Wouldn't any normal person want revenge—legal or otherwise—for the murder of a parent? Will guessed Mona couldn't have loved her father very much. The thought made him sad.

Eventually their cover-up would be discovered; someone would miss Mr. Grant. So what if he didn't have a job to go to? There was still the lady from the welfare office who came around every few months; how could Mona continue to bluff her? And, sooner or later, wouldn't someone think it strange that the truck never moved from the yard?

Will was beginning to think he should wait for Mom and Dan to go to bed, then sneak down to the trailer and have it out with Mona. It was horrible carrying around this awful secret. It made him feel dirty, dishonest. Having to lie and scam all the time made him feel like a real jerk.

What would happen to him when the truth came out? Would he get taken away—maybe locked up—right along with Mona?

Will turned off the Walkman and pulled off his earphones. The rain beat furiously on the roof outside his window. The sound gave him second thoughts about sneaking down to the trailer.

Were Dan and Mom still up? Will wondered what they knew, what they suspected. Most of all he wondered what Mom wanted to say to Dan about Mona.

There was a vent—Dan called it a register—in the floor that allowed warm air to pass from the living room up to Will's bedroom. It had a little lever to open and close the passage. Since this was August, the vent was kept closed. Will tiptoed over, knelt on the floor, and pushed the lever. Little metal slats, almost like venetian blinds, opened, allowing Will to see part of the room below. Although Dan and Mom weren't visible, Will could hear them talking.

———

Dan wanted to put Sheila's mind at ease. "The police haven't heard a word about him, at least not from anywhere in the state. Far as I'm concerned, he's vanished. Dick Bates thinks he probably went back to Long Island."

"So"—Sheila's eyes were hopeful—"that means Mr. Bates really doesn't think we need to be worried, right Dan?"

Dan knew how eager she was to hear the words that would put their lives safely back on track. Now, he was doing the cleaning up, and every bit as compulsively as Sheila. He was trying to wipe away smudges of fear and suspicion.

He couldn't mislead her though. "The chief didn't tell me to drop my guard altogether, but I don't think he's too worried, no. And neither am I."

Sheila smiled. Her eyes were almost free of worry and Dan was delighted; her nervousness was passing.

He realized the increasing amount of time he spent at the newspaper allowed her plenty of opportunity for paranoid speculation. It was important that she understood he was working: he was not avoiding her; not courting other women; not so much as contemplating abandoning her and Will. It was his job; he was doing it for the family. She had to understand.

He caught himself standing above her, looking down, smiling.

In Dan's mind it couldn't be simpler: he loved her, and he loved her son. At one time, he remembered, the word had seemed so complex, so full of subtlety, exception, and ambiguity. Now it seemed so simple. Love. It was elegant and beautiful.

He put his fingers against her cheek.

"Did you check the files at the paper, Dan?" Obviously she wasn't thinking the way he was; he had a bit more cleaning to do.

"I did, but they didn't add much to what Dick already told us." He took a couple of steps toward the glass door. "And they didn't say anything about 'little people,' if that's what you mean. Being a small-town paper, I guess they didn't go in for much speculation, and they surely avoided any lurid details …"

"Still, it's creepy, don't you think so, Dan? I mean, knowing all that stuff went on right in our house."

"I guess. But in a sense, it's not the same house it was back then. Look at it this way: We've done it all over, changed everything around. It's our house now, Sheila. What happened here four years ago, well, that was another time and another place, too. That's what I think." He took a step closer to her. "You haven't been seeing any more peeping toms have you?"

Sheila laughed. "No, no more peeping toms."

"You know who I think it was?" said Dan. "I think it was your friend, Mona. I bet she was up here checking us out."

"Oh, no, Dan, Mona wouldn't do that!" Sheila was genuinely surprised at the accusation.

"You don't think so?"

"Oh, heavens no. Mona might be a little rough around the edges, but I think she knows better than to snoop around someone's house, peeking in their windows. You don't really think it was Mona, do you, Dan?"

"Why not, unless it was that father of hers. As I recall, he's a pretty unsavory-looking character. You'll notice everything's stopped, though, since Mona's taken up part-time residence here."

"And I'm glad she does. I think it's good for her. Besides, I didn't think you minded her coming around, Dan. In fact, I thought you kind of liked it." She laughed a little. Dan thought she was forcing the jovial tone, but he wasn't sure why.

"And just what do you mean by that?" Dan said, his voice firm with mock indignation, playing along.

"Well, she is a cute little nymphet, wouldn't you say so, Humbert?"

"That's precisely the point," Dan's tone changed, became more serious. "I just don't want her and Will getting too thick. Could lead to trouble."

Sheila giggled. She sounded like a little girl. "Oh, Dan, you sound just like somebody's prudish old father. In fact, you sound just like *my* prudish old father."

Dan chuckled, too. "You want a little more wine, Sheila?"

"I've got a better idea," she spoke in a low sexy voice. "That is, unless you're feeling too prudish."

Dan moved silently across the room to her, knelt on the couch, and pulled her to him.

"Hmmmm. See how easy it can happen," he whispered.

"Oh, yes," Sheila sighed.

"Poor Will," Dan said, "see what he could be in for?"

"Poor Will," Sheila agreed.

———

The light below the register went out. A few seconds later, Will heard the stairs creaking.

He went back to his bed, feeling guilty and ashamed. *Jesus Christ,* he thought, *now I'm even spying on my parents!*

CHAPTER 14
MIDNIGHT VISITATION

At first Will thought it was a door banging.

He tried hard not to wake up, his mind fighting to protect his sleep, to blend the persistent sound into a dream.

The banging noise continued, a loud, echoing report that seemed to shake the whole house.

Will opened his eyes a notch in the dark bedroom. A heavy wind drove currents of rainwater against his window. The house rattled as a monstrous thunderclap stomped across the sky.

Squinting at the faintly glowing numbers of his alarm clock, he saw it was two-fifteen, the middle of the night.

BANG!

Somewhere, buried amid the thunder and the driving rain, another sound intruded. An unnatural sound.

Listening hard, Will tried to isolate the noise that had wakened him.

BANG!

It recurred slowly, building with a precise rhythm, like hammer blows.

BANG! BANG! BANG!

Someone was at the door!

Will untangled himself from the sheet, struggling to get up. His legs wobbled as he crossed the darkness to the door of his bedroom.

Peeking out, a movement in the unlighted hall made Will jump. The caped phantom swooping down on him was Dan, emerging from his room, pulling on his bathrobe. He tied the cord around his waist as, for a moment, his gaze locked on Will's.

Lightning flashed brightly in the hall. In it, Dan's eyes looked puffy beneath his glasses. His hair was wildly messed up, almost comic.

He fumbled for the hall light.

"Stay in your room, Will," he whispered. His tone was so emphatic Will understood there was to be no discussion. Taking an obedient step backward, he watched Dan from his doorway. The heavy banging echoed loudly among the noises of the storm.

Dan moved hesitantly down the stairs. Will could tell he was being very careful, listening and looking around cautiously in the glaring overhead light. He descended slowly, as if the stairs were unfamiliar to him, as if each step were an effort of willpower.

At the bottom Dan reached out—was his arm trembling?—and turned on the living room light. Then he crossed away from the stairs, moving toward the kitchen door, and out of sight.

Sheila came out of their room. Her stomach bulged like a colorful balloon under her red nylon robe. She blinked at the light, looking puzzled and afraid.

"Someone's at the door," she said weakly.

"Who do you think it could be, Mom?" Will whispered.

Sheila shook her head.

Will picked up on his mother's nervousness and added it to his own. His first thought was that somebody had driven off the road, maybe got hurt in a wreck. But no, their house was too far away from the highway.

In fact, their house was too far away from everything. Nobody should be around at this time of night.

Heat surged along his spine. Muscles tightened at the back of his neck, squeezing sweat from his face. As his mind became more alert, the mounting fear ignited. *What if it's that crazy guy, Nolan? What if he's come back here after all?*

But Nolan wouldn't bother to knock. If he meant to hurt them, he'd just break in.

It must be the police, then. What if they'd discovered ... ? Oh shit! Cover stories started racing through Will's mind.

He felt his mother's arm come to rest on his shoulder, hugging him a little.

He could feel her shaking.

Listening hard, he tried to hear Dan talking to whoever it was.

Your son here? Chief Bates's voice was gruff in Will's imagination.

Try as he might, it was impossible to hear any conversation above the roar of the rain. All he could make out was the rapid rhythm of Sheila's breathing.

It seemed like she was breathing too fast. Will looked at her face. She appeared a lot more worried, now. She inched toward the top of the stairs, leaned forward and looked down. Her hand was sheet-white on the banister.

"Dan?" she said softly, her voice weak and cracking. "Dan, who is it?" When she looked back at Will, fright was plain on her face. Will felt horrible seeing it there; he felt helpless, and somehow responsible.

"This is taking an awful long time," he whispered.

"It's okay, Will," Sheila said.

There was no sign of Dan. Will thought he should do something, but he didn't know what.

He remembered the aluminum baseball bat in his closet. Maybe he should take it and go down there.

Maybe Dan needed help.

Will looked at his mother, hoping for some instruction, some clue about what to do. She met his eyes, looking as if she were about to start crying.

That look of fear gave him all the instruction he needed. He had to protect her. It was his job, his duty.

Then they heard the front door close. A blast of thunder shook the house.

Together they watched the shadow of a man projected by the living room light. It fell heavy and black against the wall at the foot of the stairs.

Will held his breath. His mom's hand clenched tighter on his shoulder.

Should he make a dash for that aluminum bat?

Below them the moving shadow filled the hallway.

Let it be Dan, Will prayed. If it wasn't, he didn't know what he'd do. His eyes searched for some familiar characteristic in the silhouette's movements.

When the man appeared at the bottom of the stairs, Sheila sighed loud enough for Will to hear. Her hand was cold.

Dan hadn't put his foot on the first step when Sheila said in a shaky voice, "Who was it, Dan?"

He climbed about halfway up the steps without answering. When he stopped, he shook his head and looked up. They saw the puzzled expression on his face.

"That was Joe Grant," he said, "Mona's father."

CHAPTER 15
NEW LIGHT

"What did he want, Dan?" Sheila was staring at him, eyes wide, full of urgency and expectation. As she moved closer, arms reaching for an embrace, Dan watched her expression of fear soften into a familiar look of concern. "Everything's all right, isn't it?"

Dan hugged her, then stepped back to talk. He shook his head slowly, trying to decide if he was more amused or put off by the incident. "He said he's looking for Mona, wondered if she's up here."

"It couldn't have been Mr. Grant," Will said.

Dan looked at the boy. "Why do you say that, Will?"

Will seemed ready to say something; his eyes flashed with sudden determination, his mouth opened as if to speak. Then he stopped and leaned against Sheila, whose arm tightened around him.

"Will . . ?" Dan coaxed.

"I mean … you know … why would Mr. Grant come up here so late?"

"God, Dan," Sheila added, "I hope Mona's all right. You mean she isn't home at this hour?"

"That's what he said …"

"Did you offer to go out and help look for her?"

"No, but—"

139

"No? Dan, she might be in trouble. I mean, what's a kid her age doing out at this time of night? And in this kind of weather? I told you how very upset she was when she left here earlier."

Dan was getting impatient. "Look, Sheila, Grant was acting awful strange—"

"What do you mean, strange?"

"Well." He tried to bring the image back into his mind. Just exactly what had been so strange about Grant? "He was very unsteady on his feet; he moved as if his legs hurt him, like they were … you know … extremely arthritic, or in casts or something …"

"Da-Dan?" Will's voice was an airy whisper. "What did Mr. Grant look like?"

"What did he look like?" Dan scrunched up his face, searching for words to match the lurching, staggering picture in his mind. "That's strange, too, Will. When he heard me unlocking the front door, he moved out into the yard, out beyond the range of the porch light. He just stood there in the pouring rain, out where I couldn't get a good look at him. We had to talk to each other long distance. I asked him in, but he wouldn't have any part of it. I didn't want to get all wet so I stayed on the porch. Some of these country people are pretty weird—"

"You couldn't see his face?"

"No, it was too dark. He was a big guy, though, I could see that. He looked about the same as he did that morning at the mailbox—his general outline, I mean. But his speech was all slurred. Frankly, I think he was drunk. That's probably what he didn't want me to see. It's also why I was glad he didn't come in."

"But Dan, what about Mona?" Sheila insisted. Dan could easily see she wasn't happy with the way he'd handled the situation.

"Mona's probably at the trailer, safe and sound. I'll bet Grant hadn't even been home yet. I bet he was out at some bar, got himself loaded and came up here to check us out. If it'll make you feel any better, Sheila, I'll go down to the trailer in the morning and make sure everything's okay. Now, don't you think we've all lost enough sleep over this?"

Sheila shook her head, puzzled and clearly not satisfied. She allowed Dan to usher her back into their bedroom.

In the soft humid darkness, Dan found it difficult to get back to sleep. Will's questions bothered him. Why was the boy so suspicious? Did he know something he wasn't telling?

But more intrusive was the bizarre image of Joe Grant, standing—just standing there—swaying and droning on in that odd, raspy voice as sheets of rain splattered down on him.

———————

By first light Will was pretty sure he was cracking up. He lay there in his bed, hand on his neck, trying to formulate a plan.

First off, he had to find Mona, had to know what was going on. This whole thing—everything—had gone far enough.

Will was wide awake when Dan got up at six-thirty; by a few minutes after seven, he heard Dan go out the door. Will listened to the Renault start with a timid little roar. The tires crunched on the gravel drive.

Better wait an hour or two, he decided, *in case Dan really does stop at the trailer*. He wondered how Mona would handle it. She'd come up with some kind of story, he was sure. She was a quick thinker and could probably pull it off with no problem.

He hoped.

When he got downstairs, Mom was sitting at the table reading a writer's magazine. She asked him what he wanted for breakfast.

"Not hungry yet," he said. "Maybe in a few minutes."

141

The two of them sat silently in the kitchen. Each wanted to speak, neither could begin. He'd never felt more cut off from his parents.

"What's the matter, Will? You worried about Mona?"

He ran his finger around the smooth top of the sugar bowl. "Yeah. Plus, I didn't sleep too good."

"I'm worried about her, too. Dan's probably down there right now. I hope he is. He said he'd stop by and make sure everything's okay. I wish the Grants had a phone ..."

"That's really weird about Mr. Grant," Will said. It was the closest he could come to saying what was actually on his mind. He felt horrible concealing things from his mother, especially when she was always so straight with him.

"It sure is. Either way, I'm worried about Mona. If she really was out all night, that's a problem. If she was home, well, I might as well say it: an alcoholic for a father never did any kid any good."

Will suspected Mom might have been talking about herself a little. Although he'd never known her father, Grandpa Benjamin, and Mom rarely talked about him, Will had picked up little things here and there. For one thing, Mom seemed to know an awful lot about alcoholics, judging from some of the characters in her books.

"Will, does Mona—" His mother seemed to be concentrating deeply. When she spoke, there was a slight hesitation between each word, "Does Mona get along all right with her father?"

"I guess. Wha'd'ya mean, 'get along'?"

"I mean, does he ever ... hit her, or—how should I say it?—abuse her in any way?"

Will squinted his eyes, deliberately trying to convey that he was giving the question serious thought. "She's never said anything like that—not to me, anyways."

"Will … Mona says that Mr. Grant doesn't work, is that right?"

"I guess so, but he's never around."

"That time I met him, he said something about welfare. Are they on welfare, do you know?"

"Yeah, probably. Mona never talks about it." Something deep inside seemed to punch at his heart every time he lied to his mother.

"Of course not. I'm sure Mona's not proud of it. Then again, it's nothing to be ashamed of; it's certainly not Mona's fault."

"So why do you want to know?" he asked, even though he had a pretty good idea.

"I'm not sure," Mom said, as she stood up and went to the refrigerator to get English muffins. "Maybe if they've got a welfare worker I could talk to her."

Will panicked at that thought. "But Mom, it's not really our business, you know …"

He thought she was going to get mad at him. Instead, she had a real thoughtful expression as she poured his orange juice. "I know it isn't, Will," she said, "but I'm getting quite fond of Mona. Maybe I worry too much about her." Then she winked at Will and smiled. She put on her old lady voice and said, "That's what happens when you get old, sonny. You young folks don't know what it's like; you don't have a care in the world."

Jeez, Will thought, *if she only knew …*

———

It must have been around nine-thirty when Will headed off to the trailer.

Although it was all downhill, the short walk seemed exhausting. Will felt sick. Maybe he was coming down with the

143

flu, or something. It wasn't just that he was tired, his head was messed up.

All the secret stuff he was involved in … it was really big-deal stuff. Christ, he and Mona were covering up a murder!

Murder. He had to keep saying it, over and over, up front in his mind, to make it seem real. It was like something out of a bad movie. It was so fantastic he just couldn't believe it was happening to him, not really happening.

His mind was working so hard, he thought his brain would burst right through his skull; his head actually hurt.

He knew he wouldn't feel any better until he told his parents about Mr. Grant's body.

Then he had it. It was simple. He'd been a jerk not to see it sooner: Mona and her dad were playing some kind of sick joke on him. Before, he'd thought that only kids played dead and thought it was funny. But maybe adults could do it, too. Not Mom and Dan, for sure, but there were other kinds of adults; there were some real odd ones, and Will knew it.

The feeling that his mind was splitting in two grew stronger then. Half of him wanted to believe he'd been the victim of a stupid joke, while the other half remembered that body, sliced up the middle, insides exposed like a squished animal on the highway.

God it was awful. It was so awful. Will felt his eyes starting to sting, and he knew he was going to cry.

He stopped beside the road. A few tears squeezed out and slid about halfway to his mouth before he backhanded them away. He leaned against a tree and started to shake.

He couldn't stop.

And then he was crying like hell.

He slid his back along the tree trunk until he was sitting on the ground, and he cried and cried, just like a stupid baby.

CHAPTER 16
WRITING FOR THE WRITER

The housekeeper, Mrs. Menard, would arrive at one o'clock in the afternoon.

Sheila looked around, content that the place wasn't too unpresentable. Then she forced a chuckle at her own expense. She was actually considering cleaning for the housekeeper. *Now that really makes sense*, she thought, *like cooking for the cook, or painting for the painter*. Catching herself in compulsive behavior, she half-spoke, half-whistled, "Wheeeew."

She shook her head. "You're gettin' bad, kiddo," she said, immediately startled by the sound of her own voice in the empty house.

Now, with a few hours of privacy, she should forget cleaning; her time could be more productively spent at the word processor.

Who's going to write for the writer?

After taking a last look out the door, she started up the stairs to her writing room. As she casually slid her hand into the pocket of her jeans, she felt something.

Mona's note.

She'd forgotten all about it. She trotted up the stairs, unfolding the piece of yellow foolscap as she went. When she reached her desk, she spread the paper flat and smoothed the wrinkles with her palm.

The awkward, childlike scrawl made her smile. She felt a little embarrassed when she saw the "I's" were dotted with little hearts, and the poem was signed with a happy face.

To Sheela

To have a friend as nice as you
when I don't have no other
Is something that I'm going to miss
When god calls me to mother.

My mother died so long ago
I can't recal her face
My dad says I'm all thats left
of mother at our place.

With you jest livving up the road
and me here down below
At least now when I'm all alone
I got some place to go.

Luv
Mona

Sheila quickly folded the paper and slid it under a pile of notes at the right-hand corner of her desk. She sniffed loudly and ran her fingertips over her dampening eyes.

The simple doggerel seemed so layered with meaning. So … so plaintive.

Sheila sat and flicked on her computer, determined to write a thank-you note to Mona, one that would invite further intimacy.

She needs a friend.

But wait. Not so fast. Better think about it first. Sheila didn't want to be too aggressive and risk frightening the girl away.

Better to get my mind off it for a while.

The green screen scrutinized her; the cursor winked at her, confidentially, saying, "It's a joke, it's funny "

But it wasn't funny; it was sad. It was lonely and painful and unbelievably sweet.

Sheila knew that if she gave it any more thought she would start crying.

She rested her fingers on the keys, with no idea what she was going to type.

I'll just let it flow ...

She typed:

> Sheila Crockett
> Tenny's Hill Rd.
> Antrim, VT 05143
>
> Aug. 21
> Stanley F. Gudhausen, MD
> 2145½ State St. Suite 324-B
> Boston, MA 02116
>
> Dear Dr. Gudhausen,
> We've settled in now, and at long last I'm going to give you that update I promised you. Please forgive me for taking so long. You were so thoughtful to ask how we're doing that I feel a bit irresponsible to have kept you waiting so long.
> Everything is turning out exactly as I'd hoped. The house is finished, it's beautiful. We're feeling right at home.
> The country air is so fresh! The forest is ultra green, the sky an impossible shade of blue!
> And at night we've got stars!

Can you believe it? I'd forgotten stars, actually forgotten them!

One night I was all alone on the porch. With closed eyes, I listened to the birds and to the bullfrogs' lusty song.

When I opened my eyes, there they were! Thousands of them. A whole sky full: the little dipper, the big dipper, the North Star, and so many more, just as I remembered them.

And the fireflies! Their blinking lit up the woodland like so many tiny, white Christmas lights. At that moment I felt supremely happy, happier than I can tell you. Champagne bubbling, red balloon happy!

I'm convinced as I grow older, that happiness is precisely those crystal moments in our lives when we stop seeking and just are.

But let me tell you about the family.

Dan is caught up in the newspaper business. I think he's finding it more difficult than he'd expected; but he's busy, and when Dan's busy, he's happy.

Will starts school next month, and he's looking forward to it. Although he's adjusting well to this back-to-the-land business, he still hasn't met many people his own age—but I just bet a little romance is brewing between Will and the girl who lives down the road, Mona Grant.

… *God, that child must be so lonely …*

And me?

I think your patient is on the road to recovery. Right now the main problem (I know you want me to be honest) is that I spend too much time alone and in relative isolation.

I never guessed my social needs were so demanding. Other than the kids, our childbirth classes are my only outlet. I don't know what I'll do when Will and Mona start school next month.

It's ironic: Sometimes I feel as if my son and I are competing for the same friend—Mona.

Sounds unbelievable, right? I still haven't started my new writing project, probably I've just got too much time on my hands, too much time to think.

To be honest, I'm beginning to resent Dan's being away from home so much. I know it's necessary: I realize how much work the newspaper is for him. I suppose there's a bit of jealousy at play here, too, slipping in from some unhealed part of my psyche.

... a little jealousy ... ?

It's a new kind of jealousy, though. It's not the kind we talked about, and it has nothing to do with other women. Fact is, I'm jealous because Dan's working and I'm not.

I stay home because I want to write; I don't write because I stay home. See, they've got vicious cycles up here in the wilds of Vermont, too.

I know what you're thinking, and you're right: There's no excuse for not having started another novel. But, I think an idea is starting to percolate. If I can just bring it into focus ...

It will have something to do with the people down the road, Mona and Mr. Grant. It'll touch on rural poverty. Welfare, and ...

149

... incest ...?

... living in a trailer. It will deal with the myth of country living among newcomers and how that myth clashes with the oppressive reality among the natives.

It will ...

All of a sudden she couldn't see the screen. Everything was covered with a watery film Sheila groped for a tissue to wipe the tears from her eyes.

CHAPTER 17
BACK TO THE LAND

When Will stopped crying he sniffed and coughed and finally got himself together. He was determined to have it out with Mona. This time for sure.

Full of resolution, he walked the rest of the way to her trailer and was surprised to see Dan's Renault in the driveway.

It must have been about ten o'clock. Dan was always in such a hurry to get to the newspaper, it seemed strange he'd still be at the Grants'.

Uh-oh, Will thought, not knowing what to do.

He couldn't imagine what was going on inside. If Dan had persuaded Mona to talk, maybe it wasn't a good idea to barge in. Will stood behind a tree to watch for a while.

When Dan didn't come out, Will decided to wander back into the forest and wait by the waterfall.

Last night's rain left it damp and chilly in the woods. Will wasn't used to August being so cool. Sitting there by the pool, cold air from the falls washing over him, Will wished he had brought a sweater.

The sun was up, bright and sharp, its yellow rays slicing through the green leaves above. But it didn't warm him. Maybe he felt cold because he was so upset. Will needed to talk to someone.

Mona was really bending his mind. He couldn't think clearly, and he was scared.

He kept peering into the trees, hoping Mona would somehow know he was there and would come looking for him.

Because he was sitting so still, little animals started coming out and going about their business. Will watched a gray squirrel dodging back and forth between two trunks. The tiny creature scampered up a tree, shaking its leaves as he jumped from one branch to another. Will watched the squirrel go up one tree and down the one next to it. He had no idea what the busy animal was trying to do.

After a while, he saw some motion downstream. At first he thought it was some kind of big animal—a deer or bear, maybe—but as he watched, he became certain he was seeing people. It looked like two of them.

Will thought at once of Mona and Dan, but it wasn't them. He hoped it wasn't those jerks from town, either.

Like the squirrel, they seemed to dash from tree to tree. It was weird the way they moved, lurching and scrambling. Try as he might, it was impossible for Will to get a good clear look because they were quite far off and the bushes in between grew pretty thick.

Will kept very still, hoping to discover what they were up to. Maybe they were out fishing, or hunting or something.

They're kids! Will thought, with some degree of surprise. He couldn't tell how old they were, but he could see they weren't very big. They seemed to be playing some kind of game. Maybe they were hiding from a third kid. Will looked around, trying to spot him, but he couldn't.

When they moved across a clearing, Will got a better look. The first one dashed past the little cutaway in the bushes and quickly hid behind a tree trunk before Will got a good look at him. Will saw the second one though, saw him quite clearly.

He was naked!

It seemed so strange. Will could hardly believe his eyes. When he looked again, trying to make sure, the kid was gone.

Will guessed country kids must really get into natural activities, like skinny-dipping and sunbathing. He couldn't imagine himself, though, running around in the woods with no clothes on. Even if he'd lived in the country for a long time, he didn't think he'd ever get to that point. Besides, it was too cold.

Maybe they were queer, or something. But Will doubted it; they hardly seemed old enough for anything like that.

He waited quite a while, hoping to get another look at them. He kept watching, concentrating, grateful for something to occupy his mind. But the kids were gone.

It was then Will noticed how quiet everything had become. The squirrels were gone; the trees were still. Not even the birds made any noise. All he could hear was the rushing sound of the water.

He liked the sound of the falls, but he was too cold and antsy to relax. He thought he'd give Mona another try before heading home.

———

Dan's car was gone now, so Will marched right up to the trailer and pounded on the door.

"Who is it?" Mona's voice came from inside. It had a sing-song quality that Will found irritating.

"It's me, Will."

Will heard her pulling off the chain lock, and the door opened a crack. A draft of perfume-smelling air escaped; it was so strong it almost made him gag.

When Mona peeked out, her face looked strange. Will thought she had on makeup because she looked sickly white instead of her usual tan.

She didn't smile as she pulled the door open to let him in. Will saw she wasn't even dressed yet. She had on a light blue cotton nightgown with some silky ribbons that laced it at the neck. Will could see her round breasts moving below the cloth.

The trailer was very hot inside.

"What you doing out so early?" she asked. She seemed more put off than happy to see him. Will didn't care, though; he had things on his mind and he wanted to talk about them.

"'We gotta do something, Mona. I can't handle all this secret stuff."

"Can't live without secrets of some kind." she said flatly.

She hadn't asked him to sit down, but he walked over and sat at the end of the sofa. There was a rip in the arm through which fluffy white material squeezed out like cotton toothpaste.

Mona didn't sit beside him. She sat directly in front, in a bulky slip-covered armchair. When she plopped down, her nightgown billowed up, and Will could see her legs almost all the way up.

He didn't know how to begin. "Jeez, it's awful hot in here. You got the heat on or something?"

"Yup. Can't warm up for some reason …"

"Why'n't you get dressed? Put on a sweater?"

"Feelin' lazy. You got somethin' on your mind, William? Somethin' botherin' ya?" She kind of smiled when she said it, like she thought Will was leering at her.

He decided to come right to the point, but struggled to sound casual. "Your dad here, Mona?"

Her face flattened; her eyes flicked from side to side. She shifted her position in the chair, thrusting her breasts out against the thin material of the nightgown. "Yer the second person asked me that this morning. But you're the one oughtta know he ain't."

"Yeah? Who was the first?"

"You oughtta know that, too."

Will was getting pissed off. He was very tired; he wasn't in any mood to play games. "Come on, Mona, you gotta tell me what's going on ..."

Suddenly, he felt as if he was going to start crying again. He didn't want to do it in front of Mona.

Still, she must have noticed something in his manner. She hopped up from the chair and plunked herself down next to him on the couch. Her breasts bounced up and down as she moved. Will felt something stirring inside him, something that didn't mix very well with his growing anger.

Mona leaned up against him and spoke softly in his ear. Her voice was low and serious. "I don't know who it was come to your house last night. Coulda been anybody. Me, I think it mighta been Rapid Rollins ..."

"Who's that? Rapid Rollins?"

"He's the school bus driver. He's an old perv, and I think he's got some kind of crush on me. Always checkin' up on me an' everything. I seen him up here in his car sometimes. Wants me to go for a ride with him. But I ain't gonna; he's disgusting. When I see him, I lock the door, and pretend I ain't to home. He's a real geek; bet he's prob'ly forty years old or so."

"Why don't you just tell him to get lost?"

"'Cause I don't want to talk to him that long."

Mona had put her arm around Will's shoulder and was beginning to rub the side of his neck. Her gentle fingers found his earlobe, and she massaged it between her thumb and forefinger. It felt wonderful; it was relaxing, and at the same time it made Will feel like hugging her and pressing up against her.

"Come on, William, you're all tensed up."

She changed her position and started wrapping her arms around him and pushing her breasts tightly against the side of his chest.

Will was sweating. He tried to cross his legs so she wouldn't see how turned on he was getting, but her hand stopped his knee from moving. Will's eyes closed. He could feel her hand on the inside of his thigh; it squeezed and pushed and worked its way up to his genitals.

It made him feel so weak and relaxed that all the things he'd wanted to talk about hid themselves somewhere far in the back of his mind. All he thought about, all he wanted to do was touch her and hug her and feel their bodies close together.

Will had never made love with a girl before, but right then he had no doubt: this was going to be it. Even at the core of his growing passion, he knew what they were doing wasn't right. At the same time he knew he was going to forget all the shoulds and shouldn'ts until afterward.

Mona was kneeling on the couch facing him. She lifted the nightgown up over her head, and Will saw her naked and sweating in the growing heat of the trailer. Her breasts were surprisingly big and round. They seemed to move under their own power with each tiny motion of her body. Her dark pubic hair was silky, not kinky like his own.

Her hands came forward and started rubbing all over his body. She was breathing hard, in rapid little pants, as she took both his hands and settled back on the couch, pulling Will on top of her.

Will still had his clothes on. He felt stupid because he didn't know what to do—take them off by himself, or wait for Mona to do it. For a while he did nothing, just hugged her and felt the weight of his own body pressing her into the soft cushions of the couch.

"Warm me up, William," she said. "I'm so cold, so awful cold ..."

From the way she was sweating, Will couldn't believe she was cold. He sure wasn't. It must have been ninety degrees in the trailer, and his temperature was going up higher than that.

Will kissed her as his hands slid up and down the soft hills and valleys of her body. It was as if he were falling into a kind of trance, as if the only thing on his mind was to satisfy some strong physical need, more powerful than anything he'd ever felt before.

Her hands were on his belt, and he could feel them skillfully folding back the leather. Fingers scratched, searching for ... finding his zipper.

There was a hypnotic urgency to what they were doing. All Will's doubts, all his questions, his anger, and his fatigue were tucked away far back in his mind, hidden and forgotten along with the shoulds and shouldn'ts, the rights and the wrongs.

He could feel her warm hand between his legs; it was moist against his skin, rubbing kneading, massaging, coaxing him into position. He was almost dizzy, thrilled at the feeling of her breasts flattening beneath his chest.

"Oh God ..." Will said. He wanted to tell her that he loved her. It was right there on the tip of his tongue, but he couldn't say it. All he could do was feel.

His muscles tensed; his blood rushed; he felt as if he would explode any second. And when the wet release came, Will collapsed on top of Mona like an empty air mattress.

"Feel better now, William?" she whispered, her lips tickling his ear, her arms circling his back.

He could only sigh. He just stayed there for a while, not able to move, not wanting to. All his tension was gone. He could easily have fallen asleep. Everything seemed to be all right.

Will hugged her and spoke in a quivering little voice. He didn't know why he said it, didn't know where it came from at all. It just seemed to come on its own from out of nowhere. "Take care of me, Mona."

"Yes," she whispered. "Yes, I promise."

———————

Dan's stomach muscles contracted as if someone were squeezing him in a brutal bear hug. Vomit jetted into the bathroom sink, splattering the walls and floor. It hurt his throat as it came up, offended him with its stench.

He groped for a paper towel from the dispenser. Empty, damn. He reached for some toilet paper and rubbed it viciously against his mouth as a carpenter might rub sandpaper against an unsightly stain.

How could he have done it? He didn't understand. It was crazy, furtive, and disgusting.

He lifted his throbbing head and faced himself in the mirror. He couldn't meet his own eyes.

Outside, the sounds of the newspaper frightened him. He couldn't go back in there. He couldn't. What if they knew? What if they could somehow see?

How could he face his staff if he couldn't meet the eyes of his own reflection?

Alicia Faye tapped on the door. "Dan, you okay? You sick, Dan? Is there something I can get you?"

He cleared his throat. "No. No, I'm okay, Al. I think my breakfast didn't agree with me ..."

He'd have to put on a face to meet them all. He'd told her everything was okay; now he had to pretend it was true.

There was so much work to do at the paper. He'd just have to bite the bullet and do it.

Then he'd have to go home.

Dan could pretend. He was sure he could. But when his stomach muscles started to squeeze again, he wasn't so sure.

———————

A loud mechanical roar snapped them out of their trance. Mona sat up quickly, almost pushing Will onto the floor. A frightened look tightened her face. Will got up, freeing her to walk naked to the window.

She pulled aside a faded flowery curtain and looked out at the yard. "It's them," she said, completely without emotion. "It's Reggie and Spit. They got Norm's car."

Dazed, Will walked to the window while adjusting his shorts and pulling up his jeans.

Sure enough, the little guy, Spit, with his homemade haircut and homemade tattoo, was getting out from the passenger's side. He moved with confidence, in jerky little fits and starts.

The bigger guy, Reggie, got out from behind the wheel. Will could see Reggie's face was still a swollen mass of discolored welts, each topped by a dark ridge from where he'd been stitched up. Both his eyes were oily black and bloated nearly shut. Mona's father had really worked him over.

Each of them had an ax handle in his hand.

"Hey Grant," Spit hollered, "Hey Grant, get your ass out here. Norm sent us up with a little present for ya!"

Reggie stepped up beside him, thumping the ax handle against his left palm. Both guys faced the trailer.

"Shit," said Mona. "I knew they'd be comin' back for me. I jest *knew* it. Quick, we gotta get outta here."

Will could hardly move. He felt drugged, disoriented. More than anything, he just wanted to sack out on the couch and forget everything that was going on.

Behind him, Mona was tugging on a pair of blue jeans. She pulled a sweatshirt over her head and bent down to get into her sneakers. "Come on, William, let's get out the back way."

Hurriedly, she led him down the length of the trailer to the messy back bedroom that must have been her father's. After releasing the window and screen, she didn't waste any time crawling out and dropping the short way to the ground.

"Hurry, William," she said in an urgent whisper.

Still not sure what was going on, Will scrambled to follow her out the window. Just then he heard a crash at the front of the trailer. It sounded like they'd broken down the door.

Mona and Will ran off into the woods behind the trailer. By now Will had snapped fully awake to find himself in a real panic. He had to run very fast to keep up with Mona. For a girl, he thought, she could really move.

When they'd made a little more than a hundred yards, Will looked back. Spit was hanging out the window yelling, "Round back! Hey, Reggie, they're runnin' off!"

Like a grinning lizard, Spit wriggled out the window, ax handle in hand. Reggie rounded the corner of the trailer.

Will knew they'd been spotted; recognition of Spit's face was the last thing he saw. After that, it was head down and hard running.

He kept Mona in sight; she was tearing off to the left just in front of him. He could hear Reggie and Spit crashing along behind, yelling curses and screaming war cries like a couple of demented savages.

His sneakers kept sliding on moss-covered rocks; several times he nearly went down. More than once he saw Mona take a dive, effortlessly pick herself up, and continue.

Will didn't have much hope of outrunning them. He could think of no way they could defend themselves. His few karate lessons wouldn't go very far against two psychos with ax handles.

Worse yet, he knew trying to reason with them was out of the question.

Their only hope was to haul ass.

His breath came in violent gasps. His side started to stitch; it felt as if the muscles were ripping away from the bones. Will didn't know how much longer he could keep moving.

Mr. Grant's beating had left Reggie and Spit in pretty bad shape. Perhaps they would tire quickly.

Encouraged at the prospect of wearing them out, Will put on a burst of speed and passed Mona. "Let's head toward my place," he gasped. Keeping the brook to their left, they veered off to the right, struggling to work their way uphill.

Reggie and Spit had stopped yelling and were zombie running, arms dangling weakly at their sides. They were losing speed, tiring. Spit was making the best time; Reggie looked about ready to drop.

In any event, just as Will began to think they were really going to make it, Mona tripped and went head first into a tree trunk. She rolled to the ground. Will was afraid she'd knocked herself out, but her eyes were open.

She's okay, Will thought.

Maybe not; a trickle of blood slid down the side of her face as she sat there looking stunned.

Will lurched over to her. He was so exhausted, he wished he could fall to the ground and lay there, giving up altogether.

"You okay, Mona?"

"Yeah, I'm ..." Her eyes rolled in their sockets. Will thought she was going to pass out. She shook her head as if to clear it and began to pull herself up. Will took her hand, trying to help her. The hand felt dry and strangely cold.

The guys were still coming. Will heard their feet stomping the earth, heard the sound of twigs snapping.

Eyes glowing with fury, Reggie let out a war whoop and threw his ax handle. It turned rapidly in the air like a plane's propeller, striking the tree beside Mona's head with bark-splitting impact.

Mona gave a startled cry and was on her feet. "Move," she shouted, and gave Will a push. Eyes straight ahead, he charged off into the forest, confident that Mona was close behind.

"Asshole, Reggie," barked Spit when Reggie threw his ax handle.

Spit clutched his own weapon even tighter, fortified by its solidity. Even in his adrenaline-fevered imagination, he'd never pictured hand-to-hand combat. Instead, he visualized the Rambo-kid's face splitting like the skin of a boiled hot dog, blood spattering under the hardwood blows. He pictured the kid begging, pleading, not daring to protest as he and Asshole-Reggie took turns with the girl.

Spit's heart sank in his heaving chest when Reggie's ax handle missed entirely. It sank farther still as he watched the two chickenshits put on a new burst of speed and vanish into the woods.

Before Spit could get the dead weight of his legs in gear, a terrified scream froze him to the spot.

Fifteen feet away from him, Reggie was bellowing like a castrated pig.

Spit watched him disgustedly as he jerked and twitched, rotating his hips like he was doing some kind of fucked-up dance. "What the fuck you doin'?"

Reggie didn't answer. He flapped his arms around, flailing and furious, then reached out toward Spit.

Spit just stood there gawking at him.

Reggie kept lunging forward, toward Spit, without going anywhere. It looked as if one of his feet was stuck, as though he was caught in the mud, or maybe an animal trap or something.

But there wasn't any mud. Spit had just run through the same spot. The ground may have been a little damp from last night's rain, but it wasn't muddy.

"Help me, goddamn it," Reggie cried to Spit. "My fuckin' foot's caught."

Still Spit stood there like a statue, his arms hanging uselessly at his sides. He couldn't take his eyes off Reggie; now both his legs had sunk into the earth almost to the knees.

"Please. Give me a hand, Spit." Reggie looked entreatingly at him, then back at his own stumpy legs, invisible from mid-thigh down. "Please … somebody …"

Spit couldn't move.

"S'fuckin' quicksand, for Chrissake, Spit. Throw me a fuckin' stick …"

Reggie's terrified screams confused Spit. *This can't be happening!*

The cries brought a momentary truce; Spit forgot all about Rambo and the Grant bitch. He couldn't think of anything but the black earth sliding higher and higher up Reggie's legs. It seemed to be folding in against him, sucking at him, pulling him down.

"Christ I can't get out. Spit, pleeeease …"

Spit stood there, stupidly staring, shaking his head and saying, "Nonononono …"

The sucking earth was up to Reggie's waist now. His body protruded from the ground like a living tree stump. He was awkwardly bent over, clutching frantically at the earth, pulling at dead leaves and twigs, trying to get a grip on something, anything …

He slid down a little farther. Pushing on the ground with his palms, he tried to get some leverage, but his hands sank uselessly into the solid ground as if it were mud.

When he was chest deep, he started pounding the dirt, forcing out a shrill animal wail of defeat. "AAAAhhhhh!"

His face was pale white; he was sweating, crying. The black lines of his sutures had split open, so it looked like he was sweating blood.

When his fists struck the earth, it didn't splatter like mud. Instead, his hands came away soiled with dry clumps of dirt that sprayed into the air.

It was as if something tugged him from below. He seemed to sink an inch at a time, then stop, only to be tugged down again. His eyes were wide with terror. Spit watched his friend's mouth go under. A muffled shriek escaped. Dry dirt shot into the air.

Then he was gone.

Spit stared at a little depression in the ground where Reggie's head had disappeared.

He began backing up, inching away from the spot. When he was able to pull his eyes from the last fragments of tumbling earth, he looked up.

There, just on the other side of the fatal depression … it was the Grant bitch. Mona.

Her eyes were glassy and wild, her face bone white, and her mouth was a hideous gash, and it was grinning … grinning …

Spit raised his ax handle over his head and backed, stumbling and whimpering, into the protection of the trees.

———

Will had to work hard to keep moving. He zig-zagged between the trees like a fleeing animal.

His heart pounded; his mind was numb. He had one thought—to get home fast.

Reggie's and Spit's cries were fading. They'd probably given up, but Will didn't turn to make sure. He just kept moving, frantic and afraid.

Branches tore at his face, roots tripped him and his sneakers slid and floundered on the forest floor. Still he ran.

He ran until somebody grabbed him.

Will kicked and struggled, his arms flailing wildly. He was crying, screaming with rage and terror, but the big arms held tight, wrapping him in an inescapable coil that squeezed until he stopped struggling.

PART THREE
THE VISITOR

ECHOES

"You're looking at your cat playing with a chipmunk. You watch that cat's shenanigans: She's batting the little animal, poking it, letting it run away and catching it before it does. And all of a sudden she isn't your cute little kitty-cat anymore. All of a sudden she's something wicked, and what she's doing to that terrified little chipper, why it's ugly, it's mean. So you think, now that's a *horrible* thing, it's so vicious and so cruel and finally, something way down inside you admits it: what you're watching is evil. But when you think again, you realize it is evil, yes … but it's also perfectly natural …"

—Mrs. Elizabeth McKensie, 1983

CHAPTER 18
TELLING THE TALE

He was speaking calmly, reassuringly, his voice low and gentle. "It's okay, son. Settle down now. It's okay."

The bear hug loosened a little, and Will stepped back, still shaking, tears streaming down his face. He looked up at the man and saw he was half-smiling.

"M-m-Mona?" Will stammered.

"She's all right, son. She's right over there."

Will looked in the direction of the man's nod. Mona stepped out of the tree-tangled distance and leaned against the trunk of an old maple, fifteen feet to Will's right.

Looking back at the man, Will tried to recognize him. No—he didn't know him, had never seen him before. The stranger stood about six feet tall. He was dressed in a new blue work shirt that still bore the creases of mechanical folding. His baggy brown corduroy pants were much older. They hung loosely wrinkled, like elephant skin. The man's face was pale, as if he rarely got any sun, and he wore a tight-fitting, black knitted cap pulled down over his ears. Will immediately thought that cap was pretty weird; it was for winter, this was nearly the end of August.

Squinting at the man through tear-glazed eyes, Will wiped the embarrassing wetness from his cheeks. The man looked back. Purpose and strength combined in his gaze. Yet, there was something peaceful about him, something serene. Will felt immediately safe, nearly calm.

For a moment he couldn't catch his breath. He wanted to speak, but he couldn't. The man was patient; he didn't prod Will for information, he just waited.

"Th-they were trying to kill us." Will stammered, surprised at the wonder and disbelief in his own voice. How strange the truth sounded.

In some part of his mind, somewhere below the panic, Will was sure the man would give him one of those parental looks that say "You're just making that up." But he didn't. He just nodded, rather sadly, Will thought, as if he were real tired. Then he said quietly, "I know. But you're safe now."

Mona made her way over to Will, warily watching the stranger. "Who're you?" she asked in her flat Vermont accent. She hardly seemed upset, as if being chased and threatened was all part of her daily routine.

The man smiled a greeting as she stepped closer. "I'm a friend of Clint Whitcome's," he said. "He's the man who used to own this land."

"You see what happened to Reggie?" Mona asked.

The man shook his head. "No. Was Reggie the guy who was chasing you?"

"Nope. There was two of 'em. Spit run off. An' Reggie ... ?" Mona looked at Will for assistance.

Just what *did* happen to Reggie?

Will had lost track of everything. "I dunno." He looked around, but the three of them were alone.

"No matter," the man said. "Everything's okay now; it's all over. What say we get you two home."

As soon as she heard voices in the yard, Sheila hurried to the door. She was surprised to see an unfamiliar man with Will and Mona. She glanced around the empty yard, looking for his car.

"Hello," she said, wiping her hands on a dish towel, her voice heavy with caution rather than hospitality.

The strange-looking man in the knitted toque blinked mismatched blue eyes at her. He looked awkward in the company of children.

Will stepped forward, talking as he approached, obviously feeling it was his job to explain. "Mom, this is a friend of the man who used to live here. He just saved me and Mona from some guys in the woods."

Will winced when he saw Sheila react. She knew he'd seen the fear she was feeling. "Oh my God," she said, unhappy with the tremor in her voice, "come in, please. My God, what happened? What guys in the woods?"

Her inquisitive eyes flashed back and forth between Will and Mona. As they moved closer, she was able to see how terrible the kids appeared. Will's clothes were torn and dirty, a roadmap of black smears and red welts was scratched on his face. His eyes looked as if he'd been crying.

Mona looked just as bad.

Sheila held the screen door open, while Mona and Will walked in. "Come in, please," she said to the man. Before he entered the house, he paused and turned, taking one last look around.

Sheila tried to give Will a hug. He returned it perfunctorily. She didn't force it. "You kids are a sight," she said. "Are you all right? For heaven's sake, tell me what's going on ..."

Mona said, "You know them guys I told you about, Mrs. Crockett, the ones that're always botherin' me? They come up the trailer, chased us through the woods."

"I'd better call the police," Sheila said, but found herself looking at the man. Was she waiting for more of an explanation? Or for his approval?

As she started for the phone, Will gave a single sigh, a soft crying sound. Sheila watched her son begin to sway on his feet. His knees started to fold. "Mom ... I ... I gotta sit down ..."

She lunged for him as Will lost his balance.

The man was quicker. With a swift, precise movement, he scooped Will up and carried him into the living room. Sheila rushed along beside him, indicating the couch.

The man put Will on the couch, slowly, almost lovingly, with the gentleness of a father. Sheila was right behind him. She stepped forward and covered her son with a big lavender comforter.

Mona plopped down in the chair nearest Will's head.

"I'd better call a doctor," Sheila said. She walked over to the phone on the top of Dan's rolltop desk and picked it up. Then she tapped Morse code on the cutoff switch. *Damn.* "Phone's dead," she told them. "Wouldn't you know it."

"Prob'ly the storm last night," Mona said. She didn't seem to be suffering nearly as much as Will. A stray and pointless thought crossed Sheila's mind: she hoped Will wouldn't be bothered that a country girl might be a little tougher than a guy from the city.

Will struggled to sit up, batting at the comforter. "I don't need a doctor," Will told them. "I'm fine. Really."

Sheila was hardly listening. She wanted to act. "We'll drive into town," she said. "We'll see the doctor and the police all at the same time."

She looked at them, expecting everyone to get moving. The man walked over, stopping about ten feet in front of her. "If you don't mind me saying so, Mrs. Crockett, maybe it's best to let these kids catch their breath a minute. They've had quite a scare."

Sheila felt confused. "Yes, sure. I think you're right Mr... . Mr... . God I'm so upset, I don't remember your name ..."

The man seemed to hesitate before he said anything. He almost looked as if he were about to apologize for something. He tugged at his knitted hat and peeled it off. As if on springs, a bunch of red hair jumped out in all directions. When he started to speak, it sounded as if he was working to control his voice. "My name's Nolan, Mrs. Crockett. Eric Nolan."

Sheila felt all the color drop out of her face. The name—Nolan—jolted her like a struck nerve. She took a couple of unsteady steps backward, looking around the room, her eyes coming to rest on the phone. "Oh God," she said.

The backs of Sheila's legs pressed tightly against Dan's desk; her arms hung at her sides. She felt her right hand float up and come to rest protectively on her stomach. "What do you want here, Mr. Nolan?"

"I wanted to bring your boy back home. Otherwise, I wouldn't have bothered you. I had planned to talk to you at some point, yes. But I would have waited until your husband was here. Please, Mrs. Crockett, I don't want to frighten you ..."

"I'm not f-frightened." Sheila was so nervous she was stuttering. She looked at the dead phone again.

"Mom," Will said, "he *saved* us. He got rid of those guys, Spit and Reggie, the ones who were after us."

"Yes, yes I know." Her voice definitely wasn't warm, but she was thinking: *He doesn't seem crazy.* "I guess I should thank you for that, Mr. Nolan."

Nolan nodded, a shy smile at the corners of his mouth. "And I should give you an explanation, Mrs. Crockett. Please, try not to be nervous. No matter what you may have heard, no matter what you believe, the fact is I'm not here to hurt you. I hope you can believe that. Please sit down. We should talk."

His voice sounded calm and kind. Yet Sheila was trembling. She was afraid for the children, for herself. There was something earnest about him, she couldn't deny it. He was polite and respectful. She couldn't see what was so crazy about him; he seemed very much like some of the people she and Dan had as friends.

Sheila moved slowly to the couch, never taking her eyes off Nolan. She sat down by Will's feet and started massaging his toes, not realizing she was doing it.

Mr. Nolan sat down in the director's chair across from Mona. "I'm sure some of the things you've heard about me are true," he began. "Yes, I've been incarcerated at the hospital at Waterbury since 1983. I've been 'under observation,' as they say. Yes, I broke out—without harming anyone, I might add—and, for the last two weeks, I've been living in a cabin on Pinnacle Mountain. It's a cabin I learned about when I was staying in this house with my cousin Pamela Whitcome and her husband and their son."

Sheila found herself staring at him. She was watching for any movement that might signal danger. Tension swelled in her chest like a tumor; it spread in a prickly, itching path along her spine. As she chewed the knuckles of her right hand, she listened to Nolan's explanation, expecting any minute to hear the words that would destroy her developing trust, the irrational phrase that would justify her fear and echo with madness.

"All that is true," Nolan went on, "I can't deny it. But I'm just as sure you've heard some things about me that aren't true, too. For example, you may have heard that I was responsible for the deaths of my cousin and her family. I can see why that story got around; it's a logical conclusion: I was the only one up here who survived. Thinking I'm a murderer makes sense, I suppose. But I'm not a murderer. The only crazy thing I did was not telling the truth about what actually happened. If I'd spoken up, I might have been able to clear myself. In some ways, not speaking up

174

was pretty crazy, too, but please believe me, I had my reasons. The real story—the things that actually happened up here that night—well, that's a story that has never been told. And I promise you, it will sound crazier than anything you've ever heard."

"And just what is that?" Sheila asked.

Mr. Nolan stood up and walked over to the sliding doors. He looked out across the deck and off into the hills to the west. He spoke quietly, not looking at his companions. "If you don't mind, Mrs. Crockett, I'd like to wait until your husband gets home—"

Sheila looked at her watch.

"—It will be difficult telling it, and I'm not really sure I want to go through it more than once."

Sheila looked at Will, then at Mona. "My husband should be home any minute, Mr. Nolan," she said.

———————

While they waited for Dan, Sheila offered some minestrone soup with sandwiches of sliced turkey breast and fresh tomatoes. Will was hungry and ate his quickly. Mr. Nolan ate two sandwiches; Mona had only soup but didn't finish it all.

After they ate, the kids took turns showering and changing clothes. Will sat back down on the couch and motioned for Mona to come and sit beside him. She complied silently. Wearing one of Sheila's sweaters and a pair of Will's jeans, she looked fresh and clean. Will held her hand, right in front of Mom and Mr. Nolan. Her hand was very cold.

No one talked easily. Tension and uncertainty filled the sun-bright air of the living room.

Sheila had put on one of her classical records at low volume. She moved nervously around the kitchen and living room, looking for little jobs to do. It took her only minutes to return everything to a normal showroom state. Will noticed that she repeatedly stole glances at them and was never out of sight for more than a few seconds at a time.

He could tell his Mom was awfully frightened, and he understood why. For some reason, however, he, personally, didn't fear Mr. Nolan at all. Maybe it was the way he'd hugged him in the woods, or the way he'd brought them straight home without asking a lot of questions. Possibly it was the way Mr. Nolan had spoken right up about all the suspicions everyone was sure to have about him. Whatever the reason, Will liked Mr. Nolan and thought he was okay.

Nonetheless, Will kept a pretty close eye on him, not certain whether to trust his mother's instincts or his own.

As they waited, Mr. Nolan made frequent trips to the different windows, looking out as if he were a gangster fearing the cops might come for him any minute. That was pretty close to the truth, Will realized, but probably Mr. Nolan was just watching for Dan.

Sometimes the newcomer would poke around at the books on the shelves. He discovered a copy of *Charm Bracelet*, read the blurbs on the cover, and studied the picture of Sheila on the back. He raised his eyebrows at Will to show he was impressed. Every once in a while he'd ask Will or Mona how they were doing.

"Fine," they'd both reply, but Will wasn't so sure. Mona was uncommonly quiet. Was she just shy, or scared, or what? She'd been acting strange all day. He couldn't figure out what was going on with her.

"Are you feeling all right?" Will asked.

"Can't complain," she said.

He watched as Mr. Nolan sat down on the big wooden swivel chair in front of Dan's desk. For a while Nolan just gazed out through the glass doors into the empty yard. Then he tipped way back in the chair, folded his hands across his stomach and closed his eyes.

When the clock on the wall said six-fifteen, Will heard Dan's Renault on the driveway.

Mona pulled her hand free of his.

———————

"Dan, we have a visitor," Sheila announced as she met him at the door. Her voice was thin and cracking; he hoped it didn't signal another scene.

Dan wasn't any more prepared for guests than he was for an emotional outburst. He still felt fragile, full of self-loathing. His stomach muscles continued to hurt from their workout in the *Tribune's* washroom. All he wanted to do was relax, sit with Sheila, and drink the six-pack of Dos Equis he'd brought home.

It wasn't in the cards. Dan squared his shoulders and walked into the living room carrying the beer under his arm. When he saw Mona, he felt a rush of discomfort. *What has she said to Sheila?* He nodded coolly to her and was able to force a half-smile as she looked blankly at him.

Then he saw the stranger.

Dan braced himself before walking directly over to the man, his right hand extended. "Hi," he said, trying to sound cordial, "I'm Dan Wilder."

Dan squinted at the man. Was there something familiar about him?

Nolan stood up, and they shook hands. "It's good to meet you, Mr. Wilder—"

"Please, it's Dan. Didn't Sheila offer you a drink?" He held out one from the six-pack.

"Dan, I—" Sheila took a tentative step toward the men. "Dan, something's happened today. Will and Mona were attacked in the woods."

"Jesus, Sheila," he looked frantically at the kids, searching them for any signs of harm. "Did you call the police?"

"No, the phone's been out. But listen, Dan, it's okay … This man … well, he saved them. He brought them home."

Dan looked from one face to the next. He didn't know what was going on. Sheila put her hand on his arm. She said, "He's done us a great kindness, Dan, and now he has something he wants to talk to us about."

"Yes, of course. Shall we sit down, or what?"

They sat, but the moment Nolan introduced himself Dan was on his feet again. His thoughts bounced wildly around like the bearing in a pinball machine: *no weapons in the house; we're hostages here; is he dangerous? How can we get help?*

He looked around from his standing position in the middle of the floor. The people around him were so calm. They stared up at Dan as if he were the madman.

What's going on here? How could they even begin to trust this guy?

He had to say something. "Will, I think you and Mona should go upstairs."

Nolan cleared his throat. "Please, Mr. Wilder, maybe they should hear what I've got to say. I think it concerns all of you."

Dan looked inquiringly at Sheila. She nodded.

Nolan waited while Dan sat down. After taking a deep, calming breath, Dan opened a beer and drew a mouthful.

"This is a difficult thing for me to discuss," Nolan began, laughing a little, nervously. Dan could tell it wasn't really a laugh at all; the man was scared.

Nolan placed his beer, unopened, on the floor beside him. "I don't know how to introduce this in a way that'll keep you from thinking I'm completely out of my mind. I know how it's going to sound, but it's important that I convince you I'm not psychotic. I know where I've come from is a pretty compelling argument that I am. What I have to say might just be the frosting on the cake.

"To get right to the point, I've come here because I think you people might be in danger—"

"This is the second time we've heard that," Dan said. "The first was when Chief Bates came up here to warn us about you."

Nolan nodded, a little sadly. "The chief is a good man, Mr. Wilder. He did just what he should have done. But there are things he doesn't know. I think he'll be the first to tell you he doesn't know for sure—not for sure—what happened to my cousin's family four years ago, right in this house."

Dan glanced at Sheila as Nolan continued. "What I'm going to tell you will really tax your ability to believe. You're going to feel as if you're getting suckered into some kind of paranoid delusion, and I can't blame you; I'd feel exactly the same way myself. So, please, prepare yourselves; what I'm going to say will sound insane—I know that better than anyone—but I pray to God when I'm finished you won't think I'm crazy."

Dan shifted in his seat. Part of him was responding to the conviction in Nolan's voice. "We'll hear you out, Nolan. But, please, come to the point."

Nolan nodded. He leaned forward, wrists resting on his knees, fingertips together. "Would it be difficult for you to accept that there is a cult, a group of fanatics, who lives in hiding up on Pinnacle Mountain? Do you think that could be possible?"

Dan and Sheila looked at each other. Sheila nodded her head. "Possible? Sure. I think it could be possible. That's pretty wild country up there—"

"I've heard of stuff like that," Will said. "You know, like the Manson family, and—"

Dan thought the boy was trying to help Nolan out. He cut him off. "Go on, Mr. Nolan."

"Well, it's a fact. There *are* people living up there. The police don't know about them; nobody does. They've been living there for years, undetected, because they know all the tricks; they can stay out of sight and can cover their tracks."

Dan listened cautiously. Nolan hadn't said anything too wacked out so far. If there really was a band of rag-tag religious nuts up there—and that much was possible—then, professionally speaking, that was the sort of thing Dan wanted to know about.

"They're the ones who attacked the Whitcomes four years ago. They go crazy sometimes, working themselves into a frenzy, and the Whitcomes—well, it's pretty isolated up here—the Whitcomes were an easy target."

"Why did they do it?" Sheila asked.

"They're involved with magic and sacrifice; they wanted Pamela's son—"

'Wow!" Will said.

"My God!" Sheila echoed.

Dan stood up. He combed his fingers back through his hair. "Jesus Christ," he said, "you'll forgive me if I tell you this is a little difficult to swallow. I mean—some Satanist cult living in the woods behind our house? It sounds so—"

"Crazy? Of course it does. I know it's hard to believe. But remember, it's their craziness, not mine. Can you accept it, Mr. Wilder? Can you accept it just for a minute?"

"I don't know … without proof … ?"

"Do you have any proof, Mr. Nolan?" Sheila asked.

"Some. I think I have some. Maybe enough for you to at least hear me out." He unbuttoned his shirt and pulled out a manila envelope, which was folded in half. He dropped it on the coffee table in front of him.

"But there's something else I have to tell you first," he went on. "While I was in the hospital, I put my time to pretty good use. My therapists didn't approve of my reading all about earth magic, and cults and superstitions, but they didn't want to censor me, either. In four years I was able to learn a lot about the cult's habits and their religion. You see—and this is important—when one of them dies, they kidnap a child to replace him. They indoctrinate the child from a very young age, totally control him. My cousin's boy, Luke, was just four years old when they tried to get him."

"God that's awful," Sheila said. "You mean to say nobody knows this is going on?"

"*I* know it's going on. That's not the problem. The problem is people just won't believe it."

"What about this 'proof' of yours?" Dan said.

Nolan picked up the folded envelope and tossed it to Dan. Dan opened it. It was full of newspaper clippings.

"You see, the night these people tried to take Luke Whitcome, we killed a few of them as we tried to defend this house. Their religion requires that they maintain a specific number of members. Fallen members require replacements. I think we killed two or three of them, maybe more. Those first clippings describe kids from around here—all in a thirty-mile radius of Antrim— who have come up missing in the last four years."

Dan and Sheila crowded together and read the clippings. Dan looked up. "Coincidence possibly? Not exactly proof, Mr. Nolan—"

"I agree, Mr. Wilder, it's not exactly proof; it wouldn't hold up in court. But it's the best I've got right now. It should be enough to gain the curiosity of any good cop or newspaperman, though, don't you think?"

"Well, I must admit, I'm ... intrigued."

"With your help, I can get proof. Real proof. And together we can put a stop to this."

Sheila looked at Mr. Nolan. "In the beginning you said we were in danger ..."

"You might be, you live closer than anyone to their camp." He looked at each of them, his eyes coming to rest on Will. "Your son, William—he could be their next target."

Dan saw Will pale when Nolan said that. Sheila did, too. The expression on her face exposed her dread.

Dan was still the newspaperman; his reporter's instincts locked into place like the sights on a gun. "So, would you have me believe, Mr. Nolan, that you broke out of the state hospital, and came here, just to warn us?"

"No. Not just for that. I told you, I want to put a stop to it."

"What's in it for you? Revenge?"

Nolan looked down at his hands. He seemed to study them, as if he were holding a card with the answer written on it. Then he looked Dan full in the face. "Revenge? For a while I wanted revenge, yes. My cousin Pamela and I were very close. Anyone who saw what they did to her would have wanted revenge. But that's passed, at least as my primary motive. Now it's something else ... Something additional."

Dan didn't understand. "Something else ... ?"

Nolan held Dan's gaze. "My brother, Brian, is one of them. He was kidnapped when we were just little kids. They took him into the woods where no one could find him, and ... and he was raised by these cultists, indoctrinated into their fanatical lifestyle. You can verify his disappearance in your own newspaper, Mr. Wilder. Check the edition dated August 12, 1953."

Dan nodded. Nolan continued, "I saw my brother the night these people massacred the Whitcome family. I think the only reason I wasn't killed was that Brian intervened for me. But I witnessed the attack, I saw the slaughter—"

182

"My God!" said Sheila.

"I also believe my brother was responsible for saving young Luke Whitcome. I begged him not to hurt the boy, and he didn't—Luke is still alive.

"I think there is still some humanity left in Brian. I believed that so much I held my tongue for four years in the hospital. I wanted to protect my brother and to prevent another attack on young Luke. Now that I'm out, I want to rescue Brian; I want to get him out of there. You see, he's the only family I have left."

Everyone sat quietly. Dan looked at the sliding doors; it had grown dark outside. In the reflection Dan watched Sheila flipping through the newspaper clippings; she didn't seem to be reading them. Will sat staring at the ceiling.

"That's my story," Nolan finally said. "I know how it probably sounds, but it's true. I swear to God, it's true."

CHAPTER 19
TRAPS

I t was almost dark.

Spit was in one helluva tear to get the convertible back to Norm by nine o'clock. He'd promised, and it was a good idea to keep any promises made to Norm.

As it was, Norm would be pissed off something wicked to hear both Grants were still intact.

He'd be doubly pissed to learn they'd had a crack at Rambo and blew it.

"Jesus-fuckin'-Christ!" Spit pounded the steering wheel. He was hyperventilating. "Ah-wheew, ah-wheew." Even to himself he sounded like a leaky bicycle pump.

Gotta calm down, he thought.

With his right hand, he clutched the comforting hardness of the ax handle on the empty seat beside him, Reggie's seat.

Christ, Spit, help me …

He wanted to floor the goddamn thing, put on some speed, get the fucker moving fast enough so he wouldn't have to think, so he'd need every bit of concentration just to keep it on the road.

He finished the can of Bud, then tossed it into the back seat.

No—too much thinking was no good; when he let his mind wander, it kept drifting back to Reggie: his panicky face, his crying, his high pitched, girlish-sounding screams.

… s'fuckin' quicksand …

184

Now all Spit wanted was to get to Norm's house as quickly as possible. He wanted to tell his story and be done with it. With luck, everything would be okay. But his luck hadn't been running that kinda good today. If he started speeding, he'd probably find a statey on his ass, or worse yet, that fat fuck, Bates.

Spit looked at the speedometer: fifty miles an hour in a forty-five-mile zone. No problem, even old Master Bates wouldn't bust his ass for that.

So how would he explain it to Norm?

Spit, pleeeease ...

Could he say Reggie got stuck in quicksand? Or maybe that he'd crashed through the rotted planks covering somebody's forgotten well?

No matter what he said, Norm wouldn't believe him. Nobody would. Anyone in their right mind—that is, anyone who hadn't seen it—would say that Reggie just chickened out, took off, just like he always did. "When the goin' gets tough, Reggie gets lost." Isn't that what Norm liked to say?

Well, Reggie got lost all right.

... pleeeease ...

Spit shook his head, trying to throw off the ugly thoughts.

He'd been driving around for hours, drinking beer, not daring to stop, feeling lucky to be safe, lucky to be far away from the sight of Moanin' Mona's shit-eating grin.

It was almost as if ... as if she'd somehow caused it. It was exactly like she'd led them into a trap.

That's it! Of course! So it had been a trap. Sure. Probably something her daddy learned in the Asian jungles. Right. Vietnam was gutted with tunnels and holes and ... and, shit, it was just some gook-o trap her deadbeat father had learned to make while he was in the Army.

And the old turd had used his own frikkin' daughter as the bait. Christ, what an animal ...

185

Spit had a clear view of the dying sun directly ahead. It looked like the bead of a gun sight the way it rested in the "V" formed by two dark mountains. For a moment, Spit felt as if he were piloting a spaceship on course to some distant star.

Almost visibly the sun went down a notch.

Now it glowed like a red-hot bowl, inverted on the horizon. Trees lined either side of the road. As the darkness thickened, the spaces between their trunks grew less distinct. Soon night would fill those spaces, turning the forest into a solid black wall. A prison wall ...

There was still a while before darkness came. Spit guessed he had another twenty minutes until it would be truly dark.

He felt the cool night air whipping his hair around. It felt great. So good that for a moment he considered saying fuck Norm. Maybe he'd just keep going, running the car as far away from Antrim as the gas supply would allow.

When he looked at the gas gauge, he changed his mind—nearly empty.

His eyes flicked back at the road.

There was something up there.

Something moving.

It looked like a hazy, almost transparent object hovering above the asphalt. It was darker than the landscape behind it, a little stain on the fabric of twilight. Spit had no idea what he was seeing. It was there, yet it wasn't there. It was solid, yet it was vaporous.

Automatically, he hit the brake, slowing to a near crawl.

Something dashed from behind the object and into the bushes. Something all white and tiny. Something running on its hind legs. "What the hell?" Spit said.

The translucent object still hovered over the road. It was hard to be sure, but he guessed it was no more than a hundred yards in front of him. He squinted, trying to make sense of it. It looked almost like a black balloon.

And it was getting bigger.

NO! It was moving closer, moving toward him.

Yet, it didn't seem substantial enough to be a balloon. Its outline appeared to undulate, changing its hazy shape ever so slightly.

It was more like a bubble, shimmering, wobbling unsteadily through the air, darker than the atmosphere that contained it.

Spit's mind flashed to the soap bubbles he used to blow as a kid. They were clear, glassy, and amoeba-like. Yes, that's what it looked like—a three-foot bubble, coming right at him, apparently under its own power.

Spit tromped the gas and tried to steer out of the thing's path. When he changed direction, it changed direction, too.

His thoughts jumped again.

It's a fuckin' UFO! his mind screamed at him.

He jerked the wheel to the left, and the thing followed Spit's lead.

It was coming on fast, moving toward him like a cannonball. It was fifty feet in front of him.

Twenty.

Spit hit the brake and jounced to a near stop.

The night-black bubble floated delicately across the hood of the car, hardly touching it. It collided silently with the windshield, flattening momentarily before it rolled up the glass and poured over the visor and into the car.

When Spit's head passed into it, he didn't feel a thing. Not at first, anyway. It was no more painful than stepping into a cloud of cigarette smoke.

The trouble was, he couldn't see; it was dark, absolutely dark, inside the bubble. No light at all seemed to penetrate its filmy surface. It was as if he'd suddenly gone blind.

Spit felt the car bumping of the road, then heard scratching sounds as the vehicle tore a path through the scrub pine and brambles.

His hands jumped from the steering wheel, and he flailed wildly, trying to swat the insubstantial enclosure away from his head. There was nothing to hit, just space, just night-black space. When he took a deep breath to scream, he realized there was nothing to inhale. There was no air in the bubble!

His racing mind fought to remain rational. *What the hell is this?*

Jerking his body around, trying to pull his head out of the enclosure, Spit felt his lungs expanding with nothingness.

The car jolted to a stop. Spit couldn't see where it had come to rest.

A stray thought flashed around his mind—*Hope I didn't scratch Norm's paint job*—but the thought, like something solid and real, seemed to plunge down a deep, lightless well and disappear into the depths of madness.

Spit cried out, but he couldn't hear his own scream.

Something told him he was crazy when suddenly he realized what was happening to him. The realization didn't come as a coherent progression of thoughts; it came more as an intuitive flash: he had confronted one of the oddities of this world. Here and there, just as hollow cavities are sometimes found within solid rock masses, so too are there pockets of absolutely nothing within the atmosphere.

He had driven right into one of them.

But how come it chased him? How had it managed to block all his attempts to dodge it? How could it anticipate his movements, just as if it were ... intelligent ... ?

Or guided by intelligence?

Spit's whole chest worked as if it were a huge, frantically beating heart. It pumped sweat out of him like liquid bullets. Suddenly he was too weak to move.

His drooping eyes saw only darkness; he inhaled darkness into his weakening lungs.

When the panic had drained from him, the idea of his own death was not unpleasant. His thoughts slowed to a somnolent crawl.

Were his eyes open or closed? It didn't matter. Nothing mattered but the sound …

That sound, what was it? Did it mean the bubble was gone? He listened. It seemed so far away, so unimportant … The door of the car clicked open …

Someone had found him!

Spit tried to speak, but he had no voice. He tried to signal with his hand. It wouldn't move; it could as well have been part of the car.

Somehow, he sensed the faraway suggestion of movement. The seat moved—down, up—as if someone had jumped into the car beside him.

Reggie's seat …

Who's there? Who?

He couldn't tell.

And why was he running his fingernail slowly across Spit's throat?

Liquid? The stranger was pouring liquid all over him. It flowed, warm and viscous, saturating his T-shirt, covering his chest.

CHAPTER 20
INDISTINCT BOUNDARIES

Dan Wilder watched Eric Nolan move across the meadow and into the night. As impenetrable shadows closed around the solitary figure, Dan wondered if he had done the right thing. Had he assisted a well-meaning individual who'd been victimized by murderous fanatics? Or had he put his family in great danger while aiding an escaped homicidal maniac?

He'd surprised himself when he'd agreed not to call the police. "Your story is pretty far-fetched, Nolan," he said, "but I guess you know that. Tell you what: give me a chance to verify as much of it as I can. If any of it checks out, if there's anything to it at all, I'll do what I can for you. How's that?"

Nolan nodded stiffly.

Dan guessed it was the newspaperman in him talking. Any good journalist would have done the same thing, right? In any important story there was always an element of risk.

What about the incident in the woods? That was something else altogether. "I can't ignore it, Nolan. I'm going to have to call Dick Bates."

"If you do that, Mr. Wilder, Chief Bates will come up here. He'll find out about me."

"Look, those two punks attacked Mona and my boy. You said so yourself. The kids saw what happened, even if you didn't. We can't just forget about it. I'm going far enough out on a limb for you as it is. All I can do is try to keep you out of it."

Nolan hadn't argued too much, and his restraint seemed to show something. He'd been properly reasonable, appropriately rational. "I'm sorry," he said. "Of course I understand."

Their whole discussion had wrapped up at about nine o'clock. Sheila warmed some leftover chili. She and Mona served it with French bread, a late dinner for everyone.

After eating, Mona and Nolan collected the dishes and began to load the dishwasher.

Dan had been aware of the girl all evening. She'd been strangely quiet throughout the entire conversation, hardly moving, just staring, a faraway look glazing her clear blue eyes.

As Nolan handed her the dishes to stack, she continued to move like a zombie. She spoke only occasionally and always in monosyllables. Now and then Dan would catch her stealing glances at him. When their eyes met, she'd quickly look away.

He had to talk to her. He had to find out what she was thinking. Had she said anything to Will? To Sheila? Perhaps Dan's urgency for a private conversation with Mona accounted for his easy dismissal of Nolan.

One thing was for sure, he had to clear the air with Mona before phoning Dick Bates. What if she let something slip?

What if she ...

When the dinner dishes were loaded and washing, Dan said he'd give Nolan a few minutes to get away.

"I can't let you stay the night, not here, not with us. I hope you understand that."

"Of course I understand, Mr. Wilder." There was a hollowness in his voice, an echo of disappointment. His eyes were cast down at the floor.

Realizing he had sounded a bit too strict, Dan modified his tone. "I hope you won't mind staying in your cabin one or two more nights. It'll give me a chance to do my checking. You're welcome to come back tomorrow, of course, but only"—he added, perhaps unnecessarily—"if the Renault is in the yard."

Nolan nodded his head. He looked sad when Dan told him to leave. It was easy to guess how he must have felt. It was torture when people didn't trust you. Dan remembered all those times Sheila had been suspicious of him, all the groundless accusations, the scenes, the confrontations. He'd been guiltless, but she'd made him feel like a cad. At that time, of course, her feelings had been completely unjustified.

Now, things had changed ...

When Nolan had vanished into the darkness, Dan turned. "Come on, Mona," he said. "I'll drive you back to the trailer."

Sheila locked the door when she heard the car start. Glancing at Will, she smiled. How tired he looked sitting there at the kitchen table. *The kid's exhausted*, she thought, *he's too tired even to stand*.

"Will," she said softly, "why do you suppose Mona refused to stay the night?"

The boy shrugged.

"I'd feel better if we could keep an eye on her, wouldn't you? I do hope her father will be there."

Will nodded, yawning at the same time.

"And I hope he'll be sober," she added as an afterthought.

It wasn't a long drive, just down the hill, probably less than a mile; but it was dark outside, and Mona couldn't be expected to walk home alone.

She remained quiet as she slid into the front seat of Dan's car. Starting the engine, he cleared his throat and asked hoarsely,

"You going to be all right?" At least he had broken the silence.

"Usually am," Mona replied flatly.

"Your father know where you've been?"

"Don't know where he is hisself, half the time."

He studied her from the corner of his eye. She was just slightly visible, illuminated by the instruments on the dashboard. How alone she appeared to him, sitting there in Sheila's sweater and Will's jeans. She looked helpless, lost, afraid.

"You want me to come in and talk to your father, Mona? You want me to explain what's going on?"

"Yup. I want you to come in …"

Minutes later, when they arrived at the trailer, Dan saw the pickup in the yard. The trailer's windows were dark. Dan figured Mr. Grant must be asleep inside.

Maybe going in wasn't such a good idea; they could talk here. He didn't move. Neither did Mona.

Resting his chin in his hands, he massaged his lips with his forefinger, trying to decide what to say. "Mona," he began slowly, "about this morning—"

"It's okay, Daniel …"

"But—"

"It's nothin'. Ferget it—" The interior light flashed on as she opened the door, then went out as she slammed it shut. She walked around the car to Dan's side. "You comin' or what?"

"If you want me to."

"Yup. Want you should talk to Pa."

Dan opened his door.

"Gimme your hand," Mona said. "Yard's pretty cluttered, you'll trip over somethin'."

Mona led him across the front of the trailer and up the rickety steps to the little wooden porch. Her hand felt cold in his, yet strangely sensual. It wasn't like holding hands with a child. It wasn't a woman's hand either. It was something more, something Dan couldn't quite place. Perhaps it was some sweetly sensual memory from his own childhood.

He allowed himself to be led, docilely, as he tried to make sense of the curious sensations passing between them.

He put his hand against the trailer door so she couldn't open it. "Mona ..."

"Daniel, come on. It was just a kiss. Nothin' to worry about. How come you gotta make such a big deal outta it?"

His hand fell away. Mona opened the door—it wasn't locked—and flicked on the inside light. Dan followed her in. He looked around.

"Have a seat," she said.

"Where's your dad?"

"He ain't here."

"Not here? That's his truck, isn't it? Outside?"

"It's his truck, but he ain't here. Sit down, why don't ya."

"But you said ..." Dan's words trailed off into silence. He took a seat on the couch and watched Mona go to the refrigerator. She opened it and poked around inside. "Pa's always got a beer in here someplace," she said.

"I can't stay, Mona. I've got to get back and phone—"

"Pa'll be back. You can drink a beer, okay? Just stay with me awhile till Pa gets back."

Dan watched her move around the kitchen and stretch to reach a beer mug from a high shelf, her back arching, her breasts thrusting forward. He thought about his own youth, the flirtatious, firm-bodied girls, the teasing, the long-forgotten smells of unfamiliar bodies moving close together for the first time.

"I'm kinda scared," Mona said as she handed him the mug of beer. She sat beside him on the couch. "You think Mr. Nolan's right? You think there's people in them woods?"

Dan wrestled with the attraction he was feeling. It was wrong, and he knew it; she was too young. And Sheila ... Sheila was waiting for him at home.

"I—I don't know. It could be true ... it ..."

She snuggled up beside him, the side of her firm leg pressing against him. Arm against arm, now, her head on his shoulder. Dan tried to pass off the feeling as something noble: protectiveness, maybe. But it was more than that. There were too many emotions involved, too many sensations. Mona's hair smelled of the pine forest, and her skin, strangely cool, drew the heat from him.

"I—I should go ..." he said, but he didn't move. He couldn't.

"Please. Don't. Not yet ..." She used no force to keep him there, just the gentle placing of her hand on his thigh, just the eager look in her eyes, staring up into his. His arm dropped from the back of the sofa and onto her shoulder. He had no control over it.

At that, she moved closer, and his arm pulled her tighter still. Somewhere in the back of his mind, a fading voice told him it was wrong. Dangerous. But there was a louder voice, more urgent, primitive, commanding—it beckoned, it coaxed. Dan's lips found hers and they kissed. The boundary between child and woman disappeared.

Mona's arms were strong and demanding. They pulled him closer. Eyes closed, lips barely moving, she whispered, "I'm cold, so very cold. Please warm me up ..."

CHAPTER 21
EAVESDROPPING

"Okay, young lad, time to rise and shine."

Mrs. Menard stood smiling at Will from the doorway of his bedroom. She wore a bright flowery apron with the strings wrapped all the way around her tiny waist and tied in the front.

Momentarily confused, Will blinked his sleep-crusted eyes. He was surprised to see her.

Mrs. Menard was the woman Dan and Sheila had hired to come in three times a week to help with the housework. This was her ninth day on the job, but Will had forgotten she was coming.

"Hi, Aunt Peg," he mumbled.

Even though they weren't related, she insisted he call her Aunt Peg. "It's what everybody calls me," she'd explained the first time they'd met.

What the heck, "Aunt Peg" was okay with Will; somehow, it seemed to fit.

He got a kick out of the way she pronounced it "ant," instead of "ont," like all his relatives did. It also struck him funny that she actually looked a little like an ant. Her graying black hair stuck out all over the place, making her head look big and round. By contrast, she was skinny and very tiny; he guessed she was just five feet tall, maybe shorter. When she moved, it was in quick little motions, scurrying around the house, busily cleaning, and sorting and throwing things out.

"You know, lad, it's after ten o'clock." She ran a pencil-thin finger along the top of his bureau, looking for dust. "Round here, folks git up with the chickens."

Will almost said something wise-assed, like, "cluck-cluck," but he didn't; he wasn't feeling humorous.

"Yer mom and dad's down on the deck waitin' fer ya. Come on now, 'fore the whole mornin's wasted." She clapped her hands a couple of times to emphasize her point and dashed off in the direction of the bathroom.

After the events of yesterday, Will was surprised to discover how well he'd slept. He'd had one of those pitch-black sleeps, dreamless and long. When he woke up, it took him a minute to remember where he was.

His whole body was stiff as he pulled himself out of bed. It felt as if all his muscles had shrunk during the night. Stretching, he walked over to the window.

Below, and to the left, he could see Mom and Dan sitting on the deck, coffee cups on the table in front of them. It startled him to find Dan home at this hour, even on a Saturday. Maybe he was waiting for Mr. Nolan.

As he watched them, Will suspected they might be fighting. *Oh no, what now?*

He tried to listen; but they were too far off, and he could only catch a few words.

"… don't know *why* you'd stay down there so late, Dan …"

"… couldn't just *leave* … into town … call Dick Bates …"

"… should have been here, with us … how scared we were …"

"… talking with Mona's father …"

What? Mona's father? Will couldn't be sure he'd heard it right; he *couldn't* have heard it right. But it sure sounded as if his mom was mad because Dan had stayed at Mona's trailer too long last night. Dan seemed to be saying he'd been talking with Mona's father! What the hell was going on?

Will's drowsy mind reeled. He spun around and sat on the floor beneath his bedroom window. God! He should never have let them talk him into this—they never should have moved to the country. Everything was so crazy.

If only they could pack up and head back to Boston. Things had been so much simpler there. He'd lived on Cobleigh Street all his life, and he'd never even gotten into a fistfight. Now, in the "peaceful country," his whole life was taking a nose dive.

Will's hand spidered up his chest, thumb and forefinger probing for the arteries on either side of his neck. The silent, surging pressure comforted him, and suddenly he was thinking about his dad. His *real* dad. It was when Dad died that things started getting strange. It wasn't that Will didn't like Dan—he was a good guy and everything—but he wasn't Will's real father. Maybe something changes when your father dies. After that, things will never be natural anymore.

Certainly there was nothing natural about what was going on in Antrim. The list of strange stuff was getting longer and longer. Christ, he was covering up a murder! Two guys had actually tried to kill him, and now, to top it all off, Will's stepfather had been out talking with a dead man!

God, what the hell am I going to do?

He felt trapped in his own house, in his own mind.

Maybe Eric Nolan was somebody he could trust. Will knew he liked Mr. Nolan, even if he couldn't say just exactly why. Mr. Nolan seemed like someone he could talk to about all the things that were scaring him. Mr. Nolan might know what to do; maybe he'd have some idea what was going on.

Will had almost resolved to go find Mr. Nolan when Mrs. Menard scurried back into the room. She caught Will in his underwear as he was getting dressed. Pretending not to notice, she started pulling the sheets and blankets off his bed.

Will stepped into his pants real fast.

"So, young William, what sorts of mischief do you have planned for today?"

"More of the same, I guess." He pulled his sweat shirt over his head. "I'll knock over a couple gas stations, snatch some purses. If I get bored, I'll go into town and steal a car." He was trying to act as if everything was okay, but probably he was coming across as some kind of a jerk.

She laughed. "You kids're all the same, buncha no-goods. Here, come give me a hand, we'll flip your mattress."

Will helped her with it, thinking if she'd done it alone she'd probably get pinned under it and they'd never see her again.

An idea came to him.

"Aunt Peg," he asked, "you've lived in Antrim a long time, right?"

"Why, I guess prob'ly. I've lived here all my life, if you call that a long time. More'n sixty years ..."

"Have you ever heard any stories about people living in the woods around here?"

"Stories? What kind of stories?" She looked up at him, the smile gone from her face.

"I dunno. Just—you know—about a bunch of people living up on Pinnacle Mountain."

"Now, who's been fillin' your head fulla that kind of nonsense? Nobody ever lived up there but ole Perly Greer, the hermit, an' he's long gone. That land up there, it ain't fit for nobody at all. Even the summer people got sense enough not to buy it."

Will couldn't understand why she got so serious all of a sudden. "I dunno," he persisted. "I was talking to some kids the other day, and they told me there was a bunch of people, religious nuts or something, living up there."

"Religious nuts, eh?"

"That's what they told me—"

"Some folks'll tell you anything, they think you're gonna believe it. Don't you go lettin' em make a goat of you, now."

"But—"

"But nothin'. That's steep, rocky, no good land, an' if you're smart's you think you are, William Crockett, you'll stay clear of it. You go pokin' around up the Pinnacle, you'll get yourself hurt, sure as shootin'. You tumble off'n one a them rock ledges, nobody'll find you for a month a Sundays."

Will blinked at her a couple of times deciding not to press the point. After tucking in the sheets, Aunt Peg stood up and looked at him. "What you gawkin' at? You got somethin' else on your mind?"

"No, ma'am," he said, and saluted. He did his best military about-face and left the bedroom.

"Will, can you get that!" Dan's voice nearly shook the house. The electronic ring trilled a second time from the other side of the glass door.

"Will ... !"

Dan looked at Sheila's red-rimmed eyes. "I'd better get it, Sheil. It might be the office."

She didn't acknowledge him at all.

Dan stood up, eager to get away, but hating to leave things unresolved. "Wouldn't you know the damn phone would start working again just when—"

She wasn't even looking at him, just staring out into the trees. *Hell with it*, Dan thought, and slipped through the sliding door, snatching up the receiver on the fifth ring.

The slow Yankee tones on the other end were unmistakable, "Hello, Daniel? Dick Bates ..."

"Hi, Chief, whatcha got?"

"Daniel, them kids you called me about, Reggie and Spit? Neither one of 'em come home last night. Reggie—that's Reginald Benson the third—was last seen when he borrowed Norman Gagnon's car. Him an' Spit went out cruisin'. Nobody's seen him since. Now, this fella Spit—that's Archibald M. Shattuck—he turned up, though."

"And ..."

"And we found the car, with him in it, on Old Factory Road between six and seven o'clock this mornin'. Looks like he mighta been drunk, lots of empty beer cans in the car. Appears as though he drove off the road and plowed far enough into the bushes so nobody spotted him until—"

"What'd he have to say?"

"Whatever he had to say, he musta said it 'fore we got there—the kid was dead."

"Dead? Christ, what happened?"

"His throat was slit. Awful lookin' gash. He was a punk, but all things considered, he prob'ly deserved better'n that."

"You got a suspect?"

"Sure, the Benson kid for one. I wanna have a talk with him, if I can find him."

"And that's it?"

"Or he mighta picked up a hitchhiker. Hitchhiker mighta done it. Then again, coulda been anybody. Christ, coulda been Eric Nolan ..."

Nolan: the name cracked like a whip, silencing Dan for a second. Should he tell? "Chief ..."

"Yeah, Dan?"

"About Nolan …"

"What about him?"

"Nolan's, uh, he's, uh … Nolan's still missing?"

"No word on him yet. Don't really expect none. Funny thing, though …"

"What is?"

"The car. Why didn't the killer take the car? Hitcher kills a driver, he'll usually take the car, know what I mean?"

"Yeah, I guess that is odd. Anything else, Chief?"

"I was just gonna ask you that. You sound like you wanna tell me somethin'."

Dan swallowed. "No. No, nothing really —" He was sweating.

"You sure, Daniel?"

"Yeah, Chief. It's just that I want to thank you for keeping me posted, appreciate your cooperation. I'll stop by and check with you when I get into town."

"Look forward to it, Daniel. Somethin' you can do for me while you're at it …"

"Sure. What?"

"Bring your boy by with ya, okay? I'd like to have a little talk with him."

———

Will listened for the click on the other end of the line, trying to time his disconnect with Dan's.

He had picked up the phone in his parents' room when Dan shouted to him. More curious than ashamed, he'd listened to the entire discussion, becoming more afraid with each word.

Another murder!

A talk with Chief Bates. Holy God!

He'd never in his life eavesdropped on a telephone conversation before. He wished he hadn't started with this one.

Slowly, guiltily, he headed down the stairs.

———————

Will stepped timidly toward the deck, knowing he was interrupting an argument. With what he had to say, they were sure to turn their anger on him.

As he worked up his courage, he tried to determine the best way to approach them. In general, Mom and Dan didn't fight that much anymore. Not the way they used to when they first got married and Mom was having "her trouble." She'd had a real temper then. Always exploding. It was scary.

Lately, she might have been a little snippy sometimes—she was often tired and moody—but, she'd explained to him, that was frequently the way with pregnant women.

Since moving to Vermont, Mom and Dan only argued a little, they didn't really *fight*. Money was sometimes an issue. Mom had spent so much to fix up the house that Dan occasionally protested. Will figured his stepfather wasn't used to having as much money as Mom made off her books. He was also a little nervous the *TriTown Tribune* wouldn't do well; he wanted to keep some bucks in the bank. A nest egg, he called it.

Mom used to fight more with Will's dad. It wasn't real fighting, and it never amounted to much. Dad's temper had been worse than Dan's. He'd just blow up about something, sputter awhile, and a few minutes later he'd be back to normal. He never got mean.

When Dan got mad he tended to get quiet and stay that way for hours.

Will had never learned how to act around people who were fighting. If Mom and Dad—or Mom and Dan—were going at it, he usually made himself scarce.

Today Will had something to talk about, and he was going to have his say. He didn't care what happened; things had gone far enough, and they were piling up way too fast.

He'd decided he was going to bring everything out into the open, first at home, then with Mona. This time he wasn't going to chicken out or be put off. His good night's sleep had given him back some courage.

When Mom and Dan saw him standing by the sliding doors, they became very quiet. Mom looked like she'd been crying. Will almost lost heart when he saw how miserable she looked.

Almost. But he didn't run off.

"Can I talk to you guys a minute?"

"Will, this might not be—" Dan started to say.

"It's *gotta* be now," Will insisted. "It's important."

They looked at each other. Mom rubbed her eyes with her fingertips. Dan's face was all red and welty-looking.

"Dan," Will began, not really knowing how to say it, "did I hear you say you'd been talking to Mona's father?"

"Last night? Yeah, I spent some time with him."

"At the trailer?"

"Yes, at the trailer. What about it, Will?" He sounded angry.

Will felt his lip quivering. He was afraid he was going to start crying again. "Dan, I think Mona's father's dead. He … he got murdered … by those guys, Reggie and Spit, he …"

"Murdered?" Dan's chair scraped on the deck as he swung abound. "What are you talking about, Will?"

Will explained about the fight in town, about showing up at Mona's trailer and seeing Mr. Grant's mutilated body, about how Mona made him promise not to say anything so she wouldn't get carted off to an orphanage.

He told everything, all that he knew, all that he'd seen, and feared, and guessed. It just poured out of him, lubricated by his humiliating tears. First it came a little at a time, then nonstop, as if a dam had burst; he couldn't hold it back or stop it.

Will was sobbing heavily by the time he started to wind down. He wasn't proud of it, but he just couldn't help it. "Mona's been living all by herself down there," he cried. "I should have told; I know I should have. But I promised ... I *promised* ..."

The adults listened as if hypnotized, then Mom looked at Dan, biting her lower lip, her face filled with doubt. Dan's face just got redder and redder.

Will cringed, expecting the worst. What would they say? What would they do to him? He'd never been involved in anything like this before.

Finally, Dan stood up and walked to the side of the deck. He looked out at the mountains, holding the railing in both hands. His knuckles were white.

Feeling lost, Will moved toward his mother. She gave him a hug without moving from where she sat. He could feel her round belly against his leg. Everything was quiet for a moment.

Mom cleared her throat. It was a little raspy sound. Her voice was cold and stern, with an edge to it sharper than any knife. Will figured he was in for real trouble.

But her anger wasn't for Will at all. "So what were you doing down there last night, Dan?" she said very quietly. "Who were you really talking to?"

Dan didn't say anything. Will looked at his stepfather's back. It was tense and rigid, framed by the mountains in the distance.

"Dan?" Mom said.

"Oh God," Dan said. All the tension seemed to drop out of him. He pitched forward, folding himself over the deck railing. He buried his face in his hands. "Oh my God."

CHAPTER 22
MOMENT OF TRUTH

Will watched the whole thing.

His mom lifted herself from the chair and walked over to her husband. Dan was still leaning on the railing, his face in his hands, his shoulders quivering as if he were silently choking.

"Dan?" she said.

She reached out slowly and touched him on the shoulder. "Dan?" He shook his head. Wouldn't look at her.

"My God, Dan, what is it?"

He turned around, almost in slow motion, his expression like that of someone cringing from a bright light. His face was flushed and sweaty-looking. His eyes watered behind his rimless glasses. "Sheila, I ..."

Sheila took a step backward. Dan hadn't said anything, but she seemed to know; it was as if she had some kind of ESP. Will saw pain and disbelief in her eyes. It looked like she wanted to go to her husband but at the same time she was repelled. It was as if Dan had suddenly changed into some hideous monster right before her eyes. "I ... I don't believe it, Dan." She shook her head, still backing away. "You and that girl? You and that *little* girl ... ?"

Dan looked awful. Immobile, he leaned against the deck as a man might lean against the wall facing a firing squad. He was all alone, totally beyond help.

"Oh, Dan. God, Dan, how could you?"

He ventured a tentative step toward her, his hand gesturing plaintively, but no words came.

Will's insides were burning up; he didn't understand anything that was going on. Somehow, this thing that was happening between his parents must be his fault.

It *is* my fault, he thought. I shouldn't have told; I'd promised Mona I wouldn't tell.

"Come on, you guys. Mom … Dan … ?" He'd wanted to say something special, some magic words that would put an end to the whole ugly scene. But no words came. "Mom, Dan …"

It was as if he weren't there.

"Sheila," Dan stammered, "I don't know what happened, honest to God I don't …"

Sometimes when his mother got mad—really mad—she'd kind of turn to stone. Will had seen it before—not often—but when it happened, it scared the shit out of him. It was as if her feelings suddenly shut off, leaving a clear mind and a sharp tongue, but no compassion at all.

Will watched as Sheila pulled herself up, bracing her shoulders. Poised and stern, she gave Dan a frightful, withering look, as if he were some loathsome crawling reptile. She just held him like that, frozen in a paralyzing glare, as she spit the words at him. "It's really disgusting, Dan. It's really sick. Christ, she's all of thirteen years old. You don't need help, Dan you need …"

The stone-Sheila was starting to crumble. "… you need …" She was crying now, both hands at her trembling mouth. "… a f-fucking bullet … in your head."

Sheila's face dropped into the palms of her hands.

"Mom …" Will pleaded.

"How could you, Dan? How could you do this to me?"

"Sheila, wait …" Dan took a teetering step as she turned her back on him. "Sheila, it's not what you think …"

207

She stopped, stiffened her back, then whirled around. Her eyes were cold pebbles in her tear-splattered face. "You going to lie now, Dan? You going to tell me it didn't happen?"

"No … but, I … Sheila, wait—"

"You're disgusting. I'm not going to stay here, Dan. I mean it; there are some things I can't overlook, some things no one would expect me to forgive …"

"Sheila—"

"That's it, Dan. Period. Nothing to say."

She stomped into the house. A moment later Will heard her banging up the stairs.

Dan looked at Will with a broken, dazed expression. Then he turned away.

CHAPTER 23
OLD STORIES

Dan's mind was spinning; he was pacing like a corralled stallion.

Two or three times he started up the stairs to talk to Sheila, but he just couldn't do it. He felt dirty, deserving of all the scorn she'd directed his way. If only he could explain … but he couldn't, not even to himself.

He walked out onto the deck, turned around, came back inside, and paced some more.

The random, nervous walking made him feel more conspicuous. He wanted to hide, to turn off his racing mind. It stung him every time he saw Will's' frightened eyes looking at him. Was Will accusing him, too? He'd wanted to be an example for the boy; he'd wanted to be a good father.

Dan felt relieved when Will disappeared outside.

After about a half hour, Sheila came pounding down the stairs. Dan looked at her hopefully, but there was no hope; she was still angry as hell. He watched her, not daring to say anything, waiting anxiously for any additional punishment she wanted to dish out.

Ignoring Will, who watched from the deck, she brushed past Dan and grabbed her keys from the magnetic hook on the refrigerator.

"Sheila, please …"

She stomped toward the kitchen door. It was as if a wind were following her wherever she went.

Dan looked up at her. "Please, can't we just talk a minute?" His eyes felt wet under his glasses. His mouth was open, but he could say no more.

Sheila's voice was controlled, exact, its edge sharper than a razor. "I hope you don't imagine I'm going to wait around here, Dan. Not after this. I'm not going to have my baby born in your house!"

It was as if Sheila had punched him in the gut. He started to protest, but before his frenzied mind could formulate a sentence, she did an about-face, stiff-armed the kitchen door and was gone. She crossed the porch without breaking stride. In a few moments he heard her station wagon start up.

Will ran down the steps of the deck, around the house, and into the yard. "Mom, wait! Mom!" he cried to her.

The station wagon ground gravel as it spun into reverse. Gears growled painfully as she shifted into forward.

Together Dan and Will watched her car until it vanished where Tenny's Hill Road dipped into the trees.

———————

For the next hour or so, Dan's thoughts raced too furiously to put together a plan. All he could do was continue his endless pacing, stopping twice for shots of Canadian Club.

He banged doors and pounded doorframes. He cursed silently, and he fought his urge to drink some more.

On some buried and useless level he felt ashamed every time Will tried to approach him. He had to wave the boy away and stammer an apology in a weak and broken voice.

Soon, it felt as if the boy was avoiding him altogether.

He wondered if Mrs. Menard had any idea what the fight was about; she'd been upstairs during most of it. When she came down, Dan was standing at the front door. He held it open, staring off down the road.

"Better close that door, Mr. Wilder. Pretty hard collectin' rent from the flies ..."

Dan couldn't even look at her. He stepped quickly outside and let the door slam behind him.

———

Aunt Peg looked at Will with a puzzled expression.

"He an' Mom just had a fight." Will tried to explain.

"Good fight won't do nothin' but strengthen a marriage, William. Don't you worry yourself about it." She said it with tremendous authority, but Will wasn't so sure. Mom was pretty mad.

He felt his anger rising right along with his jealousy. He fought them both, knowing they would do no good.

Will didn't know how to tell Dan that he knew almost exactly what he was going through; he figured it would sound dumb coming from a kid his age.

He was convinced something awful had happened between Dan and Mona, just like something had happened between Mona and himself. That certainty was the source of Will's jealousy. Mona had some sort of—he wasn't sure of the word—influence? Power? Whatever it was, it was terribly strong.

When Will himself had experienced it, he'd tossed if off as simple horniness. He didn't like to talk about being horny, not the way some of his friends did; but there was no denying it, he was horny a lot of the time. The thing with Mona was part horniness, Will was positive of that, but it was part something else, too. Something weird. Whatever it was, it confused him and caused him to lose willpower; it helped talk him into things he didn't want to do.

Will was positive he wasn't making excuses, either, not for Dan, not for himself. Whatever Mona had was real. He'd felt it.

When Will was its victim, he'd figured it was simply his own weakness. But now it had happened to Dan. Wasn't that just the proof he needed? Something powerful was at work. He hated to sound like one of his own scary books, but he suspected it was something sinister, something that disguised itself as sex.

Whatever it was, there could be no doubt of its source—it came from, or through, Mona.

"Will!" Dan was yelling at him from the front yard. "Will! Come here, please."

Will moved quickly to the door with Aunt Peg right behind him. When he pushed it open, she put her hand on his shoulder.

"Will, I'm going out looking for your mother. I want you to stay here. Mrs. Menard, you stay with him until I get back, okay?"

Aunt Peg nodded her head, looking uneasy but full of purpose, eager to cooperate.

"Dan ..." Will said. "Dan, I think she'll be back. I think she'll cool off and come back ..."

"I don't know, Will. I really messed things up this time." He didn't stay to talk any more. Before Will could decide how to explain, Dan had jumped into his Renault. He drove off, spinning up gravel in the driveway.

Aunt Peg and Will stood there a few minutes. This time she was the one holding the door open, letting the flies in.

"Don't you worry, William," she said, her face tightly wrinkled. The strength of her frown pulled her bushy eyebrows together like caterpillars butting heads.

"Let me get you a glass of milk," she said. She sounded just like Mom, always wanting to feed him when he was upset. "You just sit yourself down at the table, and I'll see if I can find you some cookies to go with it. How'd that be?"

"I'm not hungry, Aunt Peg."

"That's not the point, William. You eat somethin', it'll calm you down."

She poured two glasses of milk and laid out a dozen chocolate chip cookies on a plate. Together they sat at the round kitchen table. She ate a cookie.

"It's none of my business, William. I'm just an old lady who earns a little extra money by cleanin' up your house. But, you know, I'm beginnin' to care about you folks. You're a nice young man, and I'm fond of you. If there's somethin' you want to get off your chest, well I'm here to listen."

Will was thinking very hard just then. Sure, a moment ago he'd been scared and upset. Now he had to act; his suspicions had become certainties. It was definitely Mona.

"Aunt Peg, do you know the people who live in the trailer down the road, the Grants?"

"Most folks know 'em," she said. "Most folks don't have much of anythin' to do with 'em, though."

"Why's that?"

"Ole Joe Grant, he's an on'ry cuss. He don't have much use for most people here 'bouts."

"Do you know him?"

"Know *of* him's more like it. Most men'll take a drink once in a while after work. Joe Grant, he don't bother with the workin' end of it. He's a fighter, too. A real troublemaker. They say his wife run off. Probably means she had more sense than he's got."

"He's got a daughter, you know."

"Yes, poor thing. I can imagine what kind of a life she must have. Pretty little thing, though—"

"Aunt Peg … ?"

"Yes, William?"

"Mona Grant, she's the one who told me about the people living in the woods." It was a lie, of course, but Will couldn't tell her about Mr. Nolan.

"People in the woods? You back to that now, are you?"

"I'm curious, that's all. You really never heard any stories about them?"

"Hear lots of things, can't help it. Around here, though, it pays not to believe too much a what folks say. You gotta learn to keep stories and truth in two separate parts of your head, William. You gotta learn to tell one from the other an' not mix 'em up."

"I'm just interested—"

"If I'm gonna tell you about it, William, you're gonna have to understand what I'm tellin' you is a story. I don't want you to turn around and pass it on as fact."

"Yes, ma'am."

"'You remember somethin' else, too, William: any place, be it town or city, any place at all has its stories. It's human nature. Each one of 'em prob'ly started off somewheres near the truth, but got changed around, exaggerated, by folks passin' it on and distortin' it a little to make it more interestin'."

"I understand …"

Aunt Peg ate another cookie and took a sip of milk. She cleared her throat. "Years ago, what prob'ly happened is this: Some young 'uns prob'ly got themselves lost in the woods. Maybe they got taken by Indians, maybe by coyotes or wild dogs, maybe they just wandered off. Whatever happened, they never come back to their parents. Most parents would have a hard time acceptin' somethin' like that, you know. They'd make up stories so's they wouldn't have to give up hope. They'd say somethin' like, 'I seen my boy in the woods today. I *seen* him so I know he ain't dead.'

"Then other folks'd jump on the bandwagon. Pretty quick, everybody'd be seein' kids in the woods. You see what I mean, William?"

Will blinked at her a couple of times. Her story didn't sound anything like the one Mr. Nolan had told. "Aunt Peg, you mean the story is that children are living out in the woods? Is that the story?"

"Children, little people, whatever. Everybody tells it different. There's lots of Irish around here'll tell you it's leprechauns."

"Little people?"

"That's the story, William."

Will thought of those kids he'd seen by the waterfall, the ones with no clothes on. "Aunt Peg, have you ever seen one of them?"

She looked wide-eyed, her mouth drew into a tight little line. "Now there you go, William. I'm tellin' you it's a *story*, an' you're askin' me if I've *seen* one of 'em. You can't see what don't exist, boy. Here I am, tryin' to get your mind off your mommy and daddy fightin', an' you're takin' it all as gospel."

"I'm sorry, Aunt Peg."

"Sorry nothin', see how rumors get started? See how they spread? I should take my own advice an' limit my conversation to things I know somethin' about. Folks do that, the world's be a simpler place by a long sight."

Right then Will knew what he had to do: he had to find Mr. Nolan and ask him to help sort things out. Will would tell him everything, all he'd seen, all he feared. Somehow, he was sure Mr. Nolan would know what to do.

The only problem was how to find him. He was hiding somewhere in the woods, in some old cabin, he'd said. Will didn't know of any cabins anywhere around.

"Aunt Peg," he said, "'member upstairs you said something about a hermit who lived around here?"

"What about him?"

"Did he live in a trailer, like the Grants?"

"Heck no, ole Perly Greer, he had himself a cabin—"

"Whereabouts did he live?"

Getting out of the house wasn't too difficult. Dan's instructions to Aunt Peg were simply to stay with Will, not keep him indoors. When he announced he was going for a walk, Aunt Peg looked a little doubtful but didn't say anything.

She hadn't known exactly where the hermit's cabin was—at least, she didn't admit to it. Will couldn't be positive it was the same cabin Mr. Nolan was using, but it seemed likely. It was worth a chance.

Aunt Peg's directions were very general and not too helpful: "Somewhere up Pinnacle Mountain, on the side facin' town." That didn't narrow things down much. Will couldn't prod her for more information, fearing she'd guess what he was up to.

He figured there couldn't be too many trails on the mountainside. Because Mr. Nolan was regularly going back and forth to the cabin, Will should be able to pick out his trail among the unused ones.

It was a long shot, he knew. He didn't know anything about trailing and tracking and getting around in the woods. All he had going for him was what he considered an improving sense of direction; this would be a good chance to test it.

Dan didn't keep any guns in the house. If he did, Will would have taken one for protection, or, if need be, to use as a signal. Instead, he took his Boy Scout knife and a pocketful of firecrackers he'd brought with him from Boston. He had his binoculars around his neck. In his pocket he carried one of Dan's disposable lighters, a relic from the days before he went on his health kick and gave up smoking.

Mrs. Menard watched Will from the porch as he walked off in the approximate direction Mr. Nolan had taken last night. He wished he had paid more attention to the route; he knew he was just guessing.

As he crossed the meadow, he thought about how much more at ease he was becoming in the woods. He still wasn't a real woodsman; if he were he'd have remembered things like a compass (he didn't know how to use one) and a watch (he'd forgotten it again). In front of him, in places where the trees were sparse, long shadows fell across the tall green grass bordering the forest. That gave him an idea of east and west. He guessed it must be as late as five o'clock in the afternoon.

After entering the woods, he quickly found the little brook. Instead of going downstream, as usual, he followed it up a ways until it narrowed and a natural footbridge of big gray rocks allowed him to cross without getting his feet wet.

In Will's mind, crossing the brook was *really* entering the forest. Their house, the Grants' trailer, and even the town of Antrim itself were all on one side of the brook. The woods and the Pinnacle were on the other—one riverbank was civilization, the other, wilderness.

He'd become accustomed to the darkness of the forest, and also the coolness. The air was different, too; it smelled like decaying leaves and potting soil. Now and then he could catch the sweet odor of some variety of wildflower. Insects buzzed constantly.

He quickly became tired as he climbed upward. The mountainside was very steep; it was a chore stepping over so many rocks and fallen logs and plowing his way through bushes and tree limbs.

He kept thinking how impossible finding Mr. Nolan was going to be. At most times the density of undergrowth wouldn't permit him to see more than thirty feet in front of him, and there was so much ground to cover. Before they'd moved to Antrim, Will always thought of distance as measured in feet, yards, and miles. Mostly he thought in terms of city blocks. If someone said a place was five blocks down, he'd know exactly how far to go.

Here he had to start thinking in acres! He remembered reading that an acre was about 4,840 square yards. A quick calculation told him that was about 70 yards to the side. On flat land, he figured, his stride was almost three feet. Here, moving uphill, he'd take maybe two steps to the yard. That meant it would take him a minimum of 140 steps to cross an acre, and there were hundreds of thousands of acres of woodland! He felt like one needle looking for another in a haystack.

Suddenly the whole process seemed impossible!

Will stopped for a minute and looked around. The land in front of him became steeper still, much steeper than a flight of stairs. The trees were getting scraggly-looking, with whippy little black branches that looked like telephone cables. Below his feet, rocks protruded from the soil. They were sharp and jagged, like the teeth of some buried behemoth, biting its way up through the forest floor.

He figured no man—not the hermit, not Mr. Nolan—would make this kind of climb on a regular basis. He ruled out continuing straight ahead.

On either side of him a kind of ledge skirted the abruptly rising mountain. Although he could see no trail or path, it still seemed like a more sensible route to follow.

The question was: left or right?

He looked at the ground, the rocks, the tree branches, hoping for some kind of clue. He could see no indication that anyone had passed here.

He listened. He could hear air moving in the treetops like the quiet whirring of a distant engine. Mosquitoes buzzed close to his ears.

For a few minutes, indecision locked him in place. He couldn't pick a direction. Then, to the left, he saw motion. It could have been an animal, or maybe a wind-blown branch. Or it could have been a person. Whatever had caught his eye was suddenly gone.

He almost called out, but stopped himself—what if it wasn't Mr. Nolan?

Moving as quietly as he could, he crept along the slope, binoculars ready, ears on the alert. He hadn't advanced more than one hundred yards when the trail ended. Directly in front of him the land took a sudden dip; a rocky cliff plunged straight down. Far below, Will saw a rock-strewn valley. If he'd been watching the sky instead of the ground, he might have tumbled over the side. His heart pounded a little harder as he realized how close he had come.

A scattering of pines and some trees he didn't recognize grew among the distant outcroppings. It was strange, sparse-looking land, boxed in on three sides by cliffs as steep as the one on which he stood. A crow was flying in circles above the pine trees, yet below the level of Will's eyes. Was it the crow he had seen?

He had the odd sensation that he was up in an airplane, watching the world from above. Everything seemed to be in miniature, and far away.

He squinted downward, searching among the distant trees for some sign of Mr. Nolan, or maybe the hermit's cabin. A long way off there was something moving, lurching, bashing its way through the pine boughs. It looked like some huge four-footed creature. Could it be a bear, or maybe a horse? Either seemed unlikely.

Without moving his head, Will lifted the binoculars to his eyes. When he located the figure in his lens, it was more unlikely still. Men! The lurching creature was actually two men, walking face to face, carrying a wrapped bundle between them.

Were these Mr. Nolan's religious fanatics carrying some supplies to their hideout? They definitely were not Aunt Peg's "little people." They were big and clumsy, seeming to move with great difficulty.

Will strained his eyes to see their faces; but they were looking at the ground, and they were much too far away. Still, on some level, there was something familiar about them.

One had his back toward Will, so there was no hope of getting a better look at him, but the other …

Will braced his elbows against the ground, trying to keep the binoculars from shaking. He moved the adjustment wheel to bring the microscopic face into focus. There was something about the black fall of greasy hair, about the slash of red across the indistinct features of the face, about the set of the shoulders as they struggled with the weight of the package. It was … God, it couldn't be … !

Will felt a rush of heat as he backed up, dropping the binoculars from his eyes. Feeling along behind him with a trembling left hand, Will crab-walked away from the edge of the cliff.

When he was grabbed from behind and a big hand slapped over his mouth, Will knew who had him, and he felt more relieved than frightened.

"Mr. Nolan," he said through the loosening fingers.

"Sssssshhhhh," he said. "Ssshhh."

"That's Reggie," Will whispered, pointing frantically at the lurching figure. "That's one of the kids who chased me and Mona through the woods."

Nolan put his fingers on Will's mouth, and Will was quiet.

"Be very still," Mr. Nolan said. "That's the entrance to their camp down there. I've been watching it for hours. Be quiet, Will; if they hear us, they'll kill us."

CHAPTER 24
FALLING SHADOW

Eric Nolan led the way back through the woods toward Will's house. As they walked, Will told him everything Eric listened, nodding his head, making comments, letting Will feel that he was finally doing the right thing.

The hike took a very long time; Will couldn't believe how deeply he'd penetrated into the forests of the Pinnacle.

When they got home, twilight was darkening into night. There was a faint yellow sliver of a moon. By its light Will could see the yard was empty; neither Dan's Renault nor Mom's station wagon had returned.

The whole place looked black and still; no light shone in any of the windows.

Where's Aunt Peg? Will wondered. The house appeared empty. *Did she get tired of waiting and go home? No, she wouldn't have walked all the way into town.*

Might she have gone off into the woods looking for Will? Probably not. More likely someone had come from town to pick her up. Something told Will that wasn't right, either.

Suddenly alarmed, he ran ahead of Eric, charged across the porch, and threw open the kitchen door. "Aunt Peg," he shouted. The door banged shut, startling him, but there was no answer.

He listened. Far off in the night he could hear the high-pitched chirping of crickets; they squeaked like oil-starved machinery.

The faint musical tinkling of Sheila's ceramic wind chimes sounded from the deck behind the house. That was all.

Eric came up behind Will. "What's the matter?"

Will had told Eric a little about his parents' fight, but hadn't said anything about Aunt Peg. He quickly explained.

"Let's look for her," Eric said.

Will swallowed hard and began to move slowly across the kitchen floor. He felt creepy; the house seemed strange. Everything was too quiet, too deserted. Staying very close to each other, they explored the first floor.

Aunt Peg wasn't around, not in the kitchen, the dining room, or the living room. They didn't check the basement, thinking if she was anywhere at all it would be upstairs.

She could be napping.

Eric and Will stood in the front hall a moment, looking up the stairway. The door at the top was closed. Waiting there, motionless, both of them felt something chilly, like a draft, or a passing column of frigid air. They looked at each other, but neither spoke.

To Will, the whole place had an odd feel to it, as if the air were cold and damp. It *wasn't* cold and damp, though. It was hot!

Did the chill come from nervousness?

Whatever the explanation, Will didn't want to go up those stairs. "Aunt Peg," he called from the bottom. "Aunt Peg, you up there?"

He heard a giggling sound, shrill, unnerving. Eric heard it, too; Will saw his eyes widen as his pupils darted back and forth. Beads of sweat ballooned on Eric's forehead.

"Stay here, Will," Eric said. He put his hand, fingers spread, on Will's chest and gently pushed him back.

Will watched him take the first step, very slowly. The board groaned under his weight. Eric looked totally alone. It made Will think of some guy in a cowboy picture, mounting the gallows.

"Don't go up there, Eric," he said.

"Ssshh … It's okay, Will."

When Eric had slowly progressed about halfway up the stairs, Will heard the giggle again. Then soft footfalls pounded across the upper hall, invisible behind the closed door.

Will mentally followed the running feet until they were above the kitchen. He stepped out of the foyer and looked into the kitchen. Something skidded across the rough roofing material on the porch.

Will took another step toward the kitchen. Outside, beyond the screen door, his eye caught movement: a falling shadow, nearly invisible against the unbroken darkness of the yard. It plunged from above the porch roof, briefly catching light from the kitchen, then it vanished totally into the night.

It was solid; he heard it thud when it struck the earth; he heard its feet slap the ground as it ran toward the forest.

"Eric," he shouted, "it's getting away. Eric, it's out here!"

Will darted back into the hall. Eric was surely on the second floor by now; the door at the top of the stairs was open, swinging a bit. The light in the upstairs hall was on; it cast the door's moving shadow across the patterned wallpaper like the night's edge sweeping across the land.

He could feel that strange cold air blowing down at him.

For a moment, Will was torn between his curiosity about the thing in the yard, and the security of being next to Eric. He ran up the stairs, quickly looking right and left in the upstairs hall.

Eric stood in the doorway of the bathroom, his back to Will. From inside the little room, Will could hear the giggling again. This time it sounded different, almost familiar.

He walked slowly up to Eric, trying to move noiselessly on the carpet that ran down the middle of the hall. He was shivering—from the chill? From fear? He didn't know. His teeth chattered.

Almost as a reflex, Will clutched Eric's arm as he peeked around him. Eric didn't jump; he must have heard Will coming.

The bathroom was dark. A small amount of light poured in from the hall, obscured by Eric's shadow, and Will's.

Still, it was more than enough light to see everything in the seven-by-nine-foot bathroom.

At the far end, beneath the single blackened window, wedged between the toilet and the wall, a tiny figure crouched. It twitched and giggled. It sounded like it was crazy. Then it coughed, wetly. Will heard liquid slosh onto the floor.

Eric took a step to the side, as if trying to cut off Will's view of the thing.

Will's hand automatically went to the light switch; he flicked it on.

There could be no doubt about what Will saw. The harsh bathroom light burned it permanently into his mind. The squatting, giggling, twitching creature was Mrs. Menard — Aunt Peg. She was naked, her back against the wall, her short white legs stretching into the room. She was looking up at them, her eyes glazed, her mouth slack and lifeless. Her wiry body was streaked with rusty-colored smears of blood. Her pancake-flat breasts, and the folds of her old flesh, were slashed savagely. Six, seven, red gaping wounds split her frail torso. Each incision looked about four inches long; each was a deep black trench with red meaty skin folding away from the center. Each wound was like a horrible toothless mouth, and like mouths, they were moving, contorting. One, on the left side of her stomach, twisted grotesquely; bubbles of blood hissed and popped from its interior.

Another, above her right breast, began to pucker. Yellowish fluid dribbled from it as it stretched flat again. Then, from the fleshy lips of that wound, the sound of giggling ...

Now all the slashes were moving, contorting, emitting a chorus of faint but nerve-searing giggles that backed Eric and Will into the hall.

One of the wounds spoke, awkwardly forming words with the savaged flesh. "This time we'll have your soul, Eric ..."

Another mouth spoke from her gaping side, "... and the body of young Crockett ..."

"The truce is passed, Eric ..."

"Eric ... Eric ... Eric ..." the horrible mouths echoed.

The giggles came again, from every mouth, like a choir of mindless demons.

The last thing Will remembered was Eric lunging at the bathroom door and pulling it shut. The slam echoed like a shot in the empty house.

Will vomited with great violence and pain; his nerves and muscles clutched like a fist. Pulled helplessly into a tight ball, he collapsed to the floor.

When Will woke, he was in his own bed. Eric must have picked him up and carried him into his room. He saw Eric sitting in the chair beside him. The redheaded man looked pale and tired in the misty-white light of dawn.

Their eyes met. "Will, how're you doing?" Eric tried to smile, but it didn't work.

Will blinked at him. "I'm all right, I think ..." He grimaced as the memories flooded back.

Reaching over, Eric put his hand on Will's arm. "I guess you know by now that I didn't tell you and your parents the complete story. I didn't know how much of it they'd believe, and I was afraid of losing their trust. You know the truth now, I think. You know what we're up against. It may sound fatuous, Will, but

226

what we're fighting isn't human. It's something ... supernatural."

Will shuddered; he felt the sting of reality in that word. Supernatural. There was no doubt what Eric had said was true.

"Your father's downstairs, Will. He came home sometime during the night. He's asleep on the couch."

"And Mom ..."

Eric shook his head. "Dan's alone. But we've got to tell him what's going on. You've got to help me make him believe."

Will's head fell back on the pillow, and he groaned. "Can't we just go away?" He felt his voice crack. He was afraid he'd start crying.

Eric closed his eyes and tightened his grip on Will's arm. "Yes, you can go away, Will. So can Dan and your mom. But I can't, not this time. My brother's out there with them. If I don't stand up to them, if I don't try to stop them, then ... well, you saw what happened to Mrs. Menard. You heard what they threatened to do to me. And to you ..."

Will looked at his clock. It was almost six-thirty. He tried closing his eyes, but the vivid image of Aunt Peg's slashed skin, the moving wounds, the remembered echo of those giggling voices, forced them open again.

"Dan'll never believe it." he said.

———————

When they went downstairs, Dan was asleep on the futon couch. He looked terrible. His face was shadowy with whiskers, his clothes streaked and sweat-stained. On the floor beside him, an ashtray overflowed with cigarette butts, and a nearly empty bottle of vodka lay on its side.

It was impossible to tell what time he had come in.

"Should I wake him up?" Will asked.

Eric nodded.

Will took a couple of steps toward the couch. "Dan? Dan?" he said.

Dan's head moved a little, and his eyes slid open a crack. He moaned; it sounded like he was in pain.

As Will watched, Dan's eyes opened all the way. "Will." he said. His voice was dry and distant.

Dan raised his hands, took Will by the arms and pulled him to his knees beside the couch. He hugged Will tightly. "She's gone, Will. Your mother's gone. She's left me … us. I can't find her anywhere. God, I'm so sorry, Will."

Will hugged him back as best he could, but it wasn't easy. It's not that he was angry with Dan; but he was scared, and he wanted Dan to know why.

"She'll be back, Dan," Will said. "Mom wouldn't just leave. She'll be back."

"Oh God," Dan said. He almost yelled it, pushing Will away and swinging up into a sitting position at the same time.

Then he saw Eric.

"Nolan! Christ. What's going on here?"

"We've got some more talking to do, Mr. Wilder. Why don't you take a shower, see if you can get the cobwebs out while I fix you some coffee. I think we've got a long day ahead of us."

"My wife? Do you know what happened to my wife?"

"If she's taken off, that's probably the safest thing for her, Mr. Wilder. You and Will might want to leave, too, when you learn what's going on. But for now, just be grateful that Mrs. Crockett is far away and safe."

Dan's eyes moved from one to the other of them. He looked trapped and uncertain, like a small child, helpless and afraid. When he stood up, Will stepped forward and gave him a hug. This time he did it right; it felt great. "Mom's okay, Dan. She'll be back when she cools off. She'll understand, don't worry."

CHAPTER 25

A WALL OF SAND

"So what you're saying, Nolan, is that this colony of 'religious fanatics' you told me about is actually a coven of lost children?"

Dan knew he sounded patronizing, but he didn't care. He peered at Nolan over the top of his glasses and fingered the coffee cup in front of him. It clattered on the saucer. "Is that what you're saying, Nolan? Is that what you expect me to believe?"

Eric nodded.

"And that they work magic … ?"

Eric nodded again. He held Dan's gaze with no apparent difficulty.

"And that some of them are hundreds, maybe thousands of years old? Christ, Nolan, no wonder they locked you up."

Will jumped to his feet. "It's true, Dan, honest it is." The boy was bleary-eyed, red-faced.

Dan looked at Will and tried to sound patient. "He's been filling your head full of fairy tales, Will. It's all bullshit. It's crazy."

Nolan didn't get angry as Dan expected. The word "crazy" didn't antagonize him at all. Instead, he reached out and poured Dan some more coffee.

"You're being very rational, Mr. Wilder. Unfortunately, our rational thinking is the strongest shield they have. It obscures them like camouflage, protects them like armor ..."

Dan bit his lip, trying to look impassive.

Nolan continued. "Like it or not, the facts are these: A group of little people, sometimes referred to as 'the Gentry,' is living in the wilderness of Pinnacle Mountain. They were here long before the region was settled by Europeans. In fact, they've been part of Indian folklore for thousands of years."

Nolan took a breath.

"More facts: My brother Brian was captured by them in 1953 and is now one of their number. They work magic, which is probably some form of psychic manipulation of natural objects. They require a specific number of individuals—I believe exactly eight, surely no more than nine—to operate at their fullest power. They are amoral; they are pranksters, dirty tricksters, and humans are at their mercy whenever they choose to toy with us—"

Dan slapped the tabletop. "It's lunacy!"

"It's fact, Wilder," Eric spoke sternly, with no loss of confidence. "Oh, I'd love to encourage you to toss it all off as lunacy so you can protect your self-serving concept of reality. Believe me, four years ago I went through exactly the same thing. But we can't toss it off, because of one small *additional* fact: they've targeted me, and, more important, they've targeted your stepson, Will."

Dan felt his eyes grow wide. Suddenly his mouth was dry. He felt hot. He wanted a cigarette, but thought better of it.

"You know what that means, Wilder? It means you, and Sheila, and everyone connected with this house—everyone who might stand in their way—are in terrible, unimaginable danger. Believe it, Wilder; believe it or be damned."

Glaring at Dan, Eric's blue eyes burned with conviction. He was too steady, too controlled; there was no way his words could be mistaken for lunacy.

Dan studied the two pairs of eyes that studied him: Eric's stern and insistent; Will's hopeful, yet afraid.

He felt himself begin to wither. Christ, was he starting to believe this crap? If, even for a moment, he could entertain such wild ideas, wouldn't he be surrendering something of himself? Losing some power within the situation? Forfeiting a fragment of his control and his sanity?

He fought the part of him that struggled to believe. "Why, Nolan? Why should I accept any of this? How can you *know*? How can you possibly be so sure?"

"I have lots of reasons. You can go ahead and systematically dismiss all of them as my 'lunacy' if you want. All, that is, but this one: Last night, while you were out searching for your wife and anesthetizing your wounded ego with alcohol, William and I had dealings with the Gentry. At least one of them was here, Wilder, right here in your house. They left a message for us—a warning, if you will."

"And ... ?"

"Come with me."

Dan, his interest piqued by the offer of tangible proof, followed Eric and Will upstairs to the bathroom. They showed him Aunt Peg's body. She was completely at rest now, her eyes dosed, the wounds no longer twitching. She was silent. She was dead.

Dan looked at the corpse with the detached involvement of a seasoned reporter at an especially grisly accident scene. He knelt beside the body.

Pointing at the various wounds, Eric explained what had happened.

Will swore it was true and tried to describe the horror he had personally witnessed. Dan could see the recollection was painful for the boy.

He wanted to believe the mangled atrocity—the murdered thing that had been Mrs. Menard—was Nolan's work. He knew better, though. *No man could do this. Whatever Nolan is,* Dan thought, *he's not a homicidal maniac.* More and more Dan was willing to believe it was the situation that was crazy, not Eric Nolan.

"You saw these wounds moving, Will? They actually moved?"

"Dan, I wouldn't lie, honest ..."

As a newspaperman, Dan had interviewed many different witnesses to many different, sometimes bizarre events. Through years of experience he'd developed an internal lie detector, a reasonably reliable sense of who was fantasizing and who was telling the truth.

More important, he knew his stepson.

Will was telling the truth. The boy actually believed everything he was saying.

Perhaps it was because he was exhausted, perhaps because his resistance was breaking down like a wall of sand. And, yes, perhaps he would be surrendering forever a fragment of his own sanity, but, whatever the reason, Dan's words tumbled out freely, "Okay, Nolan, what do you suggest we do about this?"

Chief Bates felt his voice rising along with his temper. "Christ, I *know* his throat was slit with a sharp instrument. I don't need you police academy boys to tell me that." He sniffed loudly and tried to calm down.

232

His town was coming apart at the seams, and all those state boys were scurrying around like ants, trying to stitch things together again.

When he spoke, it was almost a whisper. "That all you got for me, corporal? No new witnesses? No prints in the vehicle? No possessions belongin' to nobody but the boys themselves?"

He listened to the faggy-sounding voice on the other end of the telephone and tried to picture the young man he was talking to. *Christ, the stateys are hiring anybody these days. First it was females, now fags. What's it gonna be next?* Bates wondered. *Midgets? Vermont's getting almost as bad as California!* Bates thanked the Good Lord he'd be retiring in another year or two.

"Mmmm-hmmm … mmm-hmmm …" Bates mumbled, hardly listening. The death scene photos of Archibald M. Shattuck, a.k.a. Spit, were spread out like a bloody rainbow on his desktop.

Shot after shot of the gaping full-color wound told him the kid was dead, little more.

No hints in the pictures. No hints from the lab. And nothing from the boy's friends. Only two suspects really: Reginald Benson the third—a.k.a. Reggie—still missing …

… and Nolan.

"So what you got for me on Nolan?"

"Reported seen in Saratoga Springs, New York," the trooper lisped. Bates could hear him shuffling papers. "And again in Troy, Mass… ."

"Christ, I hope they're not cloning him …"

"What's that, Chief?"

"Nothing. Forget it. Keep me posted, will ya."

The fag hung up without confirming.

Bates let out a long sigh; he knew he was in a shitty mood. First he'd been simply impatient, now he was getting testy and intolerant. He'd try to be nicer to the kid if they ever talked again.

But he hoped they wouldn't; the mincing, officious tones rubbed him the wrong way.

Flipping through the gruesome array of death photos, he grappled around in his bottom drawer, hoping to find that bag of M&M's he'd stashed so quickly when the town manager stormed in this morning.

Ahh got it!

Yessir, thought the chief, *if Nolan's in Saratoga Springs or Massachusetts, so much the better.*

But, until there was a positive ID, he couldn't be absolutely sure Nolan was out of town, not with one boy dead and another missing.

Apparently two of the last people to see Benson and Shattuck were Mona Grant and young William Crockett.

I'll have to go up there again, Bates thought. *Maybe Mona and her father'll be home this time.*

And what about Wilder? Funny thing. Dan and his family hadn't been to church this morning. What's more, Dan never brought the boy around yesterday, like he said he would.

Could something be wrong up there? The question rose unbidden from that part of his thought processes the chief referred to as his "gut-sense." It was a question posed by his intuition, and such questions were usually answered in the affirmative.

After talking with the Grants, Bates decided, he'd take a little spin the rest of the way up Tenny's Hill. He'd have a talk with young William.

Bates dumped the three remaining M&Ms into his sweaty palm, shook them a few times and popped them into his mouth like a handful of Valium. Then he licked the yellow and red stains off his fingers.

Dan and Eric wrapped Aunt Peg's body in a plastic shower curtain and carried it to the basement. Will guessed they put it in the freezer, but he didn't ask; he didn't want to know.

He was glad Dan had believed their story. Still, he worried. Had Dan accepted things just a little too easily? Possibly he'd accepted nothing at all; he could simply be playing along, waiting to see what would happen. Will couldn't tell for sure.

When the men came back upstairs, they took turns at the kitchen sink, washing up thoroughly.

After drying his hands and face, Dan excused himself to phone some of Sheila's friends in Boston. "We had a little argument," Will heard him say. "She left in a huff, and I'm worried about her. If you hear from her, tell her I called, see if you can get her to call me."

Eric joined Will at the kitchen table. At first he made no attempt to talk; he was listening to Dan's conversations. The more Eric listened, the more worried he looked.

"You think he's gonna call the police?" Will asked.

"No, not really, not if he says he won't."

"Maybe he should. I mean, don't you think they can help us?"

"They could, if they believed us. But imagine Dan trying to explain everything to Chief Bates. No, I'm afraid this is our fight, Will."

Fight! Will dreaded the idea. "Why don't we just pick up and leave, get the heck away from the house?"

Eric shook his head. "You could do that, but Dan's real worried about your mother. What if she comes back to an empty house? Or worse yet, to a house full of ..."

Will didn't want to think about it. He tuned Eric's voice out, focusing on Dan. Now he was checking with the hospital in Springfield.

"... so you'll inform me at once if she is admitted? Fine. Thanks very much."

Will got up from the table and walked over to the screen door. Outside, everything seemed perfectly safe. In the bright daylight, the house, the garage, the surrounding fields and forests, all looked pretty normal.

Dan hung up the phone and walked back to the table.

Will listened to the men talking.

"What I propose is this," Eric said. "The best way I can convince you of any of this is to take you into the woods. I can show you their camp. Maybe we'll even see some of them. If that doesn't convince you, Mr. Wilder, you'll be the one who's fantasizing."

Dan thought about it. "You mean a scouting expedition?"

"Just exactly. You should know what we're up against before we—"

"Before we what? Attack them?"

"Before we make any decisions. I think we're all too tired to go up into those mountains today. I suggest we spend what's left of today resting and planning for tomorrow ..."

"Okay." Dan gave a stiff nod of his head. "That'll give Sheila a chance to come back, too."

"Yes, yes of course," Nolan agreed, but somehow he looked more worried than ever.

CHAPTER 26
ONLY A GAME

"Dan," said Eric Nolan, "let me talk to you a minute before Will comes downstairs."

Dan walked to the refrigerator and took a bag of coffee from the freezer. "Yeah, sure," he said. He began scooping tiny brown beans into the coffee grinder.

"Better not," said Eric. "That thing'll wake Will up for sure."

Dan smiled weakly. "Right." Instead he put some water on to boil. Making tea would be a lot quieter than grinding coffee.

Such mistakes were easy to make when he was so fuzzy-headed. He hoped caffeine, regardless of its source, would help clear his mind.

After poking around in the cabinets looking for tea bags, then finding them, he took a seat at the table, across from Nolan.

"Dan, I'm worried about your wife," Nolan began.

"You are? How do you think I feel?" said Dan. "I couldn't nap at all; I just kept going through the fight, over and over in my mind. She's got every right to be angry with me—what I did was inexcusable—but to take off and leave her son—"

"Exactly." Nolan locked his fingers together, resting his hands on the table. "Dan, you and I have very different points of view about what's going on here. For the most part, I know what we're up against, but my first job is to convince you. Until you're convinced, I'm afraid what I'm about to suggest may sound like more lunacy."

"Go ahead, Nolan. I've come this far, you might as well take me the rest of the way." He tried to force a smile.

"If your wife has actually left you—" Nolan began, but he was interrupted by the sound of footsteps on the stairs.

"I don't want the boy to hear this ..." he whispered as he stood up, walked to the stove, and turned off the burner under the tea kettle.

That accomplished, he turned on the coffee grinder.

———————

Will had napped fitfully. Mostly he'd tossed and turned, fighting to keep horrible images out of his head. He pictured his body as a piece of meat turning on a rotisserie; over and over it rolled, as he tried to discover a comfortable position. When his alarm finally went off, it sounded like a school bell announcing a test he was bound to flunk.

He sat up and dragged himself out of bed. After dressing quickly, he headed downstairs.

Eric and Dan were already in the kitchen. The air was rich with the smell of freshly ground coffee.

"Do you have any guns, Dan?" Eric asked as he poured steaming liquid into three ceramic mugs.

"Guns? No, we don't keep them. I, ah, I *didn't* believe in them."

"That's a problem," said Eric. He closed his mouth into a tight, lipless line. "I think we should bring weapons with us. There's a good chance we're going to need them ..."

"Why? I mean, if this is just a scouting expedition ...?"

"That's right, Dan. But if we run into the Gentry, we don't want to be unarmed, I promise you."

"I know where there are some guns," Will said, joining the men at the table. "All sorts of them. At Mona's house. They were her father's."

Dan moaned softly, "Christ, I can't go back down there. Not after—"

"Never mind," said Eric. "I'll get them. Will and I can go."

Dan looked over the top of his steaming coffee mug. "So, now that you've half-convinced me, Nolan, you can't expect me to stay here alone."

Eric smiled and patted Dan on the shoulder. "Right. Of course not. We'll all go; it's best if we stay together. Let's take the car."

After a quick supper, washed down with several cups of coffee, they prepared for the next part of the evening.

"If you've got hunting knives, or even sturdy kitchen knives, we'd better take them," said Eric. "Grab anything else we can use as weapons: hatchets, hammers, whatever you've got."

"What are we going to do?" Will asked.

"For now, just go down to Mona's trailer."

"Pretty heavily armed for a five-minute trip." Dan said.

"Better to bring them with us than wish we had them. But to tell you the truth, knives, guns even … I don't know what good they'll do."

"That sounds real encouraging," Dan said.

By the time they were ready to go, it was after six o'clock. The strong, keen light of day had passed. Shadows fell long and black across the yard.

The plan was simple. They'd go to the trailer, pick up the guns—and possibly Mona, if she was there—then return to the house and barricade themselves in for the night.

"Tomorrow," Eric said, "we'll get up early and go into the hills. We'll need a full day."

Dan armed himself with a linoleum cutter; Will had an ice pick; Eric took a butcher knife with a ten-inch blade.

239

"You got the car keys?" Eric asked.

Dan patted his pocket and nodded his head.

Will felt his heart beating rapidly. Cool beads of sweat rolled down his sides like tiny snowballs. He swallowed, trying to get some spit into his dry mouth.

Eric paused, looked at them as if to say, "Well, here goes," and he opened the kitchen door.

Mona's father was standing in the yard.

He was about thirty feet in front of the porch, standing between them and the Renault. His posture was strange; all his weight seemed to be on one foot. He was swaying unsteadily, as if trying to keep his balance.

Seeing him knocked the wind out of Will. He staggered backward, and Dan caught him.

Mr. Grant's face was deadly pale and coarse, as if his skin were molded from white sand. His eyeballs were solid black, like stones under water. The front of his body, which was ripped open from neck to pelvis the last time Will had seen it, was now covered with dirt. It looked as if the huge wound had been packed with mud. Some of it flaked off in crusty chunks as he swayed back and forth.

The dark cavity of his mouth seemed to widen and contract, not as if to form words, but words came anyway. "Stay away from my daughter, Wilder. Where's your morality? You're nothing but a child-fucker ..."

The voice wasn't human. It filled Will with dread. Somehow, he knew the words came through Mr. Grant, but not from him.

Seeing him there, watching his lips open and close like the mouth of a fish, hearing the strange hollow voice, was enough to hold all three of them in place.

When the slow grind of words finally stopped, Mr. Grant's body seemed to tremble. One leg jerked forward, and he took an uneasy, lurching step. He tottered, took a moment to regain his balance, then moved his other leg.

He was stumbling toward them!

"Stay away from my daughter ..." Now the words came from a motionless mouth. Faint laughter echoed, its source impossible to determine.

Eric jarred himself from his trance. He pushed Dan and Will back into the kitchen. The screen door banged closed. He slammed the wooden inner door, then bolted it.

"He ... he's dead," Will's voice was weak. "I kn-know he's dead ..."

He looked at Dan, who seemed paralyzed. All the expression, all the color had drained from his face. Seeing Mr. Grant must have convinced him. Now, even for Dan, there could be no doubt.

Will shifted his eyes to Eric.

"Yeah, he's dead, Will. They're just trying to scare us. They know what we're up to; they've been listening, either through the ears of that poor woman downstairs, or they've been hiding outside all along."

"Dead? How can he be dead?" Dan's voice was thin as a breeze.

"They're moving him somehow, manipulating his body with their minds. They have telepathy, Dan, telekinesis it's called. They're animating him like a puppet—their minds are the strings."

The voice from outside turned into a madman's wail. Will heard a thrashing sound, as if Mr. Grant's unstable body had tumbled onto the porch. The sound of lurching movement continued. Will couldn't tell if Mr. Grant was trying to stand up, or if he was just flopping around on the wooden floorboards.

Will didn't dare look; it would be too horrible.

"Nolan … your brother's with us, Nolan … Wanna see him again, Nolan?" Something was slapping the porch floor, maybe its hand, maybe …

Will looked at Eric, feeling confused, nearly mindless with terror. Eric held his finger to his mouth. "Sssshhh."

"Wilder … you been eatin' off your boy's plate, Wilder. What kinda man's that make you?" Now the voice was frail and raspy, like wind through dry leaves.

The three of them stood transfixed in the kitchen, not knowing what to do. Dan was shaking his head from side to side.

The first crash shook the whole wall. Mr. Grant was pounding against the outside of the door. It sounded like he was kicking, slapping, even bashing it with his head.

"Wilder …" The voice made Will tremble, nearly convulse. "Wilder … you stay away from my little girl …" The thing pounded heavily on the door. Will heard him tearing away the screen and its wooden frame. "You want her back now, Willy-boy? You want her now? Now, that we've all had her? Whyn't you let me in, Willy? Whyn't you let me in the way she done … ?"

The pounding stopped. Still they could hear him out there, heavy footfalls, stumbling around on the porch.

"Christ! Christ," said Dan, "what the hell's going on?"

"It's a game," said Eric. "They're just playing with us."

Eric looked around quickly, searching for something. Then he hurried into the living room where he snatched up a cast-iron poker from the fireplace. After trying the hard metal against his palm, he came back and stood by the wooden door. Carefully, he took the bolt in one hand, with the other he raised the poker.

"Stand back," he commanded.

Eric threw open the door.

Mr. Grant stood there, almost face to face with Eric. He seemed massive, solid as a house, but he reeled like a drunk about to collapse.

He roared, baring black teeth. Chunks of dirt dribbled from his mouth. He raised both his hands like claws.

Will was terrified, remembering what Mr. Grant had done to those three boys in town, imagining what he might do now.

A fierce, stinking wind seemed to come from him, blowing into the kitchen. It felt cold and smelled bad enough to turn Will's stomach.

Grant took a clumsy step across the threshold, teetered a bit and fell back against the doorframe.

Eric stepped into position, the poker raised like a battle ax. He brought it down into the "V" formed by Mr. Grant's neck and shoulder. It went "*thwup,*" as if Eric had struck a sofa pillow.

Mr. Grant showed no pain from the heavy blow. He just stood there, braced against the doorframe. His wide black eyes looked completely inhuman.

Eric brought the poker down again and again; its hooked, pointed edge tore Mr. Grant's filthy shirt, then ripped at his flesh.

Eric might have been slashing a sandbag. First, the horrible hollow sound, "*thwup,*" then the tearing, splitting flesh. It was as if Mr. Grant were made of dirt. Every slash with the poker opened a new rip; black dirt tumbled out. There was no blood, no muscle or bone. Dirt streamed from Mr. Grant's body, poured in wet muddy tides down his pant legs and piled up at his feet.

His face collapsed like a Halloween mask, his arms wrinkled and withered, his torso flattened like a balloon losing air.

As the Mr. Grant-thing slid down the doorframe, Eric continued to smash it with the poker. He kicked it with his heavy shoes.

Dirt sprayed in fan-shaped eruptions. Soon nothing was left where Mr. Grant had stood but shredded clothing, a smeared pile of black earth, and an ugly, empty rug of flesh.

It all happened in frightening silence. There was no cry of pain, no flailing arms, no real fight or protest. After Eric's first blow had fallen, the animated corpse lost its purpose. It simply stood there, willingly accepting the punishment, frightening Will and his stepfather to near immobility, tiring them out.

Eric looked up. Sweat glistened on his face; his chest heaved as he tried to catch his breath. "We'd better get those guns," he said.

CHAPTER 27
ESCAPE

As they drove toward Grant's place, everything was dark and tensely quiet. No one attempted conversation.

Dan's car slowed, then bounded over the turnoff to the trailer's rutted driveway. Right away Will could see bright lights blasting from the windows of every room, casting the yard and surrounding trees in an eerie white half-light.

The trailer itself, tucked into a little clearing in the pines, was a confusion of bright lights and dark shadows. It made Will think of some alien spacecraft that had landed in the middle of the forest. As Dan's Renault bounced closer, Will guessed they were all in suspense. Surely the experience was identical to what they'd feel if actually approaching a UFO. He squeezed the handle of the ice pick; his hand was moist with sweat.

Mr. Grant's pickup was still in the yard, just where Will had last seen it. An icy tremor slithered along his spine when he noticed the dirt around the septic tank; it was partially dug up again.

Eric and Will got out of the Renault. The evening air was so hot it nearly took Will's breath away. Dan waited behind the wheel, the engine and air conditioner humming in unison.

They didn't talk at all as Will led Eric across the yard and up the rickety steps to the door. Will paused midway up the steps and glanced inside through the filmy window. There was no sign of Mona.

As Will knocked at the door, his stomach muscles clenched like a fist.

Mona didn't answer.

After waiting a minute, Eric shook his head. He tried the door; it opened easily.

"Mona," Will called timidly as he stepped inside.

Right away he noticed how hot it was in there. Worse than outside. Almost suffocating. All the windows were closed; no fans or air conditioners were running. What sun had penetrated the trailer's umbrella of trees had heated the place up like an oven.

"Christ," said Eric, "what stinks in here?"

A sickly sweet scent hung heavily in the air. Perhaps it was some kind of cheap perfume or room deodorizer. Will fought his impulse to gag. Between the heat and the foul aroma, he was afraid his puking muscles were about to get another workout.

"Mona," he said, and started coughing before he could get another word out. He had to step back onto the porch and breathe some fresh air.

"What's the matter?" Dan called from the car.

"She's not here," Will yelled to him.

Dan got out of the Renault and made his way up to the porch and the safety of his companions.

In spite of the stench, Eric moved around inside, opening windows, pacing from room to room. Dan and Will walked in as Eric closed the bathroom door. "I don't know where she is, he said, "but she's not in the trailer."

"You checked all around?" Will asked.

"There's not that many places to check."

So where was Mona? Will hoped she had gone into town, or off to visit some friend or relative. Yet he knew better; a persistent instinct told him something bad had happened to her.

Could she have run off? He shuddered, thinking of the vastness of the woods surrounding the trailer.

"Why would she keep it so goddamn hot in here?" Dan asked.

Eric shrugged. "Maybe she was trying to keep warm."

Dan forced a smile but quickly saw Eric wasn't joking.

"Where do you think she is, Eric?" Will asked.

"I'm afraid they've taken her. Apparently they've been using her, just like they've been using her father."

"You mean you think she's ... dead?" Dan's doubtful expression was underscored with a private revulsion.

"No. Probably not dead. A corpse wouldn't last in this heat." Eric turned on the exhaust fan above the pan-crowded stove. "If she was trying to keep warm in the middle of August, that means the Gentry were nearby. People feel cold when the Gentry are around."

Dan blinked at him.

"Come on you guys," Will said. "Let's get out of here before I get sick ..."

Mr. Grant's guns were still standing in the corner by the couch. Eric took three of them, three rifles. He poked around looking for pistols but couldn't find any. After locating several boxes of shells and two hunting knives in leather sheaths, he handed two of the rifles to Dan and the ammunition to Will.

"Anything else we need here?" he asked.

"What about Mona ... ?" Will said.

Eric smiled at him. It was that kind, sad smile that had made Will trust him right from the start. "I don't know, Will. I hope she's safe. If not, let's hope we find her tomorrow." He looked at Dan. "None of this is her fault. With the kind of forces we're up against here ... well, a kid her age, all alone ... Christ, she wouldn't stand a chance. They could get anything they want from her, make her do anything ..."

Dan didn't answer; he looked away and ducked back outside. Eric and Will followed.

———————

By eight o'clock they had barricaded themselves in the house. Dan was visibly upset, growing more agitated by the minute. He was on the phone, making a series of frantic calls about Sheila. He phoned her friends again, sounding embarrassed and apologetic. He tried her agent in New York, even tried her editor from Allen House.

Will had to work hard to share Dan's panicky optimism. Could Mom and Mona have taken off someplace together? That seemed like a possibility. Will knew his mother had become very fond of Mona, felt sorry for her. At least that was the case until that thing happened with Dan ...

As Will mentally imposed happy endings on his fantasy scenario, he realized how unrealistic he was being. If Mom had actually run away, she would have cooled off and come back by now. Even if she'd wanted to run out on Dan, she'd never run out on Will. She was his mother; it was that simple. Will knew. Maybe they all did. Probably no one dared to articulate what he actually feared. Would Will dare speak the unspeakable? Could he voice the suspicion Dan was so obviously denying?

"Come here, Will. I want to show you how to use these." Eric was laying out the guns and boxes of ammunition on the kitchen table. Among them, Will saw a crudely drawn map of Pinnacle Mountain.

A spark ignited in Will's mind then. This was for real; it wasn't going to be a scouting expedition. They were actually entering an honest to God life-and-death situation.

He understood all the reasons they couldn't ask for help. He knew what was at risk if they called the police. But he was afraid. More afraid than he'd ever been.

The thought of setting out through the woods tomorrow morning seemed to turn his bones to jelly.

Eric caught Dan between phone calls. "Dan, why don't you get off the phone for a while, give her a chance to call here?"

"You're right. I've just about run out of places to try. Except the police ..."

"Take a break, Dan. I don't want to put off showing you and Will about these weapons. We may need them before morning, you know."

Dan joined them at the table.

———

Someone was shaking Will awake.

As his eyes fluttered open, he felt a hand over his mouth, pressing tightly. Coarse fingers squeezed his lips together, forcing his head into the pillow.

In the dim light of his bedroom he saw Dan staring down at him, his face less than a foot away. Will smelled the vague odor of alcohol.

Dan kept his hand tightly over Will's mouth and wouldn't let him speak. "It's okay, Will. Just stay quiet. Stay very still." He leaned closer, whispering directly into Will's ear. The vibration of Dan's lips tickled.

"Will, we're getting out of here. You and me—"

Will wanted to say something, but Dan was pinching his lips closed.

"This is crazy, Will. Everything about it's crazy. I should never have listened to him. I should have—"

Will shook his head vigorously from side to side and tried to use his eyes to tell Dan he was wrong.

It was no use.

"He's asleep. We're going to leave him here. We've gotta get the hell away from him, Will. I've got to take care of you. This is Nolan's battle, not ours."

Very carefully, Dan loosened his hand. He left it hovering about a quarter inch above Will's lips so he could clamp it down again if the boy spoke too loudly.

Dan's eyes were full of fright.

"No, Dan," Will whispered. "We can't leave Eric. Didn't you see Mr. Grant's body? Didn't you? What's gonna happen to him here all alone?"

Dan covered Will's lips again. His hand was moist and stunk of cigarette smoke. "You do what I tell you, Will. I may not be your dad, but by God you'll mind me. Now get up. We're getting out of here. Now!"

What could he do? He thought of yelling for Eric, but what would that accomplish? He could go limp and refuse to budge.

Although it was against his better judgment, he obeyed. He did it because Dan was his stepfather. And, the moment he acquiesced, the whole situation was out of his hands. Will's only hope was for Eric to wake up and stop them.

Dan pulled him out of bed. Will sullenly followed his stepfather down the stairs. He could see Eric's shadowy form stretched out on the futon by the far wall. He seemed to be fast asleep. Dan and Will crossed the room and made it through the kitchen door. Eric didn't even stir.

As they left the porch, Mr. Grant's clothes and flattened body were like a Halloween dummy leaning against the railing.

Crossing the dark yard to the Renault, Will decided to give it one more try. "Wait, Dan, wait," he said. "We can't just leave Eric here. What if—"

"We've got to, Will. You know he won't come with us."

"I know, I know. But we can't just *leave* him."

"He'll be all right. I'm going to tell Dick Bates what's going on. He'll come back up here and take care of Nolan. Now, get in the car, Will." He gave Will a shove that seemed a little too hard. Dan breathed rapidly, his face glazed with sweat, his eyes wild.

The engine roared when Dan turned the key. He backed up, straightened out, and headed downhill before switching on the headlights.

Will heard a cry. "Wilder, *stop!*"

Turning in his seat, he could see Eric at the kitchen door, waving frantically with his arm. He appeared red, like a devil, in the bright taillights.

Dan shifted forcefully. Tires spat gravel as they sped down the hill.

"Dan," Will pleaded, "we can't *do* this."

Dan's teeth were clenched, while both hands gripped the wheel. The Renault bounced and skidded along the dirt of Tenny's Hill Road.

There was no reasoning with him, he was too full of what he was doing.

Will kept it up anyway, hoping something he said would have some effect. He fixed his eyes on Dan's facial expression; the key was there, somewhere. If only he could find it. "Dan," he tried, "I'm scared, too. We both are, but please Dan, we can't leave him. Please."

"Shut up, Will. Just shut up."

The Renault's headlights slid over the black shadowy shapes of trees, boring a tunnel through the near-solid darkness. In the glow of the instrument panel, Will could see Dan was doing nearly sixty on this twisty dirt road.

They fishtailed around curves as Will clenched the dashboard. "Crazy," Dan was muttering. "It's all crazy. Got to get out of here."

They sped along, engine roaring, wheels grinding, headlights wrestling with the night. The mental picture of Eric alone on the porch made Will feel like a real jerk. A deserter. He closed his eyes, as if that would shut out the uncomfortable self-image.

Tires squealed as Dan hit the brakes.

Will heaved forward, nearly thrown from his seat. Clutching the dash was all that kept him from nose-diving into the windshield. As the car skidded to the right, the rear end almost caught up with the front.

Then Will saw her, nearly bleach-white, directly ahead, vivid in the beam of the headlights.

It was Mona, standing in the middle of the road. A white, loose-fitting dress hung nearly to her knees, its hem blowing slightly in the breeze. Her long legs were spread, her feet, bare. Behind her, nothing but endless black acres of wilderness.

"Oh God," Dan moaned. Both his hands snapped up to cover his face.

Will was about to open the car door to get Mona when he saw something move in the darkness. Behind her, and to the right, a small white form stepped out of the bushes. Another followed. Then one from the left.

A formation of white bodies lined up across the road behind the girl.

"Holy Mother of God," said Dan, "they're kids, they're just little kids!"

And that's what they looked like: five tiny ghostly-white children, standing naked in the road. They stared at the car with eyes as black as the knob on Dan's gearshift.

When Mona took a step forward, Dan slammed the car into reverse. He started backing up. They bounced and bashed over ruts, often sliding too close to the shoulder. But Dan did a good job; he kept them on the road as they backed up the hill. When they reached a little turnoff, Dan turned around. Then he floored it.

Eric was standing in the yard with a rifle in his hand.

"Thank God you're okay," he said as Dan and Will scrambled out of the car.

"They're kids ..." said Dan, his voice high and hollow. "They're just little kids ..."

"Maybe," said Eric. "But you see, whatever they are, they're not going to let us out of here. Not by the road, anyway, and not tonight."

PART FOUR
THE PINNACLE

ECHOES

"I don't know what, but there's something out there. Something terrible. It's as if the night itself is hungry. Waiting. Looking for a chance to devour us."

—Pamela Whitcome, 1983

CHAPTER 28
THE BALANCE OF SUPERNATURE

"They *do* look like children," Eric explained as he led Will and Dan across the deeply grassed meadow toward the foot of Pinnacle Mountain. "And that gives them a certain measure of safety. No one, at least no one in his right mind, would deliberately harm a child. In fact, for us as a species, the natural thing is to protect our children."

Above them, the sky was like an inverted riverbed, full of rolling rounded clouds that looked like gray rocks.

There's something strange about this weather, Eric thought. He hoped the sun would burn through—they could use some sunshine—but from the feel of the air, it was likely to start raining any minute.

"I should have kept going," muttered Dan. "I should've mowed them all down and been done with it."

Eric paused briefly, then turned to look downhill at the other man. "It would have been against your instincts, Dan," he said. "You see kids standing in the road, you stop. Anybody would do the same. It's a natural reaction, but it's one you'll have to overcome."

Eric looked at Will. The boy had fallen far behind. He'd been quiet all morning; he seemed sullen and preoccupied. He'd been almost ignoring his stepfather, and that worried Eric. Any conflict among them could put everyone in danger.

Part of it could be fatigue, Eric reasoned. *Will might be feeling the weight of the weapon he carried, a Mossberg bolt-action, twenty-gauge shotgun.* It's not a rifle—Eric had explained—but it's far more deadly at close range.

"If we can catch them off guard, we'll be lucky," said Dan. "Do you think there's any chance of that?"

Eric shrugged. He didn't want to fake optimism. If the Gentry had been watching them last night, they were no doubt watching now. Squinting, Eric scanned the trees on either side of them.

Will sped up a little. Apparently he wanted to hear what was being said. Eric turned, then continued up the hill with one companion on either side of him. He raised his voice a little when he answered Dan. "I don't think they'll expect any show of aggression from us; they're used to people cowering from their power. They're most dangerous when they're all together, acting in unison."

"… so they can actually team up and combine their mental power?" Dan spoke earnestly, the incredulity gone from his voice.

"That's right. It's called *coning power*. All together, acting as a team, they can focus their psychic energy through the 'lens' of their leader. He directs it, controls it. That's how they're able to make corpses walk. That's how they levitate each other. God knows what else they can do."

"But I thought it was magic." Will said.

"Maybe it is, Will." Eric stopped a minute, looked around to get his bearings, then slightly altered their direction. "Whether the cause is psychic, or whether it's some kind of magic, it doesn't change the effect."

Eric distinctly recalled the first time he had witnessed the Gentry's awesome power. Objects—soup cans, water glasses, potted plants, and even a transistor radio—had flown around his cousin's kitchen with the lethal force of cannonballs. Yet nothing seemed to be moving them. Indeed, it *had* seemed like magic.

"As I told you," he continued, "I've put a lot of time into studying them. The tradition of their rituals seems to date back to ancient Celtic practices of natural magic. The power they have is elemental; somehow, they can influence earth, air, fire, and water …"

"That's just about anything," Will said.

Walking single file again, Eric at the lead, they made their way along giant moss-covered outcroppings, through lush beds of ferns and over thick fallen trees, some of them so thoroughly decomposed that they collapsed under foot as if they were sculpted from mud. The mountainside grew steeper by the second.

After a while, Will paused and looked around. "No stone walls up here," he said. "Guess this land's so steep and rocky even the sheep farmers didn't bother with it."

Tall, wrinkly-barked trees loomed all around as they abandoned the nearly invisible trail to climb a slippery cliff. In his hiking boots, Dan didn't slide as much as Will did in his sneakers. Still, Eric heard the other man breathing hard and saw his face slick with sweat. *Maybe it'll start to rain soon*, Eric hoped; that would cool them off, releasing some of the humidity from the air.

"How many do you think we're up against?" Eric noted the fatigue in Dan's voice. They couldn't have traveled much more than three or four miles; Dan was tiring too quickly.

"Right now? Seven or eight, I'd say. They're down by at least one, we can be sure of that. For them I think nine would be the perfect number. Nine has always been considered mystical. There's a certain magical precision about it. In metaphysics and magic, nine is said to represent fullness, completeness. It's ironic, though. If their group were complete they'd be the most dangerous—but they wouldn't be raising hell like this. They'd be off peacefully doing whatever it is that they do."

He noted the worried expressions on Dan and the boy.

"We have an advantage, though," Eric tried to pep talk them. "We're on the attack, and we're at least somewhat organized. These are two conditions the Gentry won't be prepared for. My theory is their society is so highly structured that any minor confusion will weaken them. When the Gentry aren't the aggressors, when they're not pulling together, then they're vulnerable."

"Do you still think I'm targeted to be the ninth?" Will asked.

"So it would seem, Will."

"But aren't they using Mona?"

"Of course they are, but only as a tool. In their minds, Mona's disposable. You see, women are no good to them. As far as I can determine, their coven is made up entirely of males, don't ask me why."

"Sexists," Will said, trying to be funny. Nobody laughed.

"So, every one of them we take out," said Dan, "weakens the group tremendously …"

"Exactly. But we have to get them all. That's the sticky part. If we don't, they'll start recruiting again. They'll kidnap one human child for each Gentry that we kill. We've got to kill all of them."

Far in the distance, as if from some terrible beast hiding above the thick quilting of clouds, a muffled growl of thunder stopped Eric in his tracks. He looked at the sky. "Rain's coming," he said.

Dan seemed relieved that they'd stopped. He ran his fingers through his hair and flicked them, as if casting off a handful of sweat. He took a couple of weary steps toward a big gray boulder and sat down, his gun resting against a nearby tree.

Clearly, Dan was exhausted. His breathing was far too rapid. Sweat poured from him in visible rivulets.

"This is a good spot to rest awhile," Eric called to Dan.

Will walked right past his stepfather, didn't even look at him, and hurried to catch up with Eric.

"Jeez, Eric," Dan wheezed, "how come you're not getting tired?"

"I've been exercising," called Eric, smiling. "They were big on recreation back at the hospital." Fifty feet beyond Dan, Eric found a log to sit on. "But the truth is, I've been preparing for today for a long time. I've been in training, you know?"

Will sat cross-legged on the grass in front of Eric, leaving Dan alone in the distance. The boy remained quiet for some time. After a while he whispered, not looking Eric in the face. "Eric," he began timidly, "I'm awful sorry about last night …"

"What do you mean, Will?"

"About running away like that. I didn't want to …"

"Don't worry about it, Will. It's not your fault—"

"I know, it was Dan—"

"Look, Will, we really can't blame Dan, either. I think I understand what he went through better than anyone else. You know why? Because I went through it myself. Dan isn't a coward, Will. In fact, I think he's a brave man. If he weren't, he wouldn't be with us now."

"Yeah, sure. But he ran away; he left you all alone …"

"No. Listen, Will. I was exactly like that four years ago, the first time I came face to face with the Gentry. I was ready to run away and hide. I couldn't believe my own eyes and ears. Remember, Dan's a newspaper man; he deals with a reality made up of cold hard facts. Up until now, his reality never included anything even slightly resembling the Gentry.

"Dan wasn't running from the fight, Will. He was trying to escape having to rethink his whole concept of what's real. It's an honest response, I think, in the face of the supernatural. We recoil from it."

Will stared down at the ground.

261

"When Dan saw Mona and the little people standing in the road like that," Eric continued, "well, it just brought him to his senses and told him what he had to do. He's okay now, Will; he's convinced and he's with us."

Will sat silently for a few minutes more, absently plucking handfuls of weeds and tossing them into the scattering breeze.

In a while he got up and walked over to sit with Dan.

––––––

"So when am I gettin' my fuckin' car back," said Norm Gagnon, before Chief Bates was entirely out of the cruiser.

Bates rolled his eyes upward to meet those of the boy. "Now Norman, you know I can't understand a word you say when you're talkin' French like that."

Bates slid the rest of the way off the driver's seat and pulled himself up to his full six feet. His keen eyes surveyed the Gagnon property: a modest little bungalow, year-old paint job, already peeling; full porch in front, complete with lawn chairs and a porch swing. On the railing sat wooden flower boxes overflowing with colorful blossoms. On the lawn was an old bathtub, upended and half-buried in the earth—a makeshift shrine for the statue of the Virgin Mary inside. *The kid's folks keep the place up nice*, Bates thought.

He looked at Norm: loose Willy Nelson T-shirt flapping in the breeze like a ship's sail; left arm, skinny as a softball bat, with thick blue veins protruding; right arm in a cast, stained black as if with oil or grease.

"Chief, so what about my car?"

Bates looked the boy right in the eyes. "That car of yours, Norman, well, it could be a while. It's a pretty important piece of evidence, you know. We're gonna hafta hold on to it until we find out what's goin' on around here."

"So how long's that? I *need* that frikkin' car."

"I suppose you do, Norman, but we gotta keep it."

"For how long?"

"At least until I get my questions answered."

"Jeez, Chief. I told you everything I know. Told it again to the state police."

"I ain't sayin' you didn't, Norman, but maybe there's some questions we forgot to ask you ..."

"Yeah, like what?"

"Like who was doin' all the drinkin' in the car? Your back seat had enough empties to start your own redemption center ..."

"I dunno—"

"And who was smokin' all the pot? Must a been an ounce between the floor, the ash tray, and the glove compartment."

"I dunno nothin' about it. Reggie an' Spit—"

Bates looked at his clipboard. "Here's one you oughtta know, Norman. How come you let Spit and Reggie borrow your car in the first place?"

"I already told you—"

"So maybe I forgot to write it down, Norman. So tell me again, okay?"

"'Cause I got a busted arm. I can't drive too good."

"How'd you break your arm?"

"Changin' a tire. Car fell off the jack."

"Your car?"

"Jeez, Chief, I already—"

"Just tell me again. Humor me, will ya."

"Yeah, my car."

Bates studied his clipboard. "We've been all over that car, Norman. All four tires look like they're about equally worn. All the lug nuts, on all four wheels, are caked with mud. Rust patterns show they've been on there awhile. Spare in your trunk looks a lot newer than the tires on the car."

"So what?"

"So it's hard to say which tire you was changin'."

"So maybe I pulled one off, patched it, and put it back on."

"Then we'd of found the patch. Look, Norman, let me lay it out good and straight for ya: We got witnesses that your two buddies were harrassin' Mona Grant and William Crockett. Now one buddy's missin', and one's dead, apparently murdered while drivin' *your* vehicle. Now I'm not gonna say we got a lot of suspects; we don't. But of the ones we got—I might's well be honest and tell you—you're right at the top of the list—"

"Me? But, Jesus Christ, Chief—"

"Shut up, Norman. You just listen, and when I tell you to talk, you talk. And you better tell me what I want to hear …"

Norman bit his lower lip and scratched at his upper arm, inside the opening of his cast.

"Now," Bates continued, "I'm gonna forget about the beer and the pot for the time bein'. What I want to know now is why them two boys had your car, and why they was chasin' them two kids up on Tenny's Hill Road. And while you're at it, I want you to tell me where to look for Reggie." Bates held Norm's gaze for a few moments, then said, "Okay, Norman, now you can talk."

They had been hiking for more than two hours.

Conversation had stopped long ago. Now they just trudged along, single file, with Eric at the lead. He made the steep climb look effortless. Didn't he tire at all?

Will was weary and sore. He was dripping with sweat and felt certain every muscle in his body was aching. How far had they walked, anyway?

He paused, looking around at the unfamiliar forest. Trees, moss-covered boulders, and a carpet formed by many centuries of fallen leaves separated Will from the steep, rocky climb just ahead.

He didn't know if he could make it; for a moment he wished he'd stayed home.

Before they'd left the house, Eric and Dan had discussed Will's role in the climb. Dan had wanted Will to remain at the house, locked in and free of any danger.

Eric was against it. If the Gentry were after Will, leaving him alone would be just like handing him over.

Will's mind kept drifting back to their empty house. He was terrified his mother might come home, find the place deserted and fall right into the hands of the Gentry. For that reason, more than any other, he put on a burst of speed, eager to find the Gentry's camp and start ...

... *start taking them out ... Start killing them ...*

Killing. The word felt strange, uncomfortable in his mind. He stopped again, letting it bang around inside his brain.

Killing.

He remembered a couple years ago, the time Jimmy Duzak, Will's best friend in Boston, bought a new BB gun with his paper route money. The two boys had taken it out to a wooded area near Cleveland Circle and started shooting chickadees. Will recalled the tiny birds, no bigger than his thumb. They'd flit around, perching on telephone wires and bushes. They were so small, they could usually be killed with just one BB. The boys had gotten so caught up in the excitement of the hunt, had felt so satisfied with their improving marksmanship, that they lost sight of what they were really doing—they were killing ... actually killing.

Will had looked down at all the tiny feathered bodies as they piled up in the bottom of his half-gallon milk container. He remembered getting so sad he wanted to cry. The reality of what he had done splashed over him, jolting his conscience like a cold wave of seawater.

It was the same thing now. Will realized he and Eric and Dan were going out to kill the Gentry. To actually kill them.

This time there was a difference: he knew it needed to be done.

I'll bet this is how guys feel when they go off to war, he thought: *scared shitless, but full of purpose.*

His thinking had slowed him down; he'd fallen far behind Eric and Dan.

Before he hurried to catch up, he realized one bit of his physical discomfort could be easily relieved: he had to pee very badly. Probably a direct result of all the coffee he'd had that morning.

He stepped off a ways into the bushes, just a modest distance, surely no more than ten feet from the trail. A little drop-off kept him from going any farther. Bending at the knees, he carefully placed his shotgun on the ground. Then, facing a tree, he unzipped his fly.

Pain!

White stars and zig-zag lines like lightning exploded in front of his eyes. He slammed face first into the tree, clutching at it for support. The back of his head felt as if someone had taken a Louisville Slugger to it.

He felt the dirt give way under his feet.

Everything went black.

———

"Will?" Dan said, feeling the tension in his own voice.

Eric stopped and looked around.

"He was right behind me. Now he's ..." Dan stared at the empty trail and wiped the sweat out of his eyes. He waited, listening, for Will to come pushing through the undergrowth.

The red-haired man dashed past him, carrying his rifle in both hands, barrel up. He looked ready to use it.

Dan followed as they doubled back. Bushes grew thickly on both sides of the trail. They seemed to reach out and push against Dan, as he rushed to keep up with Eric.

"Hey Will!" Eric called.

"Will!" Dan echoed.

Eric stopped; Dan almost plowed into him. Both men looked into the dense foliage. There was no movement among the leaves and branches. Nothing stirred among the shadows.

"WILL!" Dan called again, this time the echo was his own voice—"Will"—answering from far away.

It was the only sound in the forest.

———

Will didn't realize he'd been knocked out until he started to wake up. Piece by piece, the world began to reassemble in front of his fluttering eyes.

His head was resting on something soft; someone stroked his hair. His first fuzzy thought was that he was at home with his mom.

Will blinked some more, trying to bring the face above him into focus; it wasn't Mom, it was Mona!

She smiled down at him; his throbbing head was cradled almost comfortably on her lap. Her warm fingers combed gently through his hair. It felt wonderful.

"You all right?" she whispered.

His head was alive with angry spikes of pain. It hurt so badly his stomach ached. After a second or two he could almost remember how to talk. When his mind finally pushed the right buttons, Will said, "Mona … ?"

Then fear seized him.

"What happened to me? Where's Dan and Eric?"

Waves of grogginess sloshed over him, putting a liquid screen between him and the world. Nausea swam in his stomach.

As he looked around, he saw that they were outside, under a thick and distant ceiling of green leaves.

"I'm awful sorry, William. I thought you was one of 'em."

"*You* did this? *You* hit me?"

"Was afraid I killed you …"

Will tried to sit up, but pain like a hammer blow nailed him in place. "Aahhh!" he said. The ache in his head hurt nearly as bad as the blow that had knocked him out.

"I hit you with a rock; I thought you was one of them boys … them little people." Mona looked down at Will with an expression of loving concern. She reminded him of his mother during the time he'd had pneumonia.

Before he allowed himself to relax, he remembered the stark and ugly scene last night: the eerie gathering revealed in Dan's headlights. His muscles seized again.

"You were with 'em," Will said. "I saw you with 'em last night."

"That was you in the car? You shoulda helped me. They was chasing me—"

"You were running away from them?"

"Yup, that's right. They'd brung me to their hideout. But I escaped—"

"How'd you get away?"

"Ssshhh, don't speak so loud. I think they're still out lookin' for me." She peered around, scanning the woodland with frightened eyes.

Will looked around, too. "Where's Dan and Eric? They were right over—" Will stopped mid-sentence, pointing. The spot where he'd left them was gone; Will didn't know where he was. Nothing looked familiar.

He closed his eyes, then settled back, trying to think.

Had he been stunned nearly witless by the blow to his head? Was the pounding headache somehow jamming his thought processes? Whatever the reason, Will accepted Mona's story. He believed it. The fact was he *wanted* to believe it.

In spite of all that had happened, Will liked Mona. He was happy to see her, comforted by her presence. He wanted to trust her. No doubt he'd have believed anything she told him just then. She looked so innocent and pure, her eyes were so bright and honest. And his head felt so good resting there on her soft thighs.

Before he could find out what happened to Dan and Eric, another wave of grogginess came over him. He felt the whole world lurching and reeling, filling with blackness.

He passed out.

The next time Will came to, things seemed a little more real.

He was stretched out on the ground behind a barrier formed by thick bushes clustered on either side of a huge rock. It was a natural shelter at the bottom of a steep incline. Will figured he'd tumbled down the hill. Then Mona must have dragged him to this hiding place.

She knelt beside him, washing his forehead with a damp cloth. Judging by the color, she must have torn it from the white dress she was wearing.

The pain wasn't so bad this time; it was more of a dull irritation. "You think you can walk?" Mona asked.

Will didn't feel much like moving, but he gave it a try. "Yeah, sure." He flexed the muscles in his arms and legs. Then he remembered. "We've got to find Dan and Eric. Didn't you see them?"

She shook her head.

"But I was right near 'em! You must have seen 'em!"

"I guess I wasn't lookin' around anymore after I seen you. I was hidin'. I heard rustlin' in the bushes. Figured you was one of them little people, so I clobbered ya."

Will sat up, cupped his hands, and hollered through them, "Dan—"

Mona lunged for him, slapping her hand over his mouth. "Quiet, Will," she whispered urgently. "They'll hear ya. We gotta stay clear of them little people. You gotta stay quiet."

"But Eric and Dan ..."

"Will, lookit." Mona knelt in front of him, her hand on his shoulder, her gaze locked on his. "I gotta tell you some stuff. Then we can go off an' look for 'em, okay?"

"Yeah ... yeah, I guess ..."

She sat down on the ground beside him and took his hand, placing it between both of hers on her lap. "Them little people, they been messin' around with me ever since my pa run over one of 'em with his pickup. 'Fore that, I didn't even know about 'em; after that—why, they was everywhere I went. They're the ones killed my pa, to get back at him. They sliced him up like they was dressin' out a deer. You seen him in the trailer ..."

Will cringed as the picture of Mr. Grant's body returned to his memory.

Mona went on. "Then they kept gettin' inside my head, makin' me do all sorts of crazy stuff."

Her gaze locked tightly on his. Somehow, he knew she wasn't lying.

"Mona," Will said. "Listen to me. We were heading up to their camp when I got separated from Dan and Eric. Eric thinks the little people want to get me. Now they'll think I've been captured for sure. We've got to find them. We've got to tell them I'm okay—"

"You hush and hear me out first, then we'll try an' find 'em. We know where they're goin', don't we?"

"Well, yeah ..."

"An' that's where I just come from. So listen to me, an' then we'll go back up there. I'll show ya; I know just where to go."

"All right, all right, but hurry up."

"What them little people want is somebody to take the place of the one my pa killed. First they tried to get me to have a baby for 'em—but I can't. I dunno why. Then they tried to get me to bust up your family—"

"So they could kidnap me?"

"No Will, not you. They wanted your ma. And now they got her. She's up there in the mountains."

My mother! Will felt the color drain out of his face like water through a colander. He began to feel woozy, as though he might pass out again.

"You hear me, Will? They got your ma. They're waitin' for her baby."

Will jumped to his feet, mindless of his wobbly knees and the grinding-glass pain in his head. "Come on," he said, "we've got to get up there. We've got to catch Dan and Eric. We've got to warn them ..."

Mona held up a flat palm. "*If* Dan and Eric's okay," she said. "You an' me's okay; that's all we know for sure."

That slowed him down. "What do you mean?"

"I mean, if we're gonna go up there and save your ma, we'd better plan doin' it ourselves. That's all I'm saying."

271

"My gun," Will said, frantically looking around. "Where's my shotgun?"

Was it at the top of the hill? Had he left it somewhere? He couldn't remember.

Gun or no gun, Will knew what he had to do. There was no question in his mind; it was as natural as breathing.

Still, the thought of going up there unarmed …

"Come on," Will said. "Let's see if we can find those guys."

The earth seemed to tremble as thunder growled across the sky. A whip of lightning cracked overhead.

The downpour finally came.

CHAPTER 29
A GRIM TWILIGHT

Rain shot down like little wet bullets.

Will trudged on mindlessly, not thinking about the stinging droplets that blurred his vision, plastered his clothes to his body, and turned the earth to slippery mud beneath his feet.

Mona tried to keep up. Often, when Will looked back, she'd be picking herself up off the ground, her white dress filthy, her long hair matted to her head.

"Wait up," she'd cry from time to time, then squeal as she took another tumble. Will couldn't wait for her. He kept climbing; his only awareness was that he'd wasted precious time while he was unconscious.

The mountain was as steep as a stepladder. Will's legs ached worse than his head, but he didn't let up—he was driven. He kept pushing his palms down against his knees, trying to give an extra boost to his weakening thigh muscles.

Maybe it was some kind of powerful instinct that kept him going. As long as he moved forward he didn't think about his mother and the horrible things that might be happening to her.

She was somewhere in these mountains; that's all Will knew. He was determined to find her.

None of the surrounding landscape looked familiar. He peered through the haze of rain, hoping to catch sight of Dan and

Eric, hoping to rediscover the ledge overlooking the Gentry's cave.

Visibility was almost nonexistent. In addition to the fierce rain, a strange darkness was falling. What time was it, anyway? Could this be twilight? that odd, unbalanced time of day that warns: Get home quick, and turn on the lights before the real darkness comes.

Trees seemed to crowd against him. Low-hanging branches slapped wetly against his face wherever he moved. Above, stretching tree limbs, heavy with leaves, flapped like wet blankets in the torrents of rain. Everything exaggerated his sense of unnatural twilight.

Will was soaking wet. He was cold.

In spite of the strong need to push on, he had to stop again to study the land.

Glancing behind him, he saw Mona, still making her way up the steep incline.

"Which way?" he shouted to her.

Apparently she didn't hear. He waited, breathing rapidly, while she persistently slogged forward, closing the hundred-foot gap between them. She groped blindly, grabbing at small bushes to keep from falling, pulling herself along.

Will watched as she tried to wedge her feet against stones so she wouldn't slide backward on the slick black soil. By now, not only her dress, but her legs, arms, and face were thickly smeared with mud. She kept wiping her eyes with the white backs of her hands.

When she caught up, she panted heavily, almost gasping for breath. Her voice was weak. "Jeez, Will, wait up, why don'cha?" Her chest heaved up and down.

"Gotta find my mother," Will told her. He squinted against the rain, trying to spot something—anything—in the vague distance.

Mona stood still in front of him. Will watched the downpour cut little white lines through the grime on her face. "I know where we're goin'," she told him. "Slow down an' let me show ya."

"We've gotta hurry," Will said.

"No hurry," said Mona. "They ain't gonna let nothin' happen to her. They want the baby, don't you understand?"

Will took a deep breath, trying to slow the pounding of his heart. He and Mona collapsed on the wet ground under a big leafy tree and let the cold rainwater splatter on their faces.

The furious tapping of hundreds of droplets did nothing to calm Will. The rain felt like an army of stinging wasps. Will thought about the Chinese water torture as he brushed maniacally at his arms.

The brief respite, though uncomfortable, allowed Will to think a little more rationally. If he and Mona could rally with Dan and Eric before storming the Gentry's cave, they might have a chance. Will thought about what Eric had said: "The Gentry were most powerful when they were all together and organized."

That was true of the humans, too. If they could get their forces back together, make a plan, work as a team …

Will wondered if the Gentry knew what was happening. Did they know there were pursuers in the woods?

He knew the Gentry had been watching last night; why hadn't they attacked then? Was it possible the little people were trying to separate the humans, break down their organization?

Then an idea—a suspicion, really—struck Will with the force of another blow to the skull. He looked at Mona. "How'd you happen to find me out there in the middle of the woods?"

She looked at him quizzically; the whites of her eyes were sparkling islands in her wet and dirty face. "Wha'd'ya mean?"

"If you were running away from the Gentry, how come you just happened to run smack into me?"

All Will's doubts about Mona came rushing back. She'd been used by the Gentry, Will knew that, even Eric said so. Was discovering Will simply a part of their strategy?

"*You* found *me*, I think," she said. "I was hidin'. When I seen you movin' through the bushes, I figgered you was one of 'em. I was scairt; guess I wasn't thinkin' too clear."

"Okay, right. So how come you saw me, but not Eric and Dan?"

She blinked again, her face flat, expressionless. "I dunno." Another blink. "You think I'm leadin' you into a trap, don'cha?"

"I don't know." Will said. "I'm afraid—"

She reached out and tried to touch him, but he pulled away. She winced. "I'm scairt, too, Will. Wicked scairt. I don't know what I'm doin' half the time. They get inside my head and buzz around like a nest of yellow jackets. They make me do what I don't wanna do ..."

"Eric told me they can't work on people's minds. All they can do is work on *things*."

"They done somethin' to me first, long time ago, last day a school. Bunch of 'em grabbed me in the woods, took me into the mountains, and fed me stuff. I ain't been the same since."

"You mean drugs? Stuff like that?"

"Coulda been. I don't know what it was. I know one thing though: after that, I started actin' funny; I jest couldn't help it. Thought I was goin' mental. It was like, you know, sometimes my body goes all numb—jest like the time I went in the Springfield Hospital to have my 'pendix out. They give me what they call a 'spinal.' My body was all numb and I couldn't move it no matter how hard I tried or how much I thought about it. It was so numb, they could cut me up an' I didn't even feel it.

"What them little folks do is kinda like that. Sometimes—an' I never know when—my body goes all numb, and all of a sudden I can't move it ... but they can. An' there's nothin' I can do to stop

it! I mean, I watch myself movin' around; I hear myself talkin' …
but it ain't me … it ain't *me* … I can't—" She looked away, staring
off at the land below them, and spoke in a whisper. "I'm sorry,
William. I'm sorry for all the stuff I done."

She started to cry then. Will knew he might be getting
suckered again, but he believed what she said; it was no weirder
than anything else that was going on. He slid closer and reached
out to hold her.

Mona snuggled into his arms, and as the cold rain poured
down, Will felt warm inside, almost peaceful.

Thunder clapped loudly in the distance; its echo rolled
around on the slopes and peaks of the surrounding mountains.
Flashes of lightning bleached the world with brilliant white light.

A few minutes passed like that. They hugged each other,
taking comfort from their combined warmth, as they worked up
the energy to go on. Will felt calmer now, less driven, but every
bit as full of purpose. Since Mona knew the way to the Gentry's
cave, he agreed that she'd lead.

Dan and Eric would be heading for the cave, too. They might
be taking some time to search for Will, but eventually they'd look
for him in the Gentry's cave. Sooner or later, all four of them
would be heading for the same spot.

With any luck, Mona and Will would get there first and wait.

It still wasn't completely dark. Could Will have mistaken a
false twilight for the real thing? In this strange, rainy weather it
was impossible to tell. Whatever the time of day, the heavy
blanket of storm clouds, the relentless downpour, and the thick
trees kept the woods in a mysterious half-light.

With Mona at his side, Will entered a huge pine forest. Here
the steep mountainside leveled out a little. The ground was
smooth and deep with pine needles. Nothing but the trees
themselves penetrated this spiky brown carpet.

It must have been a very old stand of trees, Will guessed, because their trunks were thick and dark, yet gnarled, almost deformed-looking. They towered far above the ground, becoming indistinct where their pointy tops pierced the low-hanging clouds.

Green-needled branches were the highest up. They shaded the lower branches, which, without sunlight, had long ago shed their needles and died. These dead branches crisscrossed at eye level. They were like twisted, mummified arms, reaching out to clutch Mona and Will.

The intertwining green branches were so thick they almost formed a thatched roof, stopping much of the rain. Will fought the urge to rest here, beneath the pines, where it was comparatively dry.

"Not too much farther," Mona said.

A peel of thunder rumbled across the sky. Will could actually feel it, like gas churning in his stomach.

It was easy to walk in this fairy-tale forest. The whole place made Will feel as if they'd entered some kind of prehistoric world. Everything was damp and rusty-colored, quiet as could be. Looking around, he half expected to see weird animals, or twisted little men, peering from behind the tree trunks.

"When we get outta here," Mona said, "we oughtta be able to see the pinnacle itself."

"What do you mean?"

"You know, the pinnacle, it's the highest part of Pinnacle Mountain. It's like a big stone cap on the top. I can use it as a marker to find the cave we're going to."

At the mention of the word "cave," Will felt his left front pocket for his disposable flashlight. He felt dumb enough having lost his shotgun, but he wasn't about to enter any cave without a light. It was still there, all right. Will took it out and tried it. Luckily, it hadn't broken in one of his many tumbles.

He put it away, feeling as prepared as he'd ever be for the next phase of the climb.

The pine woods ended suddenly, like the border of a shadow. One moment they were in it, the next they were stepping out onto rocky ground, high on a ledge overlooking a valley.

The valley looked familiar. Will was pretty sure it was the same one he'd watched with Eric. Now he was seeing it from a different angle.

The air and the color of the sky seemed odd, unnatural. Large mucus-colored clouds crowded the heavens. They were almost fleshy-looking. Will thought of giant sweat glands, as the cold rain splattered on him full force.

The air had a tense quality about it; it took Will's breath away. Stepping out of the pine woods was like stepping into a vacuum.

Before he had a chance to look around, light and noise erupted on the distant side of the valley.

Bang!

A tree burst into flames, spewing smoke and blazing wood fragments into the air.

Mona grabbed Will's hand, squeezing it nervously. They stood close together and watched the distant light show as jagged arcs of lightning ripped at the stormy air.

Another fiery finger jabbed out of the clouds, touched the floor of the valley, and exploded like a blinding white flashbulb. Will felt a certain excitement looking down at it, watching it from above.

Then, like the tongue of a snake, another bolt drove into the earth just fifty feet to their left. *Bang!* It sparked like a bomb blast, kicking dirt into the air. Glowing fragments rained down on them, stinging worse than the raindrops.

It was all so dramatic that it took Will a moment to react: *God, the strikes are getting closer!*

"Come on!" he yelled. Pulling Mona by the hand, he dragged her away from the tall trees behind them. They ran along the ledge between the forest and the drop-off.

Another bolt zapped a nearby pine. *CRACK!* A huge limb broke off and nose-dived toward the ground. Smoking and flaming like a crashing jet plane, it struck a rock, skidded, and somersaulted into the valley below. An acrid stench stung Will's nose as burning woodchips fluttered down around him.

Mona and Will were caught in the middle of a deadly display of fireworks.

They ran, seeking the protection of an overhanging rock.

Bolts of lightning continued to flash, cracking on every side of them like snapping whips of fire. The whole sky was alive with electricity; it crackled like grease in a frying pan.

They were under attack! The sky had opened fire on them!

Mona screamed wildly. Will cried out, too, as they zig-zagged along, not knowing where to run, not daring to stand still. Blasted trees collapsed everywhere. Spots of ground erupted left and right. It was as if they were running through a minefield.

A massive tongue of shale protruded from the face of a sheer rock cliff. It was about the size of a pool table, plenty big enough for Will and Mona to hide beneath.

When they were almost to it, Will gave Mona a mighty shove toward safety. She rocketed ahead. Will slid in close behind her, feet first, like a ballplayer stealing a base.

Another blinding bolt touched down within ten feet of Will's head. The concussion was terrible. A tingling sensation numbed his arms and legs as he tried to blink away the sparkling afterimages burned onto his retinas.

Will lay down, nearly on top of Mona, feeling the rain-soaked warmth of her body beneath him. He was shielding her. For a moment he was aware that he must appear brave in her eyes.

Thunder cracked like a volley of warning shots as they cowered, nearly motionless, protected from the rain, and—Will hoped—the lightning. His head rested on Mona's back, his arms pulled her close. He could smell her earthy odor, hear her frightened sobs. Her muscles trembled violently.

It seemed as if the storm were subsiding. The assault of lightning had ended, but rain still splattered outside their rock shelter. Will was too tired to do anything; he wanted to rest a few minutes, catch his breath, take what comfort he could from the warmth of Mona's soft body.

As he hugged her closer, he had the odd sensation that she was cooling off, that the heat was somehow draining from her body, flowing into the stone floor. He was sure of it! Beneath his hands, beneath the side of his face that rested on her shoulder, the temperature of her skin was dropping!

"Mona?" Will said, and shook her gently.

She didn't reply or move, but—there was no mistake—she was getting colder!

"Mona?"

Had she died?

"Mo-na ... ?"

Could a dead body cool off that quickly?

Will shook her again, lifting his head to get a look at her face. It was turned away from him.

He sat up and rolled Mona over onto her back. Her eyes were open slits; the irises had rolled back, and only the eerie whites were showing.

"Oh no," Will said, backing away from her, not knowing what to do. He was terrified that in his fright he had pushed her too hard. Maybe she'd hit her head, or snapped her neck!

"Mona, what's wrong?"

Her lips quivered; Will heard a bubbly sound in the back of her throat. At least she wasn't dead! Then her eyes opened more fully; the irises rolled downward, fastening on Will like twin gun sights.

Slow-moving cheek muscles stretched her mouth into a tight, glaring smile. Without the assistance of her arms, she jerked into a sitting position, folding at the waist like a jackknife.

Her filthy, raggy-looking white dress hung loosely off one mud-streaked shoulder. With coordinated precision, her hands rose to her collar, and she ripped open a couple of buttons. This allowed her to pull the neck of the dress down, over her breasts. The fabric collected around her waist, leaving her bare-chested.

"What the hell are you doing?"

She began squeezing and massaging her breasts, her muddy hands painting black fingerprints on the white skin. At some other time it might have looked sexy, but now Will just couldn't figure it out. It scared him.

"Stop it, Mona. Why are you doing that?"

The bubbly noise in her throat, air blowing through saliva, started up again. She sounded like some steam-driven machine. Her lips moved like copulating worms in front of tightly clenched teeth. It was as if she'd forgotten how to talk.

Watching her, Will felt the beginnings of panic. He thought she was having some kind of attack. Was she epileptic or something?

As he reached out toward her, her hand, like another bolt of lightning, darted from her breast and locked instantly around his wrist. With surprising strength she pulled Will's hand toward her, forcing it against her thrusting breast. The soft skin felt cold as marble.

The sound in her throat continued, while her lips moved wordlessly. The word "warrrrmmm" seemed to growl at Will from somewhere deep inside her.

He tried to pull away but couldn't. Her hand was locked on his too tightly. Now her other arm reached out, snaked over

282

Will's shoulder and grabbed the back of his neck. He struggled to move to the side, but it was no use, her grip was as strong as the cold metal hand of a robot.

Pulling Will toward her, she tipped backward, once again reclining on the rock.

Will was fastened on top of her, held tight by impossibly powerful arms. Her legs surrounded Will's now, coiled around them; her heels came together between his knees.

He couldn't move. He was helpless. It was as if she were some kind of trap, and Will had sprung it. He was locked up in her, pinned uselessly by powerful arms and legs that wrapped around him, squeezing tighter, like four boa constrictors.

Even with his head and neck in such a cramped position, Will could see out into that sandwich of space between the ground and the rock overhang. The lightning had stopped; the sheets of rain were no longer visible.

An odd kind of mist was forming, gray, dense as a cloud. Maybe it was a cloud, the kind that he'd sometimes seen swallowing up a whole mountaintop.

The mist churned, and floated and reached out in stringy white wisps, delicate as an old woman's hair.

As Will watched, trapped and helpless, something out there moved.

CHAPTER 30
SNACK TIME

Chief Bates almost missed the turnoff to Tenny's Hill Road. He hit the brake, and the tires squealed, leaving a little of themselves on the asphalt surface. He slapped the wheel, almost turning completely around in the middle of the road.

So much for daydreaming.

Maybe he should stop a minute, collect his thoughts, before continuing the trip to Joe Grant's trailer.

Indecisive, he opted to let the contents of his glove compartment be the determining factor.

Slowing the cruiser to a near crawl, he grappled around in the glove box with his right hand. His fingers recognized his ticket book, a canister of mace, the .38 automatic, his back-up weapon and ... Ah! There it is! Something soft.

Awkwardly parked at the roadside, Bates pulled out the Devil Dog, then peeled away the cellophane wrapper as it if were a banana. He took a bite.

Smiling now, he remembered how easy it had been getting information out of Norman Gagnon. The only thing in the world that kid cared about was his car. "Tell you what, Norman, maybe we can work out a little deal ..."

Another bite.

So, Norm and the other two stooges had duked it out with old Joe Grant. That showed just about how bright they were.

284

"I think you're gonna need that vehicle of yours, Norman. 'Specially if Grant takes off after you. You just better hope it can outrun his pickup."

Another bite. Finished.

It was easy to imagine Joe Grant beating up on three kids; it wasn't much more difficult to imagine him killing a few of them. God knows there were plenty of stories about Grant and his wife. He had always said she'd run off, but lots of folks had a different explanation.

And what about that little daughter of his, Mona? Bates had received more than one earful about their "special relationship"—just no evidence, no proof, not so much as a complaint Bates could act on.

"You better watch out, Norman. Stay clear of him. He comes around here, I don't want you playin' hero. You call me, understand?"

Bates wiped his chocolate-covered fingers on his tongue, then dried them on his pants.

He was almost eager. He'd been waiting a long time to get something on that scumbag Grant.

As the chief turned into Joe Grant's driveway, his gut sense told him he was getting close to something.

"I'll do what I can, Norman. You'll have the vehicle back just as soon as I can arrange it."

He saw Grant's pickup in the littered dooryard.

CHAPTER 31
ZERO OPTIONS

orms moved slowly in the fog, just beyond the point where Will could make out detail. From where he lay, pinned tightly to Mona, they appeared as little knots of fog, misty cocoons that bobbed and weaved like smoke-filled bottles floating on a stream.

One of the forms stepped closer, pushing wisps of fog out of its way. Now, even in the deepening darkness, Will could detect a suggestion of color. He saw flesh tones, muted and pale, behind the veil of mist.

He knew what he was going to see before he saw it. His muscles tensed, and he shuddered violently in a half-unconscious attempt to free himself from Mona's grip. Her snakelike limbs responded like a belt tightening another notch. Again Will heard the bubbling sound in her throat, as if she were trying to say something but had forgotten how.

"Mona, let go," he whispered, the urgency in his voice driving it up an octave. "We gotta get out of here!"

Again the noise, like moist air in a pipe.

"Mona, what's wrong with you? Let go of me, come on!"

He squirmed around, tugging, pulling, and flexing, hoping his sweat would provide enough lubrication so he could slip away from her.

When Will looked back at the moving shapes, one of them had partially untangled from the floating tentacles of mist.

Mona's grip tightened.

Now he couldn't look away, his head was pinned, immobile; more struggling seemed stupid. Will watched as a definite human form emerged from the fog and stepped closer to the entrance of the stone shelter.

For a second he prayed it might be Dan or Eric, but when the shape took its next step, Will's last hope was gone.

For the first time he could plainly see what it was; there could be no mistake. Still, the fog kept a thin veil in front of the little man.

He *did* look like a child; there was no question about it. And a very small child, at that. He must have been between three and four feet tall. His naked flesh was pale, ghostly white — the color of bones. His arms and legs were way too thin, almost like broom handles. The lines of his ribs pressed against the tightly stretched skin of his chest.

To Will it looked more like the skeleton of a child than a child itself. It was like one of those magazine pictures of starving children, the ones that always made him shudder with another kind of horror. But what made this little man especially frightening was the crop of coppery-red hair, so greasy it seemed molded to his head like stringy plastic. Will's mind reeled at the sight.

Even in this paralysis of mind and body, Will could see it was the same color as Eric's hair.

God! Will's mind veered away from the obvious conclusion.

And the eyes! Strange, completely black eyes, like polished spheres of coal were embedded in the grinning skull face.

Behind the first, other forms moved, nearly invisible in the darkness and fog. They arranged themselves around the opening of the stone shelter, appearing as vague pillars of mist magically supporting the rock overhang.

Just as the nearest figure took another step, Mona's muscles seemed to relax a little. She was letting go of Will!

Her breath quickened then. She began to feel warmer. The wet windy panting turned to a whimper of fright. As Will rolled clear of her, he saw the terrified look on her face. Crablike, she backed up, pressing herself against the stone cliff. A protective hand shot to her mouth. With fear-wide eyes, her lips worked to form stammering words, "Oh God, Will ... oh, God, I'm so sorry ..."

Will was too panicky to hear. All he could think about was escape. There must be a way ...

There was no point in standing up. If he did, he'd slam his head into the rock ceiling. There was no point in sprinting for it, at least a half dozen more Gentry were waiting less than fifteen feet in front of him.

And there was no place to retreat.

Will was a captive, the misty human columns, bars on a cage.

An oddly calm part of his mind did some rapid calculations: When he'd become separated from Dan and Eric, they probably figured he'd been captured by the Gentry. No doubt the men were looking for Will as Mona lured him away and into the Gentry's hands. If all the Gentry were right here, that could mean Dan and Eric were okay.

If so, they'd still be looking for Will. There was a chance they'd come to the rescue. It was a hope, at least.

The rest of Will's mind was less calm, as he battled the panic rising like a fire inside him.

Will backed up, too, until he pressed his spine against the cold stone and his side against Mona. She was quiet now, her fingers curled into her mouth, her eyes wide, glassy, and terrified. She just stared at the little man whose head was moving back and forth—first those black eyes locked on Will, then on Mona.

It seemed as if they stayed like that for a long time. Will guessed the Gentry were waiting for him to make some kind of move. And he was waiting for them.

He couldn't remember ever feeling quite this trapped before. When you're down to zero options, he figured, maybe some kind of little switch flicks on in your head, putting you on automatic pilot. Possibly you start doing things—brave things—things you'd never do under normal circumstances.

Will recalled a time, back when his father was alive and they were living in Boston. It was right after school. Will was in the apartment, waiting for his parents to get home from work. He wasn't alone; Tripod was with him.

At different times Mom and Dad had both told him not to tease the cat, but now nobody was around to tell him anything.

So he started chasing Tripod. He could move pretty fast for a three-legged cat, faster than a lot of normal cats. Will chased him around the kitchen table and watched him dash into the dining room. Tripod probably thought he could lose Will among the legs of the table and chairs. When Will moved a chair, Tripod took off into the living room and scooted behind the couch. Will just moved the couch and started chasing him again.

No matter what Tripod did or where he ran, Will kept it up. He never intended to hurt the cat; he was just having fun with it. Besides, he was curious to see what Tripod would do if Will gave no indication of stopping.

Will found out all right.

When Tripod ran into the bathroom, he'd reached the end of the line.

Will stood in front of the door, blocking it. Tripod was up against the wall.

Right then, Tripod probably figured he was down to zero options. Whatever he figured, this tiny three-legged cat stood his ground and turned on Will!

Will was at least twenty times the cat's size, but Tripod turned nonetheless. Hind legs spread, tail in the air, eyes wide, and teeth bared, Tripod was ready for a fight!

A frightening, snarling hiss crossed Tripod's bared fangs, and he let off the most horrible stench Will had ever smelled. It surprised him so much, he dropped his guard and Tripod bolted away.

Will had never known cats could do that, but maybe when they're scared and cornered, they've got a little bit of the skunk to them.

As he cowered there beneath the rock ledge, Will thought of Tripod's bravery. Now he knew how trapped the little animal must have felt.

Slowly altering his position, he worked his legs under him and managed to crouch. The bottom of one sneaker braced tightly against the rock wall behind him.

Will kept a steady gaze fastened on the black eyes of the little man directly in front of him. Internally, he did a quick systems check to be sure his hands and feet were free and that nothing interfered with his balance.

Then, in the same way he used to do turns in the swimming pool, Will pushed a foot against the wall and shoved off. The intent was to get as much speed and distance as he could, as quickly as possible.

Will ran in a crouch, growling loudly through bared teeth. He was careful not to charge straight ahead—that's where the drop-off was. He must have looked awfully scary, or awfully stupid, but he didn't care.

He charged past the first Gentry with no trouble, then veered off to the left. Two little men, visible only as misty shadows, sidestepped toward each other and joined hands. The gate made by their spindly arms was directly in Will's path.

He had no choice but to plow into it. The solid knot of their interlocking hands caught him in the stomach, knocking the wind out of him.

It was more an accident of balance than any real skill on Will's part, as he pinwheeled over their arms, somersaulting, almost landing on his feet on the other side of the barrier.

Almost.

Instead, Will landed on his back.

He heard a shrill burst of laughter coming from behind him. It gave him an odd, sick feeling, a feeling of defeat.

It was then, for the first time, that Will realized they were playing with him.

The line of figures began to shift, reforming into a circle around Will. They all joined hands now, moving counterclockwise. It was like some kid's game gone mad, with Will sitting in the middle.

Gentry moved in and out of the fog. Some were humming, while others chattered in gruff, gravelly voices that didn't sound at all like children. All of them continued to rotate around Will, their shiny black eyes fixed on his where he sat.

The intensity of the humming and chattering built to a maddening pitch. Then, suddenly, a grating giggle escaped from one of them.

Will started to stand up when a force like a blast of focused wind slammed him in the stomach. He fell backward onto the stone slab.

Still they circled, humming, chanting, their scrawny, naked bodies passing, ghostlike, through cobwebs of mist.

Will tried to lift his arm. The wind struck again, this time full in the back. It pitched him face first toward the exposed slab of stone he was sitting on. Will slapped the stone with both hands to keep from smashing his face.

He wanted to scream with frustration and terror, but somehow he held on. His eyes darted around from one skull face to another, looking for some weakness in that leering ring of demons.

What were they doing? Were they going to keep playing ring around the rosie with him?

Will knew Eric had been right about one thing: they weren't able to mentally force him to do anything—not the way they could with Mona—or they'd have done it by now.

Instead, they seemed to have some power over nature. Will thought of the lightning bolts that had chased them, the wind that was knocking him around.

What terrified him the most was being the center of their attention! What were they going to do to him?

His fingers clutched at the granite slab beneath him, searching for a throwing stone. As his palms explored the coarse surface, he detected a rapid change of temperature.

The rock was heating up!

The Gentry continued to revolve like a wheel, with Will as the hub. Their movement, though quite slow, was somehow dizzying; the sound of their humming chant was irritating and incredibly chilling.

Will heard Mona say something from behind him. It sounded like "Thing kathee alee … !"

The little men hardly seemed to notice, but when Will turned to look at her, one of them lifted a foot and caught him in the jaw. Will lurched to the right, again catching himself with his hands.

The stone was getting painfully hot now. It was heating up like a frying pan.

"Th'alee, th'alee," Mona cried.

Will figured she was somehow taking part in whatever ritual they were performing. Was she speaking some strange language? Some magic words?

292

"What?" Will yelled to her.

He couldn't touch the stone now. Only a thin layer of rain-damp clothing protected him from the increasing heat. The surface of the rock, just moments ago stained with moisture, was beginning to steam. Will saw what looked like shrinking shadows as the wet spots evaporated and grew smaller.

"Memba Norr!" Mona said.

Will scampered around on his hands and knees, uttering doglike yelps of pain. If he stayed still, he'd burn himself severely.

All the little people giggled and laughed in loud whiny gasps.

"Norm, 'member Norm!" Mona cried, and all of a sudden her words leaped accurately into Will's mind. She was reminding him of the time he'd attempted to save her from the three punks in the alley—"Think of the alley," she had said. "The alley, the alley"—and "Remember Norm."

Norm! God, how could he forget?

This situation was nearly the same; all the attackers were focused on Will. Mona was in the background, unnoticed; only this time she didn't have any bag of groceries to throw down to distract them.

Streams of mist rose all around him. The heat was getting terrible; it bit at him right through the knees of his jeans. Will couldn't put his palms and fingers on the rock anymore. He could only touch it briefly with the fatty butt of his hand.

"Yeah," Will cried, "Yeah, the alley … !"

Mona started screaming bloody murder. Will didn't realize she could be so loud. She came running out from under the rock ledge, her dress still dangling down around her waist.

She'd filled both hands with tiny stones. She threw all of them at once in the direction of the circle of little people. Some Gentry turned away. Some looked at her as she screamed wildly. They hardly reacted at all when she drove both hands into one of the little men. He stumbled backward, breaking the circle.

"Run, Will, run!" she cried. Screaming and waving her arms around, she jumped up and down just like a guy Will had once seen in a movie. He'd been trying to save his friends by distracting a rampaging bull.

Some of the little men looked at Will, but most were watching, or moving toward, Mona.

Will bolted, head down, running along the ledge between the cliff and the pine forest. He risked a quick look over his shoulder, expecting to see Mona not far behind him. Instead, she was running in the direction of the drop-off.

"Mona! NO!" Will cried.

It was too late. Still waving her arms as if to distract the little people, still screaming as if to freeze and startle them, she leaped into the misty space and was gone.

For a few brief moments, Will could hear her fading scream.

CHAPTER 32
AN AIR OF MYSTERY

Normally, Chief Bates wouldn't walk into a private residence without some kind of permission—either an invitation, or a warrant. Sometimes, however, on special rare occasions, he'd take his entrée from another source: his intuition.

Something about Grant's trailer triggered an intuitive reaction. Bates knew he was getting close to something.

As he knocked, he noticed that the door was not only unlocked, but it was sprung, already open a crack.

Concerned about destroying fingerprints, Bates pushed it with his notebook. The door swung some more until a stack of firewood on the porch stopped it from opening all the way.

Firewood in August?

Bates had to turn sideways and force himself through the narrow opening and into the living room. It was a tight squeeze, almost like trying to push the cork back into a wine bottle.

Grant's nearly as big as I am. How'd he get in and out?

The first thing he noticed was the smell.

Jesus Christ, smells like a French whorehouse in here.

It was as if Grant never bothered to clean the place, masking offensive odors with some heavy-duty air freshener.

"Jesus," Bates said to himself, "just the fumes alone would scare any burglar away."

Before he intruded any farther, Bates called again, just to be sure. "Hey, Grant. Joe Grant. You here?"

The silence put Bates a little more at ease. He was free to prowl and poke all he wanted. He found the light switch beside the door and flicked it on.

The place was kept a whole lot neater than he'd expected. *Must be the girl's work,* he reasoned.

Here and there ketchup and beer bottles were filled with dead wildflowers. Their browning stalks bent low, depositing wrinkled petals on the kitchen table and on the top of the TV. If the girl kept the place so neat, why didn't she replace the flowers, or at least throw the dead flowers away?

The withered blossoms suggested the place had been empty for a while. It was odd, though. Why should the place be empty when Grant's truck was outside? As far as Bates knew, Joe Grant owned only one vehicle—and that vehicle was in the yard.

If the Grants weren't here, and the pickup was, it probably meant they'd either left in someone else's car, or they were off somewhere on foot.

Where could they walk to? The only place nearby was Dan Wilder's house at the top of the hill.

Well, thought Bates, *I was planning to go up there, anyway.* Yes, he'd pay Wilder's family a little visit, but first he'd poke around some more.

CHAPTER 33
A RAY OF LIGHT

Will had no idea how far he'd run. There was no way to tell. His panic permitted no sense of distance or direction in the dark woods. He knew he'd run for a long time; he couldn't stop.

Even in daylight, he wouldn't have known where he was going. He remembered leaving the pine woods, that's all. After that he just ran, blindly. He might have been anywhere.

Still he didn't stop. All he wanted was to get away from those horrible little people and to escape the echo of Mona's dying scream as she plunged invisibly into space.

Why did she have to die? The question haunted him as he ran. Was it because she'd made an error in judgment about the location of the cliff? Or had she sacrificed herself to save Will? Could she have done such a thing?

The most likely explanation was that the Gentry had given her some irresistible urge to take to the air.

Will shuddered at the thought.

He tried not to speculate; right now reasons weren't important. All that mattered was to move as fast as possible.

He fell, then picked himself up. It was a pattern he'd often repeated, each time more battered and filthy than the last.

Slaps from unseen branches surprised him. A network of scratches stung him as he blindly plowed ahead.

The night was impossibly dark, like an unending shadow. A thick black covering of clouds hid the moon and stars. Yet the air was fresh, sweet, rich with moisture that made the night feel like a living, fleshy thing, a thing Will could not escape.

Often he thought of the flashlight in his pocket. He was afraid to stop long enough to fish it out, and he didn't dare remove it on the run, either. What if he dropped it?

He just kept running, stumbling, hoping he was moving in a straight line, hoping he was really getting away. Somewhere—he almost prayed—he'd find some feeling of safety.

His legs were heavy, lifeless weights, slowing his progress. His side began to hurt—each movement stretching his muscles to the tearing point.

He panted like an exhausted animal.

Any minute he expected the Gentry to launch some new attack. What could it be? Would the sky open up and blast him with another bolt of lightning? Would the earth yawn, swallow him whole, and grind him to hamburger with its granite teeth?

Or would it be some new form of assault? Something more horrible than Will could even imagine?

He looked up, expecting white skeletal faces to be peering at him from the branches overhead.

The fear boiling inside him was all that kept him from passing out on his feet. His aching legs told him to stop. His pounding heart told him to stop. His heaving lungs argued the same. Even his adrenaline-fueled mind tried to tune out, shut down, but his body worked independently to keep a rhythm. It just tripped along under its own inertia, sneakers slapping the forest floor.

But suddenly, he couldn't go on anymore.

Leaning against the scratchy bark of some thick-trunked tree, Will peered into the darkness. Breathing deeply, chest working like a bellows, he waited for his heart to stop pounding. It was so loud! It was all he could hear. It drowned out all other sounds, made it impossible to hear … hear what? Cars? Voices? Maybe Dan or Eric calling out for him?

When his heart started to slow down, the screech of an owl set it racing again. Will gave an involuntary gasp and was immediately terrified the sound had given away his location.

He looked around.

His eyes felt as wide as coffee mugs as he tried to drink in every bit of available light.

Nothing was distinctly visible. The trees and spaces between them blended into one vast black wall that hid the whole world. Far away—perhaps many miles—Will heard a dog barking.

He wiped the sweat away from his eyes; his hands felt gritty against his face.

He sensed that something was near.

Eyes straining into the darkness, Will saw a dim suggestion of color.

Blinking rapidly, he tried to bring whatever it was into focus.

The thing seemed to hover there, far in the distance, a faint glow, almost like a lantern.

Or a spirit …

Will watched it for a few minutes to see if it would change position. It never shifted right or left, never seemed to move any closer.

For a long time Will refused to take his eyes away from it. What if he looked away and couldn't find it again? What if it vanished?

After a while—fifteen or twenty minutes, he guessed—he felt rested enough to move. Keeping the light squarely in front of him for orientation, he inched cautiously toward it, being extra careful not to make a sound.

It vanished and reappeared each time a black tree trunk bisected his line of sight.

Will moved slowly, carefully, and, he hoped, soundlessly for a distance of some hundred and fifty yards. It took him an awfully long time.

As he got closer, the amorphous contours of the dull orange glow began to take on a definite shape. He could finally identify a rectangle—a window!

Kneeling behind a clump of bushes, Will identified the black shadow of a building. Light from what was probably a kerosene lamp poured from the window. It reflected off the ground, revealing the shape of a little cabin. Another window on the side convinced Will there could be no more than one room inside such a tiny building.

He saw a shape pass in front of the window. It wasn't anyone Will recognized, but at least it was human, and full-sized!

As desperately as he needed help, something told him to be careful. Before going any nearer, he thought he'd better take a good look around.

No cars or trucks were anywhere near the cabin. If there were, he'd have seen points of light reflecting from their surfaces.

He started to walk in a big, slow circle around the place. *Good thing there's no dog inside*, he thought, *it'd be barking by now*.

Soon he noted the dark outlines of two more buildings nearby. A woodshed and an outhouse?

When he'd almost completed the circle, it occurred to him that he hadn't crossed any driveway or road leading to the cabin. That seemed very odd.

There weren't any electrical wires, either. But he'd guessed that long ago from the kerosene lamp.

Well, Will thought, *I might as well go for it*. After all, whoever was in there was the only help around. Maybe they had a shortwave radio, or something. Will suspected not; he couldn't see an antenna.

Bracing himself, he began to walk directly toward the lighted window. He should have been tremendously relieved, he supposed, to see this tiny, kerosene-lit reminder of civilization. Instead, he was filled with some kind of dread. It was a whole new type of fear, almost a panic, and he wasn't sure where it was coming from.

He held his breath until he was all the way up to the cabin. His heart pounded loudly in his chest; it seemed dangerously loud.

Now Will was close enough to see a large, pencil-thin rectangle of light to the left of the window—the outline of a door.

He stopped, undecided.

Suddenly he heard himself panting. He was short-winded from holding his breath! Why was he so afraid? Was his subconscious trying to warn him about something?

That's when he decided not to go directly to the door.

Just to be on the safe side, he'd peek in the window first.

Holding his breath again, Will tiptoed up to the cabin. When he was close enough to touch it simply by reaching straight ahead, he positioned himself to look inside.

The window was streaked and dirty. Inside, a film of smoke buildup made the glass seem opaque.

Then his heart leaped in his chest! His pent-up breath exploded from his lungs, and Will felt a smile slicing across his face.

There, behind the filthy glass, sitting in the dim orange interior, elbows resting on a table made of old boards, were—

"Dan! Eric!" Will shouted and made a mighty grab for the door handle.

He swung the door open … and froze.

Both the men were glaring at Will. They were hard-faced, mean-looking.

Each man had a rifle pointed directly at Will's heart.

301

CHAPTER 34
SECOND STOP

*N*ow *we're getting somewhere,* Bates thought as his headlights washed over Dan Wilder's vehicle. He parked the cruiser beside the Renault.

Light poured from the downstairs windows of the house on Tenny's Hill. The bright yellow porch lamp burned a pleasant greeting.

Looks like they're to home ...

He couldn't see any movement through the windows. No problem: if Wilder and his family were in the living room, they wouldn't be visible from the yard, anyway. Maybe the Grants were paying them a visit. Bates chuckled to himself, trying to imagine such an unlikely gathering.

No, it was too awkward, too absurd; the Grants probably weren't here, at least not on a social call.

Before getting out of the car, Bates quickly reviewed the questions he had for Wilder: Why didn't you bring your boy by the office like you said you would? You know anything about these people down at the bottom of the hill—the Grants? You know where they're off to?

Then he'd ask to speak privately with the boy, William. Any details he could get about the chase through the woods, any dialogue young Crockett could remember with his pursuers, might shed some light on Spit's murder or Reggie's disappearance.

Bates grabbed his notebook and eased out of the car. The cruiser rocked up and down as if happy to be free of his weight.

He looked around. Not much to see: the dark garage, the darker trees beyond. A shrill chorus of young frogs was the only sound.

He crossed the shadowy dooryard and started up the wooden steps.

What the hell?

Dirt was piled against the newel post; it spread, fanlike, with dark spikes radiating across the new paint of the porch floor.

Bates scratched his head. *Funny.*

He picked up a pinch of the black earth, rubbed it between his thumb and fingers, then sniffed it. He almost tasted it the way his daddy used to when determining the quality of soil. *Good topsoil,* Bates thought, *moist and rich. Maybe the missis was doing some potting.*

He looked closer. A black bundle of cloth was tucked down in the "L" formed where the steps met the porch. A trouser leg extended from the bundle, draped across a nearby rose bush.

Damnedest thing.

Bates turned and walked to the door. He gave it four solid knocks, then listened for movement within.

Nothing.

After knocking again, Bates moved to the window and peered into the kitchen. Everything looked neat and orderly, except a clutter of dishes and papers on the table.

He walked to the edge of the porch and called, "Daniel ..."

Frogs in the distance stopped their chirping. Everything was silent now, as if the night were holding its breath.

Bates experienced a sudden chill. He remembered a morning long ago—December 28, 1983—when he'd made a similar trip to this house. The destruction, the blood, the mangled bodies, all covered with a dusting of new snow. And Eric Nolan, sitting on the steps, staring, motionless, like a snow-covered statue ...

Bates shook his head, rejecting the ugly images. *That was another time*, he told himself. *It's got nothing to do with now.*

He crossed the dooryard to the garage. Empty, Mrs. Crockett's station wagon, gone. Did that mean the three family members had driven off somewhere in her car?

Maybe; not necessarily.

After detouring back to the cruiser to grab his flashlight, he rapidly returned to the porch. He rapped again, loudly. Then he called, "Dan ... Mrs. Crockett."

He waited a few minutes in the silent evening.

About to leave, he paused. *Oh, what the hell*, he said to himself, and he tried the door.

It was unlocked.

CHAPTER 35
FOG BOUND

"My God! Will! You scared the shit out of us." Dan felt his tension release when he saw the grime-covered, exhausted-looking boy. Will stood as if paralyzed in the hypnotic glare of the twin rifle barrels.

Dan rapidly lowered his weapon. He smiled, taking an eager step toward Will.

"Not so fast," Eric said, interposing his gun between Dan and Will. His face didn't change; it was stony and cold. "Come in, Will, slowly."

Will stepped timidly across the threshold and into the tiny cabin, never taking his eyes off Eric's weapon.

Dan's temper flashed. "What the hell are you doing, Eric?"

Eric didn't acknowledge Dan, nor did he change his position. "Is he alone?" Eric demanded, his gun pointing directly at Will's heart.

Dan looked outside, nodded, and closed the door. Only then could he give Will a hug. He felt tears welling in his eyes. "God, it's good to see you, Will. You all right? We thought they'd taken you." He looked over at the other man. "Christ, Eric, put the gun down. Can't you see, it's Will."

Eric lowered the rifle, slowly. "Is it?" he asked, his voice flat, full of distrust.

Dan sensed how his companion felt; he was slowly learning what Eric already knew: when the little people are around, you can't be sure of anything.

Will explained what had happened, how he'd been suckered away, how they'd been attacked, and how Mona had jumped off the cliff.

Dan stared at the boy, a hand on Will's shoulder. Eric watched, a grave expression on his face, as Will chattered away, trying to tell them everything at once.

"… and they've got Mom up there," Will concluded.

"They've got Sheila …?" Dan's mind reeled. Eric had tried to prepare him for this frightful possibility. At first he'd completely dismissed the idea. Then, when he'd actually seen the Gentry standing in formation behind Mona, the likelihood of his wife's abduction had become more real. Now, hearing it confirmed, Dan staggered and steadied himself against the table. He felt as if his blood were speeding through his veins.

"Are you sure, Will?" Eric asked.

That question slowed Will down. He looked helplessly from one man to the other.

"Am I sure … ?"

Dan considered it. Perhaps the whole thing was another of the Gentry's tricks. Clearly, Will *believed* they had his mother, but how could he *know* it?

"I … I can't be sure," Will stammered, "not positive, exactly. But that's what Mona told me. She said they took Mom because they want the baby."

"How do you know Mona was telling the truth?"

Did Dan really doubt it, or was this some form of denial? Was he dismissing as a trick something he chose not to believe?

"I don't know … I mean, I don't think she was lying …" Will looked confused.

306

Dan pushed harder, "How do you know the Gentry weren't speaking through her?"

"I ... I—"

"Jesus, Dan, leave him alone." Eric slapped the wall. The alarm in his voice showed he didn't doubt Will's story. "I was afraid of this," he said. "They've been one step ahead of us right along."

Dan turned to face Eric. He tried to control his voice. "Then if it's true, Eric, we've got to go up there. If there's just a chance this in on the level, we can't wait any more. We've got to go now, tonight."

Eric sat down at the table. "No. Wait. I've got to think," he said. "I just need a minute to think."

"If Sheila's really up there, then we're wasting time ..."

Eric shook his head. "We can't. We'd be at a tremendous disadvantage. It's dark out; they can see in the dark, we can't. They're the most dangerous at night; we're at our most vulnerable."

"But Sheila—"

"She'll be all right, Dan. I know how you feel, but if they want the baby, she'll be all right. They won't let anything happen to her."

Dan felt his desperation rising, turning into anger. "You can't believe that, Eric. Think about her. She's up there all alone. Terrified. Think what might be happening to her, for God's sake. We can't just sit here doing nothing."

"Dan—"

"I say we go for help. We can't do this alone, not anymore, not knowing my wife's life is at stake—"

"NO!" Eric slammed the table. The wood split dryly under his fist. "Can't you get it through your head, Dan? We've been over it time and again: If we go for help, *that's* what'll waste time. Who's going to believe us? We'd spend the next two days talking, explaining, trying to convince professional skeptics. Even if we made up some story, by the time Dick Bates manages to pull together some inept search party, the Gentry will have abandoned their plan, killed your wife, and vanished into the woods."

"Then we've got to—"

"That's right, *we've* got to do it. We'll strike at first light. I'm not delaying, Dan. That's the soonest we'll have any chance at all."

Dan didn't reply. After a while he collapsed into a smelly, blanket-covered chair by the old wood stove.

Will stretched out on the bunk beside him. Eric stayed at the table, looking sullen and uneasy.

Dan checked his watch. Eleven-fifteen. It would be a long wait till morning.

———————

Will closed his eyes and tried to relax.

Breathing deeply, he became conscious of the air inside the cabin. It smelled bad, like kerosene, tobacco, and rot. Opening his eyes again, he saw the walls and floor were wet from rain leaking in.

In spite of the stink of mildew and the junky condition of the place, he was grateful for shelter. The cabin was lighted and dry, and—at least for the moment—the three of them were together, and safe.

Without being told, Will knew this was the cabin where Eric had been staying: Perly Greer's cabin. Will wondered what the old hermit had been like, wondered how he could survive in such primitive surroundings.

Relaxing was easier than he'd expected. It was almost luxurious being horizontal. Every inch of his exhausted body welcomed the dirty old cot. For a moment, he felt right at home.

Still, his mind wouldn't shut off enough to let him fall asleep. Questions kept banging around inside his head.

Did the Gentry know about this cabin?

Did they realize they were about to be attacked? Maybe Mona hadn't had a chance to tell them. Could she have jumped off the cliff to prevent the Gentry from finding out?

God, he missed her. It wasn't fair. None of this should have happened to her. It seemed like Mona's whole life had been a series of losses and misfortunes.

Sleep didn't come; Will kept his eyes closed and listened. No one was talking. He hadn't heard Eric get up from the table.

Dan was the only one moving. He paced around the tiny cabin, stopping at one window, then the next. If Eric hadn't been there, Dan would probably have charged right up into the woods to look for Mom.

Will knew how his stepfather felt; he'd felt exactly the same way when Mona told him about Mom. The news made him want to throw caution to the wind and go right up there to bust ass.

Will wanted to say something to Dan to make him feel better, but there was nothing to say. Instead, he just stayed quiet, letting his thoughts run their course.

The next thing Will knew, he was waking up.

———————

It was a weird, misty morning.

The window across from Will's cot was white as a cloud. On sore, unsteady legs, he stumbled over to take a look outside. A thick cottony fog pressed itself against the glass. Behind it, the sun was invisible, and the whole world was lost.

Eric had a jar of instant coffee. He was preparing three cups, using cold water from a bucket on the counter. Dan was still sleeping, stretched out on a blanket on the floor. He had a thick Sears catalog under his head like a pillow.

"What time is it?" Will asked Eric.

"Quarter to six."

"We going out in this fog?"

"Why not? It'll probably burn off before we get to the cave."

Will took his cold coffee, sipped it, and almost gagged.

"There's some bread here," Eric said. "We can make peanut butter sandwiches. I'm afraid I haven't kept the place very well stocked. I wasn't expecting company."

"I'll make the sandwiches," Will offered.

Dan groaned and opened his eyes. "I always liked a hard bed," he said, "but this is going a little too far."

He started to stand up and groaned again. His hand moved to his lower back. "Jesus Christ, I feel like I've got a hangover ..."

Eric chuckled. "With any luck we'll both feel that way tomorrow morning. I've got a feeling tonight we're going to do some celebrating."

Will smiled, too. He felt rested, and some of his confidence had returned. After all, he'd escaped from the Gentry; he'd faced them and lived to tell about it. That proved it could be done. Maybe they weren't so powerful after all.

Will ate his peanut butter sandwich, and it tasted real good. It stuck like paste to the roof of his mouth so he had to drink that horrible cold coffee after all.

———

The morning air was surprisingly cool, not warm and inviting like an August day should be. Eric shivered a little at first—was it the temperature or the anticipation?—but warmed quickly as

310

he began the uphill walk.

Although nothing remarkable had occurred this morning, Eric felt tense. Perhaps it was this new wrinkle: the certainty of Sheila Crockett's abduction. He'd hoped it was simply another of the Gentry's ruses, a psychological trick designed to make Dan and Will abandon caution for desperation.

He'd slowly become convinced that Will hadn't been programmed; the boy's uncertainty about his mother's kidnapping proved it. If he'd been programmed, he'd have been more emphatic.

At least Eric hoped so.

Fact or fiction, it didn't matter, his companions still had to deal with uncertainty and dread. Dan and Will might not be as reliable with this new dilemma on their minds.

Eric admired the boy's bravery, though, and he felt a growing respect for Dan.

He glanced back at them, recalling his own painful adjustment to the Gentry's existence. When he'd come to accept the truth, it had felt more like madness.

Yes, those two had been through a lot. Yet, Eric judged Dan and his stepson were doing—how had they phrased it at the hospital?—as well as could be expected. Better, really.

The fog hadn't broken or burned off the way he thought it would. That was a bad sign; its cause might not be entirely natural.

Natural or supernatural, the result was the same: Eric had to rely on habit, rather than visible landmarks, to find their way. He kept looking from side to side in the claustrophobic haze, expecting hidden forms to move, or maybe jump out and attack them. After a while Eric relaxed a little. He theorized that even though the Gentry could see at night, that didn't mean they could see any better than a human in the fog. Maybe the fog was an advantage ...

311

Eric wore a camouflage-colored backpack. He'd tied a red handkerchief to it, giving Dan and Will something a bit more visible to follow.

Checking one last time, he made sure his knife and flashlight were strapped securely to his belt. He touched them both to be certain, transferring his rifle from one hand to the other. *Odd,* he thought, *how distrustful I am of real objects when I'm dealing with the supernatural.* Reality's an ancient beast, dying slowly with each new minute—who had said that? He couldn't remember.

He recalled other people, though, people at the hospital: a young woman exposing a swollen breast to an invisible infant; an elderly, moderately distinguished-looking man in a bathrobe, pointing at a blank wall, screaming with terror. Who's to say the rude beast he saw there wasn't real?

Navigating with a kind of sixth sense, Eric led his companions up steep rises and through thickly wooded areas. He was careful not to get too far ahead, realizing how quickly he could disappear from view.

The fog was like cotton, not only to the eyes but to the ears. Any noise in the forest seemed blunted by the heavy air. Everything seemed otherworldly, dreamlike, as Eric pressed on.

"It's not that far," he kept saying over his shoulder. "I could walk it blindfolded."

Dan and Will were still behind him; he could tell when they chuckled at the attempted joke. Their laughter seemed nervous.

"Seems like the fog's getting thicker," Will said.

The boy was right. Now the fog was so dense that Eric could see green tree branches reaching out toward them, but he couldn't see the trunks from which they grew. Things seemed to float in the mist, mysteriously, magically.

"I think it's because we're inside the canyon," he replied. "The walls are getting closer together, cutting down the light."

"That means we're right near the cave," Will whispered.

On either side of them, piles of huge boulders, some bigger than houses, came into hazy view. The massive rocks looked like castle walls, vast and gray, looming ominously in the mist. Though their tops were invisible, and their faces indistinct in the churning fog, Eric knew they'd almost reached the end of the line.

... the end of the line? Eric shuddered at his choice of words. Yet, it *did* feel as if these sheer mountainsides were slowly squeezing together, not to crush them, but to smother them with cushions of fog.

Eric fought his growing uneasiness. It was an atavistic response, the revulsion one experiences in the presence of a natural enemy. He felt it intensify as they got nearer to the end of the canyon.

When they finally stopped moving, Will stood about five feet behind Eric, with Dan right beside him. The trio faced what seemed to be a cave. It wasn't a yawning mouthlike opening as one might expect. Instead, it was a jagged vertical slit, where towering rocks had split apart, leaving a gash never more than two feet wide between them. It made Eric think of a space between books on a shelf.

"It's a perfect illusion," he whispered to Dan and Will, "even on a bright clear day. It looks like nothing more than a split-rock cave. See, it's really shallow, five feet deep at most. No passing hunter would give it second glance. But stay close, and watch ..."

Eric turned his body, side-stepped into the gap and disappeared.

Chief Bates drove along Old Factory Road, heading toward Dan Wilder's house. It was a bright morning, not bad at all for a hike in the woods.

A natural clearing between lofty, green-leafed maples on the right revealed a scenic view of Pinnacle Mountain

Pretty as a picture, Bates thought, as he looked at Antrim's highest peak. The very top of the mountain was encased in a thick cloud, as if it were resting there, gathering strength so it could resume its journey across the sky.

Odd, thought Bates, *the rest of the sky is clear and blue.*

What the hell, he reasoned, *it'll burn off before I get up there.*

Glancing at the passenger's seat beside him, he began a quick inventory. His brown paper bag, its top neatly folded, contained three tuna sandwiches and a couple of Devil Dogs: his lunch. It tempted him already, and he'd just finished breakfast less than an hour ago.

Beside the bag, his compass and binoculars were laid out for easy access. His flashlight and notebook were ready, too.

His right hand burrowed into the slit in his shirtfront where the button had come off. He began to scratch his belly.

Settle down, he told himself, *there's nothing to be nervous about.* As he scratched, the knuckles of his hand crinkled the folded paper in his shirt pocket.

The map!

He didn't know why he'd removed the awkwardly sketched map from Wilder's table. It certainly was not precise enough for anyone to depend on. But, then again, it might mean something—it might be a clue.

Last night he'd waited a little more than an hour for Dan and his family to come home. He'd walked from room to room, not really searching the place—he hadn't opened any closets or drawers, and had just once permitted himself a quick peek into the refrigerator—just looking around. All the time he was aware his actions were highly illegal. He didn't care; he preferred to think of them as simply informal.

He'd noted what most probably was blood on the bathroom floor. Someone had been hurt—a shaving cut, some minor household wound, maybe the boy had cut himself playing. In and of itself, a bit of blood meant nothing. Someone had even cleaned up most of it; Bates had seen the scrub marks streaking the tile floor.

The downstairs wasn't remarkable. Bates saw where three people had eaten at the kitchen table. They'd left their dirty dishes right where they'd finished with them. Among the dishes, Bates had spotted the map.

It was a crude sketch on a piece of yellow lined paper. It included the house, the garage, and a trail leading across the brook and into the big circle that represented Pinnacle Mountain. Three landmarks were depicted on the mountain itself. They weren't labeled, but Bates recognized two out of three: the old hermit's cabin and a disused stone root cellar. The third mark, looking like a goal post with a big "X" in it, was positioned near the mountaintop. He had no idea what it was supposed to represent.

What is this, Bates had asked himself, *some kind of treasure map?* He'd folded it and stuck it in his shirt pocket before he left the Wilder house. Then he'd thought about it all night.

Throughout his life in Antrim, Bates had heard a hundred different stories about gold on Pinnacle Mountain. Could Wilder, hearing one for the first time, have led his family up into the woods to look for it?

Or did "X" mark some entirely different spot?

This morning, Bates was up with the first cockcrow. He was going to look in on Wilder again, try to catch him before he left for work.

On the other hand, if nobody was home this morning, Bates planned on spending a few hours in the woods. If there was one thing he hated more than walking, it was walking uphill. It was one of the less enjoyable parts of his job.

The brown bag beside him crackled as he reached into it for a Devil Dog.

Will watched as Eric stepped into the fissure. The redheaded man turned his body to the left, stooped down, took a crouching step … and vanished.

"Eric?" Will said, suddenly uncertain. Cautiously, he stepped in after Eric. The rock ledges forming the cave's outer opening hid a second opening, smaller and to the left. Taking a deep breath to reaffirm his resolve, Will ducked through it. Dan was right behind him.

All three of them crouched in a tunnel that angled downward, apparently leading deep into the earth. The passage was no more than five feet high and not much wider than Eric's shoulders. It was dark and wet. The walls, Will quickly discovered, were moist, slimy to the touch.

Eric handed Will the big flashlight he'd had attached to his belt. "Keep the light turned off as long as you can," he instructed. "When you turn it on, don't flash it around. Just keep it pointed at our feet so we can see where we're going."

Eric swung the rifle from his shoulder, his movements cramped in the tight passageway. "I'll keep us covered," he said, "but if you have to shoot, remember, I'm in front of you."

Will felt a jittery snap of nerves as Eric spoke, but he didn't let on. He just inched along in nervous silence, squeezing the handle of his knife very tightly. He also patted his pocket from time to time, making sure his little flashlight was still there. *All systems go*, he thought.

For a hundred feet, it was surprisingly light in the tunnel. Why? Will studied the walls. A strange algae growth, fuzzy to the touch, gave off a cold luminescence.

He looked at the stony floor and guessed from its smoothness that this passageway had been used an awful lot over the years.

The muscles in his legs, more than anything he saw, told him they were walking down a fairly steep incline. He guessed it was about like that wheelchair ramp back at school.

The air got noticeably colder with every step. Will kept his eyes peeled in the fading light; his ears strained against the silence. No sound but their own footfalls summoned echoes from the lightless depths.

Occasionally, Will bumped the rock wall with his shoulder and jumped in surprise; adrenaline surged uselessly. He felt the weight of the whole mountain pressing down on him as he crouched in the darkness.

"Do you think they can hear us?" Will asked Eric.

"I don't know, Will. Maybe they're listening. Maybe they're watching, too. I just don't know."

Will pressed his teeth together to keep them from chattering. In a moment he whispered, "I bet they can hear us. I bet they know we're here and they just don't care …" His voice trailed off and again the silence was complete.

Soon they didn't have to crouch anymore. The ceiling seemed higher, the sides of the passageway, wider. Eric told Will to turn on the light.

They were in an underground chamber, easily as big as a classroom. Eric took the light in his free hand and flashed it around. "You hear that?" Dan said with quiet alarm.

Somewhere, water was dripping. They listened for a while to make sure they'd accurately identified the sharp, rhythmic sound. "You've never been inside here before, right?" Will whispered.

"Never," Eric said, his eyes following the flashlight beam.

The circle of white light rippled over sheer rock walls and the nearly smooth ceiling above. It swept slowly across three openings that led from the chamber, each black as an open wound.

Another sound.

Eric jerked the light back across the tunnel openings. Suddenly the beam stopped; a man stood in the shadows.

Dan stifled a cry of surprise.

Eric tensed, but he kept the light shining in the man's eyes.

Will could see the face clearly. "God … it's … it's Reggie!"

Reggie had never looked good. Will remembered the first time he'd seen him, back in the alley with those other two geeks. He remembered the long, greasy hair, the pimply face, the too-red mouth like an ugly smear of lipstick.

He recalled the last time, too, looking through the binoculars, as Reggie and some other guy struggled to carry a big parcel through the woods.

Will knew he'd never forget the way Reggie looked in that cave. The skin of his face was sickly white, like the flesh of a mushroom. Open cuts, black and bloodless, slashed his cheeks and forehead. Each gash was lined with pieces of black thread, sutures, that dangled from his skin like tiny black worms.

His mouth hung open, slack, motionless; it looked as if his teeth were gone. A brown, dry-looking tongue lolled on his lower lip, like a dying slug. Reggie's hair seemed to have fallen out in patches, each exposed area revealing red, raw, slippery-looking skin. His clothes, torn and filthy, suggested he'd been sleeping in a bed of mud. The entire length of his arms, from where his T-shirt ended to the knuckles above his twitching fingers, was scraped and cut, dirty with dried, rust-colored blood. Yellow liquid drained from fat, open sores.

His eyes were wide, unblinking even in the intense glare of Eric's flashlight. The pupils were gone, rolled back in his head. The whites shone like dull stones.

Dan's rifle jumped like a spring and pointed at Reggie's chest. "Stay still," Eric whispered. Will couldn't tell if he was talking to them or to Reggie.

Nobody moved.

Reggie teetered on his feet, weaving unsteadily, looking as if he were about to topple. He took a step toward them.

His slack mouth didn't move at all, but a growling came from his throat. It was airy sounding, seeming to come from a long way off. And Will recognized it; it was like the sound that had come from Aunt Peg's wounds.

"We'll answer your question," Reggie hissed. "Yes, we've been watching ... yes, we've been listening. We've enjoyed seeing you work yourselves to exhaustion. A generous gesture ..."

Will and the two men stood frozen by the eerie voice.

The Reggie-thing lurched a little, rocking unsteadily. "Your gesture was kind, but, we fear, unnecessary. You see, we've had the advantage from the start."

Reggie's torso seemed to be reeling in little circles. "Now you've all come far enough ..."

Without allowing the beam of light to drift from Reggie's face, Eric handed Will the flashlight and readied his gun.

Eric cleared his throat. "Far enough for—"

"Where's my wife?" Dan blurted, his voice weak and distant.

Reggie paid no attention. Head back, white eyes pointed at the ceiling, the wispy voice blew from his motionless lips. "Each of you will submit to us, you know. You've come here to do as we say. And you *may* live, if we can find some purpose for you."

Eric took a step closer, gun poised. Reggie didn't back away; he just kept staring, slack-jawed, the frail wind streaming from his mouth.

"Brian, can you hear me?" Eric's voice was too loud in the empty tunnels. "It's your brother Eric. I want to see you, Brian. I want to talk to you."

Reggie took another unsteady step.

All the muscles of Will's body clenched tighter than fists. His mind raced, recoiling from the supernatural, begging for some human explanation.

"There is no Brian," the windy voice said.

Now, at least, Eric had gotten its attention again; it was answering their questions.

"Where's my mother?" Will said in fractured tones. When he heard himself speak, he realized he was crying.

"Your guns are useless here, as useless as your flashlights and your courage, as useless as this effort you are making. You are all very foolish. You are a trio of clowns ..."

"Brian, please show yourself. Let's talk about this. I know you can hear me. I'm your brother, for Christ's sake!"

"My brothers are with me," Reggie said.

"Can't we work something out? You have the woman with you. Let her go. Take me instead."

"She is of use to us. She stays here. Perhaps, if there is use for you—"

"Damn it," Dan screamed, "what have you done with her? What have you done with Sheila?" His voice bounced around in the rock passageways.

Other voices, gruff and mocking, picked up the chant, "Sheila ... Sheila ..." The voices came from dark tunnel openings, they came from the blackness above, they came from all around, from everywhere, joining the song of the echo.

They exploded into raucous laughter, like the demented giggling of lunatic children.

Dan pulled the trigger of his shotgun. Powder flashed. The gun's numbing roar drowned out the mocking chorus of crazy laughter.

Because Will was holding the flashlight, he had the best view of what the gun did to Reggie. It was as if a wind pulled away the shoulder of his T-shirt, and with it the shoulder itself. A disgusting red mud sprayed from the wound. At the same time, the severed arm flopped, twitching, onto the stone floor of the cave.

Reggie staggered backward; the flat, idiotic expression on his face never changed. He bumped into the rock wall and slid down to a sitting position. Red mud gushed from his shoulder like excrement.

When the echo of the shotgun had passed, the cave fell into a shattering silence.

Again Will heard the bubbly sound, like air in a drainpipe. Once more, Reggie began to speak.

"You will do as we say," the wheezing voice began. "You will come to obey us, either as men and of your own volition, or as senseless sacks of obedient earth. To us it makes no difference; to us they are the same."

Will looked in disgust at Reggie's mutilated corpse. Now terror mounted as the eerie voice continued, "The decision, of course, is ours; you have sacrificed the freedom of choice."

Little people appeared, two of them stepping into each of the three tunnel openings. By reflex, Will turned around, looking back where they'd come from. The redheaded Gentry, the one he and Mona had seen near the drop-off, blocked their path of retreat. They were surrounded.

"Shoot!" Will cried in a panic, jerking the light in all directions. "Quick, Eric, shoot the damned things!"

CHAPTER 36
FAMILY TIES

"Shut up, Will." Eric waved the boy silent. He didn't sound angry, but he sounded like he meant it.

Dan's eyes scanned the shadow-slashed forms waiting in silent pairs at the tunnel openings. *We're surrounded*, he thought; *we're trapped*.

He looked at Eric, hoping for some clue about what to do. It seemed their only chance was the guns they were holding.

Eric didn't appear as rattled as Dan felt. He stood straight and firm, enviably calm. Turning around slowly, Eric faced the redheaded Gentry behind him.

Head cocked to one side, the spindly little creature squinted up at Eric.

Beyond the copper-colored hair, their differences were disturbing. One was tall, blue-eyed, and apparently confident. The other, Eric's shriveled, shrunken clone, had solid black eyes that collected the light from Will's flashlight, but reflected none of it. Dan focused on those eyes. They were cold, passionless, dead. The eyes of a shark. In contrast, the sickly white skin surrounding them evoked the image of a skull.

Dan couldn't look at it.

"You're smart, Eric," the little man's voice grated uncomfortably, like metal against stone. "Smart enough to find us, smart enough not to test your weapons. Still, Eric, your intellect will fail you; you'll never be able to survive what you're doing here. You're like grandfather's minnows, remember? They'd swim into a trap, then they couldn't find their way out ..."

Dan studied Eric's face. The muscles around his eyes seemed to struggle, trying to maintain some kind of control. If Eric relaxed those muscles, what would appear there? Terror? Anger? Tears? Some unnamable emotion, some distorted feeling of kinship, an aberrant attachment for the warped child-man that taunted him?

"Brian," Eric was almost choking. For the first time his stalwart veneer began to crack. Dan heard something like fear in his tone. "Brian, I—"

"Four years ago, Eric, it was agreed: we'd abandon our cousin's boy unharmed. We thought you understood it was a truce; you were not to come back here. We had a pact, Eric. You violated it."

"Brian, look, I've done this ... I've come back here ... Because I want to take you away ... I want you to leave this place ..."

High-pitched laughter split the earthy-smelling air. It was the mocking laughter of monstrous children.

The little man's head cocked even farther to the side, almost resting on his shoulder. "We'll leave when you do, brother."

Another bleating chorus of laughter rang through the darkened tunnels. A crouching hump-backed figure smirked from the shadows, chanting tonelessly, "... 'cause you won't be leaving at all, at all ..."

The skin at the back of Dan's neck tightened. He felt, cold, clammy with sweat.

"I want to help you, Brian, you're my ... you're still my brother." The uncertainty in Eric's voice had turned to pleading. Dan looked away.

"Our brothers are here. We'll not soften to you again, Eric, we've grown too much. There can be no more bargains—"

"This ... this thing that has happened to you, it wasn't your fault, Brian. Whatever they've done to you, maybe it can be cured, maybe—"

"It needs no cure! We're now beyond the touch of disease. Now our only inconvenience is the intrusion of you and your kind."

"Brian—"

"*You* are the contagion, brother. We are the cure ..."

"Brian, listen ... if you won't come with me, why don't ... why don't I stay with you? I know you need help, someone who can ... go among men. All I ask is that you let these people go."

"And Sheila," Dan broke in. "What about Sheila?"

The little man ignored Dan, continuing to address Eric.

"You are misguided, 'brother.' Your sense of self-importance will not permit you to believe how insignificant you are. You have nothing we want. You are nothing we want. The only thing useful to us is the woman, and she is already ours."

"Why . . ?"

"Because she is the Last, until the Last comes—"

"Where is she?" Dan blurted, jerking his gun to his shoulder.

"No, Dan," Eric cried.

Brian laughed. It was a bubbly, high-pitched laugh. For some reason, it made Dan think of a fish screaming under water. "If you fire that gun, we will be on your wife before the echoes die."

"He's right, Dan. I think we'd better put our guns down ..." Eric started to bend over, about to place his rifle on the stone floor of the cave.

Dan couldn't believe it—their only hope was the weapons! Could Eric be so blinded by familial devotion that he'd surrender their one chance for survival? It was stupid; the Gentry weren't about to discuss a bargain. Apparently all they wanted was amusement.

Dan realized then the size of the blunder he had made: he had stupidly allowed Eric to lead them into these frightful caverns. Now they were helpless. All he could do was stand by, watching, as Eric turned over their defenses.

A sickening realization jolted Dan: Eric was crazy after all!

He wanted to say something to stop Eric from letting go of the gun. Before he could open his mouth, Eric snapped upright again, gripping the rifle in both hands.

The gun barrel moved almost too quickly to see. Dan watched it catch Brian across the throat. The little man flew backward, bounced off the cave wall, but had no time to tumble; Eric scooped him up in his arms and dashed into the tunnel from which he'd entered.

Vanishing into blackness, Eric shouted something, but Dan couldn't hear. The garbled words reflected from the sheer stone walls, distorted, useless.

He's abandoned us, Dan thought. Eric had run off with his brother, leaving his companions to face the remaining Gentry.

Anger welled in Dan—Eric had used them.

Stepping forward, Dan placed himself between Will and the three dark tunnels where the Gentry lurked.

"Go ahead, Will, follow Eric."

"But, Dan—"

"Get out of here, Will!"

Will took a step backward, flashing the light around. In the shadowy distance, ghostly forms pressed themselves against the tunnel walls. Some of their eyes reflected red, like animal eyes, some reflected not at all.

Will remained in a half-crouch, his shotgun trained on the hiding Gentry.

Slowly, the small red fox approached the strange thing. Greatly cautious. Eyes alert. Ears erect. Legs poised. Ready for a sudden retreat.

The thing didn't move.

The fox's black nose wrinkled, sniffing the air, searching for some familiar scent.

Still no movement. The little fox pressed its muzzle tentatively against the sprawled and mangled thing. It was big, draped over piled stones, partly covered with dirt.

There was a smell, strong and familiar. The fox knew it was human—a thing to be feared. But there was another smell, too. A strange smell—the sweet odor of death.

The little animal's muzzle inched along the white, twisted arm, moving upward, looking for a place to bite.

When its sharp teeth pressed torn and bloody muscle, the thing twitched.

The fox darted away, scampering into the safety of the bushes.

A transformation came over Dan.

As Will watched, the fear, the doubt, the uncertainty all disappeared from his stepfather, like ripples vanishing from a pond.

Suddenly, Dan appeared very frightening. He looked like he'd had enough.

Will got another surprise when Dan spoke. "I don't much care which of you bastards gets on this first, but I want all of you out here where I can see you. Right now."

None of them stirred.

"If you sonsabitches don't move, I'm going to start firing. I don't know if this gun can kill you, but I bet it'll tear you up a little. I'm willing to see, if you are."

Nothing.

"You think I'm bullshitting?"

Will believed him, even if the Gentry didn't. None of them rushed out into the light, but they weren't backing off into the tunnels, either.

As brave as Dan was, Will still worried about his mother. What Brian had said really scared him: if Dan fired the gun, they'd be on her.

On her ... ? What could that mean?

Dan must have been thinking the same thing. He started inching toward the tunnel on the far left, taking care not to lose sight of the other two openings.

"Now, which one of you is going to show me where my wife is?"

The two creatures in the leftmost tunnel stood perfectly still, like rats peering out from little rat holes. They looked as if all life had left their bodies. They were mummified children, wrinkled, shrunken, starting to decay.

"You think I'm fucking bluffing?" Dan pulled the pump on the twelve-gauge Winchester. Its precise mechanical click echoed in the tunnel.

For a moment there was a tense silence.

Will jumped when Dan pulled the trigger. Roar piled upon roar as the sound ricocheted around the stone chamber. At the same instant, Will witnessed what could only be described as a savage wind. It blew across the two cowering Gentry, tearing their flesh away, pocking their skin with tiny seeds that instantly blossomed brilliant red. Both collapsed like punctured balloons.

Will's stomach heaved. A hot flash rippled across his face. His ears hurt wickedly; the horrible shotgun blast reverberated inside his head.

Face taut, eyes blazing, Dan whirled, waving the gun barrel at the other cave openings.

"I'll keep these guys covered, Will. You go look for your mother."

"What about Eric?"

"Fuck Eric. Give me a flashlight and get going."

Without looking around, without lowering his gun, Dan reached out and took the flashlight from Will's hand.

Will slipped his own disposable light from his pants pocket and started moving toward the undefended tunnel.

Because he was moving through unknown shafts, he wanted to proceed slowly and with care. He was afraid of drop-offs, booby traps, possibly a stray Gentry or two, unaccounted for by Eric's population theory.

At the same time, he wanted to hurry. How long could Dan hold those four creatures at bay? Long enough for Will to find his mother and get out of there?

God, he hoped so.

She felt pressure. Something pinching her cheek. She wanted to raise her hand, feel her face, see if anything was touching her skin … but she could not.

She sensed movement inside her head. Tiny explosions, like miniature bubbles, bursting, tickling her brain.

She tried to open her eyes. No—they were already open. She couldn't blink. Couldn't see. No way to tell where she was. No way to know if she was sitting, standing, or lying down.

She was close to ... something. Was it sleep? Or death? She couldn't tell. Her mind wasn't working right; she couldn't follow a thought, even a simple one, to its conclusion.

If she could only force her brain to work, then she'd be able to move her body.

The bubbles again. Like soda pop. Inside her skull.

They were words—some kind of words—demanding to be understood.

One stung as it made contact, exploding like an electric spark. A tremor cut slowly through her body, slicing along her spine.

Her eyes tried to blink in response. For a moment, for the tiniest fragment of an instant, she could sense herself: She was lying on her stomach. Her eyes were open. They were packed with gritty sand.

Another bubble popped. It was a word. Her name.

Something was calling to her.

———————

The passageway snaked around a bend where its appearance changed. Suddenly it looked less like a natural tunnel through solid rock and more like a mine shaft. Now it seemed man-made, with ancient black support timbers at regular intervals.

The ceiling was sandstone and dirt. Stringy roots hung down here and there like wet clots of hair. Wispy cobwebs woven among them looked like hairnets on a corpse.

A big black rat, fat as a woodchuck, scampered across Will's path. The beam of his light drove the animal quickly out of sight. If black *cats* were bad luck, Will wondered what that beauty held in store for him.

He could almost feel spurts of adrenaline keeping time with his heartbeats. He took a deep breath, trying to calm down, trying to force his mind to control his fear. *I'm okay*, he told himself, fingers on his throat, *I'm okay*. He had to think clearly; he had to figure out where to look for his mother.

The explosion came with his next breath.

More vicious than thunder, it was a hundred times louder than Dan's shotgun blast. Will felt the concussion like a hammer blow and staggered under its impact.

The shock wave shook the tunnel. Dirt tumbled from the ceiling like gritty hailstones. Dangling roots and cobwebs shimmied eerily.

Dan! Will's terrified mind screamed. He whirled around.

Smoke filled the passageway behind him. It rolled toward him like a ghostly tidal wave.

Then he heard feet. Running feet.

A form plowed through the wall of smoke, cyclone-shaped fumes swirling out of its way.

Will backed against the wall.

For a split second he didn't recognize his stepfather. Dan's face was cut, bleeding, black where his skin and clothes were burned and streaked with soot. His shirt was ragged. He held the flashlight like a club.

"Move it, Will, they're right behind me!"

But they weren't.

Will and Dan ran for a few yards until they dared to feel alone in the passageway.

Dan's eyes blazed in his scorched and bleeding face. He leaned against the wall, panting, eyeing the tunnel behind them.

"What happened, Dan?"

He gasped hungrily for breath. "The fucking gun exploded. It started heating up in my hands. Damn thing got so hot it touched off the shells. If I hadn't thrown it down and run, it woulda killed me. I don't know what the hell happened —"

"They can do that," Will explained.

"What?"

"They can heat things up, just by thinking about it."

"Oh Christ, that's just great," Dan slapped the rock wall. "So now we got no gun, just a couple of flashlights, and —"

"I got my jackknife ..."

"Yeah, right. Me too." Dan looked around. "And there are plenty of rocks." He patted Will's shoulder, "Come on, let's go find your mother."

CHAPTER 37
THE CALL

A gain, no sign of life at Dan Wilder's place.
Dan's car hadn't been moved; his wife's hadn't returned. The pile of dirt on the porch had fanned out a little, spread, no doubt, by last night's wind. Looking through the porch window, Chief Bates saw the dishes from yesterday, three place settings, were still on the kitchen table.

His last hope was to try the door. He knocked loudly, then opened it a crack and shouted.

Nothing. No one.

Bates's heart sank; now he couldn't avoid making the long hike up Pinnacle Mountain. Oh, he could probably assign the task to a younger man, maybe even convince the state boys it was their job, but convincing would be tough, possibly embarrassing. The problem was he had no real evidence, no hard facts at all, just a crudely scrawled map and a belly full of instinct.

By the time he'd crossed the stone wall at the edge of Wilder's yard, he was sweating. When he'd walked up the hill to the little brook, he was puffing like a plow horse. After he'd crossed the water, jumping from stone to stone like an elephant playing hopscotch, his heart was pounding like timpani.

Will and Dan walked along that dank underground passage. They crouched when necessary, skirted stagnant pools of discolored water and often scratched their already tender skin against the rough rock walls. They moved quietly, whispering when they talked. Any noise they made flew through the tunnels like frenzied bats through a conduit. *That could be good, though,* Will thought. If the little people tried to sneak up on them, they'd know by the sound.

Of course, the Gentry were at home here. They could move through the darkness as easily as Will could cross a lighted room.

Right now—and he tried to force the idea from his mind— they could be nearby, watching from unseen cracks in the walls, or peering from shadowy nooks.

Will and Dan stayed close together, using only one of the two flashlights in order to conserve battery power. What if their lights went dead and they got lost down here? They'd be, in effect, buried alive. Which would get them first, the little people or the inevitable madness …

Once, just as an experiment, Dan flicked off the light. Will had never experienced such darkness. It was as if the eyes had suddenly vanished from his head.

More and more he realized how difficult it would be to find his mother in such a lightless labyrinth. If she was really down there she could be anywhere. The tunnels seemed to go on forever.

In any threatening situation, Will's mind would invariably create all sorts of strange possibilities. Now, he was wondering what the little people actually *do* when they're all together, and not terrorizing human beings. From the looks of his surroundings, Will concluded that they built tunnels.

But why? To what end?

If, as a race, the Gentry were as old as Eric thought— thousands of years—they'd have had time to create an unending network of tunnels. What if all of Pinnacle Mountain was honeycombed with these mysterious, seemingly useless passageways?

Will had never visited any foreign countries, but he guessed if he were walking through some ancient Greek ruins, or maybe the Colosseum in Rome, he'd get to thinking about the people who used to live there. What were they like? What was important to them? What did they do with their time?

It was the same way with these tunnels.

What were the Gentry all about? He couldn't figure it out. It didn't make any sense at all.

Dan must have been thinking the same sorts of things because after a while he whispered, "I feel like we're wandering around in some kind of ant hill."

Dan was right; Pinnacle Mountain was like a huge ant hill or termite mound. In school Will had done a report on the differences between ants and termites. He'd learned a lot about them while he was at it. Both had one thing in common: they protected the one responsible for reproduction—their queen.

Will didn't think his mother was the queen of the Gentry, but it looked as if she was responsible for reproduction.

In the mud nests of South African termites—which Will recalled looked very much like miniature mountains—the royal chamber was typically in the center, the least vulnerable and most easily protected spot. Galleries and connecting passageways surrounded the queen's chamber, many constructed as dead ends to trick invaders lucky enough to have penetrated that far.

Perhaps the little people's mountain stronghold was designed along the same logical pattern.

If they could just find their way to the center of things ...

It made a kind of sense. They agreed it was worth a try.

Will had recently learned to trust his talent for direction. With him in the lead, they would follow downward paths, avoiding left turns.

They moved a little more rapidly now, feeling a clearer sense of direction and purpose.

———————

The Call wouldn't stop. It tugged at her mind, a persistent irritation, pulling her away from the womblike safety of blackness.

She'd been so comfortable there, so warm, for the first time really and truly at peace. She fought The Call and clung to the warmth. Her mind screamed, "No!"

Then the shiver of cold.

Again, The Call, pulling her in different directions. It wanted her to move, get to her feet, follow the summons.

There was something she had to do, some obligation she had to fulfill.

She tried to move, but the comforting blackness called her, too: "Stay still," it said, "stop holding on. Let it happen ..."

She seemed to be floating now, drifting on a gentle current of warm air, high above her own motionless form. Was that really her down there? Was that her body, twisted and bloody, smashed on that mattress of stone?

"Don't look at it," the blackness said. "Let it go. It's over. Be done with it."

But she couldn't stop looking. It was fascinating. It was as if she were a reflection, an image in a mirror, looking out through the glass at her physical self.

The Call sounded again, and she was falling.

Again The Call. It forced her back into that ugly tangle of blood and flesh and bone.

Help us.

She tried to move and found it impossible.

Help us.

She was responding, not through the strength of her own determination, but by the will of The Call. It coursed through her, cell to cell, nerve to nerve, like an electrical current. Useless muscles twitched. Blood bubbled and spat from open wounds. Bones, cracked and splintered, rubbed against each other like dry sticks.

She wasn't causing any of it, but it was happening.

Help us.

She wanted to close her sightless eyes, to float away again. Above her body. Beyond. Into the beautiful sky and the bright warm sun.

She wanted to die.

Her senseless limbs quivered, shook, and finally moved. *No!* She screamed silently, but The Call didn't hear.

———————

As Will and Dan continued downward, the passageway seemed to narrow; the ceiling suddenly wasn't high enough to walk upright. Will glanced back at Dan and saw he was crouching.

Reflexively, Will ran his hand along the ceiling so he wouldn't bump his head.

Soon he was forced to his hands and knees.

The rock walls pressed tighter and tighter all around him. He imagined hundreds of feet of tightly packed earth above his head, weighing heavily on the earthen pipe through which he crawled. His progress was slowed, and it made him nervous.

He felt like an insect in a test tube, with Dan right behind him, sealing the exit like a cork. If anything came at him from the front, he'd be done for.

"Maybe we oughtta turn back, Will," Dan said. "This can't be leading anywhere."

Will was about to agree; it was probably a cleverly engineered dead end, and he really wanted to get out of here.

Then he heard the sound.

He couldn't tell where it was coming from; it seemed to be everywhere. It seemed to come from behind, from in front, from within the very walls. It was a high-pitched moaning sound that seemed to go on and on.

Something in Will's mind responded to that sound.

His mother used to tell him that if there were a hundred babies in a room, a mother could always recognize the cry of her own. Maybe the same was true in reverse.

"That's Mom," Will said to Dan. "You hear it?"

Dan put his hand on Will's leg as if to say, "Quiet!"

They both held their breath.

The moaning sound rose and fell. It had a mindless quality to it, like a madman's monotonous drone. The notes chilled him, like tiny icicles driven into his heart.

What were they doing to her?

What had they already done?

Will started to crawl rapidly forward, but Dan squeezed his leg. "Wait. It might be a trap."

Will didn't care. Trap or not, he knew his mother was around here someplace. She was very near; he could hear her.

Jerking out of Dan's grasp, Will scurried forward on hands and knees. His palms hurt from grinding them against the stony floor of the cave. It didn't matter.

Behind him, Dan held the light. The bright beam kept projecting Will's shadow over spots where he wanted to see, his own silhouette blinding the tunnel directly in front of him.

Still he wormed along.

If he'd been walking on two feet instead of crawling, he'd have gone right over the edge. As it was, his left hand skidded on the rim of the drop-off, and he pitched forward, smashing his elbow on the sharp ledge.

Will muffled a groan.

The tunnel had suddenly taken a right angle, straight down. Directly ahead there was nothing but a solid wall.

Somehow Dan squeezed up beside Will, and they both hung their heads over the hole, peering down.

The flashlight illuminated a vertical shaft that led straight down for about five feet. It was like a chute, with no rough and ragged contours like the passage they'd been crawling through. It actually looked as if it had been polished, either by flowing water over thousands of years, or — could it possibly be the work of the Gentry?

Now that they were directly over the hole, the melancholy moaning sounded louder. The tunnel acted as a megaphone.

The perfectly round opening at the bottom of the vertical chute suggested it led either to another passage or into a chamber. Will could see a floor, maybe fifteen or twenty feet below. It seemed like an awfully long way.

"End of the line," Dan said. He noiselessly tapped the unyielding floor with his fist.

"But *Mom's* down there ..." Will insisted. He tried hard not to yell out to her. They were so close, why risk it all by giving away their location with a shout?

The problem was how to get down to her. Will thought of Eric's backpack. The rope it contained was no good to them now. It had vanished with Eric. Then he thought of their belts. Maybe they could buckle them together. Dan could then lower Will down far enough to drop safely to the floor.

"It won't do any good, Will," Dan said.

"Why not?"

"Because we'll never be able to get you back up. It's a long drop. We can get you down there, but—"

"But nothing, I gotta help Mom." The constant moaning tortured Will's ears; it was like a razor slicing across his brain, cutting to his soul.

Dan put his hand on Will's shoulder. "I know Will, but ... wait a minute! It is a trap. That can't be your mother down there."

"It's Mom. I can tell. Can't you hear her?"

"Will, Sheila couldn't have fit through this hole. Her stomach's too big. This *has* to be a trick. That can't be her down there" —his eyes sparkled in the dim light—"unless—"

"Unless there's another entrance!" Will experienced a surge of joy at the realization. "They must have taken Mom in there some other way."

"Let's back up, Will. Let's go find that other way."

Will hated the idea; it would take forever with all those crazy passageways running helter-skelter through the mountain. Here they were so close; they must have been within fifty feet of her.

"Dan, if you lower me down, it'll be easy to find the way out from down there. Mom may even know the way ..."

"I don't know, Will. It's awfully dangerous. We'll be separated ..."

"Wouldn't you do it if I could lower you?"

Will saw the shadows on Dan's face change as he frowned. "Of course I would. But I can't ask you—"

"You're not asking me, Dan, I'm asking you."

He nodded. "Let's do it, then."

It was fortunate that they both habitually wore their belts a little too big. Will's was thirty-four inches, Dan's forty-five. When they'd fastened Will's loops to Dan's buckle they had almost seven feet of belt. That would get Will through the hole, but there was still more than a ten-foot drop to the floor. Dan's arm, fully extended, would add another two, almost three feet. Add Will's heights to that, and …

If Dan could hold Will with just one arm, they could do it.

Will lowered his feet and legs into the hole until the only things keeping him from falling were his elbows resting on the rim.

"Take it real slow, Will. We still can't be sure it's not a trap. Some of them might be down there, waiting."

Will nodded his head and wrapped the end of the belt securely around his hand.

"You yell 'pull!' I'll have you back up here in a second."

"Okay."

"And don't be too quick to let go. Once you're on the floor, Will, there's no turning back."

"I'll be careful."

They looked at each other, eye to eye. Then Will braced his knees and feet against the sides of the chute. Dan kept the belt taut as Will began his slow descent.

CHAPTER 38
HUNGRY DARKNESS

Will passed through the five-foot stone chute with no painful scrapes or cuts. When he looked up, Dan was watching; when he looked down, he saw the nearly invisible stone floor getting closer and closer.

The only sound was the rise and fall of his mother's tortured whine.

The belt bit into his wrist, and his right arm—the one suspending him—hurt something fierce. It felt like it was tearing from his shoulder. But the discomfort of holding on sure beat the pain that would come from letting go and dropping into the dark.

The disposable flashlight was in his left hand. With it he could see he was descending into a stone chamber, rather than another passageway.

He hung there like a puppet suspended by one arm, looking around. The room below was domelike in shape, from thirty to fifty feet across. As Will swept the floor with the light, he could see the shadow of his own feet falling heavily on the ground. He tried to take everything in at once. The circle of light slid over dark mounds and knobs; he couldn't make out the details— stones most likely. He hoped so.

Almost directly below was a circular stone structure like the built-up wall around the opening of a well. All it lacked was the little peaked roof, a crank, and a wooden bucket. It was about four feet high. Maybe it actually was a well, Will couldn't tell. When he turned the light toward it, he couldn't see anything inside.

The walls of the cave itself were another thing. They were sheer and dark, here and there covered with strange markings. Not pictures exactly, but odd symbols like these:

He had no idea what they meant. Others were equally strange. Probably they were some kind of writing.

Two openings led out of the chamber. They weren't like the half-circular mouths of natural caves. Instead, they seemed man-made. Heavy pieces of very old wood framed each opening like a doorway. To Will they looked exactly like the entrances to mine shafts, identical to those he'd seen in so many western movies.

As Will jogged down another notch, he passed completely through the shaft. Now he dangled in midair about six feet above the floor.

The eerie, high-pitched whine stopped abruptly.

Will flashed the light around, trying to see where the noise had been coming from. It was impossible to tell. Sound, bouncing around on the domed ceiling, seemed to come from everywhere.

At the farthest wall of the room, beyond the well, he could discern a stone bench or table. There were two stubby candles burning on it, their dim light hardly noticeable in the hungry darkness. Behind the stone slab, on the cave floor, he saw what appeared to be a big bundle of white cloth. He couldn't get a good look at it because the table was in the way.

"How you doing, Will?" Dan whispered from above.

Will looked up. He could see Dan's arm and part of his shoulder stretching as far as possible down through the hole.

"I'm okay. Should I let go now?"

"Wait a second." Little by little Dan let out more of the belt in jerky fits and starts. Will inched closer to the floor.

"That's it," Dan said when there seemed to be only about five feet of space between Will and the ground. "Be careful, Will."

Careful is right. All Will needed now was to jump and twist his ankle or break something.

Dan's flashlight, balanced on the rim of the hole, was bright enough to see by. Will slowly slid his own back into his pocket; that way he could hold the belt with both hands. He wanted to redistribute his weight in order to drop straight down and land on both feet.

Will's distorted, truncated shadow swung this way and that on the smooth rock floor. It gave him the creeps; it was like the shadow of a Gentry.

Holding his breath, trying to steady himself, he looked up at Dan one last time, then down at the floor, concentrating.

Here goes, he thought.

He let go.

Dan rolled over onto his back and rubbed his arm. The pain was excruciating. Tiny invisible needles pricked at his muscles from strain and inhibited circulation.

It was then he began to realize the position he'd placed himself in the moment he'd let go of Will. He was forced to remain there, alone, in the unfathomable darkness. He had to wait until his stepson could direct him to the chamber below. It was likely to be a long, grueling wait, without so much as the comfort of his flashlight.

As soon as Will's light turns on, I'll shut mine off, Dan thought.

It wasn't like being *completely* alone, Dan reminded himself. He and Will could communicate through the connecting tube. That was at least something. But what good would it do if Will were in trouble? There was no way Dan could get down there to help him.

He had to struggle with himself not to speak to Will immediately.

Are you all right?

What do you see down there?

What about Sheila?

Trying to control his own fear, Dan realized once again how brave the boy was. He felt very proud of Will, but the feeling was quickly displaced by a more demanding sensation; as the circulation improved in his arm, he felt the muscles begin to cramp. He sat up, shaking the arm as if he were flicking a thermometer.

The motion stirred the damp air in the tight passageway, and the moving air felt strangely cold—colder than a moment before. The new cold seemed to spread all over him, seeping through his clothing, stinging the corners of his eyes.

Dan stopped massaging his bicep and sat very still. He listened acutely. Was that Will moving around down below?

No. It was something else. Something behind him.

What could it be? What was scraping along the passageway? Right behind him. Getting closer.

———————

When Will's feet struck the floor, a jolt of pain shot up both legs.

The flashlight jumped out of his pants pocket as he staggered to the right, catching himself against the rock wall surrounding the well.

Could this have been where the moaning sound had come from? Balance restored now, Will turned his attention to the circular opening.

A horrible stench rose from the dark interior. It was as powerful as ammonia, but had a rotten, almost sickish sweetness about it. It made Will's eyes water, and he turned away, looking for his flashlight.

He quickly retrieved it from the floor, then switched it on, but it didn't work. "Shit," he hissed through clenched teeth. When he pounded its plastic case a couple times against his palm the beam sprang back to life.

Will shone the light into the well.

Far below the level of the cave floor, where the surface of the water might have been, he saw a churning, rolling layer of mist. If heat had been rising from the well, he'd have thought the water inside was boiling. But there was no heat, and the mist didn't seem to separate and float from the opening. It seemed almost like a solid thing, a moving, breathing layer of discolored foam.

Will picked up a nearby stone and tossed it into the well. It silently broke the smoky surface and dropped out of sight. He listened really hard but didn't hear a splash. He didn't even hear it strike solid ground.

Strange, he thought. He might have tossed another stone, but the smell was making him sick. Besides, it was obvious his mother wasn't down there.

Will reminded himself to stay more alert; in his momentary distraction, he had dropped his guard.

Looking around the cavern, he was suddenly all too aware that anything—any *thing*—could be lurking in the shadows behind him.

There were plenty of places the little people could be hiding. The fact that candles were burning on the stone table made him think they were nearby.

Cautiously Will walked over to the stone table. *It's an altar*, his mind kept telling him. That's what it looked like, some ancient sacrificial altar like the ones in all those mysterious South American ruins.

The blood in his veins felt like it was running cold, freezing his guts into hard sluggish lumps. He was tense, aware of every heartbeat.

As he moved closer to the table, huge brown spiders scurried off into the shadows. Will jumped back, sickened. God, some of them were as big as his fist and twice as hairy!

Will braced himself and stood beside the table, shining his light on the white bundle. The moment the beam struck it the sound started again. The whining ...

It was close now.

Too close.

It was coming from the bundle itself.

Will blinked a few times, trying to make sense of what he was seeing. The bundle was covered by crawling things, spiders of various sizes. As the light struck they slithered away or ducked out of sight beneath folds in the white fabric.

Tearing his attention away from the spiders, he tried to take in the overall picture. The bundle wasn't really an amorphous pile of discarded cloth; it had definite shape, human shape. It looked like a freshly wrapped mummy, or perhaps a burn patient covered head to toe in white gauze.

But it wasn't gauze—the spiders still crawling here and there on its surface told Will that. It was a cobweb, a gigantic cocoon, the monumental cooperative effort of dozens of spiders.

On one end of the bundle, something glistened.

Eyes ...

Eyes buried in the delicate strands. Will turned his light directly on them, and they winced. The whining stopped.

A half-step closer and he could make out the face. Strands of cobweb, like the fragile wisps of an old woman's hair, ran this way and that across the pale features. All the same, the face was recognizable.

Mom.

In that instant of recognition, something electric happened in Will's body. It was just as if a surge of current passed through him, paralyzing him for a second.

"Mom," he whispered, kneeling down beside her. "Oh God, *Mom.*"

Her gaze locked on Will, round staring eyes that offered no hint of familiarity. Her mouth, open but slack, made no motion to speak. Only her tongue moved a little, like the sluggish movement of some dry pink snail struggling from its shell.

Frantically he began to tear at the garment of cobweb. It was strong and thick, binding her tighter than any ropes. It felt horrible, sticky, like that disgusting hairy stuff some people put on their Christmas trees.

As Will's hands ripped and pulled, spiders scurried away. He slapped at them, almost enjoying the feeling as their little bodies exploded wetly below his palms.

The whiny sing-song started coming from Sheila again, "Oooooh ..." It was mindless, and for that reason, chilling.

"What is it, Mom? What's happened to you?" He shook her gently, hoping for some reaction, some sign. "It's Will, Mom. Come on, say something. Help me get this stuff off you." The sticky, wispy strands clung to his hands as he wiped tears from his eyes.

Sheila was partially uncovered now. Will saw she was naked under the cobwebs, her stomach fat and smooth and tight.

He tried to get his arm under her shoulder. "Can you get up?" he choked. "Do you think you can walk?"

He could feel no cooperation from her slack muscles.

Will's attention was yanked away from his mother when he heard the sharp cry from above.

"Nooooooo!"

The sound of Dan's voice thundered down through the stone chute. It seemed to flood the whole cavern.

"No, no get *away* … !"

A crash echoed crazily through the cave. It sounded like metal and glass against stone. It was so loud it hurt.

Sheila blinked. Her tongue lolled to the side of her mouth, and the whining increased.

"Noooo," Dan's voice boomed from above. "No, Damn it. Get *off* me!"

All was silent.

Will ran quickly to the spot below the opening and looked up. The chute was like a huge dark eye. There was no sign of Dan's light anywhere.

"DAN!" he hollered. There was no answer, only the sound of his own voice bouncing and fading. "Dan … 'an … 'n … 'nnn …"

He looked back at his mother. She hadn't moved at all, hadn't reacted to the commotion. Will realized that even without the cobweb straitjacket, she was going nowhere.

What had they done to her? Had they somehow destroyed her mind? Will knew that exposure to these filthy surroundings alone was enough to do her great harm. But it was more than that …

What should he do? She didn't look like she could walk, and he wasn't strong enough to carry her.

And what about Dan?

In Will's panic and frustration, all he could do was tip his head back and scream. "Daaaaannnn!" Then, "Eeerrrriiiic!"

The sound of his voice, like a sky full of thunder, filled him with a sense of his own powerlessness. He dropped his head, unclenched his fists, and went back to where his mother lay. He just sat down beside her, stroking her hair for a while. Then he held her hand.

After a few minutes her whining stopped, and the cave was quiet. Will turned off his flashlight to conserve the batteries.

Candle flames danced like distant, dying souls.

Will and his mother huddled together in the candle-lit dampness, staring into the silence that seemed to last forever.

He felt an odd sort of calmness, now that there was nothing at all he could do. They were done for. Beaten. This was the end.

In a while the Gentry would come. After that … ? He didn't know. He didn't dare imagine.

When she woke up she was crawling. Her body—coaxed onward by some deep-rooted suggestion planted long ago when her brain was fine-tuned and powerful—had covered much distance while she had been asleep.

Help us.

The Call … it was a promise she had made. A promise she had to keep.

She tried to look around to see where she was, but she could not; her muscles no longer took their orders from her. She watched her arms, moving as in a dog paddle, trying to pull her erect; hand over hand, they climbed the limbs of a dead tree. Upright now, she tried a step, fell, and hit the earth with a thud. Her legs wouldn't support her. The right one bent like rubber where the bone had split in half.

"God help me," she said, surprised to discover she could speak.

In a while Will heard a muffled clumping noise; someone was coming through the darkness. He took his mother's head in his arms and hugged her to him, as if that would somehow protect her. He kept the flashlight turned off and peered into the tunnel nearest to where they crouched.

The sounds grew louder.

He guessed some switch in his brain had turned off, some generator shut down. He couldn't summon the energy to fight anymore. It was as if all his strength were gone. He couldn't run away, either, not with his mother helpless and unable to come with him.

Three forms gradually emerged from the tunnel, a tall one with two stubby shadows on either side.

It was Dan. The Gentry had him.

At least he wasn't dead—that's what Will had been afraid of—but Will's heart sank when he saw the rope coiled around his stepfather's neck. The two Gentry held the ends of the rope. They yanked him along, a step at a time. The belts he had used to lower Will into the chamber were tied around his wrists.

Will was sure the Gentry could see him, huddled there with his mother; he was making no effort to hide. He wasn't even moving.

Although Dan's face was barely visible in the dim light, Will could see it was blank and pale, as if his spirit were missing. *He's given up, too,* Will thought.

Unthreatened by Will's presence, the little men walked Dan up to the wall and fastened the rope to a metal loop imbedded in the stone.

Only after he was tightly secured did they turn their attention to Will.

At that point Sheila started making noise again, as if she knew her captors had returned. She flipped her head from side to side, moaning in a long hopeless sound that tore at Will's heart. He hugged tighter but couldn't tell her everything was all right.

One of the little men stepped forward. "Come, boy," he said, motioning with his hand.

Will couldn't move. The beckoning Gentry seemed older than some of the others. His arms and legs were more fleshy, and his head seemed too large, bulbous, and swollen. Dark black eyes stared at Will from unblinking sockets.

Will shook his head, *no*.

The second Gentry, more childlike in his appearance, stepped up beside the first. They jumped at Will. Each grabbed him by a wrist and pulled. They were surprisingly strong, easily yanking him to his feet. Their hands felt like ice-cold metal handcuffs.

"Mom." Will heard himself saying. He tried to pull away, but it was no use. He kept thinking, *this whole thing was a trap. They used Mom for bait.*

They hadn't had a chance from the start ...

On some level Will knew it was true. All of them were here now, his whole family, captives. He just couldn't understand why the Gentry didn't kill them and be done with it.

They pulled him to the wall, stood him next to Dan, and tied his wrists together with a piece of scratchy rope. Then they tied the rope to another rusty loop on the wall.

Without speaking to anyone, or to each other, they moved through the darkness to where Sheila lay. With what seemed like no effort at all, they lifted her onto the stone table.

God, Will thought, *they're going to sacrifice her!* His mind flashed to a grotesque and bloody image: the Gentry carving the infant from his mother's womb.

351

He worked his wrists frantically trying to loosen the ropes. Tiny sharp fibers bit into his skin like thousands of miniature teeth. Soon his flesh was raw and bleeding.

Two more Gentry entered from the tunnel to the left of the stone table. One carried what looked like a jar made of clay, as big as a half-gallon milk carton. All four of them surrounded Sheila, who remained silent and unmoving.

It was eerie the way they worked around her, in perfect coordination, like a highly trained surgical team, not talking at all. Will knew they were communicating with their minds, making it impossible for him to guess what they were up to. He watched, helpless, filled with a mixture of dread and horrible fascination.

One of them locked the stubby fingers of his hands together. With his palms he pressed Sheila's head against the stone. Two others spread her legs while the fourth held the clay jar over her and began to pour.

When the golden liquid, thick as honey, touched Sheila's stomach she heaved and gasped, but the three Gentry held her in place. In the faint candlelight, Will could see the liquid glistening on her skin. It seemed to evaporate the cobwebs that covered her abdomen and upper legs. Wisps of steam rose from her as if she'd just stepped from a hot bath on a wintry day.

As the little man continued to pour the viscous stuff all over her enlarged stomach and inner thighs, Will saw her muscles begin to ripple just as if live things were crawling around under her skin.

She started to sweat and gasp. Will knew she was in tremendous pain as she convulsed on the stone slab.

He pulled wildly at the ropes. His wrists were slick with blood. "Stop it!" he screamed. "Leave her alone!"

Beside him, Dan sat staring dumbly. "Dan," Will cried, "Dan, do something, please ..."

Will didn't know what he expected Dan to do. His stepfather looked so out of it, head slumped forward, feet spread, leaning against the wall like a piece of discarded furniture. The scariest thing was his face; it was blank, expressionless, as if he were asleep with his eyes open. As Sheila's screams grew louder, Dan never even blinked.

Suddenly, as if the four Gentry were responding to a signal Will couldn't hear, they stopped what they were doing. All four of them turned and faced right, watching the opening of the tunnel. They stayed that way for a split second, motionless, like ugly little statues. The one holding Sheila's head moved his hands down over her eyes. Her body became limp, as if she'd passed out.

In perfect unison, the four lifted her down behind the table where Will couldn't see her anymore.

As if responding to an unheard command, they all left the table and lined up in front of the tunnel opening. In a few minutes Will heard someone coming.

Eric! he thought. Eric was coming back to help them!

"Eric, no, stop! It's a trap!" he shouted.

The Gentry on the end, the oldest-looking one, whirled on him, a glare of hatred on his contorted face. His hand shot out, fingers spread, as if he'd hurled something at Will.

Will saw nothing leave the hand, but something warm struck him in the face; it seemed to engulf him, smother him. It was a cloud of stench so powerful that he gagged reflexively. Burning tears filled his eyes. His stomach heaved as if to throw up. He fought to take a breath, hoping to control the urge. As he tried to inhale, a horrible realization stunned him: he couldn't breathe! His lungs couldn't pull in any air.

Will yanked desperately at the ropes. Frenzied now, he pulled with his arms and bucked with the strength of his entire body. The fibrous cords cut into him like dull knives; the back of his head bashed against the unyielding stone wall. Still he couldn't jar loose whatever prevented him from breathing.

Sweat flooded his skin. He flushed with a tingly heat, while his pulse raced. A terrible pressure built behind his eyes.

His chest seemed about to explode.

This is it, he thought, *my heart! Just like Dad ...*

His hands jerked automatically toward the throbbing artery in his neck, but the ropes held him fast.

He wanted to scream, opening his mouth to let it come. But there was no wind to drive it out.

"Be still," a voice said inside his mind, and something released; sweet air flowed into his starving lungs.

Will stumbled back against the support of the cave wall—he'd been warned. The four Gentry were together, organized; he knew they had the power to deny him fresh air.

Will watched helplessly as two new figures came into view. Flickering shadows bounced along the tunnel walls as two shapes emerged, one straight and tall, the other squat and twisted.

Eric appeared, carrying a flaming torch in one hand, his shotgun in the other. Beside him, the redheaded skeleton who was his brother.

"We will stop this now," Brian said in his grating, high-pitched voice. "It is over."

Oddly, it flashed into Will's mind that the strangeness of Brian's voice resulted not from physical deformity, but from disuse.

The other four, standing in formation, echoed in unison, "... over ..."

Brian continued, "My brother has made a pledge. He will stay; he will ... work for us. The others will go."

Relief swept over Will like a refreshing breeze. Eric hadn't deserted them, he'd—

Wait. Something was wrong. Why were they speaking? They didn't *need* to speak …

"Your first task, Eric: You may give them the woman. We are done with her now."

"Where is she?" Eric asked, his voice weak but steady.

Brian pointed, but not at the stone slab concealing Sheila. Instead, he indicated the round stone well. "She is there."

Will wanted to cry out as Eric obediently approached the circular wall. *He's lying!* But fear of psychic retribution locked the words in his throat.

Eric turned his back, then approached the stone wall. The instant his hand touched the masonry, the Gentry were on him.

With the savage speed of a pack of hungry dogs, they grabbed his legs, lifted him, and tried to wrestle him into the well. His shotgun dropped uselessly to the floor.

"Brian!" Eric shouted, terror screamed in his voice.

Snarling like a dog, Brian jumped at the arm carrying the torch. Eric tried to yank it away. The four other creatures pushed at him.

"Feed the earth," they chanted in squeaky, giggling voices.

Eric clung mightily to the stone wall, balancing there, as tiny hands shoved and prodded at him.

He kicked at the spindly arms surrounding his legs and swung the flaming torch at the fiendish faces.

"No," he cried. His flexing legs lost purchase; they flopped out of sight inside the rim. The strength in his left hand was all that kept him from tumbling out of sight. Grappling at the wall with his right hand, he let go of the torch.

It fell, striking the wall. One of the Gentry grabbed for it. The chubby hand connected but missed getting a hold. The torch rolled across the top of the wall, teetered on the edge, and disappeared inside.

At that moment the Gentry released Eric and backed away from the wall. Will watched as Eric scrambled out of the well.

A fountain of fire erupted from the opening. A *whoosh* of searing-hot air filled the chamber.

Eric had barely tumbled safely outside when the gigantic tongue of flame licked at the cavern's ceiling. It filled the darkness with bright orange light. Will felt the singeing heat where he stood; it warmed his face like a sunburn.

Faster than a lizard, Eric crawled over to Will. He cut the ropes with a quick flick of his hunting knife and ordered Will to free Dan.

It was the Gentry's turn to look terrified. They ran around chaotically, crying out—"Orudu! Mentifil!"—and screaming as if the erupting fire were burning them.

Will cut Dan's ropes and freed his belted wrists. Unfettered now, Dan teetered on his feet. Thinking he'd fall, Will grabbed him and shook him. Looking directly at him, Will urged, "Dan, come on, help us."

One of the frenzied Gentry dove at Eric, tackling him around the legs. Eric picked him up like a sack of flour and tossed him in the direction of the open well. The little man cried out as his tiny body bashed against the stone wall. Before he could tumble to safety, a tentacle of fire scooped him up and pulled him toward the opening.

He didn't fall. The flames tossed him around in the scorching air above the hole like a leaf over a bonfire. Will watched, unbelieving, as shimmering waves of heat moved the tiny squirming body in and out of focus; sometimes it was gone, sometimes partly hidden by smoke and brilliant red peaks. Will saw the body blacken and blister. The little man gave a nerve-tearing shriek as his eyes and stomach exploded. Then he dropped out of sight.

Among the terrified cries that filled the cave, Will heard Dan cough. "The gun," he choked.

Will made a dash for it. One of the Gentry saw him and dove. Will collided with the round wall and, somehow, found the shotgun in his hand.

Will pointed the weapon at the charging figure; it stopped.

The two of them were motionless amid the chaos. Will's mind blotted out all else, concentrating on the little man in front of him.

He was very much like a child. He must have been one of the newer ones, the ones who hadn't yet completed the transformation. His eyes were not totally black; they reflected the flames behind Will. And they were still capable of human expression. Will saw they were pleading.

"N-no …" the creature said in a voice not yet distorted from disuse. It was the voice of a child.

Will closed his eyes and squeezed the trigger. The gun kicked hard against his shoulder; its roar was painful. When he opened his eyes, the little figure was twitching on the floor.

Eric was suddenly at Will's side. He took the weapon. "Help Dan with your mother," he shouted.

Will started toward the stone slab, but something he saw there stopped him in his tracks.

Something moved among the shadows.

A figure lurched toward him.

It materialized out of the darkness the way a swimmer appears from the depths. Too tall to be a Gentry, it moved with a stumbling, lunging gait. Will blinked as light from the belching pit fell over it.

Its bare and filthy body was torn, streaked with blood. The calf of its right leg was split wide; a shaft of bone poked from the wound. Still it moved, taking a step closer. Its arms were contorted as if the bones inside were broken in a dozen places. Somehow, those arms reached out, clutching at Will.

When it touched him, he wanted to pull away. He couldn't. He was held in place, fascinated by the powerful alien presence of the thing.

Its face was black, ripped, gory as a slab of meat. One dangling eye had flattened like a grape against a protruding cheekbone. The other eye was wide, pain-filled, staring.

It was on him now. Palsied arms circled his neck; a flayed cheek touched his face. It wasn't until the thing spoke that Will recognized her.

"I ... I'll help you, Will ... I'll ..."

Mona! Her mangled mouth sought his.

"I'll take care of you, Will ..."

From behind, Eric shouted, "She's dead, Will. Get away!"

He couldn't move. Something in him cried out to her, ached to help her. She was his friend, his—

"WILL!" Eric screamed.

In spite of everything the Gentry had done to her, she had saved his life.

"Mona ... ?"

In a second Eric was beside him, the shotgun raised.

"It's another corpse, Will. It's a trick ..."

Her savaged lips touched his.

Will couldn't tear his eyes from Mona as Eric pulled her off him and shouldered her away.

"I ... I promised ..." she said, stumbling backward. "... I love—"

"Eric, NO!"

The gun roared. A deadly wind swept across her ruined body.

A huge tear, black and ragged, ripped through her stomach. She flew back, slammed against the cave wall, and slid to the floor.

Will stared in disbelief. No earth tumbled from the wound, just brilliant blood and wet, slippery-looking organic matter.

"Come on, Will," Eric yelled, and pushed the boy toward Dan. Mechanically, Will tried to help Dan get Sheila to her feet. Eric kept watch.

Another Gentry—the one Will had shot—was being tossed in the soaring flames. As the tiny body sank into the open pit, the flames sank, too. In minutes the fire was gone.

In the sudden darkness, Will slipped the disposable light from his pocket and flashed it around the room.

There was no motion, no noise. The four of them were alone. Brian and the two remaining Gentry had vanished into the dark, quiet tunnels.

"Come on," said Eric, "we've got to get out of here."

CHAPTER 39
DECISIONS

I t was obvious someone had been there, and recently.

Standing at the door, Chief Bates scanned the interior of the little cabin: a near-empty jar of peanut butter on the table, an old, rusty-handled kitchen knife protruding from it; beside the jar, half a loaf of white bread in a plastic bag.

Other indicators: water bucket, almost full; a few cans of food near the dry sink; on the floor, a brown grocery bag containing garbage.

Bates staggered across the room, the floor boards screeching painfully under his weight. A worn-looking sleeping bag was rolled up at one end of the little cot. *Tempting*, thought the chief; he was so exhausted from the hike that he wanted to lie down and rest. Instead, he sat at the table, reached into the plastic bag and pinched a slice of bread. *Not stale*, he decided.

He stretched mightily, bending so far forward that his massive gut flattened against his upper legs, and grabbed the water bucket with his fingertips. He slid the bucket to him, then picked it up with both hands, as if it were a giant's water glass, and drank. He wiped his mouth on his shirt sleeve.

From his back pocket he pulled a dark blue handkerchief, already saturated with sweat. He dragged it across his forehead, rubbed his cheeks with it, and wiped the back of his neck. *If I wring this thing out*, he thought, *I could refill the water bucket.*

He sat there until his breathing quieted and his heart stopped pounding. Then he got up to pace around the cabin some more, looking for some clue to corroborate his suspicion: Nolan was staying here.

Bates had to make a decision now. Should he hike all the way back down the hill and call for backup? Should he keep going, following the map until he found the three-sided box with the "X" in it? Or should he look for a place to hide in the surrounding bushes and wait for the cabin's occupant to return?

He took the rusty kitchen knife and, using it as a spoon, helped himself to a bit of the peanut butter. Working it slowly between his tongue and the roof of his mouth, he contemplated his options.

CHAPTER 40
HOMECOMING

It was a frightening walk, out of the echo-haunted caverns and through the dark woods. The moon was bright, hanging like a naked light bulb on a black ceiling of sky. All around, the trunks of trees and their shadows made Will feel trapped; they were like the bars of a prison, one he hadn't yet escaped.

Luckily there was plenty of light, enough to find their way back to Eric's cabin without using the flashlight.

The moment they'd carried Sheila out of the cave, she'd seemed to wake up a little. A momentary clarity returned to her eyes. "Will," she'd said, a flicker of surprise in her voice. She passed out again before recognizing Dan or Eric.

Dan tried speaking to her, but it was useless: she couldn't hear.

With Eric's help, Dan carried his wife over the steep, rocky ground. They'd fashioned a stretcher from two saplings strung together with their shirts and belts. Still, they had to make frequent stops to rest. When they started to move again, it was Will's job to lead, carrying the shotgun at the ready.

Watching the men struggle with the stretcher, Will thought of the time, just a few short days ago, when he'd seen the walking corpses of Reggie and Mr. Grant carrying his mother toward the cave. If only he'd known. If only he'd put a stop to it then.

Now he didn't dare drop his guard, not even for a second. What if the surviving Gentry were watching now from behind moonlit trees or bushes? What if they were waiting, planning, preparing for another attack?

"I'm not too worried," Eric said, "with just three of them left, their psychic power is probably shot."

"I hope you're right," said Dan.

When the low, dark form of the cabin came into view, everyone brightened. Dan and Eric eased Sheila to the ground so Eric could go on alone. "I'll check to be sure the place is empty," he said. "Everybody keep quiet, okay?"

The tiny cabin looked like home to each of them. Joining together, working noiselessly, they moved Sheila inside. Dan and Eric gently placed her on the wobbly old army cot.

They busied themselves around her. Eric heated water, and Dan bathed her and covered her with a ratty old blanket.

When she seemed to be sleeping comfortably, Eric and Will stepped outside, to give the couple some privacy.

Dan knelt by the cot, massaging Sheila's swollen feet. When he looked over his shoulder, he saw Will and Eric had left the room. He turned his back, then positioned himself between his wife and the partly opened door.

Lowering his face to hers, he whispered, "Sheila?"

She didn't respond.

He took the wet cloth from a nearby basin of water. He wrung it out, used it to wipe away the tears that were forming at the corners of his own eyes, then, gently, he washed his wife's face.

"God Sheila, God I'm so sorry," he whispered.

He saw a nearly invisible twitch of her nostrils as she breathed.

Hoping not to be overheard, Dan continued, "I know it's my fault, Babe, but I … I hope you understand … it was all … all … You've got to understand, I just couldn't help it."

His eyes were stinging again. He wiped away the tears, then gently stroked the tangled hair from Sheila's face.

"Oh God, Sheila. I know you can't hear me, but I've got to tell you: I don't know why I did it. I'd never do anything to hurt you. Not intentionally. Sheila … I … I …"

Her eyes flickered open. She looked right at him. A delicate smile bent the corners of her mouth. Suddenly her hand was on his cheek.

"I know, Dan. I understand better than anyone what they can do. But let's forget it now. Let's thank God it's behind us."

"Sheil …"

"I love you too, Dan."

She grimaced. Then she was asleep again.

Outside, they couldn't help listening through the partly opened door. Sheila gasped loudly. "You think she's gonna be all right?" Will whispered to Eric.

"I think she's okay, Will. Dan's taking good care of her."

"What did they *do* to her?"

Eric shook his head.

Every few minutes Sheila would cry out in her sleep. Her body would jerk, then relax, as if prodded occasionally with jolts of pain.

Will stole a glance at the couple. Sheila kept reaching out— still fast asleep—and stroking the side of Dan's face.

In a while, when she seemed to be resting peacefully, Dan got up and paced over to the window.

Will stepped inside and took Dan's place by the cot, wanting to spend some time beside his mother. He sat in a straight-back wooden chair and looked down at her. It hurt him to see her in such condition, her dirty hair slicked back, her body wrapped with a smelly blanket, her face so familiar, her mind so far away.

He must have been drifting off to sleep when he felt something touch him. He opened his eyes; his mom was holding his hand, looking up at him with a weak grin on her face. "It'll be all right, Will," she said, just as if he were the one who was suffering.

Smiling, Will bent forward to hug her. He stopped when she tensed with a new seizure of pain. Her face contorted. Regaining consciousness had made her aware of the pain. Her body cramped. She bit hard on her lower lip, sweating wickedly.

Will squeezed her hand.

Somewhere behind him, Eric was whispering, "Can you tell how much longer?"

"No. There's no way to tell. Minutes? Hours? I really can't say."

"Can we get her down to the house, do you think?"

"Not a chance," said Dan. "We're lucky we got her this far."

Will sprang to his feet, whirling around. "You mean she's gonna have the baby? Not here! We can't let her have it *here!*"

———————

Dan placed a rough, blistered hand on Will's shoulder and led him outside. The air was cool and fresh; bright stars twinkled in the clear sky.

"I think that stuff they poured on her somehow induced labor."

"Can't you stop it?"

"No. There's nothing we can do, Will. It'd be dangerous to move her any more."

"I could run to town. I could bring help."

"It's too dangerous. Besides, I'll be right there with her, you don't have to worry." He tried to appear sure of himself.

Will nodded, but he didn't seem very confident.

"I think the best thing," Dan said, "is for you to sit right out here next to the door. Eric and I will have our hands full for a while. Our minds have to be on your mother. If you could stand guard out here it would ease things up on us a little."

"Okay, sure."

Sheila let out a loud, sharp scream.

"I think it's time, Dan," Eric called from inside.

———————

The scream woke him up.

For a couple of confusing moments he didn't know where he was. Everything was dark. Above his head—that wasn't the ceiling of his bedroom! It was treetops!

Jeez, I was really down for the count, Bates thought. *Can't take it the way I used to. I musta been asleep for hours ...*

His back and legs ached from lying on the damp ground; his shirt and pants were moist with dew.

He rolled onto his stomach, pulled the bushes apart and looked at the cabin. He had a clear view of the back and one side.

There was light in the window; Nolan had crept back in while Bates was asleep.

The chief raised his binoculars and trained them on the window. They weren't very useful at night, but—

There! Red hair. That's Nolan, moving around inside, passing by the window!

So who screamed?

Merciful Christ, he's got somebody in there with him.

Bates unfastened the retaining strap on his .357 and waited, watching, preparing to make his move.

Will sat outside the door, weapon across his lap, peering into the night. He was intensely aware of every small sound, every movement.

The really scary sounds, however, were coming from inside the cabin. Each time his mother screamed, Will felt it, too.

What the hell's he doing in there? Bates wondered. *Sounds like he's got a woman with him; sounds like he's torturing her.*

His legs had cramped so badly it felt as if his muscles were tied in knots. He hefted his bulk and tried to get to his feet. Standing in place, unsteadily, he shifted his weight from one leg to the other, trying to get the circulation going.

As soon as he could regain control of his limbs, as soon as the numbness was gone, he planned to cross the dooryard to the back of the cabin. From there he could look through the window and better assess the situation.

The .357 slipped easily from his holster; it felt good in his hand, cool, solid, dependable.

Pain still pulling at his muscles, he quietly crossed to the rear wall of the cabin.

Bates chanced a quick peek through the dirty window. *That's Nolan all right.* The redheaded man was bending over someone stretched out on the cot. It was a woman with a blanket covering her.

She flailed around, thrashing, flinging her arms this way and that.

What the hell is he doing to her?

When she tossed her arms, the blanket peeled back, exposing naked breasts.

Bates fought the urge to push his weapon right through that filthy window and put a stop to whatever Nolan was doing. It wouldn't be wise, though; there was no way to be sure Nolan didn't have some sort of accomplice. Before doing anything, Bates would creep around the cabin and make sure of the odds. Then he'd enter through the door.

He squatted down, let his head drop below the level of the sill, and moved away from the window.

When he began to stand up, something grabbed him around the neck. His left hand shot up, too late to stop it, just in time to feel the rawhide band bury itself in his flesh.

Something smacked solidly against his right wrist. Pain flashed. The revolver thumped to the ground.

Bates tried to cry out, but the rope locked the sound in his throat. It locked the fresh air out.

He tried to step forward, devoting all his weight to the task, but the unyielding rope pulled him backward.

Something was right behind his legs.

He stumbled over it. He was falling …

Bates struck the ground like a falling tree.

———————

Alone again.

How much time had passed? He felt uneasy, as he strained his ears and tried to detect alien sounds in the surrounding woods.

His mother's cries filled his head. Sometimes, between screams, he could hear Dan talking to her, "Good, Sheila, good. You're doing just fine. You're doing great."

She must have been in terrific pain. Every wrenching cry made Will feel cut off from her and useless. At least now she was alert, she kept talking to Dan, gasping out the words.

"He's coming, Dan. I think he's coming ..."

"Yes! Yes, I see his head," Dan cried. "No. Sheila, *breathe*, don't hold your breath! That's it ... that's right ..."

Sheila screamed.

In a few moments, Will heard the baby cry.

CHAPTER 41
AFTER THE STORM

Dan and Eric sat at the crude wooden table, sipping tepid coffee from jelly glasses.

Sheila was in bed, holding the little baby, both of them sleeping peacefully.

Will felt drained, full of irritating aches and pains, his skin covered with a network of scratches and livid, puffy-looking welts. When he allowed his mind to wander, it filled with ugly memories and torturous speculation.

He needed to sleep.

For a while he sat next to the cot, smiling down at Mom and the baby. A disquieting possibility tugged at him. The baby's head looked funny. It was somewhat pointed, and the face was all wrinkled and red and covered with cheesy-looking film. It didn't seem to bother Mom though; she seemed right at home, comfortable and content.

Through the dark window, he could see a suggestion of brightness in the eastern sky. A couple hours more and it would be day. They could make the trip back to the house and call a doctor. Will prayed everything would be okay.

Will knew sleep would be impossible; he—like Dan and Eric—was running on nervous energy. Still, a few hours of rest before leaving was important for Mom and the baby.

The men were talking in quiet voices. Will joined them at the table.

"The thing I really *need* to understand," said Eric, "the thing I just can't seem to get through my head is this: Whatever that monstrosity is, it definitely isn't my brother. There's not so much as a suggestion of Brian left. Something else is inside his body, something savage, and without a soul. It hasn't been Brian since they kidnapped him thirty years ago."

"But what *is* it?" Will asked. "What happens to those kids?"

Eric shook his head. "I still don't know. The kids they capture change, rot away from inside. Somehow they embrace the earth, and ... Christ, I understand less now than when I got into this." He chuckled mirthlessly. "It's funny, you know; I really thought I could save him."

"You saved *us*," Dan said.

Eric smiled at him "Thanks. You probably thought I'd deserted you when I ran off with Bri—, with that ..."

"*I* sure did. I—"

Dan cut Will off. "Not for a minute, I just figured they'd somehow turned the tables on you. I was afraid you were dead."

Eric looked sad. "The awful part is, I believed him. I trusted him. He promised he'd let all of you go."

"... *if* you stayed with them, right?" Dan said it so as to suggest Eric should never have offered to trade his life for theirs.

Eric pressed his fingertips firmly against his closed eyes and massaged. Then he looked up, blinking at Dan. "Sounds pretty noble, doesn't it? It wasn't. Fact is, I was at the end of my rope. I knew Brian had no intention of coming with me. So what options did that leave? Where could I go? It was back to the hospital or life on the run. Naw, no thanks. I guess I was as well off with the Gentry as anywhere. At least that's what I tried to make myself believe. I thought, in time, I could coax him away, possibly help him. Now I think … I don't know … Christ, Maybe I am crazy. I actually believed I could …"

Eric's words trailed off to a contemplative silence.

For a few moments no one spoke. The soft sounds of Sheila's breathing filled the cabin.

"The thing I can't understand," said Dan, "is what it's all about. The motive. I mean, overall, the big picture. What do they want? What do they do?"

Eric chuckled sarcastically. "More a philosophical than practical question, really. I mean, what do *we* want, what do *we* do? We make buildings and pave roads; they dig tunnels."

"I guess so …" Dan looked away. "Christ, I'm too tired to think about it."

"But what was that thing in the cave?" Will blurted.

"Which?"

"It looked like a well. The thing the fire came out of?"

Eric looked thoughtfully at the boy. "Whatever it is, it was a surprise to me. It could be the key to all this."

"What do you mean?"

"During that short time when I was alone with Brian, he argued that they *had* to kidnap children; it wasn't a matter of choice, it wasn't even a matter of right and wrong. He told me the Gentry are the guardians of the fire, gatekeepers, actually. Over the centuries it has been their mission to protect the world from dangerous earth spirits bent on destroying mankind. He could have been talking about the thing in that well. Possibly — and Brian tried to convince me of this — the Gentry are the unseen allies of man. He told me their efforts are all that stand between us and the powers of darkness."

"So he wanted you to think they're some kind of guardian angels or something, is that it?" Dan said. "So if they snatch one of our children now and then, that's perfectly okay, right? That's just the dues we have to pay to keep your … your 'fire-demon' in its pit. Christ, it sounds like something out of Machen or Lovecraft, or—"

"It's probably just as much a fiction. Why would Brian tell me the truth?"

The first rays of golden sunshine flooded the little cabin. A window-shaped rectangle of light fell across Sheila and the baby as they slept on the cot.

Will couldn't wrench his mind from the memory of that stone well at the center of the tunnels. Again he saw the almost-living fire belching from the opening. In some ways it resembled the geyser he and his father had seen a long time ago at Yellowstone Park. Could it be some kind of natural wonder? A geyser of fire, or a miniature volcano?

He pictured the flaming tentacles reaching out, plucking the squalling Gentry from the stone floor. Perhaps it was some kind of god to the little people. Did they worship it? Sacrifice to it? He remembered them chanting, "Feed the earth."

Will wondered if somehow it was their motivator, the thing that sustained them and gave them their power.

There definitely *was* something about it, something that seemed—Will wasn't sure—alive? Intelligent? What if it could get out of that well? Rise up like a snake? Escape through the smooth vertical tunnel through which Will had entered the chamber? It was almost directly above the well; could the fire-thing go up, and out, and keep on moving?

If Dan and Eric had killed all the Gentry, would the fire-snake be free to roam around on its own?

Will glanced through the window of the cabin, wondering if the thing was out there.

Or were the surviving Gentry powerful enough to keep it in its hole? Hopefully that's what they were doing right now. With luck it would keep them busy for a while.

Despite his curiosity, Will knew he'd never have the courage to return and investigate.

A loud yawn startled Will; his reverie evaporated. Eric was standing up, stretching. Bleary-eyed, he walked over to the door and opened it to the new morning.

"Beautiful day," he said in a tired voice, and stepped out into the sunlit yard.

Through the open door Will watched him looking around like a proud farmer surveying his land. The bright sunshine emphasized the paleness of his cheeks, the redness of his hair.

A dark form dropped from the roof of the cabin. It hit the ground with a *thwuck*.

Eric whirled around just as a second form landed beside the first. Two Gentry, naked and bent, dirty as animals, positioned themselves between Eric and the cabin.

They held long spears, taller than they were, with shafts thin as arrows, and copper-colored tips, sharpened to deadly points.

Dan lunged for the shotgun. At the same time the two Gentry leaped toward Eric. They moved with a fearless precision, quickly placing both spearpoints against the soft tissue under Eric's chin.

They laughed.

One looked over his shoulder, his black eyes, wide and hateful, glaring at Will. His snarling mouth exposed animal teeth. "You move," he growled, "and we'll skewer his brain."

Eric stood nearly on tiptoes. His neck stretched away from the spearheads. He remained straight and still, hands in front of him, palms outward. Terror had returned to his features.

A dark bubble of blood slid down the coppery point of a staff. Dan and Will were powerless; there was nothing they could do for him. If they moved, Eric would die.

Behind Eric's back, a third figure emerged from the protection of a three-foot outcropping.

Red hair announced that it was Brian. He carried a five-foot spear that towered two feet above his head. Eric couldn't see him as he crept up from behind.

Will wanted to cry out, to warn him, but feared the quick upward thrust that would drive a pointed stick into Eric's brain. "Turn and face your 'brother,'" Brian said.

Eric's eyes registered surprise; no other part of him moved. Then, slowly, he turned around. One of the two Gentry repositioned the point of his shaft at the back of Eric's skull. The other stepped aside and stood like a castle guard, spear at his side. He never moved his black eyes from Dan and Will.

"Now we are the ones who will state the terms." Brian's grating voice brought gooseflesh to Will's arms and spine; he felt a tingling at the back of his neck.

Brian stood directly behind Eric where Will couldn't see him. Nor could he see Eric's face.

"Wha-what do you want?" Eric's voice was so fragile Will could hardly hear him.

"The child, Eric. Only the child. That which has been ours from the start."

Eric struggled to hold still. His arms and shoulders twitched. The point of the wooden spear made a circular indentation at the back of his neck. When he spoke, his trembling voice seemed far away, "… and if we agree?"

"Not 'if,' brother, never 'if.' Your fate rests with us now. We say you have already agreed. You agreed the moment Rool's staff kissed your flesh."

The Gentry behind Eric snarled, as if recognizing his name.

"So, what is your bargain, then?" Eric's voice cracked. His neck stretched impossibly.

"Only this," Brian said invisibly, "you will give us the child, and we will give you … to the earth!"

The three little men giggled like murderous children.

"That's not *fair*, Brian." This time Eric sounded loud and commanding.

"Not fair?" Brian roared—Eric staggered backward a step as if pushed by Brian's stick—"'Fair' is your language, not ours. You have cost us, 'brother.' You have invaded our dwelling place, you have destroyed our kin, and you have distracted us from our purpose. Such is your gift to us."—Eric staggered backward another step—"This gift, in all *fairness*, we are obligated to repay …"

Eric's entire body seemed to twitch all at once. He slumped forward. His knees sagged, his back hunched. His hands were invisible in front of him Still he blocked Will's line of sight to Brian. "Brian …" Eric gasped, "the child … the child is no good to you … the child is a girl—"

"It is *not* a girl!" Brian bellowed, his rage thundering through the air.

Eric stumbled backward, his progress stopped by Rool's spear at the base of his skull. He lurched to the left, then shuddered.

Will saw a bulge appear at the back of Eric's shirt. It grew, forming into a little teepee. Within a second, the sharpened point of Brian's staff, redder than any pain, tore through the fabric.

376

Turning more to the left, Eric grabbed the staff, trying to keep Brian from pushing it farther. His pale and perspiring face mouthed inaudible words.

Rool let down his own staff. He began to turn, transferring his attention to Dan and Will. Smiling horribly, he reached up and grabbed the bloody spearpoint where it protruded from Eric's back. With a powerful throwing motion, he pulled it all the way through.

Eric screamed. Impossibly, he remained on his feet. He tottered, unsteady, about to pitch forward.

It could have been an accident of balance. It could have been a final show of strength—the ultimate courage of a dying man.

Instead of falling to the ground, Eric pitched forward. Springing from his buckled knees, he collided with Brian and locked his hands around the tiny throat.

The pair tumbled. Brian squealed as Eric fell on top of him.

Chief Bates inched forward, keeping close to the cabin's foundation, pulling himself along with his elbows. He felt woozy, lightheaded. He hadn't been able to get a decent lungful of air since he'd regained consciousness.

The pain was awful; it felt like someone was inside his chest, playing his ribs like a xylophone.

Fuck the pain, Bates thought, *you don't die from pain*. He knew he'd been lucky. Nolan's accomplice, whoever it was, had left him for dead. It was a good thing, too, otherwise they might have tied him up and taken his weapon away.

The fuzzy world around him seemed to rock back and forth like the deck of a ship. He knew he couldn't stand. Everything seemed unstable. His tear-filled eyes could hold nothing in focus.

Right now the only thing in all of creation that seemed solid and real was the .357 in his right hand.

Bates dragged himself another foot.

His head felt awful, as if some demented butcher were tenderizing his brains with a wooden mallet. His eyes crossed and uncrossed, struggling to hold everything still.

Yet he crawled, inching toward the tortured cries and maniacal laughter coming from the front of the cabin.

Once, immediately after he'd come to, he'd let his hand venture to his throat. He wished he hadn't; his neck was slick with blood. His sticky fingers discovered a tight rawhide band imbedded in his flesh. The meat on either side of it was raw, electric with searing, white-hot nerve endings.

Now the leather garrote seemed very much part of Bates's anatomy. For a split second he considered removing it, but then thought better of it. What if it were holding the blood in, like a tourniquet? If he removed it, God, he might die.

He scraped forward another foot.

Each breath was a tremendous effort, rewarded with terrific pain. He knew his air passages were jammed up, maybe crushed. It was like trying to breathe through an opening no larger than the eye of a needle. Bates had considered performing an emergency tracheotomy on himself, but quickly abandoned the idea.

He was alive, that's all that mattered. And he had a job to do.

He had to help the tortured woman on the cot.

Taking as deep a breath as possible, he hoped it would sustain him. He braced himself, preparing for a confrontation. Then he crawled around the corner of the cabin.

Holy shit; it was Nolan all right, just as he'd thought. The son of a bitch was kneeling on the ground, straddling …

… straddling some little kid!

Some naked little kid.

Pervert, fucking pervert. Christ, the maniac was choking the little kid.

Bates tried to speak—*Hold it right there, Nolan*—but no words came.

Instead, he squeezed the trigger.

———

It was as if a stick of TNT exploded inside Eric's head. Bright blood arced toward the sky like a crimson rainbow. Eric collapsed on top of Brian.

The two standing Gentry rushed the cabin.

Will cried out and kicked the door closed.

Dan snatched up the shotgun. Fired. The shot ripped a twelve-inch hole though the wooden door. It flew open, torn against its hinges.

Outside, one of the Gentry squirmed on the ground, its tiny body covered with open, bleeding sores.

Behind Will, the baby wailed.

The other Gentry, Rool, charged through the open door, head down, snarling like a beast. He held his spear with hands spread slightly apart, as if it were a bayonetted rifle.

Dan turned the gun on him and pulled the trigger. It clicked lifelessly.

Reflexing backward, Dan tried to dodge the Gentry's spear; it was aimed directly at his solar plexus.

Without thinking, Will launched himself with his left leg and pivoted to the left. His right leg, straight and stiff, delivered a perfect karate kick.

His foot connected with the staff, exactly between Rool's two hands. It snapped in half like a toothpick. The impact hurled the little monster against the wall of the cabin.

Before Rool slid to the floor Dan was on him, hammering with the gun stock. The bone-crushing blows sounded like music. Outside, the Magnum roared again.

Will turned to the open door.

Eric was moving!

"Dan!" Will cried.

Dan stopped what he was doing and looked up. They watched Eric Nolan jerking and twitching where he lay in the dooryard.

Dan ran to assist the other man with Will at his heels.

"Holy Christ!" Will said in disbelief.

On the ground, beneath the body of Eric Nolan, the fallen Gentry, his hair like copper in the morning light, was sinking an inch at a time into the earth. In a moment he was gone.

Eric Nolan lay dead atop a child-sized depression in the solid ground.

CHAPTER 42
A CYCLE OF SECRETS

They kept to themselves, twice venturing into town for essentials, exchanging only the most superficial of pleasantries with outsiders. It was what they'd agreed to do.

Three suspenseful days passed before they heard from Chief Bates.

When Dan saw the cruiser arrive, he walked out into the yard to meet the policeman.

"Daniel." The chief nodded stiffly in greeting.

Dan caught himself staring at the big man, mentally listing the changes he saw. A collar of white bandages surrounded the chief's neck. The material was sweat-stained, damp-looking. The chief's complexion was as pale as the gauze. His face looked uncomfortably drawn, almost thin compared to the rest of his bulk. The skin around his eyes was so dark he appeared to be wearing a mask.

"How you feeling, Dick?"

Bates choked out a halfhearted laugh. "Can't complain," he said in a painful-sounding whisper. "Prob'ly the only time in my life I was lucky to have this collection of chins. If I was skinny like you, I'd probably be dead right now."

Dan could see the humor was forced.

The chief moved slowly, painfully, across the dooryard and up to the porch. He talked as he went. "Had to let Doc Clawson win three straight games of chess and work his way through the better part of a bottle of Black Jack 'fore he was willin' to believe I got my neck tangled up on a barbwire fence. Didn't get drunk enough to forget to bill me though."

Will met them on the porch, holding the screen door open.

Bates nodded a somber greeting to Will and to Sheila before lowering himself into a kitchen chair. Dan joined them at the table.

"You folks ain't said nothin', right?" The chief's voice has hoarse and faint. He swallowed frequently as he spoke.

"Not a word," said Dan. Sheila and Will shook their heads. Baby Sarah hiccupped from her place on Sheila's lap.

"Okay then," said the chief, "I ain't said nothin' myself. Trouble is, I'm afraid I'm gonna hafta. But before I say anything at all, we gotta decide how we're gonna handle this whole stinkin' mess. First off, what I want you to do is go over everything one more time."

"Chief, we've been over it a—"

"I know Daniel, but just humor me, will ya? I wanna be sure I ain't leavin' nothin' out. We can't have no loose ends, you know."

Dan's story unfolded, an episode at a time. Will supplied the transitional details to which Dan had not been a party. The story took a long time to relate. It filled the kitchen with a kind of hopelessness. Dan communicated his discouragement to everyone; soon they wore it on their faces like scars.

While Dan spoke, the chief didn't take a single note. His clipboard lay like a brown raft on the expanse of empty blue tablecloth. No pen or pencil was anywhere in sight.

The story ended with three little men vanishing; two sank into the earth like water into sand. A third turned to ashes on the cabin's floor.

When Dan finished, he glanced around, first at Will, then at Sheila. No one had anything to add.

Dan studied the noncommittal expression on the big man's face. Without giving any due about what he was thinking, Bates lifted himself out of the ladder-back chair and stood up. He walked silently across the kitchen and stood in front of a closed door.

"This the basement, Daniel?" he asked.

Dan nodded.

When Bates disappeared down the cellar stairs, Dan felt Sheila's hand tugging at his. He accepted it gratefully. Across the table, Will looked very much alone.

Moments later Bates returned. His complexion seemed even paler now, but his expression was no more revealing.

He looked Dan in the eyes. Dan tried hard not to look away.

Finally, the chief shook his head sadly and let out a long noisy sigh. His left hand came up to the bandage around his neck. With two fingers he tugged at the white collar of gauze.

"You expect me to believe all that, Daniel?"

This time it was Dan who nodded.

"You swear to me Nolan didn't kill the old lady?" The chief flicked his head toward the cellar door.

"Nolan didn't kill anybody."

"And you swear to me that Joe Grant and his daughter are both dead?"

"I'm afraid so."

"'That makes quite a pile up of bodies, don'cha think?"

The chief pressed his lips together until their redness curled invisibly into his mouth. "By God," he said at last, "I ain't never seen nothin' like this before." He took a painful breath. "Let me ask you somethin', Daniel," he said, sitting back down with the family at the table, "you gonna report what happened in your newspaper?"

Dan hadn't thought about that. Days earlier, when he'd ventured into the woods with Eric and Will, he'd hoped to come back with a story. Lately the idea had lost its importance, slipped unnoticed from his mind. At last, Dan said, "I have no intention of turning the *Tribune* into some supermarket scandal sheet. "Homicidal Leprechauns Found in Vermont Woods." A story like that could be suicide for a paper our size, and besides—"

"Besides? It's the 'besides' you'd better pay close attention to, Daniel. What's gonna be the repercussions for everyone involved? What's gonna happen if more folks go pokin' around up there on the Pinnacle? What's gonna happen to each of us if the real facts get out?"

The chief nervously fingered the brass badge pinned to his sweat-darkened shirtfront. His big fingers dug at the back of it until it slipped free into his hand. He placed it face down on top of his clipboard.

"What I'm gonna say to you folks, I'm not saying as a police officer, you understand that?"

"Yes ..." They all said it together.

Bates looked directly at Will. "You sure you understand what I'm saying son?"

"Y-yes. I think so."

"Well, you better be sure, William, because what I'm about to say's gotta stay right here. It don't leave this room, not now, not ever. You with me, son?"

"Yes, sir," Will said meekly.

"Okay then, here's my deal. You run this story in the *Tribune*, nobody's gonna believe you, right?"

Dan nodded.

"Same for me. Supposin' I report everything you say happened out there, includin' the stuff I seen myself. I could prob'ly delay turnin' in my shield for, oh, let's say another month or so while they're puttin' me through a whole battery of their

384

goddamn psychological workups. They're gonna think I'm crazier than a shit-house rat—'scuse me, ma'am. Tell you the God's truth, I ain't got the time nor the inclination to prove to them I ain't. That's what we done to Nolan, you know, back in eighty-three. That's what they'd do to you folks, too, if you was to tell them what you told me."

The chief shook his head and looked down at the badge. "Hindsight's always twenty/twenty, as they say, but you know, I never felt just right about what they done to Nolan. I wisht I'da trusted my instincts better back then, when I had the chance. I'da done that, Nolan'd be alive today and I wouldn't have nobody's death on my conscience. Tell you one thing though, I ain't never gonna make that kinda mistake again."

Bates looked infinitely sad. Dan guessed he was thinking about Eric Nolan. The big man shook his head, slowly, from side to side. He gazed from eye to eye. "Now you folks ... I can't say I know any of you all that well, but a man in my job gets to know people in gen'ral, gets a gut feeling about what people say and do. Fact is—and I hope you hear this good, 'cause I ain't never gonna say it again—fact is, I like you folks. I trust you. The point bein', I believe you one hundred percent."

Dan leaned back in his chair, relieved.

The chief continued, "I believe somethin' else, too. I believe what we got here ain't a matter for the law. The law was made to protect *people*, not them ... them goddamn little pissants up there on the Pinnacle. So what I'm gonna suggest is this: First, Daniel, either tonight, or some night pretty quick, you an me's gotta give Peg Menard a good Christian burial. She deserves better, but we're gonna do as right by her as we can."

Dan agreed.

"Then," Bates continued, "I'll go ahead and fess up to my run-in with Nolan. I'm gonna say I played a long shot and tracked him up to Perly Greer's cabin. I may even give Nolan credit for the damage to my neck. I'll say a fistfight resulted, and I was forced to fire on him. I'll say I mighta winged him, but I don't know for sure. Then, I'll tell 'em, he run off into the woods."

"You think they'll believe you, Dick?" Dan asked.

"Maybe they will, maybe they won't. They got no reason not to; I've always done right by this town."

"So you're going to blame all the murders on Eric Nolan?" Sheila's expression showed she didn't like the idea.

"Nope. I don't figger I gotta do that. I'll let somebody else make them connections. The simple fact is, you people are the only witnesses, the only ones who know anything at all about what's been goin' on. And I ain't plannin' to bring you into it, not for corroboration, not for anything."

"But Chief," Will spoke up, "Eric was a hero. He got us through it all. Now nobody'll ever know."

"I'm afraid that's true, son." The big man dropped his gaze to his linked hands on the tabletop. Without looking at the others, he went on. "I'm gonna leave my badge right where it is. I'm gonna tell the town manager he can find himself another cop, and I'm gonna take me an early retirement to Florida."

Then he looked up. "And you folks? Well, what you're gonna do is just as tough. Now, I know you folks no more'n come to town and all, but you're gonna hafta sell that newspaper of yours, Daniel. And you folks are gonna have to pack up and head back to Boston—or any place you want, I don't care, long as it ain't Vermont."

Sheila and Dan glanced at each other. Will was impassive.

After a breath, Chief Bates went on, "Getting out of here will be the best move for all of us. It'll make all this crazy stuff that's been happening hereabouts a little easier to forget. Oh, I know none of us is gonna be able to forget it, but one thing is sure: after today none of us is ever gonna talk about it again.

"So that's my deal. That's my offer. You got maybe fifteen, twenty minutes or so to think about it."

A thoughtful silence settled over the group. Never in his life had Dan been a party to a cover-up. Until today he'd been emphatically opposed to them—but this time he could clearly see the wisdom of censoring the news. He wondered how many other Antrim residents had pacts of silence, how many had some ugly secret, very like his own, that would never be discussed.

He looked at Sheila and raised his eyebrows to ask what she thought.

She transferred her gaze to Chief Bates. "We're all lucky to have come through this," she began. "And I appreciate what you're offering, Mr. Bates, but I don't like it. I mean, we've done nothing criminal; we have no reason to run away, we haven't done anything wrong—"

"But Sheila—"

"Please, Dan, let me finish." Dan settled back as his wife spoke. "Dan, you've worked too hard to establish the *Tribune*. You've gone a long way toward making it the newspaper you want it to become. It wouldn't be right to abandon it now.

"And look at Will, he's beginning school in a couple weeks; we can't expect him to uproot again, not when he's becoming such a woodsman and nature enthusiast." She smiled at her son.

Will returned the smile.

"And what about our house?" Sheila asked. "Look at all the work and money we've put into it. Look how far we've come toward making it our home ..."

"And what about you, Sheila?" Dan asked.

"Me?" Sheila smiled. "You and I have a daughter to raise, Dan. And"—her eyes twinkled—"I've got a great idea for my next book." Bates fidgeted, as if he knew what that idea might be.

"So," Sheila concluded, "if, as Mr. Bates says, he's not going to bring us into the story, I see no reason why we should run away."

Dan turned to his stepson, "What's your vote, Will?"

Will looked at his mom, then at the policeman. "I dunno," he said, "I guess I could probably get into this country living."

Three sets of hopeful eyes were on the chief.

"What do you say, Dick?" Dan asked.

Bates emptied his lungs, blowing air through pursed lips. "A'course you're right, Mrs. Crockett, you folks got every right to stay on here. Lord knows you went through enough hell so's you oughtta be able to keep your home. I'm just scared about the truth getting out …"

"I understand, Dick." Dan smiled. "But you said it yourself— who's going to believe it?"

In the thoughtful silence, everyone listened to the baby cooing contentedly on her mother's lap.

AUTHOR'S NOTE

Guardian Angels was my second published novel. My first, *Shadow Child*, did so well that the publisher asked me to write a sequel.

But I didn't want to.

At that time, my ambition was to write two more books that would complete what I thought of as my "Vermont Trilogy": *Shadow Child*, *Lake Monsters*, and *The Gore*. Each addresses a different aspect of Vermont folk horror.

But the editor's enthusiasm and the promise of an immediate book contract enticed me to change my plan. I could delay my "Vermont Trilogy," first tackling the requested sequel.

But I still didn't want to write a sequel.

After some negotiating, we agreed that I'd write a standalone book as long as it took place in the same town and featured the same villains, the Gentry.

The plan changed: there would be a second and maybe even a third book in the "Gentry Series." My thought was to present them as a progression of genres. The first book, *Shadow Child*, was horror; the second, *Guardian Angels*, would be closer to fantasy; and the third—working title *Alien Skies*—would have been science fiction, with the same villains in each. There are clues within *Guardian Angels* setting this up.

But again, plans changed. The third book was never written. And it's just as well. In time, I got to do what I wanted to do in a much more ambitious and horrifying novel, *Deus-X: The Reality Conspiracy*.

But the *Angels* still fly...

What you have read is not exactly what I had originally submitted to the publisher. The completed first draft of *Guardian Angels*—originally titled *Screams of Angels*—was written in the first person. It was Will Crockett telling his story.

Somehow, I got it into my head that I wanted to write what you might call a horrific version of *The Adventures of Huckleberry Finn* or *The Catcher in the Rye*. I gave it a good shot, too, but editor Wendy McCurdy was able to talk some sense into me. "With multiple viewpoints," she said, "we'll be able to get to know the other characters so much better." Or something like that.

Anyway, I think she was right. Hate to admit it, but editors often are. The good ones want the same thing the writer wants: to make the best book possible.

But the original copy still exists, in case I ever need a reminder... And I want to thank Crossroad Press and editor David Dodd for allowing me to show you a chapter from the first draft of that first-person manuscript. The book that might have been...

I am proud of a few things that carried over from the first draft (*Screams of Angels*) to the published novel (*Guardian Angels*). For example, I introduced a couple of horrific concepts.

First, black-eyed children, long before they became a staple of supernatural pop culture.

And second—and this one especially pleases me—the golem. For some reason, those who have recently revived old horror standbys like werewolves, zombies, mummies, and vampires have overlooked the nightmarish potential of the golem. Did you overlook it, too? Take another look at what became of poor Joe Grant.

Oh, and about Joe Grant... In *Shadow Child*, you may recall that the menace was entirely supernatural. In writing *Guardian Angels*, I decided I could not ignore the component of human evil.

And so the enigmatic Joe Grant was born. Joe's character is so foul, malignant, and malevolent that a reviewer from Woodstock, Vermont, denied—in print—that we have any such people living in the state. Well, I'm not so sure about that, but I know Joe is the most despicable character I have ever created.

Some readers may have noticed my habit of throwing friends' names into my books as a sort of joke or salute. Chief Bates, for example, was no accident. But I had some trouble coming up with the right name for the loutish lummox, Mr. Grant. What could I call him and not risk inadvertently offending someone?

I decided the safest thing was to name him after me.

Joe Citro
Windsor, Birthplace of Vermont
July, 2025

SCREAMS OF ANGELS
CHAPTER 1
WILLIAM CROCKETT'S NOTEBOOK

W hen I first saw the place on Tenny's Hill, I thought it was nothing but a dirty old farm.

That was in April, when Dan and Mom and me came up from Boston to look at it. I was really surprised when Dan made an offer on it. "Twenty-five thousand dollars, for a house and fifty acres, it's a steal!" he told us on the ride home.

Maybe it was, but I couldn't see why anybody'd want to steal something that wasn't any good. I mean the windows were bashed in, the front door was boarded up, the whole place needed a paint job. Inside, it was dark and damp and smelled like the dirt basement of our apartment in Boston.

"It ain't been lived in for about four, five years," Mr. Carey, the real estate man told us. And I could see why. Who'd want to live so far out in the boonies? You'd have to take a bus to school, and there was no place to walk to—no video stores, no library, not even a goddamn shopping mall. I was never one to hang out in the malls, but I *did* like TV. There wasn't even any cable TV, just that old, twisted antenna on top of a broken-down windmill. It would pull in channel 3 out of Burlington when the wind was blowing just right.

"So we'll get a satellite dish, how does that suit you?" Dan told me, and I felt a little better.

"But what about my karate lessons?" I asked him. "I bet there's no place around here to practice."

"That's because people around here don't fight," Mom said. I could tell from that how much she knew about karate.

I argued the best I could, but they bought it anyway. And I've got to admit, when August came, and we moved in, the place looked a whole lot better. It was all covered with a bright colonial-red aluminum siding, and they'd had a deck built on the west side, facing the mountains. The inside was all done over. They'd had the dingy linoleum pulled up and the floors sanded and polished. Everything shone with new paint and brand-new wallpaper. Sliding glass doors opened onto the deck and gave us a great view of the countryside, if you go for that sort of thing.

Okay, maybe it looked great, but it was still five miles out of town. I didn't know anyone around, so I pretty much had to plan on a solitary summer with not much of anything to do until Dan got the satellite antenna hooked up.

During our second week on the hill, Mom was working in the living room, trying to hang some kind of plant with long green leaves from these little hooks in the ceiling.

I watched her standing on the chair. Her stomach looked really big as she stretched toward the ceiling. Dan kept telling her she should rest more. The move itself had been pretty hard work for a pregnant woman. Now that was all over, but Mom had always been really hooked on housework. What I knew, and Dan didn't, was that she wouldn't be able to rest at all until everything was just so.

"Why don't you let me help you hang those plants?" I asked.

She looked down from the chair and smiled. "You must be awfully bored if you've stooped to helping with the housework."

Mom knew me as well as I knew her. Probably better.

I took the red-clay flowerpot and she got off the chair. I took her place, picking up the plant by the attached strings. It was easy for me to loop the string over the ceiling hook. I'm almost six feet tall—pretty good for fifteen years old. I'd been taller than Mom for about two years, and she's pretty tall for a woman, almost five-nine.

"What else you want me to do?"

"You want to ride into town with me? I'm going to do a little grocery shopping. I want to have something special for dinner tonight. Kind of a celebration."

"How come?"

"Cause all the papers are signed. Today is Dan's first official day as owner of the *Tri-Town Tribune*!"

Big deal! I thought, but I didn't say anything. See, that was part of the master plan. It's not just that we moved from Boston to Antrim, Vermont. My stepfather, Daniel Crockett, had just bought this country newspaper, the *Tri-Town Tribune*. He used to work for a real paper in the city, *The Olympian*, but ever since he and Mom had gotten together, he'd been talking about how great it would be to move to the country and run his own paper. Pretty soon Mom started talking about the same thing.

Then it became a plan.

Then we actually did it!

So now he has to get a paper out every week, and pretty much all by himself, too.

I always liked to write, myself. I probably got it more from Mom than from Dan, but they both encouraged me. Dan even said I could do a column for the *Tribune* once school started. I'd be the reporter assigned to school news. I guess I liked that okay, though. It was something to look forward to.

Mom is a writer, too. She's had three books published. She said she was writing them for teenage girls, but all of a sudden grownups started reading them and they really caught on. Her first book, *Popbeads*, got really good reviews. She sold her second, *Charm Bracelet*, to a filmmaker for lots of money, and her third,

Toymaker, got such a big advance we could buy this house outright!

After the baby came, she planned to start another book, and in a year she wanted to open up a daycare center. She really likes kids and she'll really be good at it. But she better do it in town. Nobody's going to drive their kids way out here.

We sat down together on the deck and had lunch. Mom made the sandwiches and I mixed some of that iced tea from an envelope, with the sugar already in it. "So, are you going to ride into town with me after lunch?"

"Yeah, sure. Why not?"

"Will..." She always began a sentence with my name whenever she was going to say something really serious. "Are you really as bored here as you're trying to act?"

I thought about it a minute; maybe I wasn't all that bored. "It's just that there's nothing to do. I don't know anybody."

"You'll meet people fast enough when school starts."

"Yeah, I know. But I just don't see what you're supposed to *do* around here."

"What do you suppose country kids do?"

"Who knows? Go walking in the woods maybe?"

"Or hunting, or fishing..."

I had a feeling she didn't know what country kids did, either. She seemed to think about it a long time. She sipped her iced tea, never taking the glass from her lips, just tipping it back a little every now and then, and she looked out over the mountains. They were different shades of green, depending whether the sun was directly on the trees or coming through the clouds.

Finally, she said, "I guess it's a matter of what we can and can't do. To tell you the truth, I don't think I can enjoy all these simple country pleasures, either. I mean, I can't enjoy them right now, but I want to *learn* to enjoy them. Do you know what I mean?"

"I guess so," I told her. I really did know what she meant.

"It's a big change of life for all of us, you know?"

I nodded, and polished off my tea.

"So, you coming into town with me or not?"

"Maybe not. Maybe I'll try going on one of those hikes in the woods."

Mom seemed a little surprised that I hadn't accepted her invitation. She stared at me a second, like she was trying to tell if I was serious or not. When she decided, she said, "Do you think you really should be going off into the woods by yourself. You're really not used—" Then she started laughing. She really cracked up, and I didn't know why.

Finally, she said, "What a pain in the ass us mothers must be, huh? First, I tell you to start getting into country life, then when you do, I tell you not to. No wonder adolescence is such a mixed-up time." She gave me that pretend stern look of hers. "You be careful if you go hiking, though. I mean it. You're not used to the woods."

"Yeah, yeah," I said, and we both laughed a little. It was all right.

I decided to take my camera with me. It's a little 35mm made by Canon. Dan and Mom gave it to me six months ago as a wedding present. They said I had gotten married, too, so why should they get all the gifts?

I hadn't thought about it that way, but I guess they were right.

Dan is not my real father. My own dad died three years ago of a heart attack. He was only forty-two at the time. I guess that's pretty young to have a heart attack, but I suppose you can have them at any time. I don't really think about my own heart all that much. I used to, right after Dad died. I used to spend a lot of time with my fingers on my neck, feeling my pulse, just making sure it was beating the way it's supposed to. At night, I discovered that if you lay on the pillow just right, you can hear your heart beating in your ear. I used to spend a lot of time listening to it before I went to sleep. It thumped away at a pretty regular beat, and when I was sure it wasn't going to stop, I'd fall asleep.

But I don't worry about that anymore. I think about Dad quite a bit, though. I remember he used to say, "When your time comes, that's it."

I guess he was right.

Of course, Mom was real upset for a long time afterward. She spent hours at her writing, seeming to vanish into it, and when she came back, she was tired and cranky. I was twelve years old back then. I guess I didn't realize how hard it was for her; I was too busy thinking how hard it was for me.

I think that's when she got really interested in housework. She cleaned all the time when she wasn't writing. I bet we had the cleanest house on Cobleigh Street, maybe in all of Boston. That's the one thing about Dad's death that she hasn't gotten over—she still cleans an awful lot. But I guess that's okay.

Dan teases her about it sometimes. Once at dinner he said, "Your mother depends on that vacuum cleaner the way a kidney patient depends on a dialysis machine."

I wasn't sure what he meant, but I laughed anyway. Mom seemed to get offended and was struck funny, all at the same time. I guess it was a good joke.

Dan's okay. I really like him, actually. Maybe at first he tried a little too hard to get me like him, always wanting to play catch, or take me to Red Sox games. Finally, we discovered we both liked Sherlock Holmes, and science fiction, and stuff like that. Not too many people even know who H.P. Lovecraft is, but Dan knew. He even had some Arkham House editions of Lovecraft's books and he gave me one of them. That was great. All of a sudden we had something to talk about.

We started going to horror movies instead of Red Sox games, and by the time Mom and Dan got married, he and I were pretty good friends.

The woods started about a hundred yards from our house. I walked out behind the garage where a kind of trail led across some flat land to a stone wall. Dan told me the stone wall was for sheep, that this whole area used to be big on sheep farming before Vermont became a dairy state.

I hopped over the stone wall and started walking between the trees. Right away I noticed how much darker it was in the forest. If I walked to my right, the land got steeper and led up to Pinnacle Mountain. We own a lot of that mountain, but not the whole thing.

To my left there was a brook. I could hear it, but I couldn't see it yet. I decided to take a look.

Maybe two hundred yards or so into the forest I could see the brook, winding between the trees. The water splashed over brown-looking rocks and sprayed a mist into the air, for about six inches or so, like a halo. Stray beams of sunlight came through the opening in the trees above the water so you could see a little rainbow in some of the halos.

I thought it might be a good thing to get a picture of, so I laid down and tried to fix it right in my viewfinder. I snapped a couple and got to thinking about fish.

As I stood up I wondered what kind of fish might be in this water. I really didn't know that many types of fish. Cod, mackerel, perch, and stuff like that. Dan sometimes talked about trout fishing, so maybe it was trout that lived here.

I jumped out to a big rock in the middle of the stream and sat down. A pool of water collected around the downstream side of the rock. It looked pretty deep, maybe twelve or fifteen inches. Too much sun on the surface made it almost impossible to see what was happening underwater. Everything was all sparkly.

My shadow fell across the pool and that killed some of the reflections. Now I could see rocks and leaves and stuff down below.

Maybe if a fish came by, I could get a picture of it.

I must have sat there for thirty minutes waiting, but nothing swam by, so I decided to follow the brook down to see where it went.

In some places it had cut so deeply through the earth that trees and bushes grew right up to the water. When that happened, I jumped off the bank and hopped from stone to stone. One time I slipped and got a sneaker full of really cold water.

After a while I got kind of thirsty, but I wasn't sure if this water was okay to drink, so I just rubbed some on my face. It felt real cold and nice.

Pretty soon the running water started to sound very loud. Fifty feet or so in front of me, the stream funneled between two huge ledges and disappeared.

As I got closer, I saw I was above a waterfall. I climbed up onto one of those ledges and peered over the side.

The water shot downward about twelve feet. It bubbled and frothed at the bottom where it collected in a big pool.

That's when I saw the girl.

She was stretched out on a flat rock at the side of the pool. The sunlight was bright on her. I think she had just been swimming because the T-shirt she wore was all wet and sticking to her. She was lying on her stomach, but I could tell from the way the shirt clung to her that she wasn't wearing a bra or anything.

I figured she couldn't see me because I was SO far above her, and besides, she had her face buried in her folded arms. She couldn't hear me because the waterfall was roaring so loud.

I watched her for a while. I even thought about taking her picture, but somehow I just didn't feel right about that. I didn't really try to hide myself, but I laid down on the rock to get comfortable. If she could see me at all from down there, it was probably only my eyes and the top of my head. I figured my brown hair would probably blend in pretty well with the colors of the forest, so I wasn't too worried.

I couldn't tell how pretty she was because I couldn't see her face. Her back looked nice, though, and her legs were long and real tanned. Besides the T-shirt, she had on real short denim shorts. Nothing else, I mean, no shoes or anything like that.

When she rolled over I got a better look at her. I watched the way her tits moved under the T-shirt. From way up there, I could see that her nipples were hard and brown-looking below the white cloth. The T-shirt had some writing on it, but I couldn't see what it said.

She stood up and pulled off that T-shirt. I really wanted to take a picture then, she looked so pretty and everything, but I felt funny doing it. In fact, I felt kind of funny watching her like that.

Her breasts were pretty big. Part of me wished I had brought binoculars instead of my camera. I really wanted to get a better look at those breasts. I've got to admit it, that was the first time I'd ever seen a girl's breasts.

Back home some of the guys said they had seen them. Some of them probably had, too. Their sister's or something. Most of them were just bragging, I'm pretty sure, especially the guys like Phil Lubio, who said he'd actually done it with some high school girl. I don't believe it.

Anyway, this girl on the rock took off her shorts too. I got a quick peek at a dark patch of hair between her legs before she jumped into the water. Then I could hardly see her at all, the way the water was churned up.

I watched her for a minute longer, then I got to feeling really funny, like a pervert or something.

I thought once more about taking a picture, but I didn't. I just went home.

ABOUT THE AUTHOR

Joseph A. Citro is considered an expert in New England weirdness. In over a dozen publications – novels and nonfiction – he has guided readers through a dark, disturbing, and often sinister landscape that's traditionally portrayed with sunny skies and quaint villages. His ever-expanding canon includes five terrifying novels that explore folk horror themes, fourteen collections of New England's strange-but-maybe-true tales, a book of regional humor, a memoir, and even a comic book. He is a popular lecturer, teacher, and media personality whose writing has been adapted for radio, stage, TV, and movies. Taken together, his work presents a uniquely dark and mystical side of the Vermont experience.

A lifelong Vermonter, he resides in Windsor, the Birthplace of Vermont. He can be reached via the electronic Ouija, i.e., Facebook.

Book List

Fiction

The Gore – 2025

Guardian Angels – 2025

Lake Monsters (Collector's Edition) - 2023

Shadow Child (Collector's Edition) - 2018

Deus-X: The Reality Conspiracy

Possibly Not Fiction

Vermont Ghost Guide - 2025

Vermont's Ghostly Gallery – 2023

Vermont's Curious Encounters – 2022

Vermont's Creepiest Classics – 2022

Loose Ends (a memoir) – 2022

Vermont Monster Guide – 2020

Joe Citro's Vermont Odditorium – 2013

Vermont's Haunts – 2012

Weird New England – 2005

Cursed in New England: Stories of Damned Yankees – 2004

Curious New England – 2003

Green Mountains, Dark Tales – 1999

Passing Strange – 1996

Green Mountain Ghosts, Ghouls & Unsolved Mysteries – 1994

Other

Vermont Air (Editor) – 2002

Vermont Lifer (Parody, Editor) - 1986

Curious about other Crossroad Press books? Stop by our website:
http://crossroadpress.com
We offer quality writing
in digital, audio, and print formats.

Subscribe to our newsletter on the website homepage and receive a
free eBook.

www.ingramcontent.com/pod-product-compliance
Lightning Source LLC
Chambersburg PA
CBHW030803260626
47169CB00001B/165